CATCH YOUR BREATH

O'LEARYS 4

SHANNYN SCHROEDER

DEDICATION

To Trouble,

I love you even when you talk too much

ACKNOWLEDGMENTS

No book is really written in isolation, and this holds true for this book more than any other I have written. This was the first book that I truly had to write under deadline, and I was nervous. Not only did I have to write under a real deadline, but I also had to start the book over the summer while my kids were home. Then, two writer friends, Erica O'Rourke and Clara Kensie, came up with the brilliant idea for Summer of All the Words. The concept was simple—every night, writers would meet on Twitter from 10 to 11 to get words on the page. Without that motivation and support, I'm not sure writing would have been as much fun, so I owe a huge thank-you to Erica, Clara, and all the writers who showed up nightly all summer long. Next, as always, thank you to my critique partner Paly, who is never afraid to tell me when I'm screwing up my characters. To Hanna Martine and Pamala Knight, who beta read the book and gave me excellent insight under pretty tight deadlines—I owe you guys. And finally, to all of the book bloggers and readers who have taken the time to read about the O'Learys: without you, I wouldn't be able to have such a great job.

1

———

Jimmy O'Malley sat in the commander's office, knowing that one day, he'd move into the space. Today, however, he was waiting to hear why he'd been summoned. He hadn't been a detective long enough to screw up, so the reason eluded him. He'd been working doggedly on some property crimes that went nowhere. Most of the detectives from his class had gone on to investigate violent crimes. He'd been relegated to burglary and vandalism.

Commander Elks hung up the receiver and stood. "I hear good things about you, O'Malley."

"Thanks, sir."

"I've been contacted by the mayor about a special assignment."

Jimmy tried not to get excited. "Special" could mean anything from initiating a new task force or babysitting a dog. He really hoped for the former.

Elks sat on the front edge of the desk. "You'll be going undercover to gather information."

Undercover sounded good. "Information on what?"

"A possible theft."

"Possible?"

Elks shook his head and crossed his arms. Jimmy realized the commander wasn't happy about this assignment.

"The mayor has a friend who was burglarized. He wants us to quietly look into it."

"Did he file a report?"

Elks shook his head. "Like I said, it's a special assignment."

A sinking feeling hit him. Not the good kind of special.

"Here's the deal, O'Malley. The mayor's buddy was robbed, but he didn't report it. I'm still not clear as to why, but the mayor thinks his friend is not the only victim."

Jimmy shifted. "He thinks?"

"These people are high society. They have something stolen, they just replace it, I guess. I don't know. I told the mayor that without a formal report, we couldn't do much. What I did promise was that if he provided access, I would provide a detective to investigate. If you come up with other victims, we'll form a task force. If he's right and someone is targeting the city's wealthy, it could be a career-making case."

"And if he's wrong?"

Elks shrugged. "We lose some man hours. You get to rub elbows with the upper echelon of the city and attend some fancy parties."

Fuck. Getting dressed up to hang out with a bunch of snobs was not his idea of a great career move.

Elks reached around, picked up an envelope from his desk, and handed it to Jimmy. "You'll be attending a gala tomorrow night. It's black tie, so get a tux. You're going in as James Buchanan, a friend of Mayor Park. You've just moved to the city, and he's extended his societal pull to you. He'll be there to introduce you around."

Jimmy looked at the invitation, which felt more like fabric than paper. The script was fancy calligraphy. Elks went back to his side of the desk and Jimmy stood.

Before leaving, he had to know. "Sir, if you don't mind my asking, why me?"

"You're a low man in the ranks and no one knows you. I can't afford to pull a detective off a homicide to make the mayor happy."

Disappointment stung. Part of him had hoped that the extra hours he'd put in on going nowhere cases had made an impact, that people higher on the ladder had noticed. Instead, he could've been a total idiot and still been chosen for this assignment.

At least he'd get face time with the mayor. That couldn't possibly be a bad thing. Make a positive impression there and he'd have pull down the line when he'd need it.

Jimmy went back to meet up with his partner, Gabby. She'd been reinterviewing a witness to one of the burglaries they were trying to solve.

When he found her, she sat at her desk, staring at a file.

"Hey."

"So what'd Elks want?"

"I got a new assignment." He explained the details and her mouth opened.

"And he chose you? What the hell, man? I wouldn't mind attending a party. Although the heels would probably be a killer. But the champagne and caviar? Might be worth suffering through heels and a dress."

He shook his head at her. "I'm there to get information, not to get drunk."

"Lighten up, O'Malley. There's no rule against enjoying

your job. If you don't find some spark, you'll burn out inside five years." She closed the file in front of her. "At least your case will get me out of here."

He raised his eyebrows.

"I get to be your backup."

JIMMY WALKED through the front door of his childhood home and tripped on a hockey skate. What the fuck? His brothers weren't twelve anymore. You'd think they could manage to pick up their shit. He went straight to his bedroom upstairs to hang up the tuxedo. If his brothers caught sight of it, they'd never stop ribbing him. They'd assume he had a date.

Not that he'd waste dressing up on any of the women he'd been with lately. His life plan was right on track, except for that one part. Finding the right woman had not been working out.

"Hey, Jimmy. You home?" his baby brother Tommy screamed from the kitchen.

Rather than yell back, Jimmy walked back downstairs. "What's up?"

"Your turn for dinner."

Shit. He'd forgotten. He eyed the phone and wanted to call for pizza, but he knew his dad had probably eaten crap all day, so he'd have to cook. His brothers cheated enough on their days. "Where's Dad?"

Tommy pulled a beer from the fridge and shrugged. "I just got home a little while ago. He wasn't here."

"Sean around?"

Another shrug. "Haven't seen him."

Jimmy checked the contents of the fridge. He didn't have

the energy to go shopping. If their dad wasn't home anyway, pizza would be fine. The old man's diet would be shot for the day. Jimmy just hoped he was smart enough to check his blood sugar while he was out. He tossed thirty bucks on the table and grabbed a beer for himself. "Call for a pizza. No anchovies."

Tommy snickered. He was the only one in the house who ate anchovies, so when given the chance, he ordered them on pizza so he wouldn't have to share. Sometimes Jimmy let him get away with it. The kid was on the scrawny side. Always had been.

Jimmy took his beer back upstairs. After his brothers had moved out, he turned the two attic bedrooms into an apartment for himself. If he had to be stuck living at home with his dad, he might as well be comfortable. He hadn't counted on two of his three brothers moving back in.

They'd moved into the basement. At least they had a separate entrance, so it gave the appearance of an apartment. Until you walked into the unfinished basement anyway. Neither Tommy nor Sean did a damn thing to improve the space. They lived in a concrete dungeon, and it didn't seem to bother them a bit.

After a quick shower, he sat at his computer to research Mayor Park's friends and the charity event he had to attend. He didn't go into any situation unarmed.

Moira O'Leary scanned her closet for the right gown for the fund-raiser for Children's Memorial—correction: Lurie Children's Hospital. It didn't matter if she'd grown up knowing it as Children's Memorial. If she didn't get it right in the article, she'd be a laughingstock.

"Ooo...what about this one?" Her friend Kathy pulled out a simple little black dress.

"Not formal enough. I need floor length for this party." It looked like she needed to make another trip to the consignment shop.

"Rough life you have. Getting dressed up and pretty in order to drink with a bunch of rich people who are donating money for a good cause. Shoot, how do I get in on that gig?" Kathy replaced the dress in the closet.

Moira smiled. All anyone ever saw of her life was the glamorous parties. "Yeah, that's my charmed life. Champagne and bonbons."

She laughed it off. It was easier than trying to convince anyone that she held a real job. No one ever saw her at three in the morning struggling to get words on the page to meet a deadline. They all forgot the years she wrote obituaries and suburban city council meeting articles.

"Really, Moira. Can't you get me in to one of these parties? I'm thinking it would be a great place to meet a guy. It would be like *The Millionaire Matchmaker* without Patti being mean to me." She plopped on Moira's bed.

"If I had an extra invite, I would. I get one, and I usually have to beg for that. Plus, I've yet to see an unattached guy who I'd like to date." She'd been to enough functions to realize that having money didn't make those guys any better than the ones they'd meet at her family's bar or her brother's bowling alley. "Come on, I need to go shopping. I can't wear the same dress I wore last week to tomorrow's party. I need to spread them out or people will notice."

Kathy stood and Moira felt a twinge of jealousy at Kathy's height. Her friend stood a good six inches taller. Moira hated having to get every garment tailored.

"You're going to show me your secret shopping places?

Do I need a special invite or do they let lowly people like me in?" She flashed a bright smile and gathered her wildly curly hair in a ponytail.

"If they let me in, I'm sure they'll love you." Moira grabbed her purse and did some quick mental calculations to see how much she could afford to spend and still make rent. She couldn't wait to make a real name for herself so she wouldn't have to worry about how much a dress cost.

She grabbed two bottles of water from the fridge and tossed one to Kathy, who was holding the invitation for Moira's ten-year high school reunion.

"Going?" she asked.

Moira shrugged. "Maybe. I don't know if I'm up for it."

"Go. It's fun. I told you I had a blast at mine last month. If nothing else, you get to poke fun at all the people who haven't done as well as you have."

"High school all over again." The problem with that was Moira hadn't done as well as she'd expected. Although she had a decent job, she hadn't gotten the recognition she'd hoped for. She also hadn't gotten married and had no family. Shit, she didn't even have a boyfriend. It *was* like high school all over again.

"I know that look. You've done well for yourself. Just find some really hot guy to go with you."

"Easy for you to say. Come on, we have dresses to buy."

THREE STORES LATER, Moira found the perfect gown. The emerald green fabric held just a hint of shimmer. She only needed to have it shortened. For a change, the bust and waist both fit, an anomaly for which she was grateful. Usually, she needed to take in the waist and shorten it, or figure out how to let out some room in the bust, which was hard, so she tended to opt for sizes much too big for the rest of her body. She'd gladly give up a couple of cup sizes to add a few measly inches in leg.

As she carried her new dress into her apartment, her phone rang. She juggled the keys and phone with the dress as she opened the door. "Hey, Ry, what's up?"

"How's my favorite sister?"

She rolled her eyes. Ryan liked to think he was the only one who knew when people were calling for a favor. "Right now, I'm the only sister you have on this continent. Not too hard to be the favorite. What do you need?"

"A babysitter for tomorrow night?"

"Sorry, no can do. You know I love baby Patrick, but I have a work thing tomorrow night." She tossed her keys on the coffee table and hung the dress on the back of her bedroom door. "How about Sunday?"

"I have to be at the bar on Sunday."

Moira sighed. Ryan always did stuff for the rest of them. "How about during the day? I can spend the afternoon at your house and head out to the party from there."

Ryan went silent and she knew he was considering the option. "That might work. Let me talk to Quinn."

"Let me know." She disconnected and called her mom, seamstress extraordinaire. "Hi, Mom. I bought a new dress. Any chance you can hem it for me?"

"When do you need it?"

"For tomorrow?"

Her mother tsked like she always did.

"I just bought it today, and it fits really well. Except for the length, of course."

"But when did you know you needed a dress? When did you go shopping for it?"

Mom had her there. So she procrastinated. In her

defense, had she gone shopping earlier, she probably wouldn't have gotten this perfect dress. "You should be used to it by now. It's not like I became an adult and suddenly started procrastinating. I've waited until the last minute for everything my whole life."

"Come for dinner and I'll do it after."

"Thanks, Mom. You're the best."

Her mom disconnected without acknowledging her gratitude. Her mother would make a real dinner, so Moira was getting a double bonus.

Unfortunately, this was a pretty typical Friday night for her. For a long time, she thought things were good—she was getting where she wanted to be. But now, she watched her older brothers all find love and she felt like she was missing out.

Like when she was a teenager and they all had girlfriends. Many girlfriends. But they scared off any guy who came looking for her.

She liked having protective brothers, but damn, she wanted a little taste of what they had. No, a taste would never be enough. She wanted the whole shebang, her own fairy tale.

Hanging out with her mom on a Friday night wouldn't get her there.

~

ON SATURDAY, Jimmy dressed in the rented tux and tried not to feel trapped. He was still getting used to wearing a suit on a daily basis. A tuxedo felt so formal and stiff, like being in a straitjacket. He walked downstairs to check on his dad before heading out.

"Where the hell you going all dressed up?"

"Work," Jimmy answered. "Did you check your blood?"

His dad nodded and drank from a glass. Jimmy eyed the liquid to determine what it was.

"Diet root beer," Dad said. "And before you ask, yeah, I ate dinner, even my vegetables."

If this was what being a parent felt like, maybe he wasn't cut out to be a father. Jimmy could barely control his temper over his dad's attitude about everything. It's not like Jimmy wanted to mother him.

"What kind of case makes you dress like a damn penguin?"

"Undercover."

"There's the reason I stayed in uniform. Things are black and white. None of that shite." He slugged back more of his root beer.

While his father had been a good cop, Jimmy knew Dad hadn't been particularly ambitious either, which had been the main reason he'd stayed in uniform his entire career. Jimmy wanted more. More money, more respect—he wanted it all.

Dad couldn't understand, so they clashed pretty often when it came to talking about work. Jimmy avoided the topic whenever possible, but at the same time, he knew Dad loved to have a small piece of his life back by talking over a case with Jimmy.

He took the Blue Line downtown and walked the few blocks to the mayor's office. The tuxedo irritated the shit out of him. He tried not to claw at the tie and hoped the stench of the El didn't stick to him.

Gabby offered to drive, but it didn't make sense for her to drive to the Northside when she lived south. They planned to meet at the mayor's office and he'd ride with the mayor. Gave him a chance to get chummy with the man.

As he turned the corner in front of the building, a long, high-pitched whistle broke the air. Gabby stood, leaning against her car, smiling at him.

Christ. It's going to be a long night.

"You clean up good, O'Malley. Maybe this should be your new uniform. You're not as scary in a tux as you are in your suit."

He took in her clothes—jeans and comfortable shoes—and wished he had suggested that she take this assignment. She did have seniority.

But backup didn't impress people. The guy who went through the door first was the one everyone remembered.

He was determined to be that guy.

They walked to the mayor's office and sat in the reception area waiting together. They were on time. Why couldn't everyone else be?

When the mayor emerged from his office, wearing a tux that looked much better than his, Jimmy stood. "Mayor Park, it's good to meet you."

"Detectives O'Malley, Ruiz." He nodded at them and pointed at his office. "Join me a few minutes before we head out."

Once they were behind closed doors, the mayor's countenance changed, relaxed. "Look, I know my request was strange and the two of you probably think I'm crazy. But a good friend of mine lost some very expensive jewelry in the theft. I don't think he's the only one. I've heard rumors of other burglaries, and I think we have a sizeable theft ring running in the city, targeting wealthy men."

He paused and waited for a response.

Jimmy asked what both he and Gabby wondered. "Why haven't the burglaries been reported? Alert other members of the social circle to be aware, hire extra security..."

"I don't know about other cases, but I know in my friend's, he was in a compromising position that he didn't want to get out. These are important men with deep pockets and reputations they need to protect."

The muscles in Jimmy's jaw tightened. As if men with less money didn't have reputations worth protecting. "What do you hope will come from this operation, sir?"

"I'm thinking that if I bring you in, you'll see or hear things I don't. You'll be able to build a case and put these men's minds at ease." He pressed his lips together, then inhaled deeply. "I don't like to waste city resources and I don't take this lightly. Give me a few weeks. By then, you'll have had the chance to meet people and be accepted into the circle. If you find nothing, that'll be the end of it."

"Yes, sir."

The mayor moved forward and clamped a hand on his shoulder. "And starting right now, I'm Bill, not sir. Am I right, James?"

James would take some getting used to. He'd only been James when he was in trouble growing up. In the recesses of his memory, he could hear his mom calling *James Matthew O'Malley*.... He stopped the memory from going further and focused on becoming James Buchanan.

Some tech guy in the department created a whole online life for James Buchanan and Jimmy had spent the day memorizing enough to be able to pass basic conversations. James Buchanan had led a charmed life.

Hours later, he still felt strangled by the bow tie and he'd shaken so many hands that he probably had a lifetime of germs on his palm. How did politicians do this day after day? Mayor Park—Bill—had introduced him to many men, and in the few moments they had between introductions, Bill had pointed out the men who were rumored to have been robbed.

Now Bill left him standing with Stan Decker, some guy who was in real estate using hard sell tactics on James. Jimmy listened with half his attention, while scanning the remaining guests. Through the crowd, he caught a glimpse of a woman with a great rack. Her tits were spilling out of the top of her green dress. Not obscenely so, but enough to draw attention.

Jimmy stared at the milky white globes barely contained by the slippery material. His eyes wandered across the expanse of skin up over her collarbone and to her face.

And then his heart stopped.

What the hell is Moira O'Leary doing here?

As if she felt him staring, she started to turn his way and he ducked a little to the side. Fuck. So much wrong with the entire situation. Forcing his tongue to work, he said, "Sorry to interrupt you, Stan, but I need to make a call."

Jimmy fumbled for his phone and dodged out of the way before Moira made eye contact. He jostled through the crowd, zigzagging like he would on the football field. He spared a moment to glance over his shoulder and saw Moira heading to where he'd left Stan. A crowd stood in front of the elevators, so he veered toward the stairs and dialed Gabby.

"My cover's blown. Meet me out front." He hung up before she could rattle off questions.

He couldn't believe it. Of all the people to show up at this party, it had to be Moira O'Leary. He hadn't expected any of the O'Learys to be there—they weren't part of this circle any more than he was—but in the back of his mind, he knew seeing Griffin Walker was a possibility. He was one guy from the neighborhood who had made it big. He also knew Walker would keep his mouth shut.

Moira was a completely different story. That girl talked a mile a minute to anyone, anywhere, anytime. He'd made it a few measly hours into his special assignment before being blown out of the water by Moira. The girl was a menace.

Some things never change.

As he pushed through the revolving door in the lobby of the hotel, the image of Moira's tits stuck in his head. He tried to push the picture away. He had no right to ever think about her that way. She was Liam's little sister, for Christ's sake.

Nothing looked too little tonight, though. Blood stirred in his body where it shouldn't and he clenched his jaw.

Yeah, some things never change.

2

---

oira strode across the room, sure she'd seen Jimmy O'Malley talking to Stan Decker. She'd avoided Decker for the first few hours of the party. The man hit on her relentlessly, and whenever he talked, he spoke directly to her chest. She had no idea how he managed to sell so many properties if that's how he treated clients.

But right now, her curiosity got the better of her and she had to see if it was Jimmy. She'd barely caught a glimpse, but something about the man made her believe it was him. Like on an instinctual level, her body knew.

Which was just plain silly, and she knew it, but she couldn't help it. She'd been in love with Jimmy since the age of ten and he'd never given her the time of day. Except to tell her to scram because she annoyed him.

She approached Decker with a friendly smile, not that he'd notice. "Hi, Mr. Decker. How are you this evening?"

"Good, and you?"

She tried not to inhale, forcing her boobs higher and

closer to his face. "I'm fine. The man you were just talking to, was that—"

"James Buchanan, new to town. Friends with the mayor."

"Oh." Why the news should disappoint her made little sense. Maybe part of her wanted to see a friendly face in the crowd. A real friend, not the phoniness of people who wanted their picture taken. Jimmy might not be a real friend, but being Liam's friend, he would probably put in the effort to be nice to her. Probably.

Moira made her rounds, talking to donors and visiting with the parents of sick kids. Listening to their stories was both inspiring and heartbreaking. One thing she took away from it, though, was the strength they displayed. Especially the couples. Trying to hold a family together while caring for a sick child had to be devastating. Watching them hold hands and support each other while talking about their families gave her hope.

One day, she'd find the man who would hold her hand and help her meet her dreams and goals. They'd build a life together, have a family, find happiness. She wanted what her family had. Sometimes she thought she was born in the wrong decade. If only she could be like Bogie and Bacall or Tracy and Hepburn.

Life in a black-and-white movie with witty banter and true love.

She wandered through the crowd looking for James Buchanan. Thinking back, she realized her imagination had simply run away from her again. Not every good-looking man was Jimmy. Maybe Mr. Buchanan was actually better looking. Plus, he probably had money. She wanted to introduce herself and definitely include him in her article.

"Mr. Mayor," she started. Then she realized he might not remember her. "Moira O'Leary."

He smiled and nodded. "I'm not doing interviews today, Moira."

"I was wondering if you could point out your friend James Buchanan. I spoke with Mr. Decker who mentioned you and Mr. Buchanan are friends. I'd like to interview him, if possible."

The mayor shifted as if surprised she would ask about Buchanan. She always asked about new players. *Curious.*

"I'm not sure if James would want to be interviewed. He's rather private." The mayor peered over the top of her head and scanned the crowd. "I'm not seeing him just now."

Moira pulled a card from her purse. "Well, when you do see him, please pass on my card. I'd love to chat."

The mayor pocketed the card, but she knew the look. Her card would be dropped in the nearest trash can. Now she had a mission. Something was up with this Buchanan and she planned to find out what his juicy little secrets were. Moira liked to have a mission. It wasn't like she didn't enjoy her job. On the contrary, she loved it, but every now and then the boredom bug bit her. Today was one of those days.

Trailing after a sexy, rich man new to Chicago wasn't a bad way to spend some time. If she happened to get a story out of it too, well, that was just a bonus.

LATER THAT NIGHT, face scrubbed clean of makeup and beautiful gown hanging back in her closet, Moira stared at her computer screen. James Buchanan had very little information online. His Facebook page didn't have any photos. A whopping three blogs mentioned his name, always after the mayor's name.

Something was definitely up. She tried every directory and search engine she could, but still came up empty. Desperate, she scrambled to think if she knew anyone who would be able to dig deeper.

Griffin would be able to find information. Although he made his name and money as a video game developer, she knew he could hack into anything. The question became whether a possible goose chase was worth breaking the law. She thought about baby Colleen and decided that satisfying her curiosity was not that important. She wouldn't want Griffin to get into any trouble.

Maybe she'd e-mail Griffin and see if he knew the guy.

As she crawled into bed, she tried to conjure up the image of the man she'd seen. He had a beard-in-progress thing going on and his hair was cropped short. Jimmy never had facial hair, so why would she think it had been him? The look was more sophisticated than any guy she'd known growing up. She fell asleep with images of Jimmy O'Malley floating in her head, dreaming about how she wished he'd give her a chance, just once.

JIMMY AND GABBY stood in Elks's office.

"DAMN IT, O'Malley. How could you have screwed this up in a matter of a few hours?"

Jimmy bit down on his response.

"Who is this woman who saw you?"

Jimmy unclenched his jaw. "Moira O'Leary. She's a reporter."

"Fuck. And how do you know her?" Elks paced the length of his office. Gabby stood at attention, like she expected the ax to fall.

"I'm friends with her brother. We grew up on the same block."

"And you didn't think it important to inform us of that when we brought you in?" Elks's face turned an unnatural shade of red, nearing purple.

"She's my friend's little sister. I knew she was a reporter, but I had no idea she'd be at the party." He'd made a point over the years to try to ignore everything about Moira O'Leary. The girl spelled trouble. Now she managed to get him into hot water without even trying.

"You're sure she made you."

Jimmy shrugged. "I left as soon as I saw her. She was headed in my direction, so I think she did. I didn't stick around."

Elks pulled out his chair and sat. "You and Ruiz pay her a visit. See her reaction. Find out if she told anyone your real name."

Shit. He'd rather do just about anything than ask Moira for a favor. He and Gabby left the office. "You need to take point on this one."

Gabby stopped in her tracks. "If she's your friend, why would I take lead?"

Jimmy didn't answer.

"What's the story here?"

He didn't know what to tell her. "She's my friend's kid sister."

"Did you sleep with her? Is that why you're avoiding her?"

"No." Like he needed Gabby's help putting that image in

his mind. "We tend to...butt heads a lot. If I say the sky's blue, she's going to argue it's purple. Just to fight. If she knows that keeping her mouth shut means doing me a favor, she'll run down the street screaming my cover." He turned back to head out the door.

Gabby's footsteps clomped behind him and she grabbed his jacket. "I'm not buying it, Jimmy. You must've done something to make her want to fight you."

He shrugged. He had no idea why Moira pushed his buttons. She'd been doing it most of her life. He remembered when she was little, she'd look up at him with those big baby blues and she was the sweetest thing on two legs.

Then she hit puberty.

He hadn't been able to look at her like a little girl anymore, and he had no business looking at her any other way. So he'd stopped talking to her unless he absolutely had to. He wasn't rude to her, but he kept his distance. It was like doing so just drew her closer. She was always looking for ways to get at him, talk to him, rile him up.

"I don't know, Gabby. You have younger siblings. You know how it is. They bug you just to bug you."

"I guess." But she didn't sound convinced.

They drove to Moira's apartment. After they parked, he scanned the street, but realized he didn't know what kind of car she drove these days.

They walked up to the building and climbed three floors to her apartment. The entire building was completely unsecure. He wondered if Liam knew she lived here. Not only was there no security at the main entrance, but the front door didn't even lock. Anyone could get in. What the hell was she thinking living in a place like this?

Gabby took lead and knocked at Moira's door. Jimmy stood to the side out of sight of the peephole. With any luck,

Gabby could talk with her without Jimmy ever having to show his face.

Moira swung the door open quickly enough that she probably hadn't even checked the peephole. "Hello."

Not an ounce of wariness in her voice.

"Moira O'Leary?"

"Yes."

Gabby flashed her badge.

"Oh, my God. What happened? Who's hurt?"

Gabby's hand flicked up. "No one, Ms. O'Leary. I have a few questions for you about a function you attended last night."

"What about it?"

Jimmy heard her tone change, like she was preparing for a fight.

"There was a guest there, James Buchanan." Gabby paused.

Jimmy listened for Moira's smart-ass remark, but none followed.

"Mr. Buchanan is part of an ongoing investigation, so I'm here to request that you not include his photo in whatever article you might print about the party." Gabby shifted closer, standing a full head above Moira. "Did you take any photos of Mr. Buchanan?"

"Hmm...surprisingly, he disappeared as soon as I was heading over to meet him."

Jimmy heard the smirk. She knew. He rolled his shoulder off the wall and pressed his palm against the door, widening the opening to reveal himself.

Moira let out a little yip and jumped. "I knew it. I only saw you for a second, but I knew. Why the hell did you run out? And what's up with the phony name? Oh. You're undercover, right? I bet it's something good. Tell me—"

"Moira." The single word came out sharper than he'd meant, but it worked. Moira's jaw snapped shut.

Gabby continued, "Ms. O'Leary, did you mention to anyone that you saw Detective O'Malley at the party last night?"

"No. I thought it was Jimmy, but by the time I made my way through the crowd, he was gone and Decker said he was James Buchanan. I thought I'd imagined seeing you."

Although Moira spoke directly to him, Gabby interrupted her. "Ms. O'Leary." When she had Moira's attention, she went on. "Detective O'Malley is undercover and it's imperative that no one know his real name."

Moira slid her gaze back to Jimmy, and being the oldest of five, he knew what was coming.

"What's in it for me?"

"The thanks of the Chicago Police Department," he answered.

She snorted. "That's not gonna pay my rent. I want an exclusive. I'll keep my mouth shut and you give me the details before anyone else."

"How about you keep your mouth shut or I'll haul you in on obstruction charges?"

Gabby touched his forearm, but he refused to back down. No way was Moira going to get the better of him. He'd never bowed down to any reporter and he wouldn't start now.

Moira stood, staring at him with her arms crossed defiantly below her full breasts, daring him to threaten her again.

The problem was, legal threats weren't crossing his mind just then. Luckily, cooler heads prevailed and Gabby stepped between them.

"Ms. O'Leary, we can't promise you'll get the story first,

mostly because there might not be much of a story when we're done with our investigation. But we'll do our best." She pulled a card from her pocket and handed it to Moira.

She accepted it and smiled up at Jimmy, who glared at her over Gabby's head. "What, Jimmy, no card from you? However will I contact you?" She snapped her fingers. "Oh, yeah. I can probably knock on your dad's door."

He stiffened at the implication that he couldn't support himself, mostly because Moira knew the truth. He'd moved back home to take care of his dad. Shit, she'd been there to help him move in. Gabby stepped back and he either had to move or knock her over.

"Thank you for your cooperation, Ms. O'Leary," Gabby said.

Moira moved back inside her apartment and wagged her fingers at him before closing the door. Her smile returned to the sweet one that he found so hard to resist. He listened, but she didn't lock the door. Gabby turned and started down the stairs. She looked over her shoulder. "You coming?"

"In a minute." When Gabby hit the landing and turned the corner, he grabbed the doorknob and turned. Sure as shit, it turned without any resistance whatsoever. What the hell was that girl thinking?

He opened the door and strode in. She had the radio on and he knew she couldn't hear him. He leaned against the wall in the hallway at the epicenter of the apartment and waited. She wouldn't be able to go anywhere without seeing him.

Within a minute she emerged from her bedroom wearing a skimpy robe while reading the label on a jar. Although he hadn't moved, it was like she felt his presence and looked up. Everything froze. Her eyes widened.

Then she screamed, threw the jar at him. The bottle bounced off his chest and he grabbed it from the floor. Wax.

Jimmy let out a chuckle.

~

MOIRA'S HEART lodged in her throat before recognition hit. *Jimmy? What the hell?* Air flooded into her lungs and her heart steadied, but her blood boiled. "What the hell are you doing in my apartment?"

"You didn't lock your door."

"I certainly didn't leave it open either. There was no invitation to enter." Her voice rose steadily and she jabbed a finger in his direction. "You had no business coming in. I should call and have you arrested."

He raised a hand in defense. "When you closed the door, I listened for you to lock up and you didn't. I turned the knob and let myself in."

"You scared the shit out of me. What the hell is wrong with you?"

"Me scaring you is the least of your worries. What if I was a rapist or murderer? You're making yourself an easy target. This building has zero security. It *is* like an invitation for some creep to come after you." His voice stayed quiet and strong, and was somehow way more menacing than her screaming rant.

She took a step back and crossed her arms again. She suddenly realized that she wore nothing but her bathrobe, which was currently gaping. Tugging it closed and pulling the sash tighter, she stared at her feet.

Could she get more embarrassed?

Jimmy's hand holding a jar filled her field of vision. Her wax. "I think you dropped this."

Yes, her night just got more embarrassing. She curled her fingers around the jar and tucked it into the pocket of the robe. His feet nearly touched hers and she focused on his scuffed dress shoes in front of her bare toes.

They stood in silence and Moira noticed that they breathed in rhythm. He stood close enough that the heat from his body permeated the thin material of her robe. Holy shit. Jimmy O'Malley never got this close to her. If she leaned forward, she could rest her face on his chest.

She couldn't look at him. It was bad enough that he scared her half to death, but now he'd seen her freak out while half naked, all while he was holding her leg wax. And she might actually die if he realized she was just fantasizing about him.

"Hey," he said softly. Nothing else. He waited silently until her eyes met his.

She expected to see his usual ridicule, but instead, there was something else. Kindness?

"I didn't mean to scare you." He paused. "Well, I did, but only because I want you to understand how completely unsafe you are. I wouldn't want something to happen to you."

Her heart, which had been making its way back to its normal position, plummeted to her feet. Jimmy stood so close, mere inches separating them. How many times over the years had she dreamed of being in this exact position? And he was here because he *cared*.

She leaned forward and was certain she'd seen the look on his face shift. His eyes darkened and she knew he wanted to kiss her. The knowledge sent tingles through her body.

He suddenly stepped back, turned, and walked to the door. Opening it, he said over his shoulder, "Make sure you lock up."

Then he was gone.

Moira stood frozen in place for a second.

"Now, Moira," he yelled from the other side of the door.

She scrambled to the door, flipped the dead bolt, and collapsed against the wood. *What the hell just happened?* Moira closed her eyes and replayed the scene in her mind. When she'd first come out of her bedroom, all she saw was a hulk of a man standing in her hall.

Thinking back now, she should've recognized him immediately. Jimmy had a way of standing, he had this air around him that was a constant buzz of motion without having to move. He hadn't been threatening, just leaning against the corner of the wall. And she had to go and throw wax at him.

But what happened after—now that she could work past the embarrassment—she hadn't imagined. She could still feel the warmth of his body even though they hadn't actually touched. And while she would never claim to be an expert on all men, and certainly not one on Jimmy O'Malley, she knew a lusty look when she was on the receiving end.

That was no one-way lust.

Moira pushed off the door feeling lighter than she had in a long time. Jimmy O'Malley almost kissed her. She didn't know how or why it had happened now, but she knew she wanted to be in that position again.

With the jar of wax thumping against her thigh as she walked back to the bathroom, Moira developed a plan. They needed each other. She could help with whatever investigation Jimmy had going on and he could help her get a story that was more than high society fluff. And if she was lucky enough to get lucky with him, well then, that would be all the better.

JIMMY STOMPED down the stairs and out into the fresh air. Or what would've been fresh air if it wasn't July in Chicago. He dragged in a deep breath from the wall of humidity. He didn't know what he'd been thinking. He just wanted to teach Moira a lesson about personal safety.

He wouldn't want to face her brothers if something happened to her and he could've prevented it. Never had he expected to find her wearing nothing but a skimpy robe. The woman was like a quick-change artist. He might not have even noticed how short the robe was or how the pale skin on her chest was sprinkled with freckles, but she got all feisty and started poking at him, which caused the opening of the robe to widen.

Even then, he kept himself in check, but he made the ultimate mistake of getting too close to her. The look in her eyes when they met his undid him.

He almost lost his fucking mind and kissed her.

Shaking his head, he slid into the car beside Gabby.

"'Bout time. What the hell were you doing? Gettin' lucky?"

His head jerked back. "No. I wanted to make sure she locked her door. That apartment isn't safe."

"Dude, it takes three seconds to say, 'Lock the door.'" Gabby snickered.

"It takes longer than five minutes to get lucky if you're doing it right."

She continued on as if he hadn't spoken. "Plus, you're looking totally guilty right now. What's the story?"

"There is no story. Moira's like a little sister." The lie made his stomach turn. He wanted to think about her like a little sister, but he hadn't been able to for years. Which was why he avoided her.

Gabby pulled out into traffic, a smile still hovering on her lips.

"What?" he snapped.

"Nothing. You want me to believe she's like a sister, so be it. But the attraction in the hallway was like snap, crackle, pop."

"Not attraction, annoyance."

"Whatever."

Gabby drove back to the station so they could discuss a game plan. Last night had been a waste of time. He was supposedly new to the city, and no one was quick to befriend him. How was he supposed to get people to talk about being robbed? This whole thing reeked of a wild goose chase.

If these rich assholes wanted to take the loss, let them. They obviously didn't trust the police to do their jobs.

They let the commander know they talked to Moira, who at least appeared to be cooperative. Then after a long-ass day of accomplishing exactly jack shit, Jimmy drove home.

Elks told him he'd be in touch with the mayor to decide how they would proceed, but Elks gave the impression that Jimmy's days of being James Buchanan weren't quite over.

BY THE TIME he got home, the last thing he wanted to do was deal with his dad. He walked through the front door and tripped over the same damn hockey skate. He picked it up and hurled it across the room. It whizzed by Tommy's head as he came in from the other end of the room.

"What the fuck, dude?"

"That's what I was thinking. If you can't pick up after yourself, find somewhere else to live. I'm not your goddamn maid."

Tommy grabbed the skate and shoved it under the table. "You're not my mother either, so stopped acting like it."

"Be an adult and I won't have to."

"What the hell crawled up your ass and died?"

What the hell indeed? Jimmy didn't know what the hell was bothering him. Yes, he did. A hot little redhead made his blood boil every way possible and made him crazy. "I'm having a bad day."

"I'll say. Maybe you need to get laid. Always sets me straight. You wanna go out?"

"Maybe later. I have some work to do. Have you checked on Dad?"

Tommy shook his head. "He was asleep when I came in."

"Asleep?" Not a good sign.

"He was breathing, but I didn't wake him."

Jimmy stuck his head in his dad's bedroom. The man's snore sounded like a Mack truck. He counted the empties surrounding his dad. Eight beers. Enough that his father wouldn't have thought to check his blood. Probably not for the entire day. Jimmy thought that once he got in as a detective, he'd be able to keep a better eye on his dad. It didn't help that Tommy and Sean didn't see his drinking as a problem. If he offered them a beer, they'd sit and drink with him.

No matter what he told them, they didn't get it. They still looked at Dad like he was an invincible superhero instead of a diabetic old man.

Jimmy gathered the supplies and tested his father's blood. As expected, his blood sugar was low, so Jimmy roused him enough to take a glucose pill. Then he went to the kitchen to make some real food.

Most weeks Dad did a good job. He watched what he ate and stuck to a couple of beers a night. Something would trigger a binge like this, but Jimmy didn't know what the trigger was. And it wasn't like Seamus O'Malley would ever admit to his sons that he had a problem.

3

M oira schooled her face and practiced what she wanted to say. *Treat it like an interview. Be professional. And don't think about Jimmy O'Malley.*

She tugged on her T-shirt to straighten it, knowing it was a silly habit, especially since no one would see her over the phone. One more deep breath. Game time. She dialed quickly before she lost her nerve.

"Hello."

"Hi, is this Detective Ruiz?"

"Speaking."

"Hi, Detective. This is Moira O'Leary. Do you have a few minutes to talk?"

"Sure."

"I have a proposition. I know this afternoon I was...less than professional. I apologize. I definitely would never do something to intentionally cause problems for the police." She inhaled slowly and reminded herself that Jimmy was the police, and although she liked to cause as many problems for him as possible, she couldn't this time. "Anyway, I'm sure Jim—I mean Detective O'Malley explained that we grew up together. You know how it is when you've known someone your whole life. You get on each other's nerves."

"Okay."

"Let me get to the point."

"Please do."

"I take it from last night's fund-raiser that Detective O'Malley needs to be accepted in this social circle for whatever case you're working on. My guess is, that needs to happen fast. I'm offering my help."

A slight pause and then, "Go on."

Ha! I knew this would work. "I know this crowd. I've been writing about these people for a year now. We might not be friends—they're never going to invite me out for coffee or anything—but they trust me. I make them look good. When they want press, when they have a cause they feel strongly about, they call me." Moira shifted the phone to her other ear and clicked to open her e-mail. Her invite to the Lincoln Park Zoo benefit had arrived. This was one party she really liked.

The zoo was one of her favorite places. She had excellent memories of going to the zoo as a kid with her whole family.

"How do you suppose you could help, Ms. O'Leary?"

"Uh…" Shit. She'd gotten distracted again. She hadn't come up with a plan for Jimmy. She just knew she could use his situation to help herself. "I can talk to him in front of the others. Make it seem like I know all about him so he doesn't appear to be such an outsider."

"And you think that'll be enough?"

"If you can have your tech guys, who I'm assuming created Jimmy's phony online life, create a few news articles dropping his name. They have to be out of town events for it to be realistic. These people read the newspapers and blogs that celebrate themselves. While they might excuse not noticing Jimmy at one or two events, they'll know if he keeps saying he was somewhere, but *no one* remembers him."

"In truth, we were hoping no one would notice."

"They will. If I act like he belongs, offer to interview him as a new Chicagoan, the others will take notice. I'm not saying they care about what I think, but they'll notice. Between that and being the mayor's friend, he should be able to blend." Moira sounded good even to her own ears. She was getting good at the bullshit.

"And what are you looking for?"

"Excuse me?"

"Cut the crap, Ms. O'Leary. You're not calling me and offering help out of the goodness of your heart. You're after the story."

"Well, I am a reporter. This is how I make my living."

"I can't make you any promises."

"I didn't think you would. I can promise not to write anything without permission, but I want the exclusive."

Detective Ruiz sighed heavily. "I'll run it by the commander, but it's probably doable. It might not pan out to be much of anything. There might not even be a story."

Moira doubted that. Jimmy wasn't the kind of guy who spun his wheels on a pointless job. "What's the next event he has to go to?"

"There's something going on tomorrow night. A fundraiser for I don't know what."

"You need to narrow it down more. I have at least two to three things on most nights I could go to."

"Animals!" Detective Ruiz yelled.

"The animal shelter?"

"Yeah. That's the one."

Moira scanned her schedule. She hadn't planned on attending. It broke her heart to see all those dogs waiting for adoption. She always wanted to bring them all home, and her building wouldn't let her have a pet at all. She sighed. "Okay. I'll be there." She added it to her schedule. "You know Jimmy's not going to like this, right?"

"Of course. That's why you called me instead of him, even though you grew up together."

"He would shut the whole idea down. He wouldn't want to accept any help from me."

She heard what sounded like a snort of laughter. There was nothing funny about pissing off Jimmy O'Malley. Maybe his partner hadn't learned that lesson.

"Call me after you break the news to him. Will you be at the fund-raiser?"

"Not where you can see me. I'm purely backup."

Backup, huh? Was Jimmy into something dangerous? He hadn't made it sound dangerous. He'd just sounded like he didn't want her anywhere near him. "Okay, then. I'll talk to you tomorrow. Oh, and this event is business casual. Tell him to leave the tux at home."

Moira disconnected and danced through her living room. She popped the top on a beer and took a swig. Things were looking up. Having his partner deliver the bad news to Jimmy could only be sweeter if she could watch. It would almost make up for him scaring the shit out of her in her apartment.

She smiled as she took another drink. She'd definitely learned her lesson, though. She'd never forget to throw that lock again. After all these years, Jimmy O'Malley was still looking out for her.

JIMMY ADJUSTED the waistband of his pants again, shifting his gun to a position where it couldn't be seen.

"No good, O'Malley," Gabby said. "I can still see it. Why don't you take it off? It's not like you're going into a gun fight."

He grunted. He wasn't going anywhere without his gun. Untucking his shirt, he bloused it out. "Gonna have to do."

The polo he wore still held the creases from being new. Gabby laughed about it. Like it was his fault he didn't wear preppy clothes. He blamed the whole thing on Moira.

Thinking about her irritated him all over again. He knew she wouldn't be able to keep her nose out of his business. The mayor sent a car to pick him up. He briefly wondered if this was one of those bills being passed on to the citizens of Chicago. He'd just as soon drive himself, but apparently a wealthy businessman wouldn't drive an SUV unless it cost more than Jimmy made in a year.

Gabby rode with him again, but planned to attend as a server for the caterer. That way, she could listen in on conversations where he wouldn't be invited. They'd be able to cover twice as much ground.

He stepped from the car and Gabby said, "See you inside. Be nice."

The event was being held in a park. Shelter workers were all wearing blue polos, a shade darker than what he wore, thank God, so they were easy to spot and avoid. Most of them walked dogs on leashes and stopped to talk to guests about the dog in their care.

As he took a glass of champagne from a waiter drifting by, he kept one eye out for Moira. It was hot out, and if she wore another dress that showed off her chest, he might have to pull her out of the party.

"James," someone called.

Jimmy turned to see Stan Decker walking toward him. He wasn't sure if he should be relieved that someone sought him out or irked that the man would try again to sell him a property he wouldn't be able to afford in five lifetimes.

He forced a smile and extended his free hand. "Stan, good to see you again."

"I didn't know you were going to be here tonight."

"It was a last-minute decision. Bill told me about it and I figured why not? I'm still trying to get settled and meet people. Hard to do that from behind a computer screen, you know?"

The fucking phony stream coming from his mouth made him want to puke.

"Yeah, I understand. Come this way. I have some people you should meet."

They turned and skirted around a dog doing his business and the shelter worker cleaning up after. Jimmy kept his eyes on the ground in case everyone wasn't as diligent in his job as that girl.

Stan pulled up to a high top table, which seemed totally out of place in the middle of the park. Jimmy looked around and saw a handful of similar tables. Then he realized each table held some paddles for the auction. Stan put a hand on Jimmy's shoulder as if they were old friends instead of two guys who had just met.

"James Buchanan, meet Nick Starlow, Len Bitger, and Marcus Higherly."

Each man nodded at him and then silence fell. Jimmy should've taken a class on making small talk. This night was going to be more painful than the last, and he'd been stuck in a tuxedo then. Luckily, Stan liked to talk.

"James just moved to our city. He's friends with Bill."

Len's eyebrows shot up. "You are?"

Jimmy nodded and studied the three men. All three, four counting Stan, were contemporaries of the mayor, older than Jimmy by a good ten to fifteen years. They were also men that the mayor felt had been targeted for theft. He needed to get in with this group to ferret out information. "We met in Boston. His sister is a client of mine."

He kept his story vague enough that no one would question it. If they were Bill's friends, they would know he had a sister in Boston, but wouldn't push it.

Stan let out a whistle. "Love to see that one coming and going."

Jimmy followed Stan's line of sight to see Moira walking by. She wore a bright yellow dress. It was sleeveless, but covered her chest to her neck. He was wrong—not seeing the cleavage didn't make her less sexy. This dress clung to all her curves.

Her mouth tilted up at the corners.

Stan leaned over. "I think she's eyeing you, James. She came asking for you the other night. It'd be great if you could put a good word in for me."

Jimmy stiffened and wanted to smack Stan Decker, but Moira's eyes shifted to tell him not to. Had she heard what this asshole said?

"Mr. Buchanan, it's so nice to see you again. I've been trying to track you down for an interview." She paused, her smile widening. "Moira O'Leary. Please tell me you haven't forgotten me."

"How would that be possible?" He took her hand and

leaned over to kiss her cheek. It was every bit as soft and smooth as he imagined.

Stan looked astonished. "You two know each other?"

Moira looked him in the face, which was quite a feat because the man continued to stare at her chest. "We met a few months back when he was visiting Mayor Park. At the time he was considering moving here and we spent some time talking about the city. I'd like to think I had a hand in his decision to move here."

"Really?" Stan elbowed him like they were frat bothers.

"Yes. His wife was so lovely. She couldn't wait to get involved with some of the charities here."

Wife? What the hell is Moira doing? He didn't have a goddamn wife. She just threw him under the bus and destroyed their entire operation.

"Your wife, huh?" Stan snickered.

"When will she be joining you?" Moira continued. "I was hoping to be able to interview the two of you together."

Jimmy unclenched his jaw. "Soon, I hope. She had to tie up some loose ends in Boston."

Moira waved a hand in the air. "Can't you hire someone to wrap things up? At the rate she's going, she'll miss all the best events. There's nothing like summer in the city."

She glanced over her shoulder. "Oh, I have to go. I'll be in touch about that interview." She leaned up as if to kiss his cheek, but whispered, "Play along with them. Laugh at their crude humor. You'll fit right in."

And then she swooshed away.

"Please, James, tell me you got a piece of that."

His anger returned twofold and his blood ran hot. Stan Decker was an asshole. "What?"

"Come on, wife's out of town, and that little number is hunting you down."

Remembering Moira's advice, Jimmy eased into his best playboy smile. "Not yet. But I have high hopes for this interview to work out to be one on one."

"We definitely want the details," Len said.

Nick waved at someone across the lawn. "Looks like the wives want our attention, gentlemen."

Marcus extended his hand. "Good to meet you, James. Enjoy your freedom. Once our wives meet yours, you'll be stuck in the pack."

Jimmy gnawed on the idea for a while. He left his glass of champagne on the table and decided to walk through the park. He spied Gabby serving hors d'oeuvres. She made a beeline for him with her tray.

"Anything interesting?" she asked.

"I'm going to kill Moira and then I might follow up on you."

"What happened?" A crease formed in between Gabby's eyebrows.

"She told these guys I had a wife. How the hell am I supposed to produce a wife?"

Gabby handed him a napkin. "Did you think maybe she had a reason?"

No, he hadn't had any thought, other than Moira wanted to fuck with him. He snatched a crab cake from the tray and moved on. He stopped and listened to a woman talk about the terrier that yanked on a leash doing everything possible to get away from Jimmy. He knew the feeling.

He finally caught sight of Moira again and followed. If she was working, she had an odd way of doing her job. She stopped to pet every dog that walked in her path. By the time he caught up with her, she was crouched on the ground nose to nose with a beast of an animal. The dog looked big enough that it could easily maul her, but she cooed and giggled when the thing licked her face.

Jimmy tucked his hands in his pockets and watched for a minute. Moira interacted with the dog like she'd found a long lost best friend. She laughed and played and looked completely out of place with all of the other women. She sighed and stood, taking a moment to brush dog hair off her dress.

When the dog walker moved on, he sidled up next to Moira and tried to hold on to his anger. If he let the gooey look on her face affect him, he'd be useless. "We need to talk."

She looked up at him, using one hand to shield her eyes from the setting sun. "I thought we already did. Do you want to set up that interview now?" Her eyes held an evil glimmer, as if she knew what he'd said to Stan about the interview.

He grabbed her elbow and guided her away from the crowd, around the back of the tent that held the auction items. Fighting to keep his voice low, he said, "Why the hell would you tell everyone I have a wife?"

She eased her arm from his grasp and narrowed her eyes. He'd expected the sweet fuck-you smile she liked to throw out when she caused trouble. "You have no idea who you're hanging out with, but I do. Those four are all married. They bring their wives to every function and event. Or I should say their wives bring them. They stand around and ogle every female in sight."

"Yeah, I got that."

"The thing is, if you want in, the wives are going to have to approve. The wives like Mayor Park since he's such a good wholesome guy, so they'll be inclined to accept you, but in their world, having a wife makes you safer."

"Safer?"

"Less likely to bring a bunch of single women around, making it easier for their husbands to cheat."

"They're surrounded by women at these events."

"I didn't say it made sense. Their friendship extends beyond attending fund-raisers. The wives are here to keep an eye on them, but they don't follow them everywhere. At least I don't think they do." She shifted so his shadow blocked the sun and looked up at his face. "I'm not trying to screw things up for you. Trust me. I understand these people."

He believed her, but it didn't make the truth any easier. "Where the hell am I supposed to get a wife?"

She huffed out a breath. "Am I supposed to do everything for you?"

Her irritation wouldn't last. She had a hot temper, but once it blew, she went back to being sunny Moira. And she wasn't even pissed right now, so when she turned to walk away, he followed.

He walked beside her, as if they were there together, which he knew he shouldn't, but since she'd talked about interviewing him, he figured he could get away with it. She waved to various people and stopped to chat with others.

With Moira, though, it wasn't bullshit small talk. She asked real questions. She knew details about people's lives, and they respected her for it. They opened up around her, which would be a huge asset for her job. An asset he'd have to avoid.

When they were walking a stretch alone, he asked, "Why doesn't it bother you?"

"What?"

"The way Stan Decker talks about you." Remembering

the comments made him angry again. "I know you heard him, but you acted like it was nothing."

She shrugged. "Because it was nothing."

He stopped and touched her arm to halt her. "That's not true. No one should talk to you like that."

"He wasn't talking *to* me. It's not his fault I have excellent hearing."

Jimmy thought back. In truth, Stan had been respectful, at least in his words while talking to Moira. "He stares at your chest."

She laughed so hard her shoulders shook. "Really?" She spread her hands in front of her chest. "He's far from the only man to do that. It happens so often, it doesn't faze me anymore."

Jimmy made a point of looking into her bright blue eyes. No sign of anger or hurt. It would make him nuts if he saw men staring at his woman's chest instead of her face.

But Moira's not mine.

"Doesn't make it right."

She shrugged again and he saw a hint of something that she covered quickly.

"You should totally get a dog."

"What?" The abrupt change of subject rattled him.

"All of these dogs need homes. You live in a house. Your dad is home all day, right? Think about it. Having a dog would give him someone to hang out with when you and your brothers aren't home."

He immediately shook his head. "I don't have time for a dog."

"What time? I'm not talking about a puppy that needs training." She looked over the lawn. "I know just the one. I saw him before."

"Moira, no."

"You can at least look at him. He's a big dog. Part shepherd, part mastiff."

"I don't want a dog." But she'd already grabbed his hand and tugged. As much as he wanted to dig in his heels, he enjoyed the feel of her hand in his too much. When he started to walk, she released her grip. It was best that they not seem too friendly and he knew that, but he liked her touch. He followed her across the lawn. It couldn't hurt to look.

4
___

Moira wrapped the last bowl of salad and shoved it into her mom's refrigerator. This was the only part of the annual summer block party that she absolutely despised. As soon as she'd grown tall enough to see over the kitchen counter, she'd been expected to help with the preparations. The annual tradition had been going on longer than she'd been alive, and it was her favorite part about summer.

The block party was the celebration of the season. While their soiree wouldn't compete with the champagne shindigs she attended for work, it was more fun than all of the other events she went to combined.

And she was pretty sure that Jimmy would be there this year.

He'd missed half a dozen block parties while he was in the army, and since his return, he only showed up if he had the day off. He probably never requested the day off like everyone else in the neighborhood. He would rely on the luck of the draw.

This was her chance to work on him in a relaxed

atmosphere to get information about the case. Although the entire block would be filled with families, the O'Learys and the O'Malleys always hung together. Liam and Jimmy had been friends since kindergarten, and much to her dismay, she and Jimmy's younger brother Kevin had been in the same class through elementary school. Plus, they were the two big families of the neighborhood. Most others only had two or three kids. The O'Malleys had five and the O'Learys six, so they created the foundation for the football game.

The block party brought everyone back to the neighborhood where they grew up. They returned with spouses and significant others, kids, and pets. From early morning until past midnight, it was the ultimate reunion.

Satisfied that the bowls of food were balanced and the fridge door would close, Moira washed her hands and pulled her hair into a ponytail. The guys were all outside setting up tables and grills and party games for the kids. The older kids—not that there were many—were tasked with filling water balloons. When her jobs were done, there was nothing about this day she wouldn't enjoy.

She stepped outside and took a deep breath. The air was warm but not terribly humid, the sky clear blue, and the sound of kids laughing rang in the streets.

The day would be perfect.

Liam came thumping up the steps with bags of groceries and mumbled a hello as he went into the house. Moira's mouth watered at the thought of one of Liam's burgers. Colin and Ryan were flipping over the folding table they'd assembled. Quinn stood by with a rag and spray bottle to clean it. Griffin and Indy spread a huge blanket on the grass. The scene reminded her just how much things could change in one year.

Last year, Colin had returned home, Ryan and Quinn

were only friends, and Griffin and Indy barely knew each other. Now, they were all paired off and both Ryan and Griffin had kids. Which made her an aunt twice over. She began to wonder where her life might be in another year.

"Hey," she called. "Where are Michael, Brianna, and Elizabeth?"

"Michael's on his way," Ryan answered.

Colin looked over at her. "Elizabeth's at the bar. She'll be here later."

"Man, I was counting on having her for the football game."

Colin laughed. "Trust me, you don't want her playing football."

"Stop being mean, or I'll tell her you said that."

He shrugged. "Go ahead. It's not like she can deny being dangerous."

"How about you, Quinn? Are you playing?"

Quinn's eyes widened. "Football? I don't think so. I'll watch the kids."

"I'm in," Indy called from the blanket where she set up a tiny tent to house the babies. She started braiding her hair, and as soon as she had it pulled aside, Griffin kissed her neck. Being surrounded by all these couples caused a surge of jealousy. She wanted this for herself. Why couldn't she find the right guy?

Without thought, her gaze went to the O'Malley house across the street. She saw no movement, but it didn't surprise her. They weren't planners or preparers. They usually set a cooler on their front porch whenever they got moving and then pulled their grill from the yard right about when it was time to cook.

A revving motorcycle engine drew her attention. Sean O'Malley pulled up in front of his house. Moira walked over to remind him not to leave the motorcycle on the street. Knowing him, he forgot about the party and didn't even notice the construction horse that he had to drive around to get down the block.

Sean climbed off the bike and looked around.

"Hey," she called.

He waved. "Block party today, right?"

"Yep. I figured you forgot. You might want to move your bike so kids don't knock it over when they're playing."

"It'll be fine."

"You guys are going to play football today, aren't you?"

He shrugged. "Guess so. I better call Kevin and remind him it's today."

"You don't have to do that." It might be nice if she didn't have to suffer through Kevin's relentless teasing for one block party.

Sean laughed and pulled out his phone.

"You need help getting ready?"

With the phone to his ear, he answered, "Nah. Jimmy will have food in the fridge. I'm sure he's got it covered."

That answered one question she had. Jimmy was going to be at the block party. She turned away to head back to her family's house. "Game starts in two hours."

Even as she crossed the short distance, more people started filling the street. Kids ran with water guns, and the new family at the end of the block was filling a bounce house with air. Moira snickered. They would regret it once the drunk adult males decided to hop in.

Jimmy filled the cooler with ice and beer. He didn't know why he bothered. His brothers always hoarded their beer and headed down the street where the O'Learys would have a keg set up. Same with the food. Liam would be on grill duty and Jimmy's burgers could never compare, especially since his were packaged and frozen.

He shoved the frozen patties back in the freezer, grabbed a couple of bags of chips, and checked his wallet. He'd give Liam some money to cover what his family would eat. If necessary, he'd run to the store for more supplies. One of these years, he'd plan better. Maybe by the time he had his own kids running the street.

He sighed and dragged the cooler out the front door with the chips balanced on top. Once the cooler was in place, he glanced down the street. Sure enough, the O'Learys were already sitting in lawn chairs and laughing. Moira stood in front of her siblings acting something out that had them all in stitches. Liam stood back at the grill, arranging charcoal.

Sean sat at the curb next to his bike.

"Hey, you might want to move that into the garage for the night."

Sean looked over his shoulder. "Yeah, Moira already reminded me. I want to change the oil first."

"Hurry it up, then. We have a game to play."

The football game was the best part of the block party. It gave him a chance to play the game he loved. He'd played in high school, and probably could've in college if he had gone. After becoming a cop, he tried out for the police league and made it. For a very short season, he represented the boys in blue on the field.

The remainder of the block party turned him into one big ball of stress. Kids ran around unsupervised because the parents were all socializing and having a good time. Parents were drinking, sometimes too much. Grills were on...there were too many things that could go wrong.

He made his way to the O'Learys and did his level best to keep his eyes off Moira. When he reached Liam, they shook hands and Jimmy offered him money for food.

"Put that away."

"Every year my brothers all come over here, eat your food, and drink your beer. Let me cover some of it."

"We always plan extra. It's tradition. I don't want your money."

Jimmy stood there feeling frustrated. Not paying for his share made him feel like a kid again. People had never really known how to react to him. They tried to be nice, but he saw the pity in their eyes. He was the boy whose mom had been killed; therefore, he and his brothers could do whatever they wanted. His past became a ticket to skate through life.

And it had made him nuts.

He tucked his money away only because he knew Liam had refused out of friendship not pity.

"Hey, Jimmy," someone called.

When Jimmy turned to look, he saw a crowd had gathered behind them and he immediately knew it was football time. The O'Learys stood on one side, facing his brothers Tommy and Sean. Jimmy scanned the crowd. No Kevin? He never missed a block party.

Liam covered the grill and slapped Jimmy's back. "Let's go. Time for the O'Learys to beat the O'Malleys."

"Shit. In your dreams."

They joined the crowd on opposing sides. As usual, Ryan O'Leary was captain, although Colin obviously offered direction. Jimmy took his spot in front of his brothers.

Tommy said, "Kevin will be here in five."

Jimmy counted the O'Learys. They had added a bunch

of new faces, but lucky for him, they were all women. "We'll take Griffin."

"Griffin's an O'Leary. You can't have him," Ryan said.

"His last name's Walker."

Ryan shook his head. "You try that every year. I brought him to the party, so I get to keep him."

True, Jimmy did try to get Griffin every year. He did it to annoy Ryan more than anything. They took turns grabbing up their old neighborhood friends until they had two teams.

Then the entire crowd made its way down to the end of the block and the field where they played. Standing on the rough, dry grass was like coming home for Jimmy. This was where his father had first taught him to throw a football, and where he got his first tackle and his first kiss. Summer wouldn't be summer without a football game on this field.

The game they played wasn't regulation anything. It was supposed to be touch football, but it often got out of hand. They didn't call plays because most of the players wouldn't have a clue as to what any of it meant. He took the spot as quarterback, hoping no one would notice.

Of course, Moira opened her big mouth.

"No way, Jimmy. Rules are, you can't play quarterback. It's cheating."

"I haven't played quarterback since high school. I think we can erase that rule."

She shoved her hands on her hips, trying to look tough. "But you're still playing football. You play for that special cop league. You're a ringer and it's not fair."

Her head tilted with attitude while she spoke, but she wasn't really angry.

He threw his hands up and took up a spot on the defensive line. It made him a little crazy that they didn't use positions. Everyone just stood on the line and either ran for the ball or ran to stop the opposing players. The lack of structure irritated him.

The O'Learys won the coin toss. The ball was snapped and Moira came running through the line. She was easy enough to spot with her flaming hair, but no one else on his team seemed to notice. Some were breaking through to get at Colin, who played quarterback, and others were already piled up on the line.

Jimmy dropped back and ran after Moira, glancing over his shoulder. Sure enough, the ball headed her way.

He bore down on her and waited a half second. If she caught the ball, all he had to do was tag her, but he couldn't figure out where to reach that wouldn't get him slapped, so he decided to try for an interception. He turned to reach for the ball, but Moira switched gears and they collided.

He saw it happening in slow motion but couldn't stop, so he did the next best thing: he wrapped himself around her to protect her. They landed with a loud *oomph*.

Jimmy pushed up on his elbows and looked into Moira's eyes. They were still bright blue and smiling. His hand cradled the back of her head and her leg wedged between his. He was suddenly very uncomfortable. All of her soft places lined up where they shouldn't be.

Someone smacked his shoulder. "What the hell, O'Malley? This is supposed to be *touch* football."

He eased his hand out from under her head and shoved up to his knees. He looked at Ryan. "Yeah, well, I was trying to figure out where to *touch* her when she changed course."

Moira started to giggle and parts of her jiggled along, so he looked away. He stood and held his hand out to help her up.

"I'm fine. Jimmy was a total gentleman and made sure to

cushion my fall." The syrupy sweetness in her voice made him want to forget being a gentleman.

Kevin did it for him. "Some gentleman. I'd like to cushion your fall, sweetheart."

"Stop being an ass, Kevin," she tossed out before brushing grass from the seat of her denim shorts.

As everyone went back to the line of scrimmage, Jimmy took an extra minute to slow his breathing and regain control. He would let the O'Learys score ten touchdowns before he would lay another hand on Moira.

5

An hour later they were all tired, but laughter filled the field. No one could agree on the score, so Jimmy and Ryan called it a tie. Moira decided she could live with that as long as she got away from Kevin. After the first play of the game, when Jimmy landed on top of her, Kevin had taken over guarding her. He taunted her nonstop until she finally stuck out a foot and tripped him.

The O'Malleys of course called a penalty on her, not that they used any real rules, but she couldn't argue. That man had been getting under her skin since the first grade. Every year they were in the same class and he always had the seat behind her. God forbid the teacher do something other than alphabetical order for the seating chart.

It started with him tugging her pigtails in the first grade and it hadn't stopped since.

The group went back to their respective homes to throw the first round of food on the grills. Except for the O'Malleys. They joined her family. They were an odd mix. The O'Malleys were mostly younger than her siblings. Colin, Ryan, and Michael were all older than Jimmy. The entire

O'Leary clan was older than Sean and Tommy, and Norah who didn't live in Chicago.

But somehow, they always hung together. She guessed it was a little like having an extra extended family.

With the help of Quinn, Indy, and Brianna, she got all of the salads brought outside in one trip. As they peeled back the plastic wrap, Quinn asked, "So what's with Kevin O'Malley?"

"What do you mean?"

"I watched the game. There's something going on there."

Moira snickered. "Yeah, a massive case of annoyance. You know that kid in class who's worse than the class clown? He makes everyone laugh, but at the same time, he just makes you nuts?" She didn't wait for a response from all of her new sisters. She was sure every class had a Kevin O'Malley. "That's him."

Needing to avoid any questions that would lead to confessions, Moira checked her watch and called out to Liam, "Hey, do we have time for the water balloon toss before the food's ready?"

Liam nodded and waved with his tongs. She used the excuse of a water balloon toss to escape any further discussion of the O'Malleys. If they pressed, she would spill her guts about being in love with Jimmy for most of her life. She knew it was silly and probably wouldn't really be considered love, especially since it was one-sided, but when she thought about Jimmy, she always thought she loved him.

Moira lined up kids and adults alike for the water balloon toss. She grouped the kids and started their toss, which ended quickly. She handed out cheap prizes and then stood in line with the other adults. Their game offered no prizes, just bragging rights, which she'd held for more than a decade.

Her partner, Olivia, one of Maggie's friends, lined up across from her. It rarely mattered who partnered with her. What she lacked in football skills, Moira more than made up for in skills for throwing a water balloon gently.

Colin whistled to announce the start of the toss. After the first lob, the lines took a step back.

Olivia asked, "When's Maggie coming home?"

"She was here at Christmas. Didn't you see her?"

"Yeah, but I thought she'd be back by now."

Moira shrugged as the balloon came back to her. Another step back, widening the gap between players. Balloons were dropped and handled too harshly. Women squealed as cold water splashed against them. It only took another ten minutes until they were down to the final three couples.

Olivia released the balloon into a high arc as someone yelled, "Hey, Moira."

Moira looked next to Olivia and saw a second balloon in the air. This one coming like a line drive at her. What the hell?

She tried to keep her eye on her balloon, but the other reached her first and smacked her on the chest, exploding with cold water. In the meantime, her balloon landed at her feet, soaking into her gym shoes.

The cackling laugh sounding behind Olivia told her exactly who had thrown the balloon. Kevin. She was going to kill him. He ran down the block, laughing, so she took off after him. They neared his house and he whipped by Jimmy.

Jimmy stood and stopped her progression. "Don't you think a wet T-shirt contest is a little inappropriate?"

She looked down at her chest and realized how exposed she was. Leave it to Jimmy to embarrass her. She clamped down on her jaw and held tight to her anger. "You think this was *my* idea? It was a water balloon toss that I haven't lost for over ten years. If your stupid ass brother didn't attack me with a water balloon, I would've won."

"Kevin did this?"

"Doesn't he always?"

She plucked the material from her skin and allowed a calming breath to ease past her lips.

Then Kevin made the mistake of yelling from his porch, "Looking good, Moira."

Her rage returned tenfold and she leaped for him, but got nowhere. Jimmy had swooped in and scooped her up by her waist. She scrambled like a cartoon character with her feet off the ground.

He whispered in her ear. "Why don't you go change? I'll deal with Kevin."

She smacked his chest and he set her down, but didn't allow enough room for her escape. "Change into what? Unlike you, I don't live at home. I don't have clothes here."

"Borrow something of Maggie's."

She laughed. "Have you ever taken a look at my baby sister? There's no way her shirt would fit me."

He sighed and his eyes darted everywhere but at her. Then he reached over his head and tugged his shirt off. Moira lost the ability to think. Whoever said Chicago cops carried a spare tire around the middle and ate nothing but doughnuts had never laid eyes on Jimmy. Lots of delectable muscle.

The shirt landed on her shoulder.

"Here. Lucky for you, I do live here and can get a new shirt."

Her brain came back online and she said, "Thanks." He

always took her off guard when he did something nice. She couldn't quite read him and it annoyed the hell out of her.

"Whatever. I'm sure your brothers don't want everyone staring at you. I'm saving you some embarrassment."

And he's back. The Jimmy she was used to, treating her like the bothersome kid sister who needed to be protected.

JIMMY WATCHED as Moira's expression changed. Her face fell and he felt like an ass. He hadn't wanted to hurt her feelings, but he never knew what to do with her. He spoke the truth. Her brothers would keel over if they saw her looking like that. She turned and headed toward her house.

He turned to his. Kevin hovered in the doorway, just like he did whenever he stirred up trouble and expected to be hunted down.

"Why are you always fucking with that poor girl?"

"It's fun. I like her mad."

Jimmy could relate. Moira was one hell of a spitfire. She always had been. Even when he'd had her off the ground and at a disadvantage, she kept kicking.

"One day I'm gonna do just the right thing for her to get mad enough to throw herself at me." He slapped Jimmy on the shoulder.

"Dude, if you really think that's a possibility, I failed at teaching you to read women." Plus, it would only complicate his life if anything happened between Kevin and Moira. He had a hard enough time avoiding her. He went upstairs to grab a fresh shirt. When he came back down, Kevin was sitting on the steps. "You need to apologize to her."

"Hell no."

"You're being an asshole." Not much better than Jimmy

had been. Taking a page from his own book, Jimmy headed across the street to find Moira.

It was easy enough; her red hair acted like a beacon. The shirt he'd given her should've swallowed her body because he dwarfed her, but she did one of those girl things where she tied it in a knot at her waist. A sliver of white skin peeked out where the shirt met her shorts. Her expression appeared only slightly guarded when she saw him. He wondered how she managed to be a reporter when she wore her every thought and emotion for the world to see.

"I'm sorry," he said.

"For what? You didn't throw the balloon. Tell Kevin to watch his back."

He couldn't stop his smile knowing she was plotting revenge against his brother. "What I said to you came out wrong. I was an ass."

Her hands settled against her heart. "Be still. Did I hear right? Did an O'Malley not only apologize, but actually admit to being an ass?"

"I do know how to apologize. Your brothers would've been pissed to see you looking like that, but you have nothing to be embarrassed about. It's just..."

She squinted up at him. "What?"

"Nothing." He didn't know what he planned to say. Or how to explain what she did to him. He turned and walked over to the grill where Liam was pulling off burgers. "Need some help?"

"Nope. I'm good. Help yourself." Liam placed the last cheeseburger on the platter.

Before Liam had the chance to set it down, Jimmy grabbed two buns and burgers. Liam's burgers would disappear quickly. Jimmy glanced over at Kevin who still stood on the porch. He picked up a burger and waved it at his brother. Served him right for not apologizing.

Moira caught his wave and glared at Kevin. Jimmy skirted to the other side of the table. He loaded his plate with salad and fruit and a handful of chips. Then he went back to his lawn chair in the middle of the block where he could watch all the action. He'd gotten a text from Gabby saying she'd be there soon.

He normally didn't invite people to the block party the way most families did, but Gabby had overheard him talking to Liam about it, so he felt he had to. She was always bugging him about meeting his family anyway. He sank his teeth into the first bite of the burger and he got another text from Gabby.

Where the hell am I supposed to park?

Wherever you can find a spot.

Smartass.

And that's why he liked partnering with her. She was a straight shooter.

Tommy and Sean set up a couple of chairs on the lawn in front of the house and yelled for their dad to come out to eat. Jimmy had no idea what his dad had been doing in the house all day. He'd invited him to come watch the football game, but Dad didn't want to. At the same time his dad decided to make an appearance, Gabby strode down the block.

Jimmy figured it would take all of three minutes for Gabby to realize why he never asked her to socialize with his family. He waved her over and she sat on the curb. "You can have my chair. I can get another from my garage."

"Nah. I'm fine." She looked up and down the block. "So who's who?"

He gestured directly across from where they sat. "That's

my house. My dad and two of my brothers, Tommy and Sean, are right there. Kevin is hiding somewhere." He pointed down to the O'Learys house. "The O'Learys live there."

Gabby snorted. "The O'Malleys and the O'Learys? What is this, Little Ireland?"

He shrugged. "The neighborhood's pretty Irish, but there are other people. The Schultz family lives down there, the Polks live two doors down, and the Fosters are on the corner."

"Yeah, a real melting pot."

"Whatever. You've met Liam. His family owns O'Leary's Pub, and they have a keg if you want a beer. And if you want one of Liam's burgers, you better move fast."

"I ate already. I just wanted to come and hang out for a while. Maybe talk strategy."

Another reason to like Gabby. She didn't mind talking shop on her off time. She was damn near the perfect woman. Too bad she was a cop and he wasn't the least bit interested in her.

"What are we going to do about getting you a wife?"

"Looking to get married, Jimmy?" Moira said as she sat beside Gabby.

Beer almost spewed from his lips. "Thanks to you, I'm looking for someone to pretend."

She smirked. "It's sad that someone has to pretend."

Gabby laughed.

"I thought you might want a beer." Moira handed Gabby a plastic cup.

"Thanks." Gabby took a sip and then said, "Now tell me why you invented an imaginary wife for Jimmy."

Moira brushed her hands on her lap, which drew

Jimmy's attention to her bare legs. To distract himself, he studied his burger.

"I don't know who you're investigating, and let me tell you, it would be a whole lot easier to help if I did know, but I saw the group he was standing with. They're all married pervs. If he wants in, he kind of needs to be like them. Birds of a feather, you know."

That caught Jimmy's attention. "Besides the obvious fact they ogle you, why do you call them pervs?"

"They do more than ogle."

He hadn't expected that. The thought of one of those assholes manhandling Moira pissed him off again. "What did they do?"

"Nothing to me. Sometimes they forget I'm there or something. Which never happens with the wives. They're always on top of it, making sure they say just the right thing. The men, on the other hand, get a few drinks in them, and they chat with each other regardless of who might be standing around."

He rolled his eyes. What he wouldn't give for a straight answer. "Get to the point, Moira."

She shook her head and talked to Gabby. "They cheat. Every last one of them. Their wives probably know, but I don't have confirmation. I mean, they can't be that clueless, can they? Or maybe they just don't care."

Moira had given them the link they'd been searching for. If these guys were all adulterers and were robbed while with a mistress, it would explain why they wouldn't come forward to report the crime. They didn't want to account for their whereabouts. He could kiss Moira.

She gave him an odd look. "I know, 'shut up, Moira, you talk too much.' Forget it. I'm going to get a burger."

She stood before he could process his thoughts.

Gabby moved closer. "You thinking what I'm thinking?"

"They're being targeted when they're with their mistresses. The wives don't know, so they don't report."

Gabby took a gulp of beer. "The thieves must be pretty sophisticated to follow these guys around to know when they won't be home. That's a lot of surveillance."

Moira came back and sat beside Gabby, looking pitiful with a plate full of salad.

"I thought you were getting a burger," he said.

"They're gone. I knew I should've grabbed one, but I saw Gabby and wanted to bring her a beer. Then, as usual, I got distracted talking. You'd think by now I'd know better."

He thrust his second burger at her. "Here."

She stared at it.

"I only took one bite." He waved it a little to get her to take it.

"I'm not taking your food."

"I already had one. You know you want it."

She took it and sank her teeth in, not bothered by the missing bite. Moira was a girl who liked food. She gave a moan of appreciation over the burger.

"I can't wait until Liam opens his own place and I can eat like this whenever I want."

Jimmy picked at a chip. "Is he finally looking?"

"Not really. He's thinking about it. If he thinks much longer, he'll be eighty by the time he decides." She took another bite.

"He's being cautious." Something Moira knew nothing about.

Gabby interrupted. "Back to getting you a wife, O'Malley. What are we gonna do?"

"Marry me, Gabby."

"Go to hell. Why would I marry you knowing you hang out with adulterers?"

"You guys are weird," Moira said with a mouthful of burger.

Gabby turned her attention to Moira. "So tell me more about the pervs."

"What do you want to know?"

"Are there more than the four that Jimmy was hanging with?"

"Nope. Just the four, I think, but I don't go to every event and watch them." Her eyebrows shot up. "Are you investigating them? What'd they do? Corporate espionage? Fraud? Ooo...murder?"

He couldn't believe she was getting excited talking about possible crime. "We're not telling you."

"Come on, Jimmy. I'm trying to help. I haven't said anything to anyone. Nothing. I think I deserve information based on that alone. You know how much I like to talk." She chewed on the burger and chased it with beer.

He remained silent. Telling Moira details would make her rabid. She never could keep a secret.

"Go get me a refill, Jimmy." Gabby put her cup in his face.

He stood and set his plate on his chair. Looking pointedly at Moira, he asked, "You need a refill too?"

"That would be lovely, thanks." She held her cup up to him.

He walked to the keg with all three cups in hand. After getting the refills, he looked back at the women. They huddled together in deep conversation like they'd known each other for years. Not surprising, since Moira made friends everywhere.

When he returned to his spot, he asked, "So what'd I miss?"

"Girl talk," Gabby answered, taking her cup from him.

Moira's cheeks were pink as she accepted her cup. Maybe they hadn't been discussing the case. What were they talking about then? They didn't know each other, and the only thing they had in common besides the case was... oh shit. Him.

He quickly grabbed his plate and mumbled, "I'm going to talk to Liam."

No way did he want to have anything to do with whatever Gabby and Moira were talking about.

6

―――――

"**A**re you sure there's nothing going on between you and Jimmy?"

Moira stared at Gabby. "I'm sure." She hoped she covered her crush. "Why do you ask?"

"I've never seen him this bent out of shape, and I don't get what's causing it."

Moira laughed. "I have that effect on him. I have since adolescence. He finds me annoying."

"Annoyed is only a fraction of what he's feeling. We haven't been partners long, but we've logged a lot of hours. I was sure he had something going with you and it was throwing him off his game. Especially after he stayed in your apartment the other day."

Moira felt her face flush. Damn pale skin gave everything away. "Don't go there. I didn't lock my door, so he let himself in and scared the crap of me."

"He did what?"

"You heard me. He just stood in my hallway, waiting for me to come out of the bedroom." Moira shook her head at the memory. "I screamed and threw my leg wax at him."

Gabby spit beer out as she laughed.

"It's not funny. I was mortified." Moira smacked her on the arm.

"Not a very effective weapon. Unless of course it was hot wax?"

She shook her head again. "A jar."

Tears streamed down Gabby's cheeks. "What..." She took a halting breath. "What happened then?"

"I yelled at him."

"I would've paid to see that. No one yells at Jimmy and lives to tell the tale."

Moira thought about that for a minute. Jimmy had always been a tough guy, but not for a second did she feel afraid around him. "If he did anything to me, he'd have to answer to my brothers." She pointed in the direction of the O'Leary boys.

"I think he could hold his own."

Something about the way Gabby talked about Jimmy made her think that maybe something was going on between the partners. But Jimmy wouldn't date his partner. He wouldn't cross those lines. At least she didn't think so.

"Can I ask you something?"

Moira looked at Gabby who had finally regained her composure. "You've been asking me things since you got here. Why stop now?"

"How hard is it going to be for me to blend with this crowd as Jimmy's wife?"

Moira noticed the uncomfortable shift in Gabby's eyes. She was nervous. Maybe she had a thing for Jimmy. "I don't know. I've never had to blend. I have to play a part. Lord knows I wouldn't dress like that if I weren't at one of those parties. But once you know the players, it's easy. You learn one or two things about each person, and you always have a starting point for conversation. Let them take the lead."

Gabby's lips thinned.

"What? All you have to do is look pretty, pretend to be in love with Jimmy, and make superficial small talk."

"I don't think I can pull it off. I'm not the dress up and look pretty type." She stared at her cup. "Shit. I'm empty again."

"I'll get refills."

Moira walked down the block. A breeze kicked up, knocking strands from her ponytail. She swiped at them with her forearm and looked at the sky. The weather hadn't called for any rain, and she hoped a storm wasn't rolling in. They still had to start a bonfire and roast marshmallows. And she was nowhere near drunk enough yet.

At the keg, she filled their cups and eavesdropped on conversations. Quinn and Ryan were arguing about how much longer they were going to stay. Griffin paced with his phone to his ear. Then she heard the low timbre of Jimmy's voice, so she strained to listen. He was talking to Liam.

"Try dating someone your own age," Liam said.

"I have. At our age, women are set with careers. I want a wife who will build a home and raise our kids."

Damn. Hey, Jimmy, 1950 called. They want their ideals back. Beer overflowed the cup and trickled on her fingers.

"Shit, Moira. Didn't anyone ever teach you to pour a beer?" Colin asked.

"I got distracted." She licked the drops from her hand. "Elizabeth here yet?"

"On her way."

"What kind of guy sends his girlfriend off to work while he parties? Isn't it your business too?"

"I told her the place would be fine for one day without us. You know how she is." He filled his own cup.

"Tell her to find me when she gets here."

"Who's that you've been talking to?"

"Jimmy O'Malley's partner."

"You've been talking to him a lot lately. What's going on?"

"Nothing. I bumped into him at a work function. That's all." She left before Colin could ask more questions. Although she was better at keeping secrets than anyone gave her credit for, she wasn't good at lying to people, especially her family.

She sat back on the curb next to Gabby. She should go dig out more lawn chairs. They were all getting too old to be sitting on concrete all night.

"Are you going to be at the Lincoln Park Zoo fund-raiser thing next weekend?"

"Yep. It's one of my favorites. I go every year."

Conversation across the street drew Moira's attention. Sean O'Malley was talking to some guy. While Sean's voice was low, Moira read his body language. Something heated was going on.

"Hey, why don't I introduce you to Jimmy's younger brother?" Moira hoped the interruption would cool things down. Having a fight break out during the block party was never a good thing. Most years they were fine, but every now and then, someone got drunk and belligerent.

Drunk and belligerent meeting an O'Malley never ended well.

When they crossed the street, Moira said, "Hi, Sean. This is Gabby, Jimmy's partner."

Gabby raised a hand in greeting, but Sean didn't notice.

"Who the fuck do you think you are, asshole?" Sean's voice was tight and controlled. He wasn't drunk.

The other man—Foster?—from down the block wove in place. "Shut up, jagoff."

Gabby tugged her sleeve. "Go get Jimmy."

Moira looked at Gabby, who was well on her way to buzzed. "You get Jimmy. I know these guys." Moira pointed her in the direction where she'd last seen Jimmy sitting with Liam.

When Gabby took off at a stumbling jog, Moira stepped between the two men. "Hey, guys, how about some more food?"

"Moira, step out of the way." Sean stood a foot taller than her, like all the O'Malleys. His right hand was already bunched in a fist.

"Sean, please. Don't ruin the party with a fight."

Foster stood behind her and slurred, "Listen to the little lady. You don't want to get your ass kicked."

From the corner of her eye, Moira saw Jimmy running over. Two seconds, that's all she needed to stall, but even as she had the thought, Sean reached past her.

"Sean," Jimmy yelled loud and sharp.

Sean turned his head slightly. It was enough of a distraction that drunk Foster thought he'd get in a cheap shot. He stepped around Moira, and when he pulled back for the punch, his elbow smacked into her head, knocking her on her ass.

Moira wasn't sure if he connected with Sean because that boy moved fast. Sean was on him and pounding away. Jimmy yanked Sean off like he held a kitten by the scruff. Foster scrambled back like a crab. His lip was bleeding.

Jimmy barked orders. "Liam, walk Bradley home."

Liam helped Bradley Foster stand, practically lifting him

under his shoulders. As they passed her, Liam asked, "You okay?"

She nodded. A throbbing pain beat on the side of her head, but she was okay.

Jimmy continued yelling. She assumed he was aiming for Sean until he lowered himself to meet her face. "What the hell did you think you were doing?"

From behind him, Sean said, "It wasn't her fault, man. She was trying to diffuse the situation."

Jimmy barely glanced back, but snapped, "Stay out of this."

"I sent Gabby to get you. I was trying to stop them before it got physical."

"How? With your face?" His fingers traveled along her jawline.

She swatted him away. She couldn't hold on to being mad at him if he was gentle. Her head might explode if she saw both sides of Jimmy at once. Pushing up from the ground, she felt the throbbing worsen.

Jimmy grabbed her elbow to help her stand. "You're a damn menace."

"Everything was fine until you distracted Sean. That gave Bradley his opening. Sean wouldn't have thrown a punch with me standing in between them."

"Hell, no, I wouldn't. The O'Learys outnumber everyone."

"But you didn't account for the drunk in the equation." He held her chin and tilted her head to see if there was damage.

"I said I'm fine." She yanked away from him. What she really needed was some ice and another beer. Her cup had been a casualty of the brief fight, the red plastic cracked in multiple spots.

As she walked away, she saw her brothers all running toward her. She rolled her eyes. They all looked pissed. She thought to stop them, but remembered Jimmy and Sean were big boys. *Let them deal with it themselves.*

Colin and Ryan led the pack. All she heard as she walked by was, "What the fuck, O'Malley? How the hell did our sister get hit?"

She definitely needed a beer.

JIMMY SENT Gabby after Moira to make sure she put ice on her head. He needed to deal with her crazy brothers. Sean already stepped out in front of it, explaining what had happened. He apologized, but quickly pointed out that he didn't throw the first punch or hit Moira.

They calmed down. Irritated, but accepting of the situation. Colin, Ryan, and Michael headed back to where they were setting up a fire pit. Tommy and Kevin had emerged from wherever they'd been hiding, and Sean began telling them about the fight.

Jimmy crossed his arms as he stood beside Liam. He watched his brothers reenact the brief brawl and then looked over at the O'Learys, who were simultaneously checking on Moira and rallying the family to make s'mores. "Do you see what I see?" he asked Liam.

"What do you mean?"

"Look at your family and look at mine. Is it any wonder why I'm looking for a wife who will be at home to raise my kids? We're pretty fucked up." His brothers were congratulating Sean on his win, if that's what you could call it when fighting a drunk.

"Our families are different, but my mom worked,

remember? She worked at the bar all the time when we were young."

"But she was always there for you guys. I remember your mom always being around."

Liam shrugged. "Your mom would've been around if she could've. Having a job isn't what killed her."

"I know, but if she hadn't been forced to work to help support us, she wouldn't have been walking home late at night. She wouldn't have gotten mugged. She wouldn't have been killed."

"That's some faulty logic. She could've just as easily been attacked coming home from the grocery store."

Jimmy didn't have an answer. He knew it didn't make sense, but he needed to have some control over the variables in his life. He could provide for a family. It's what he wanted to do.

"Come on. I'll buy you a beer. You look like you could use one."

Liam led the way back to the fire pit and pulled up two lawn chairs. The plastic weave was old and fraying, and Jimmy worried about whether it would hold him. He sat and immediately regretted it. The spot put in him Moira's line of glaring. And she was shooting some dirty looks in his direction. What the hell had he done to piss her off? He didn't hit her. He hadn't even been part of the fight. He'd simply pointed out the carelessness of her actions.

Yeah, that's what a woman wants to hear when she's hurt. Tell her how it was her fault. Dumb ass. Jimmy knew better, and if it had been anyone else, he still would've been upset, but he would've held his tongue. Something about Moira made him cross the line. Every time.

He couldn't tell her the panic he'd felt seeing her get hit.

Brushing aside the thought and the image that went

with it, he took a gulp of the beer Liam handed him.

Griffin's wife, Indy, stood from her spot in the grass and said, "Okay, most of the kids are gone or they're with their parents at their own fire. I think it's time for some fun. What game should we play?"

Moira's eyes narrowed. "Truth or dare."

"Ooo...that's good. I'll start." She tapped her lips like she needed to plan something. "Moira, truth or dare?"

Moira got a cocky glint in her eye, and he knew he was in trouble. "Truth."

Indy's face lit up. "Who was the last guy you made out with and was it any good?"

All four of her brothers plus Griffin cringed. Liam spoke for them all. "You can't ask those kinds of questions. We don't want to hear any details."

Colin added, "She's a virgin until marriage."

Moira snorted. "First"—she made eye contact with each brother—"you all need to recognize that I am a grown woman. Second, his name was Rick. I picked him up at a bar. We made out next to my car, but he didn't do it for me. I'm still looking for the guy that can make my toes curl with a kiss. Elizabeth swears such guys exist."

A woman with long dark hair, Colin's girlfriend, he believed, answered. "Well, I was referring to your brother, so maybe it's genetic."

Moira screwed up her face. "Ewww. Now that's gross."

Elizabeth laughed and Colin kissed her.

"My turn." Moira scanned the group. "Jimmy. Truth or dare?"

"I'm not playing."

"You have to."

"No, I don't."

"Come on, Jimmy. Lighten up," Gabby said.

He shot her a look that told her to shut up. He knew playing this game with Moira would be a mistake. There was no way for him to win.

"Ask someone else."

"You're here, so you have to play." She leaned forward in her chair and put her elbows on her knees.

"Then that's my cue to leave." He stood and picked up his beer from the ground.

"*Bawkk, bawkk*...who would've thought Jimmy O'Malley would be afraid of a kids' game?" Moira taunted.

He walked toward his house and heard her ask Liam a question about his social life. Glad to have escaped the fire, he sat on his porch. The spot put him in the shadows as night fell.

He had all of a minute of peace until Moira sauntered up. It was a fabulous thing that she no longer lived with her mother. He'd never survive if he still had to live across the street from her and her relentless hounding.

She leaned against the wobbly wrought iron rail of his porch. Which reminded him he needed to fix it.

"How's your head?"

"What's your problem with me?"

The words were meant to sound angry, but he heard the hurt behind them. "I don't have a problem with you."

Other than you make me insane.

"Then why are you mean to me?"

"I'm not mean to you."

She crossed her arms, and he thought of her being about eleven and doing the same thing when he convinced Liam not to bring her with them when they went to the park or the mall. He was mean to her.

"I don't mean to be mean to you."

"Why'd you leave the fire?"

"You told me I had to play the game if I stayed. I didn't want to play." He set his beer on the cement step behind him. He shifted over to make room for her to sit.

"You didn't want to play, or you didn't want to play with me?"

"Honestly?" He waited for her to nod, as he knew she would. "It was mostly you."

"Why?"

"What would you have had me do for a dare?"

"I don't know."

"Liar. You had a truth and a dare ready for me before Indy even picked you."

Even in the dark he saw the corners of her mouth quirk up. "If you picked truth, I planned to ask why you don't like me."

"I like you."

She snorted again. He'd heard that sound countless times as a teenager.

"What would've been the dare?"

"I was going to dare you to kiss me."

Air locked in his lungs and his heart stopped. He had no way of responding. At least his instincts had kept him safe by retreating from the game.

"The thought's so awful you can't even speak?" Her voice, usually so strong and full of energy, became quiet and meek.

"Why would you want me to kiss you? Trying to get your brothers to beat my ass?" With any luck, his joke would break the spell she wove between them. He needed another escape.

"I'm looking for that kiss. The toe-curling kiss while fully dressed."

"So you're sampling every guy you can get your hands

on?" He picked up his beer and took a long drink to wet his overly dry throat.

"No. I have a feeling about you. I'm thinking the kiss would be like fireworks. Everything between us tends to be that way, so why not the kiss?"

She shifted closer and he was grateful for the dark. He didn't want to be able to see her eyes.

"It would be a mistake, Moira. You know that."

"Yeah, you're probably right." She nudged his shoulder. "Friends?"

"Of course. Is your head really okay?"

"Yeah. Foster hits like a girl."

Laughter and relief flooded his system, and it felt good to let it out. She joined him, and as their laughter filtered out to the street, they got a few looks from the campfire crew.

"Let's go back and have some s'mores. I promise not to make you play truth or dare." She stood and held her hand out to him.

He accepted it, not wanting her to think he was being mean again, but he enjoyed the feel of her palm against his far too much. "I'm sorry I yelled at you before."

"Which time?"

"Every time. I worry about you. You fly through life without thinking half the time. It makes me crazy that you put yourself in danger, and it comes out the wrong way."

She released his hand and nudged his shoulder again. "Aww, Jimmy, you care."

Her face remained in shadows, but he knew her smile was flirtatious and her eyes would be bright blue.

He needed to wrap up this case and get as much distance from Moira O'Leary as possible before she convinced him to act on her dare.

7

———

Moira sat with Kathy at the bar for their usual girls' night out to catch up and gossip. Kathy sipped on a cosmopolitan and Moira had a beer.

Their drinks alone spoke volumes.

"Sorry I missed the block party. Was it fun?"

She considered the question. "Interesting would be a better word. We had the usual football game, barbecue, and water balloon toss."

"And the interesting?"

"Jimmy was there."

Kathy set her drink on the bar. "Jeez, girl, not him again."

"He lives across the street from my mom." Moira left out how much she'd hoped he'd be there this year. "But that was the interesting. We shared some intense moments."

"Intense, how?"

"I spend my day with words, so I should be able to explain it to you, but I can't. There were these fleeting moments, where it was more than Jimmy and Moira, childhood neighbors. I was more than Liam's kid sister. But then, like a flash, it disappeared." She drank her beer and avoided Kathy's gaze.

"You need to give up on him. He's been back home for how long? Like five years? If he hasn't shown interest yet, he ain't gonna."

"Excuse me," a deep voice said behind them.

They both turned. A tall man, early thirties was smiling at Kathy. Of course.

"Can I buy you a drink?"

"I'm good, thanks. Maybe later."

Then Moira saw the wicked grin. The one Kathy only pulled out when she was about to start something.

"Wait a minute," she called.

Moira lowered her voice. "Whatever you're about to do, please don't."

The man turned back and took a step closer.

"Take a look at my friend here."

He looked at Moira and smiled. She bit her lip and shook her head.

"She's pretty, right?" Kathy didn't bother to wait for a response. "She's hung up on some guy who's her brother's friend. She's known him, like, her whole life. Speaking as a man, if he had any inkling of being interested, he would've acted by now, right?"

The man cocked his head and studied Moira for another minute before speaking. Nothing like being under the microscope.

"Depends."

"That's a cop-out."

"No, hear me out. If it was just some guy she grew up with, I'd agree. But you said it was her brother's friend? That adds a layer most guys aren't going to tangle with. He might be interested, but not willing to act because of the brother."

"Ha," Moira blurted.

The man's smile widened. "Glad I could help. I'll be over there if you change your mind about that drink." He pointed over his shoulder and backed away.

"I'm going to kill you. I can't believe you asked a total stranger about this." Her beer couldn't cool her throat fast enough.

Kathy shrugged and tossed her hair over her shoulder. That toss was like a mating call. At least three guys turned in their direction. "It was an objective opinion. And still just an opinion. I don't want what he said to give you some false hope. Jimmy is never going to get off his ass."

"I just want...God, I want to be in love. Real love, like the once in a lifetime kind. I see my brothers all finding this incredible happiness, and they weren't even looking. It's so freaking unfair."

"Maybe the universe is telling you something. Stop searching so hard and let it find you."

"I can't sit back and wait. It's not my style."

"So look, search, seek, but not Jimmy. We're surrounded by guys. Pick one."

They both spun on their stools to survey the options. A few guys made eye contact, but no sparks zinged through the room. She wanted sparks.

And if she said that, Kathy might pull out a Taser.

"You have to promise to give a guy a chance without thinking about the keeper list."

She drank from her bottle and avoided Kathy's eyes. "Don't know what you're talking about."

"Please. We made up that crappy list as college freshmen."

"I've updated it since." Her keeper list was a list of ideals she used to recognize whether a guy was a keeper.

"You mean you've moved beyond sexy arms and excels at cunnilingus?"

Moira's beer snorted up her nose, but she prevented its escape. With her nostrils burning, she grabbed a cocktail napkin and wiped her face. "Warning next time."

But the laughter felt good. She was glad she had a friend like Kathy.

"As important as those things are, and don't fool yourself into thinking you don't still look for them," Moira responded, "I have added to the list. He has to like the same movies I do and enjoy a quiet evening at home. I spend too much time socializing for work. He absolutely has to have a steady job. That is nonnegotiable. Too many losers." She took another sip of beer to soothe her throat. "And he has to be supportive of what I want in life."

"Not bad, as far as lists go, but you can't figure those things out on a first date. If you're running a checklist instead of really getting to know a guy, you're not giving him a fair shot." She bumped Moira's shoulder. "Remember when you introduced me to Ryan? Sure, he had the sexy arms and steady job, but he was not paying attention to anything I said. It made him appear self-absorbed. Is that how you would describe him?"

Moira had tried to get Ryan and Kathy together and spectacularly failed.

"No. I got your point. I'll try. But the list is there. It's not like I can forget it."

Kathy tugged her sleeve. "Finish your drink and let's go dance. We'll find a guy for you to kiss and make you forget Jimmy."

Moira sucked down the rest of her beer, but didn't

believe for a minute that anything would erase Jimmy from her mind.

She followed Kathy to the dance floor and checked out her prospects en route. Something Jimmy said Saturday night struck her. If she wanted to find the toe-curling kiss, maybe she did need to sample as many guys as she could. She didn't need to sleep with them. A kiss should tell her what she needed to know. The kiss was at the top of the list.

And if she could find the sparks before her class reunion, that would be better. She'd spent an inordinate amount of time staring at the invitation. High school hadn't been horrible, but it certainly hadn't been the best years of her life either.

Her life wasn't quite where she'd thought it'd be. By now, she believed she'd have found her guy. If anyone had asked her in high school, she would've said that she'd beat all of her brothers to the altar.

Ten years later, she not only hadn't found Mr. Right, but she wasn't a famous journalist either. She hadn't traveled any farther than the suburbs to hunt down a story.

She shook off depressing thoughts and danced beside her friend. Before the first song had ended, they had guys joining them. Moira was determined to kiss at least one tonight.

Her journey of a thousand kisses—hopefully it wouldn't really take that many—would begin tonight.

JIMMY JOLTED AWAKE AND LISTENED. Something woke him, so he waited. At first he heard nothing but his own slow breathing. Then he heard the clinking. Someone was in the house. He grabbed his gun and headed toward the stairs.

Both Sean and Tommy knew not to come through the main house after midnight. They came and went through the back basement entrance.

That way, he never had to be woken thinking they were burglars and he never had to deal with their drunken mess.

He edged down the stairs quietly, straining to hear where the person might be. Another slight jostle. The kitchen? It sounded like the refrigerator door closing. Probably wasn't a burglar, but one of his dumb-ass brothers.

Jimmy rounded the corner and saw a nearly naked ass staring back at him, backlit by the refrigerator. He flicked on the light. He knew that ass. He set his gun on the counter.

When the room brightened, Leena spun and offered him a smile. She held out a beer to him. "Hey, Jimmy. Took you long enough."

She crossed the room with extra sway in her hips, as if her kind of crazy could ever tempt him again. When she reached him, she ran the neck of the beer bottle down his bare chest.

"How did you get into my house?"

"Aren't you glad to see me?"

He took the bottle from her hand, set it on the table, and grabbed her elbow. Looking around the small room, he asked, "Where are the rest of your clothes?"

The basement door opened, and Sean said, "Leena? What the hell's going on?"

Jimmy froze. Leena slid from his grasp.

He turned to look at Sean, who stood in his boxers. "She's with you?"

"Where else did you think she came from?"

"She—" Jimmy stopped, not liking where his thoughts were headed. Maybe Sean picked her up at a bar and brought her back here and maybe she didn't remember the house. He took a step back and looked at Leena, who continued to stare at him. Fuck that. She knew exactly what she was doing. "I thought she broke in."

"In her underwear?"

"I guess she didn't tell you. Leena and I used to..." Words escaped him. He didn't want to say they'd dated because they really hadn't. They barely made it out of bed. When he thought about women he'd dated, he considered women he believed had possibilities. They were wife potential.

Leena would never be that. At least not for him.

"What?" Sean asked, crossing his arms and waiting for Leena to answer.

"We used to have a great time." She licked her lips. "We still could."

"What the fuck? You think I want my brother's sloppy seconds? Get the hell out."

She tilted her head and smiled. "I wasn't looking to sleep with you. I would've—you're not bad looking or anything—but when you told me your last name, I figured I might have another shot at Jimmy."

Heading toward the basement stairs, she tossed another smile back at both of them. "Have a good night, boys."

Jimmy rolled his eyes.

Sean lowered his voice. "What the fuck, man?"

Jimmy pointed to the basement. "You might want to follow her out. Make sure she doesn't help herself to anything."

When Sean disappeared downstairs, Jimmy popped the top on the beer Leena had given him. He'd had a good time with Leena a few years ago, before Sean and Tommy moved back home. The sex had been great, but after a couple of weeks, he'd known something was wrong. He tried to dismiss it because they'd agreed to have a casual relationship and enjoy each other's company.

But then he noticed small things missing from his room: a paperback from his nightstand, a CD, and one of his CPD T-shirts.

When he'd confronted her, he tried not to be accusatory, thinking she might've borrowed his stuff. She flew off the handle and started throwing things at him. He never took the time to figure out what her problem was; he didn't want to deal with her baggage.

Sean came back upstairs. He grabbed a beer from the fridge. "Maybe you should make a list of every girl you've ever screwed and post it on the wall. That way, me and Tommy can try to avoid them. It would be really handy if you could put a star next to the crazy ones."

Part of Jimmy thought Sean would be angry about the entire scene, but he should've known better. Sean usually took things in stride. He was often quick with his fists, but never against one of his brothers.

"Don't know what to tell you. I think most women would put that out there when you tell them your last name. They'd at least ask, right?" He took a pull on his beer. "I think she was the weirdest."

"Good to know."

The back door opened and Tommy walked in. Before Jimmy could reprimand him for using the back door after midnight, he held up a hand. "I saw the light on and knew you were up." He pointed to their bottles. "Having a party without me?"

Jimmy kicked out the chair next to him. "Pull up a seat. We're talking about crazy women."

Tommy turned the chair around and straddled it. "Are you giving lessons on how to find them?"

Jimmy kicked Tommy's thigh, but he wasn't angry. It felt good to sit around having a beer with his kid brothers. He was glad they were adults and could fend for themselves. Jimmy finally had the time to build the life he wanted with a family of his own.

But this, right here, was something he wouldn't mind replicating. For all of the fights and arguments and petty bullshit he'd dealt with when it came to his siblings, they always had each other. They might not be the O'Learys, but they weren't totally fucked up either.

MOIRA SAT at her desk typing furiously to meet her deadline when her phone rang. She wanted to ignore it, needed to ignore it, but she couldn't. She always feared missing out on something. Maybe something great.

She looked at the screen. It wasn't a number she recognized, but since it was local, she didn't think it was a telemarketer. "Hello?"

"Hi, Moira, it's Gabby Ruiz. I have a favor to ask."

"Shoot." She saved the article on her computer and stood and stretched.

"I have no idea what I'm doing for this Lincoln Park Zoo thing this weekend. Jimmy acts like it's no big deal. I just show up on his arm and it all works out." A heavy breath filled the air. "This case is important. We're working for the mayor. Don't tell Jimmy I told you that. Bottom line, I don't want things fucked up because I can't be a society woman." Gabby's voice held an edge of panic.

"What do you need?"

"Everything. Clothes, directions, information on people. I need to be able to fake it."

Moira remembered Gabby's concern when they talked at the block party. "Does Jimmy know you're calling me?"

"It was his idea."

Bingo. That was exactly what Moira had hoped. "What's in it for me?"

"What do you mean? You already have an exclusive if this case develops."

"That was for me helping Jimmy." She stared at the invitation stuck to her refrigerator. The reunion was at the end of the summer and her prospects for a date hadn't panned out. At least not yet.

"Name it. Although it's a little mercenary of you to bargain when I'm desperate."

She snickered. "I'm the second youngest of six. Being mercenary was the best way to make it out of childhood alive. You're gonna need to get Jimmy on the line for this bargain."

"This doesn't bode well for me." Gabby sighed again, but Moira heard her calling Jimmy. "Okay, Moira, you're on speaker."

"Here's the deal. I'll help Gabby get ready. I'll even lend her clothes to wear if she needs them, or I'll take her shopping. I'll feed her information so she can wow any guest she needs to."

"And in return?" Jimmy's deep voice came across the line.

Moira almost lost her nerve, but she thought about going to the reunion alone. It was bad enough she wasn't the world-class journalist that she'd thought she'd be by now. But to face everyone and not even have a date? She would feel like an awkward freshman all over again. Plus, Kathy said find someone hot. Jimmy more than qualified. "I need a date to my class reunion at the end of the summer."

"No."

That was all he said. No explanation. No excuse. No negotiation. Like one word would be enough. "You only have to agree to be my backup date in case I don't find someone else. It's not like you would be my first choice, O'Malley."

He grunted.

"Being a backup isn't asking so much, Jimmy. I'm sure Moira gets asked out a lot. When's the reunion?"

"Mid-August."

"So there's more than a month. That's plenty of time to find a date." Then Gabby added, "I'll help her find a date."

"You can't find yourself a date. How are you going to find one for her?"

Moira heard some shuffling, like Gabby moved or covered the phone. She heard the whisper, "I don't think I can do this on my own. Please."

Another all-suffering sigh, this time from Jimmy. "Fine. I'm backup only. Don't count on me actually taking you."

"I'll meet you at my mom's house on Saturday, Gabby. That way, when I have you all dressed up, Jimmy can get you from there. You won't have to worry about leaving a car at my apartment and having to pick it up later." As she spoke, she went back to her computer and sent the e-mail to respond to the reunion invitation. She now officially had a date.

"See you."

They disconnected, and Moira wished she could be a fly on the wall to see and hear Jimmy's response.

Her unfinished article stared at her. She poured another cup of coffee and thought about the zoo fund-raiser. It was one of the best events of the summer. Lots of people came out to support the zoo. Everyone liked to help keep the zoo open and free to everyone.

Her night at the bar had fallen flat. She'd only kissed one guy and it definitely hadn't gone further. But she remembered what Kathy had said about using these events to find a date. As long as she didn't write about the man she was dating, why couldn't she go out with someone from that circle?

Instead of focusing on her article, she began to think about the perfect outfit for Saturday. Maybe she wouldn't need Jimmy as a reunion date after all.

MOIRA SPENT Saturday afternoon hauling outfits over to her mom's house. Gabby had said she didn't have anything to wear, but Moira wasn't sure if her clothes would work. Gabby was taller, but her chest was smaller. Moira hoped her mom might be able to temporarily take something in so Gabby could wear it.

When the doorbell rang, Moira hadn't expected Gabby to look so nervous. The woman fidgeted like she was about to have a root canal with no painkillers. She led Gabby upstairs to her childhood bedroom. The room across the hall, the one Michael and Liam had shared, had been turned into a sewing room for her mom. Maggie still had most of her stuff in this bedroom. She left whatever she didn't need for traveling in Europe.

Even her baby sister managed to travel places Moira had only dreamed about.

Gabby plopped on the bed. "Where do we start?"

"Let's pick an outfit first because I think my mom will have to alter it for you. She can work while we do the rest of our magic." She reached into the closet and pulled out the first two dresses. They were cocktail length, one in blue and one in black. "You don't even own a little black dress? Everyone owns one of those. What do you wear to funerals?"

"Pants."

Yay. Someone else who offered one-word answers. This was going to be a long and painful tutorial.

Gabby nodded at the black dress. Moira laid it over the back of a chair and reached for two more dresses. One was the green one she wore the first night she saw Jimmy under-cover. "I think this one will look good on you, so I'm putting it in the yes pile for you to try on."

Gabby sighed but didn't argue.

After they had five dresses chosen, Gabby stripped down and stepped into the black dress. It was an obvious choice. Everyone looked good in a black dress, but Moira wanted something snazzier. Gabby needed to draw attention during her first outing as Mrs. James Buchanan. Eyes would be on her. Moira didn't say it out loud because it would only worsen Gabby's nerves.

When she had the dress on, Gabby gasped. "Oh, God. This is never going to work," she moaned. She stared down at the gaping front where her chest didn't fill the cups.

Moira rolled her eyes. "Relax. My mom will alter it. We had this conversation." She went behind Gabby and pulled the dress taut so they could see what the dress would really look like.

"I like it," Gabby said. "Let's use this one."

"Are you sure you're a girl? You have to try on the others. You might like one of them better."

Moira got her to try on all of the dresses, and they decided that the green dress was the best choice. She called her mom in to do her magic with pins, and when her mom went to the next room to sew, Moira pulled out some of the pictures she'd printed out from past zoo events.

She spread the photos on the floor. "Now, obviously, I don't know who's actually going to be at the fund-raiser tonight, but based on past attendance, I picked some for you to get to know." She pointed at the top row. "I'm guessing you already know those guys because Jimmy was so interested in them. Right below them are their wives."

Moira ticked off small conversation starters for each of the women. Little things like hobbies or other charities that the women were involved in. "I'm sure you can handle this part. All you have to do is get them talking. They'll take over."

"Okay. I can handle that."

"And smile. Lots of smiling. You need to be friendly. If you look like a bitch, they won't approach you."

"My default look is bitch."

"But they're going to want to check you out because you'll be with Jimmy and they've all been wondering about him." She pulled out makeup she bought for Gabby and sat on the bed. "Let's get your makeup done."

When Gabby sat next to her, Moira said, "I guessed about colors. We can't use my makeup on you. You'd end up looking like a ghost if I used my pasty white complexion powder on your glowing golden skin."

"Shit. I didn't even think about makeup. Tell me what I owe you and I'll pay you back."

"How about you just tell me about the case? It's killing me to not have details. My imagination runs wild and then I have unsubstantiated stories running in my head. Put me out of my misery."

Gabby closed her eyes and let Moira apply makeup. "It's

not exciting. The mayor thinks there's a possible theft ring targeting Chicago's wealthy residents. We're looking into it."

Not nearly as exciting as Moira had hoped. Still a quality news story, though. "And the pervs that Jimmy's so interested in? Are they the thieves?"

"Victims, we think."

"Think? You don't know who the victims are?"

"I can't say any more. I shouldn't have told you that much. Don't tell Jimmy."

Moira worked in silence. Once the makeup was done, Moira began to play with Gabby's hair. The thick mop didn't have much style, but there were enough layers that Moira was able to pile most of it on Gabby's head and leave a few sexy tendrils dangling down.

"Here, Moira. Have her try it on now." Her mom stood in the doorway of the room holding the green dress.

Gabby stood and looked at herself in the mirror. "Oh, my freaking God."

Mom's mouth thinned to a straight line.

As if she felt the glare, Gabby shrank down. "Sorry. It's just that I don't even look like me."

Moira took the dress and had Gabby step into it quickly. She knew her mom would get it right on the first try. She always did. Moira zipped up the back, and when Gabby turned, Moira's mouth dropped.

The woman was stunning.

Her mom came around and tugged at seams and moved Gabby's body in different directions to check her handiwork. Satisfied that it was good enough, she gave Gabby a stiff nod and left.

"Your mom's not much of a talker, huh?"

"Only when she has something to say."

"Then where did you get the talking gene?"

Moira laughed. "My dad. He owned the bar. He loved to talk to people. He was a natural bartender."

Watching her dad engage people at the bar was where she'd learned most of her tricks she used as a reporter. She learned to get people to open up.

She glanced at the clock. "I better get myself dressed."

Gabby sat carefully on the bed, almost like she thought she might wrinkle.

Moira stepped into her dress. She'd found an awesome deal on it. The bluish purple color shimmered, and she felt like a princess wearing it. After applying a hint of makeup, she pinned her hair in place in a hairstyle similar to the one she'd given Gabby.

Just as she gave herself a last once-over, the doorbell rang. "I think your husband's here."

"Moira," her mom called.

"We're coming." She turned to Gabby. "You look totally hot. You know I would've helped even if Jimmy didn't agree to anything, right?"

"I hoped so, but it's good to know."

They made their way down the stairs that led into the dining room. Jimmy stood in the living room, staring out the front windows. For a brief moment, she imagined he was waiting for her. Gabby stepped down behind her and said, "Hi."

Jimmy turned as they walked toward him. His eyes bugged and he swallowed hard. "Wow."

Gabby blushed. "Thanks. Maybe I'll have to have Moira teach me to do this more often."

"Ready to go?"

Gabby nodded and he looked at Moira.

"I'm driving myself. You don't want to show up with me in your car. I'll see you there."

They turned and walked out. Moira gave herself a mental pat on the back. She'd done a good job getting Gabby ready. A small sigh escaped. When Jimmy stared at Gabby, Moira felt a huge hit of jealousy. What she wouldn't give to have a guy look at her like that.

She gathered her purse and slid in a notebook for taking notes. Time to look for the next guy to kiss.

8

"Okay, you can pop your eyes back in your head and roll up your tongue," Gabby said as they settled in the car. "I'm still the same Gabby."

Jimmy adjusted his expression, glad that Gabby believed he'd been looking at her. When the women had come down the stairs, he was struck stupid looking at Moira. He covered by staring at Gabby, who had in fact made a huge transformation. But to him, she remained Gabby, his partner. Moira had become the woman he'd drooled over the first night he played James Buchanan.

He didn't need to fuel that fire.

He did his level best to push Moira from his mind while he drove to the zoo. He was sweltering in his suit and wondered how long he'd have to wait to at least take off the coat. The air-conditioning in the car blew full blast, but his blood remained hot.

At the zoo, they made their way to the pavilion. Waiters eased through the crowd with trays of champagne. Would anyone notice if he went to the bar and ordered a draft? Would it make him stand out as not belonging?

Gabby grabbed a glass but didn't drink. They studied the crowd.

This group was more diverse than previous events he'd attended. Although it was still a ball, the crowd seemed to have more than just the wealthy in attendance. And in fact, some were drinking beer. He glanced at Gabby, who turned the glass in her hand nervously. "I'm going to grab a beer. I'll be right back."

She clutched his forearm. "Don't leave me."

"Beer. I'll be right back." He thought he'd have to peel her fingers away, but she dropped her hand.

At the bar, he found what was rapidly becoming his usual crowd. Stan Decker and his friends all held bottles of imported beer. Not his usual, but better than champagne. He ordered and then said, "Hi, Stan, how are you?"

"James, good to see you again."

The bartender delivered his beer and Jimmy raised it to Stan, Nick, and Marcus. "My wife loves animals, and as soon as she visited the zoo, I knew she'd want to attend."

Stan chuckled as a man who suffered a similar fate.

"Let me ask you something, Stan. Man to man." Jimmy shifted closer. "Are the wives part of every social function around here?"

"Most. Why?"

He shrugged as if uncomfortable in order to project a level of trust. "While she was out of town, I was enjoying not being watched. You know how it is. She's probably shooting daggers at my back right now because I left her to get a beer."

"Where is she? I know Karen has been dying to meet her."

Jimmy pointed over his shoulder and hoped he knew Gabby as well as he thought. "Dark hair, green dress."

Stan looked over and laughed. "Yeah, she looks ticked off. I know what you mean about being watched. It's not so bad once all the wives get together. They do their thing; we do ours. Come on, let's get your wife into the group so you can enjoy your evening."

When they reached Gabby, she painted a smile on her face. "Hey, sweetie, look who I ran into at the bar. Remember I told you about Stan Decker and how he's been so welcoming."

Gabby extended her hand. "So nice to meet you."

"Likewise. We were starting to believe James made you up." Stan looked around. "There's my wife Karen. She's been wanting to meet you."

Stan led the way, and after another painful introduction, Stan tugged him away from the women. Gabby looked at him with pleading eyes. He smiled and shrugged. He followed Stan, but before they got too far, he heard Moira's voice.

"Mrs. Buchanan, is that you? Oh, my goodness. It's so good to see you again."

Jimmy didn't need to turn to know she was in full actress mode. Back at the bar, he indulged in another beer, knowing it would be his last for the night. From his position, he could keep an eye on Gabby, who appeared to be doing better thanks to Moira jumping in. He'd lost sight of Moira, though.

The mayor approached, and Jimmy found himself stiffening out of habit and forced his body to relax.

"James, good to see you."

"Bill, glad you could make it. Do you have a minute?"

The mayor nodded, and Jimmy led them away from the crowd and noise. "Mr. Mayor, this isn't working. We don't have enough to go on here, and no one is about to open up about a robbery they were afraid to report."

"What if I can convince my friend to come forward and file an official report?"

Jimmy tucked his hands in his pockets. "That would help, but we need details. We don't know where to aim our investigation right now, so we're just spinning our wheels."

"I understand. I'll see what I can do. Give me until the end of the week."

Jimmy shrugged. Like he was going to say no to the mayor? Besides, there wasn't another event he'd be forced to go to during the week. Most of his week, he was able to just be Detective O'Malley.

The mayor walked away and he went back to the bar. No sooner did he lean against the hardwood when he saw Moira. She stood at the opposite end of the counter, looking gorgeous with a broad smile on her face. She was talking to a man whose face he couldn't see. Then she leaned forward and patted his arm.

She was flirting with this guy.

As soon as she made that simple move, the guy had his opening. He reached up and toyed with a lock of hair that framed her face. He was much too close and Jimmy straightened with the intention of breaking up the intimate party. But then he stopped himself. James was a married man tonight, and Moira was no one to him other than some reporter that he knew casually. Blowing his cover wouldn't be a smart move.

Stan starting talking about real estate again and excellent locations for James and Gabby. He acted as though Jimmy had already hired him to find a place. Jimmy listened, at least halfway, but his gaze tracked Moira. She'd left the bar and mingled through the crowd. She stopped and talked to no fewer than five different men. None wore a wedding band.

When she left the pavilion with one guy, Jimmy had had enough. "Excuse me, Stan, I'm going to take a walk. Save us a spot at your table for dinner, and you can tell Gabby all about your ideas for where we should look."

"Will do."

Taking his coat off and carrying it over his shoulder, Jimmy hoped to find a breeze to cool himself down. Then he realized it wasn't the weather making him hot, but Moira's teasing.

Once his eyes adjusted to the dark outside the pavilion, he glanced around and found Moira and bachelor number six. He followed from a safe distance. Until the guy slid his hand around Moira's waist. Then Jimmy picked up the pace until he was almost alongside them.

"Moira? Moira O'Leary?"

She stopped in her tracks and turned. Although she smiled, her eyes spoke volumes of irritation. "Mr. Buchanan, nice to see you again."

The man beside her dropped his hand from her body and held it out. "Mike Thornton."

"James Buchanan." He returned his attention to Moira. "I'm glad I ran into you. I've been meaning to talk about that interview you wanted to do."

She opened her purse and pulled out a business card. "I'm sorry. I thought I'd given you my card. Feel free to call me at your convenience."

He made no move to take the card. "Actually, I was hoping you might have a minute now." He looked pointedly at her companion.

"I'll head back to the party. I'll see you inside, Moira. Save a dance for me."

Once Mike was out of earshot, she asked, "What the hell are you doing?"

He glanced over his shoulder at the number of people still milling around. He grabbed Moira's elbow and guided her farther away.

She struggled in his grasp, which caused her dress to gap and then tighten in all the places that shouldn't draw his attention but did.

"Let go of me. What are you doing?"

When they were safely ensconced in shadows, he released her. "I was going to ask you the same thing."

"I'm doing my job. Same as you." The moonlight peeking through the foliage made her white skin glow. Her chest rose and fell fast; he knew she was getting wound up.

Well, so was he. "Your job is to flirt with every single guy you come across?"

"What do you care who I flirt with? You barely like me."

Why did she keep going there? "I told you I like you just fine."

"Funny way of showing it. You ruined a nice walk I was having with Mike. I don't need another big brother. I've got that covered."

He wasn't looking at her like a little sister right now. In fact, he was having a hard time remembering she was a little sister. "You're making me nuts. What are you trying to do?"

She sighed heavily and leaned against the rock outcropping behind her. "My friend Kathy—"

"Hendricks?"

"Yeah. She pointed out that the events I attend have plenty of bachelors."

Christ. She was taking dating advice from Kathy Hendricks? The woman briefly dated Kevin, which didn't say much about her taste.

"Then something you said the other day stuck with me. Remember at the block party, you mentioned kissing every guy possible to find the one who would set off fireworks? Well, that got me to thinking. Maybe I was being too selective in trying to find the right guy. So I figured I'd give it a shot. It shouldn't be a conflict of interest if I don't write about the guys I date. And I might be able to find the one to make my toes curl—"

He lost the ability to think. Dropping his coat, he pushed against her, one hand bringing her hips toward him. He braced an arm against the rough rock to keep balance as he lowered himself to align his mouth with hers. His movement caused blessed silence from her except for a quick, sharp intake of breath.

God, she tasted just like he'd always imagined: like sweet sunshine and smiles. Pushing his tongue into her mouth to seek out hers elicited a moan from her, and it made him want to take more. His hand traveled up her back, pushing her more firmly against him and the softness of her chest pressed against his.

As her arms twined around his neck and her fingers rubbed his head, he could've sworn that he did indeed see fireworks. Like some damn kid.

He nipped her full lower lip and was about to dive in for more when the sound of laughter behind them caught his attention and he remembered where they were.

Shoving away as quickly as he'd moved in, he mumbled, "Fuck."

"Not quite, but that was a hell of a start."

He heard the smile in her voice, along with a hint of *I told you so*.

He took a full step back. "I'm sorry. That shouldn't have happened."

"Just what every girl likes to hear after being kissed senseless. Why not?"

"You mean besides the fact that you're Liam's little sister?"

"Definitely besides that. Liam doesn't decide who I date, much less who I kiss or sleep with."

He couldn't think about her kissing or sleeping with anyone right now, even him. Especially him. "I'm supposed to be married, remember? Fuck. I don't know how I let you do this to me."

"So sorry to be an inconvenience." Her voice didn't hold an ounce of apology.

"I need to get back to the party."

"So do I." She took a few steps away from him until she stood in a pool of light. Her skin continued to glow and her hair was still in place, but her face was flush and her lips kiss swollen. "I've had some interesting conversations. You know, if you tell me what kind of information you're looking for, I can probably find things out for you."

Fury crept in quickly and he grabbed her elbow. "Stay out of my investigation."

"I'm a reporter. I ask questions. It's what I do for a living."

"I'm not kidding, Moira. Stop playing Lois Lane. Leave it."

Again with the snort. "If I'm Lois, that makes you who? Superman?"

"We don't know what we're dealing with. You'll get your damn story. Stay away from it."

"Whatever. I have people to meet." She turned away to leave again.

"No more men tonight, Moira."

"We'll see," she said without turning around. And he

was certain she added a bit of sway to her hips just to make him crazier.

He watched her walk away and took a deep breath. Then he retrieved his coat from the ground before heading back to find Gabby. She was already sitting at a table with Stan, who monopolized the conversation. More daggers shot his way.

"Hey, sweetie. Sorry I took so long. I ran into a few people and needed to say hi." He took his seat.

Gabby didn't respond except for a raised eyebrow as if she knew what he'd been doing. Some famous chef prepared dinner, but Jimmy didn't taste much. And the portions were so small, he was still hungry when they pulled away his empty plate. He carried on conversations half-assed as he kept an eye out for Moira.

When the band struck its first chords, he looked for an escape. The case was stalled without more information, and he didn't know if he could continue this charade while Moira flirted. When Stan's wife pulled Gabby to the dance floor, Jimmy went back to the bar. Enough alcohol had been consumed that everyone became friendlier.

Stan had followed him, and if Jimmy hadn't been sure he had information about the thefts, he would've told Stan to back off. Jimmy decided one more beer would be fine and then they could cut out. As he took his first sip, he heard Moira's laugh. Full-throated and enticing. He turned to see her. Stan followed his eyes.

"That one has eyes for you," he said.

"Hmm?"

"The O'Leary reporter. She's been watching you all night like you're a chocolate dessert."

"I don't think so."

"Trust me. She hasn't given anyone a look like that." He

leaned closer to Jimmy. "And if you're interested, I can say she'd be safer than some you'll encounter."

Jimmy froze. Stan's words held plenty of implications. Safer how? He wanted to ask, but Gabby came rushing up to him.

"I need a drink. These women know how to party." She grabbed Jimmy's beer and took a gulp. Then she turned to the bar and asked for a glass of water.

"You almost ready to go, honey?"

"One more dance."

"I'll be here."

She gulped her water and danced off. Stan began a conversation with someone else at the bar, leaving Jimmy to ponder the cryptic message.

MOIRA DIDN'T KNOW what she hoped to accomplish. Sure, when the night had started out, she had a plan, but Jimmy managed to blow it to bits with a single kiss. And she'd been right. The man could make her toes curl with a kiss. Now she was just playing, and maybe part of her wanted to see if he'd get jealous.

It was a little childish, but the man ticked her off. He kissed her and then apologized. What the hell did that mean?

She spent the remainder of her evening collecting phone numbers, but the thought of kissing any of these guys did nothing for her. Especially when she remembered the raw power of Jimmy's kiss. He was always in control of everything. Just once, she'd like to see him lose control. Even when she annoyed him, he kept his voice, his emotions, everything in check.

Jimmy stood at the bar with creepy Stan. Stan had to be an integral part of whatever theft Jimmy was investigating. Would it be asking too much for Stan to land in jail? Probably.

She noticed a gold band on Jimmy's finger and wondered where he'd gotten it. When he wasn't holding his beer, he toyed with the ring, the only sign that it was an unusual part of his wardrobe. In the span of him finishing his beer, after Gabby left him, Moira counted three different women enter his space to flirt.

He didn't acknowledge it, not the way Stan did. But Moira found it interesting that being married made Jimmy more popular. Why would women go after someone who was supposed to be unattainable? Was it the chase? Just to see if they could?

She shook her head and went to find her next bachelor. If Jimmy wanted to believe their kiss was a mistake, that was his choice. She'd find someone who actually *wanted* to kiss her.

As she finished her evening, she waved to Gabby and Jimmy, and a nagging thought about all of the flirtatious women grabbed hold of her brain. There was something there—she just needed to find it.

Hours later, Moira sat up in bed, unable to sleep. At first, thoughts of kissing Jimmy revved her hormones. She couldn't stop feeling his hands roughly hold her in place. Her mouth remembered his slick, hot tongue sliding along hers. His hard body pressed against her, his soft, bristly hair brushing her palm, everything leaving her wanting more.

Then there was the oh-my-freaking-God feeling because Jimmy O'Malley kissed her. She'd never seen it coming, even with their brief encounter in her apartment. With great effort, she pushed all images away. She didn't know what to do about Jimmy. She'd loved the man more than half her life, but he would laugh at her if she ever confessed.

She sought something else to focus on and returned to that same nagging thought, like a major breakthrough sat just out of her reach. She needed some caffeine to charge her brain, and then maybe it would come to her. Two a.m. and a pot of coffee gurgled on her kitchen counter while she scrolled through files of photos.

Something familiar about one of the women who had approached Jimmy tugged at her, but for the life of her, she couldn't place the woman. She must've been a guest at the occasional event, but not one of the regulars. Moira couldn't put her together with any of the usual faces.

By the time Moira finished the pot of coffee, she had a nice caffeine buzz going, and she'd flipped through thousands of photos. Every time she caught a glimpse of the mystery woman, that's all it was—she was always in the background. Moira had never interviewed her, and her name appeared nowhere in any of Moira's articles.

Moira didn't even know why it seemed to matter so much, but now it felt like a challenge. She made a file of pictures of the woman and then opened the file and spread the photos across her screen. Long auburn hair, always left down and flowing, as if to conceal her face from cameras. She was tall, at least five foot eight, judging her beside people Moira knew. The collage of faces stared at her, and Moira closed her eyes.

Had she ever spoken to the woman?

She thought back to the events where she knew the woman appeared. Early on, when Moira first started covering fund-raisers and charity events. One of her first, in fact. Moira's eyes popped open with the recognition.

Jimmy had to hear about this. Standing in front of her

computer, she looked down at herself. Okay, so a quick shower and change of clothes were in order. Regardless of what Jimmy said about not wanting her, his kiss said different, and she refused to give him fuel to forget her. She checked the clock. By the time she was ready, Jimmy would be up. The military had taught him to be an early riser. He and Liam always joked about it because Liam was not a morning person.

Moira was out the door and in her car before six. The only time she ever saw six in the morning was when she pulled an all-nighter. She made a stop at Starbucks and drove into Jimmy's neighborhood. She probably could've gotten away with calling him, but she had the feeling he'd brush her off if she called. She'd be harder to ignore in person. She parked in front of his house and looked up. No lights were on. She didn't want to ring the bell and risk waking up his dad.

She sat sipping her coffee until she heard a motorcycle rumble behind her. Had to be Sean.

Stepping out of her car, she took a long look at him. "Taking a walk of shame, Sean?"

"Hey, Moira. No shame here. It's all good."

"Do you know if Jimmy's up yet? I didn't want to wake your dad."

Sean glanced at his phone. "He'll be out running. Like clockwork every morning. He'll turn the corner any minute."

He tapped her shoulder and pointed to the end of the block. Sure enough, there was Jimmy running toward them. Sean stepped up on the curb. "I'm off to bed. See you later."

Moira followed him and sat on the front steps. Excitement bubbled in her chest. She knew the information she had would help Jimmy. She didn't know quite how, but her gut was rarely wrong.

She leaned over and looked down the block. He had slowed to a walk now, arms up, as he cooled down. The T-shirt he wore was wet with sweat and pulled tightly against his chest and around his biceps. She swallowed a healthy gulp of coffee and lust simultaneously.

He pulled up short when he saw her on the steps. Pulling the earbuds from his ears, he said, "What are you doing here?"

She stood, swallowed, and focused on her mission, which was *not* imagining him naked. "I had this idea that kept bugging me last night after the zoo party. It nagged and kept me awake, and I knew if I focused, it would mean something."

He released a heavy breath. "What would mean something, Moira? I need to get in the shower."

She fumbled her coffee. Pictures of a wet, naked Jimmy were not helping. Then he lifted the edge of his shirt to wipe his forehead. His stomach muscles flexed and her brain shorted. "Uhh...I think I have something that might help your case."

He dropped the shirt and straightened. "I told you to stay away from my investigation. You have no idea what you're doing."

She took a slow, deep breath, one she was told would help control her snap temper. "I didn't do anything to your investigation. But I still came up with something that I think will help."

She sucked down the last of her coffee as he stared at her. *Lois Lane, my ass.*

"Can I take a shower and then we can talk?"

"I'll wait if you buy me breakfast."

"Fine." He jogged past her up the stairs. "You coming in?"

No, it would be better to keep barriers between her and a wet, naked Jimmy. "Nah. I'll wait here."

He took her empty cup and went inside.

While she waited for him, Moira studied the neighborhood. She'd spent most of her life here, but she never thought about how different it looked from this side of the street. It was a different perspective, and she wondered what Jimmy saw when he sat here.

Her daydreaming was interrupted when Kevin dropped a bag at her feet. "Finally here to declare your love for me?"

She rolled her eyes. "What are you doing here? I thought you were the only one with his own place."

"The laundry room in my building is a mess. I need clean clothes. The real question is, why are you here? Don't you belong across the street?"

"I'm waiting for Jimmy."

"For what?"

"I need to talk to him."

"You can talk to me." He hefted the bag over his shoulder.

She shifted over so he could get by. "You're the last person I'd want to talk to. I'm still pissed about the water balloon."

The bag thumped against the sidewalk again.

She squinted up at him and waited.

He rubbed a hand across the back of his neck. "About that. I'm sorry. I thought it would be funny. I didn't think about what you were wearing."

Moira froze at the sight of Kevin apologizing.

He didn't say anything else or wait for a response. He grabbed his bag and disappeared into the house.

Moira continued to stare at the spot where he'd stood. The only other time in their tortured relationship that she could remember Kevin ever apologizing was when they were ten. She had blossomed early and had a chest before most of her classmates. And not just little buds either. Over that summer, she had bloomed straight into needing more support than a training bra.

And of course, Kevin O'Malley sat behind her as he had every year. She had no idea what bug had crawled up his ass that day, but he poked and prodded and then went to snap her bra strap. He started making jokes about how she'd needed an industrial strength bra to hold up her hooters.

She'd never been so embarrassed in her life. Not being able to hold back the tears made it worse. She ran all the way home with tears streaming down her cheeks. Her throat hurt from running and crying.

When she'd gotten to her house, Jimmy and Liam were sitting on the front porch. Liam grabbed her arm and asked what was wrong. She yelled that she hated the O'Malleys and went to her room to finish crying.

An hour later, Kevin O'Malley stood beneath her bedroom window because she'd refused to come to the door. He yelled at the top of his lungs that he was an idiot and he didn't deserve to even sit behind her at school.

Moira remembered peering under the shade of her window and watching him. He rubbed his neck, just like he did today, and it was like Jimmy stood behind him holding him in place by his neck.

Kevin never said Jimmy made him apologize, but she'd known it. That was the day she fell in love with Jimmy O'Malley.

9

———

Jimmy came out the front door and Moira was in the same place. He'd passed Kevin on the way out and Kevin hadn't said anything, but Moira had a look now, a little misty-eyed, that made him think Kevin had done something. Again.

"Hey," he called. "Ready to go?"

She shook her head. "Yeah."

"You okay?"

"Of course." Then she smiled in that way that could compete with the sunrise. "Maybe a little too much caffeine..."

"Let's walk to the diner." As they stepped onto the sidewalk, he asked, "So what do you want to tell me?"

"Well, it started last night. Before you left, you had a lot of women talking to you. You have to admit I was right. Having a wife made you safer—they accepted you more because you were one of them, right? Anyway, there were a couple of women I didn't know, but I recognized. It kind of bugged me, but I was busy, so I pushed it out of my head. Then I got home and I couldn't sleep—" She stopped suddenly as if she just realized she needed to breath.

"Exactly how much coffee have you had?"

She waved a hand at him as if it didn't matter. "A pot to keep me up while I worked and then the one I finished when I got here. Anyway—"

"Did you sleep at all?"

She shrugged and rolled her eyes. He stopped. She kept walking.

It took about five steps for her to notice that he was no longer beside her, so she turned and walked back. "What?"

He studied her face. "Why didn't you sleep?"

"That's what I'm trying to tell you. Come on. I'm starving. Keep walking while I talk." She tugged his hand, but let go as soon as his feet started moving. "Once I had my first cup of coffee, my brain engaged and I started trying to figure out where I knew this woman from. I scoured every photo I had from every event I've attended over the last year. And you know what? She wasn't really in any photo. I mean, I have glimpses of her, but never a shot of her with friends or an interview with her name. But she's there."

Jimmy tried to hold his patience. He knew Moira. She needed to gear up to her point, but he suffered from the same lack of sleep she had. Except his wasn't from finding a lead in the case. His insomnia was directly related to her and her mouth against his. That damn kiss haunted him all night. He thought for sure a run would fix him, but it barely eased the burn. Finding her at his doorstep didn't help.

They turned the corner and headed down the next block to the diner. Super Cup wasn't exactly great food, but it was close and they knew what to expect. "Where are you going with this?"

She threw her hands up. "Let me have my moment,

would you? I spent all night racking my brain trying to remember. This woman, this nameless woman who doesn't want to be photographed—I think she's an escort."

Jimmy reached for the door of the diner and stopped. "Escort, like hooker?"

"I don't know the specifics of it, but we're not talking streetwalker, though."

He held the door for her. His day did just take a turn in the right direction. Watching Moira's ass in some short shorts was pretty nice.

They grabbed a booth and sat. Before they even opened the sticky menus, a waitress arrived at the table with two glasses of water.

"Can I get you some coffee?"

"Yes," Moira answered too quickly.

Jimmy shook his head. "You've had enough coffee. Two glasses of orange juice and a milk for her."

She rolled her eyes again but didn't seem bothered by him changing her order.

He set the menu to the side.

She did the same. "Milk will go better with brownie à la mode anyway."

"You're eating a brownie and ice cream for breakfast?"

"I'll eat the brownies here any time, any day. They are *the* best. Chocolatey, gooey, and fudgy all at the same time. If I could find a man to make these for me, I'd be his love slave."

Jimmy choked on the water he'd been attempting to drink.

She leaned forward against the table, pressing her breasts up, and Jimmy focused squarely in her eyes. "So here's the deal. I have an imagination. I told Gabby that without details, my mind wanders and I make things up." She raised a hand quickly. "Don't worry. I don't actually ever publish those things, but the ideas are there. So I started thinking about the guys you're hanging out with at these parties. An idiot could realize that they must figure prominently into your case. That led me to think that since they like to hit on every female they see, and they have a habit of cheating on their wives, maybe it wouldn't be beneath them to hire an escort. To do whatever." She took a quick drink of water.

Jimmy stared at her. Sure, it was completely unfounded and they had zero proof, but her working theory closely matched what they'd developed. The difference was, Moira knew these people. It hadn't occurred to him and Gabby that rich people would hire escorts. Maybe Chicago had its very own Mayflower Madam.

"Uh-oh," she muttered.

"What?"

"You're giving me that look again."

"What look?" Shit. Had he been looking at her mouth? He hadn't been actively thinking about kissing her, but the thought never strayed far from his conscious mind whenever she was close.

"The look that says, 'Shut up, Moira. You don't know what you're talking about.'"

He smiled. "I wasn't thinking that at all. In fact, I rarely do, even though you push my patience to the limit."

The waitress returned with their drinks and took their order.

He wanted to get this information from Moira without giving her any details. If he let her know they were on the same track, she wouldn't be able to keep her nose out of it. When they were alone again, he continued. "Why did this woman make you think of escorts?"

"Because she approached me at one of the first events I

covered. I'm pretty sure it was her. She handed me a card with a phone number and told me she'd get me more money than my current employer paid."

He choked on some orange juice. Drinking during this conversation didn't seem like a smart move. "She thought you were an escort? Why?"

Her mouth curved into a smile as she sat back and waved her hands in front of her chest. As if that was supposed to be an explanation. She sighed. "I guess I look like a hooker. I don't know."

Jimmy had known Moira to look a lot of ways, but as a hooker appeared nowhere on the list. "Interesting ideas you have, but I told you to stay away from my investigation."

Her face fell.

He didn't quite understand her disappointment. It's not like her job was riding on the success of this case. His wasn't either, exactly, but when the mayor asked for a favor, he expected something. "Do you still have the card or the phone number? Name of the company?"

"I don't know. I'll look. But that means you think I'm onto something."

He shot her another look.

"Come on, Jimmy. Give me something. I'm trying to help you."

"I don't need your help. Believe it or not, I'm capable of doing my job."

She started fidgeting with the salt and pepper shakers and then the packets of sugar, organizing them by color. He wondered if Moira knew how to sit still. Definitely a smart move to cancel the extra coffee.

They sat in silence until the waitress returned with their food. His stomach turned at the sight of the sugar mess Moira immediately dug into. "How can you eat that?"

"How can you not?" She looked at his plate. "I eat food like this too. If my mom makes it." She snagged one of his pieces of bacon. Then she scooped up a piece of brownie and offered it to him.

"No, thanks. I'll stick with my breakfast."

"You don't know what you're missing."

He watched as she attacked the brownie and ice cream like she'd been denied dessert for a year. It took considerable effort to ignore her mouth, especially when her tongue swirled around the fork to catch a drip of fudge sauce. Tearing his eyes from her, he focused on his own plate. Their conversation was nonexistent and he preferred the silence. Anything else might land where he didn't want to go.

She finished her brownie in record time, leaving a blob of melted ice cream on the plate. After draining her glass, she spun it in circles while watching him eat.

"You can go if you want. You don't need to wait for me."

"No, I'm fine. I'll walk back with you."

He waved the waitress over to get their bill while he finished his last few bites.

"Tell me something else about the case."

"No."

"Come on, Jimmy. I'm trying to be helpful. Give me something and I can generate more good ideas. My theory is gonna break your case open, just wait and see." Her cocky grin put him on edge.

"A theory doesn't solve crimes. I have to do real police work for that to happen."

She folded her hands in front of her on the table. "I'm like Yoda. I show you the path, but you need to seek your own answers."

"You're going to crash so hard when the caffeine and

sugar wear off." He dropped cash on the table to cover the bill and a tip and then he stood. "Ready?"

"Yep." She bounced out of her seat.

He shook his head. He'd never known anyone as bouncy and bubbly as Moira. If she could bottle it, she'd be rich.

Once they were outside, she opened her arms in a wide stretch and inhaled. "Gorgeous day. Don't you love summer?"

He shrugged. He didn't have any preference for one season over another. Just having seasons was enjoyable.

"So about last night."

His step shuffled and he hoped she missed it. He'd also hoped he'd escape having this conversation.

"You kissed me."

"Yeah."

"Why?"

He thought of a slew of reasons: she was beautiful and sexy, he wanted to stop her from flirting with other men in front of him, he wanted to capture a hint of the vivacious-ness she exuded. But what came out of his mouth was, "I needed to get you to shut up somehow. You weren't listening again."

"Usually you just say, 'Shut up, Moira.'"

He shrugged again.

She put a hand on his forearm to stop their progress. He turned to look at her, afraid of where she was headed.

"You know, I can't read you. I'm good at seeing people and understanding them, but not you. You run hot and cold with me, and I don't know what to do."

"Nothing."

"But I think we both want to do something about it."

"Don't." He turned to walk away and she grabbed him

again. He pulled his arm from her grasp and she jumped in front of him.

"Do not blow me off. I felt it in the kiss last night. That was not a shut-the-fuck-up kiss. There was heat and passion and attraction. It's a pity if you can't recognize it."

Her cheeks were pink again and her blue eyes sparked. Every emotion with Moira was extreme.

After a beat, she took a step back. "Or maybe you just don't want to be attracted to me. Is that it?"

That was a minefield if he ever heard one, so he didn't answer.

"So we're back to you pretending like your mouth doesn't work?"

"It works fine. I don't know what you're looking for here."

She stepped closer to him again, and he smelled her perfume, soft and flowery. "Tell me the real reason you kissed me last night."

"Because I wanted to. You were beautiful and you kept flirting with all those other guys."

"You were jealous?"

Fuck yeah. "I have no business being jealous."

"But you kissed me."

"We've already established that."

"Kiss me again."

"No."

She sighed at him and a look of pity came into her eyes. "Afraid? That's really too bad. Maybe you can't top the kiss from last night and then I'll know you're a one-hit wonder." One side of her mouth tilted up in challenge.

He shouldn't touch her. He knew he should keep his distance, but he was also never good at backing down from a challenge. Taking a half step forward and invading her space, he wrapped a hand around the back of her neck and lowered his mouth to hers.

He took his time sampling everything about her mouth.

He tasted the sugary sweetness of her breakfast. She was soft and warm and inviting. Her hand came around and rubbed its way up his back, exploring, pulling him nearer. Her pulse tattooed a rapid beat against his palm as his thumb stroked her jaw. Everything about Moira was soft.

His heart beat faster than it had on his run, and something primal took over.

Take.

Mine.

He jerked back from her with the thought. What the hell was he doing?

Her eyes fluttered opened and she tilted her head back as if looking for another round. He held her at arm's length in an attempt to clear his head.

"Why do you do that?"

"What?"

"Pull away. I know you wanted that kiss as much as I did."

His hands slid down her arms and he let her go. Then he took a full step back. "Because we shouldn't. *I* shouldn't."

A look of complete bewilderment crossed her face. "Because of Liam?"

"That's one reason." He moved to her side and began walking toward his house again.

"Liam wouldn't care." Her shoes slapped the pavement as she ran to catch up to him. "I'm serious. Of all my brothers, Liam would be the last one to hassle someone about dating me."

"And if we end things, how would he react if I hurt you?"

Her grin turned wicked again. "Who says I'd be the one to end up hurt?"

Deep down, he knew she spoke the truth.

She didn't wait for a further response. She turned and began skipping—honest to God skipping—down the street. Stopping in front of his house, she called, "Are you working today?"

"Not sure yet."

She squinted in the sunlight. "I'll pick you up at seven."

"For what?"

"Our date."

"What date?"

"The one I'm taking you on tonight. We're going to go out and have a great time." She walked to her car and opened the door without a key. Of course she hadn't locked it.

Just as he was about to yell at her, she revved the engine and pulled away. He made a mental note to yell at her later as he climbed the stairs to go inside. Kevin met him at the door.

"What the hell was that?"

"Hurricane Moira."

MOIRA DROVE HOME in a haze of pleasure and frustration. Jimmy's kiss had been heady and wonderful and strangely soothing. But also frustrating because he kept pulling back from her. It was a bizarre dance. He'd initiate and pull away. She'd step forward and he'd retreat further.

He hadn't shot down the idea of them going on a date, though. Not that she'd given him much chance. By the time she parked in front of her apartment, she felt the sugar crash. Maybe a brownie for breakfast on top of all the caffeine hadn't been the best idea. Still the best brownie, but now her system was shutting down in need of rest.

She climbed the stairs to her apartment and went straight to bed. Falling asleep proved difficult because her brain was preoccupied with imagining possibilities with Jimmy for the night. She heard their conversations and saw their date as a movie in her head.

She drifted off seeing a smile on Jimmy's face while he looked at her, which would be a nice change of pace. He didn't smile nearly enough around her.

HER PHONE RANG, waking her. Glancing at the time and the caller simultaneously, a small jolt of panic hit her. Why was Mom calling? Was there family dinner today? As she answered the phone, she did some quick calculations and realized that family dinner was next Sunday.

"Hi, Mom. What's up?" She did her best to make it sound like she'd been up for hours so she wouldn't have to hear the reprimand about sleeping the day away.

"Was that your car I saw parked in front of the O'Malley house early this morning?"

Moira's mind was not up for battle with her mom. She knew Mom phrased it as a question to trap her in a lie. "Yeah."

The tsk came clearly across the line and Moira knew her mother thought she'd spent the night with one of the O'Malleys. "I was up early and had to talk to Jimmy. I had some information he needed for work."

"So you were up early, across the street from me, but you couldn't come to mass?"

Hell, no. "Jimmy took me to breakfast. We had to talk

through the information I had. It needed some explanation."

"And I suppose the explanation required you to be kissing him at the corner."

Busted. Moira didn't even try to explain. She flopped back onto her pillow and wished she'd never picked up the phone. She knew better than to have a conversation with Mom without her brain firing on all cylinders.

"I received a call from Mrs. Flaherty telling me that my daughter was in a passionate embrace with one of the O'Malley boys." Mom paused for effect, as only mothers could do. "That's how she phrased it—*passionate embrace.*"

"It wasn't like that, Mom. Yes, we kissed. And we have a date later tonight." She briefly wondered if her brothers received phone calls like this or if Mom reserved it for her. Sometimes, she really missed Maggie. As the youngest, Maggie took more heat than anyone.

Her mother sniffed. "Still should've come to mass. See you for dinner next Sunday."

Then Mom hung up, as she always did, without really saying good-bye.

Although she wasn't fully rested, Moira decided she could function, so she got out of bed. She had to finish her article on the zoo fund-raiser so she could submit it before her date. Thinking the word date in relation to Jimmy sent a shiver through her body. For so many years, she'd imagined him asking her out. Not once did she consider asking him. Maybe she should've done this a long time ago.

She sat at her computer and stared at the photos she'd left up of the mystery woman. Although Jimmy hadn't outright dismissed what she'd said, she didn't really know how useful it would be for him. He'd asked for the business card from the woman, but looking for that would have to wait. She'd been so sidetracked thinking about the woman that she was behind in the work she needed to do.

Perusing the scant notes she'd taken, Moira realized she hadn't been on her game at all last night. Flirting with single guys and watching Jimmy had taken so much of her attention that she'd missed out on a lot of the details she normally included. Maybe her editor wouldn't notice.

Her fingers flew over the keyboard as she immersed herself in the moment. Even without notes, she could close her eyes and picture the people she'd seen and spoken to.

When she hit her word count, she saved the article for a final read through later and opened the news. If she wanted a job people respected, she'd need a new story, one she could investigate while Jimmy worked his case. She wasn't good at waiting for things to happen. One of the perks of working as a freelancer was that she had some choice about what she wanted to cover. She'd made enough connections over the past year that she could continue to write for society pages for various editors, but she wanted more.

She thought more about Jimmy's case. She couldn't report on the thefts, but the escort angle might work as a story. Jimmy didn't seem too interested in it. If Chicago had a ring of high-class hookers, how were they getting away with it? Where did they operate? Who did they hook up with?

Suddenly, finding that business card became a priority. If she could contact the mystery woman, Moira could get information that could lead to a full exposé. By the time she wrote about the prostitution and who the clients were, Jimmy's case would be done and she would have that exclusive. Two powerful stories would put her in an excellent position.

Before she knew it, she was digging through every

drawer in the house. She tended to save things because she never knew when they might come in handy. While she searched, her imagination took over and she saw her name and articles associated with nighttime news programs and a movie of the week.

She had to find that number.

Hours later, her apartment looked like it had been ransacked, and she still hadn't found the damn business card. She kicked at a pile of books. It was time to get ready for her date. Her heart pounded at the thought of a date with Jimmy. A date with Jimmy was the stuff of her teenage dreams.

Adolescence wouldn't have been so bad if she'd gone to a regular high school, but since she was the first girl in the O'Leary family, everyone was overprotective, and her parents thought it would be better for her to go to a Catholic high school, which meant an all-female student body. Her prospects for finding dates were limited to guys she met on the bus. She couldn't even meet a cute boy at the mall because one of her brothers would always show up and ruin her fun.

So that left the neighborhood.

And Jimmy.

She picked up the pile of books and set them on a shelf. Then she surveyed the rest of the mess. Screw it. She'd deal with it later.

She stepped out of the shower, and her phone buzzed with a text from Jimmy.

Stuck at work. Won't be able to meet.

Moira's stomach sank. She'd been able to put Jimmy out of her mind and get work done. But in the back of her thoughts, in her heart, the thrum of excitement and anticipation hummed all day. Her eyes welled.

She swiped at them. It was stupid. She'd gotten her hopes up that if he gave her a chance, *they* would have a chance. He hadn't even agreed to go out with her, but he was the kind of guy who would've gone through with it. At least she'd thought so. Now, she'd reduced him to making up stories to get out of a date with her.

That spoke volumes because Jimmy wasn't a liar.

10

Jimmy pocketed his phone and waited, thinking Moira would respond. He didn't know which to feel more guilty about: the fact that he'd actually been looking forward to spending time alone with Moira or canceling a date they should never have.

She was due to pick him up in a little over an hour, but he knew he'd still be at the mayor's office. Park had finally convinced his friend to come forward to talk about the theft. The man refused to come into the station, but agreed to meet in the mayor's office. And while Jimmy arrived on time, the mayor's friend hadn't. The mayor still hadn't even given them the guy's name.

Even Park thought the man might back out. Jimmy paced the hall outside the office, tired of sitting in the reception area. He wanted Moira to call or text him back.

The elevator dinged, and Jimmy turned to see Len Bitger get off the elevator. When he saw Jimmy, his back shot up and his eyes widened. "James?"

"Len." Shit. He should've waited in reception so Bill had

to tell him. "Bill's waiting for us." He pulled the door open and waited for Len to walk through.

The mayor emerged from his office. "Len, I see you've met Detective O'Malley."

"Detective?"

"We hadn't gotten that far yet, sir."

"Let's take this into my office."

Len shifted like he was going to bolt. Gabby followed Park, and Jimmy waited for Len to move forward. This was the first real break they'd gotten. He wasn't about to lose it now.

In the mayor's office, Len and the mayor took seats across from each other. Jimmy and Gabby chose to stand.

"Len Bitger. This is Detectives O'Malley and Ruiz. I asked Detective O'Malley to go undercover to see if he could get any information about the thefts."

Len's eyebrows shot up.

"We've all heard the rumors. It concerned me enough to bring in a detective. You're the only person I know who has been robbed, though."

Jimmy crossed his arms. "Why didn't you report the crime when it happened?"

The mayor's lips thinned, and Len shifted in his chair.

"I thought Bill already explained why. I can't have this get around. It would ruin my marriage." He stared at his shoes.

"Who were you with? A mistress?"

Len shook his head.

Thinking back to Moira's theory, he asked, "An escort?"

Len nodded. Gabby took a seat beside Bitger, obviously irritated with Jimmy's interrogation tactics.

"Mr. Bitger, I understand how difficult this is, but we need as much information as you can give us so we can stop this from happening again. Did you bring her to your house?"

He shook his head.

"Did she have access to your house ever?"

Again, he shook his head. This was like playing twenty questions with a three-year-old. They needed narrative. Len needed to open up. He immediately thought of how easily Moira got people to talk.

Jimmy asked, "Where did you meet her?"

"What do you mean?"

"When was the first time you met her?"

"She approached me at a charity event. She flirted. At first, I thought she was one of those young things looking for a sugar daddy." He paused again, then rushed to add, "Not that I was looking for that. I'm happily married."

"So she approached you. Did she give you a number or a card?"

"No, she asked for my cell phone number. I didn't expect her to actually ever call me, but a week later, she did. Crystal wanted to meet on my usual poker night with the boys." He shrugged and stared at his hands in his lap. "I thought once couldn't hurt. My wife was out of town."

"When did she tell you she was an escort?"

"When we talked on the phone. I almost hung up, thinking she was a prostitute, but she assured me that she was simply an escort. She'd introduced herself because she was attracted to me. She wanted to meet and maybe have drinks. See if the attraction was mutual."

Len shoved out of the chair and paced with his hands in his pockets. "We met at the bar of the Drake. We hit it off. I asked her if she wanted me to get a room and she agreed." He sighed. "I probably should've known then that something was up."

Gabby stood and looked at Jimmy, pleading with her eyes for him to let her finish. He nodded.

"Mr. Bitger, did you spend the entire night with Crystal?"

"Yes, we had breakfast together in the morning."

"What was taken?"

"My wife's diamond necklace."

Jimmy started. He'd assumed the escort lifted something from him while he was asleep. This added a whole new dimension. "Where was your wife's necklace?"

Len looked at him like the question was ridiculous. "In my wife's jewelry box in our bedroom. I've asked her to keep it in a safe, but she refuses because she says she likes to be able to look at it whenever she wants."

Jimmy stepped closer. "So this theft happened at your house while you were screwing Crystal at the Drake."

Len and the mayor both cringed.

Gabby stepped between Jimmy and Len. "Was she with you the whole night? Is it possible she left after you fell asleep?"

"I don't think so."

"Could she have lifted your key and passed it on to someone?"

Again Len shook his head. His cheeks turned scarlet. "We were busy for most of the night. And she fell asleep in my arms."

A surge of excitement plowed through Jimmy. This was turning into the exact career-making kind of case he wanted. They had a theft ring made up of escorts targeting wealthy Chicago men. He imagined the headlines now. Which immediately made him think of Moira, who still hadn't called him back.

Gabby continued with questions. "What makes you think Crystal had something to do with this?"

"Well, I haven't heard from her since, her phone is no longer in service, and she hasn't been at any event since the one where we first met. I don't believe in that much coincidence, do you?"

No, he did not believe in coincidence. Not like this.

His phone buzzed in his pocket and he checked the urge to pull it out. They'd finally made some headway on this case and he couldn't afford to split his attention. Gabby fished for more information from Len, and Jimmy's phone vibrated again. What the hell? He knew Moira was impatient, but the least she could do was give him a few minutes to respond, especially when he'd already told her he was working.

Another minute and another text buzzed his thigh.

This was getting ridiculous. He pulled the phone from his pocket and nodded at Gabby. Out in the hall, he checked the screen. Not one call from Moira. He'd missed two calls from his baby sister Norah and then a text from Sean.

You need to get home now. Norah's here.

What the hell is Norah doing home? She only came to visit at Christmas. He shot a text back to Sean letting him know that he was working.

Before the message had even sent, he got a text from Norah.

Ignore Sean. He's overreacting.

Not a good sign. Sean didn't overreact. Norah was trying to hide something, and he didn't have the time to deal with bullshit.

He called Sean. As soon as he answered, Jimmy said, "What the hell is going on?"

"Dude, you need to come home. You're not going to fucking believe this."

"Is anyone dead or bleeding?"

"Not yet."

Jimmy blew out a heavy breath. "Keep it that way until I get home. I have to finish this up. Don't let Norah out of your sight."

"Shouldn't be a problem." Sean disconnected.

Something didn't sit right, but Jimmy didn't have the time to examine it. He needed to get back to the mayor and Len.

When he reentered the office, it looked like Gabby had finished. She'd pulled out her notebook, so Len must've come up with some more details. Len slunk out of the office without meeting Jimmy's eyes.

That was one tough lesson for the man to learn.

When the door closed behind Len, the mayor stood. "Now do you have enough to work with?"

"We have a starting place," Gabby said. "It's more than we had last week, but in truth, we were kind of working down this path as our theory. Now all we have to do is get Jimmy to look like he'd be an easy target." She grinned at him.

"We'll meet with Commander Elks in the morning to come up with a plan, sir."

"Thank you. I appreciate your discretion on this."

Gabby and Jimmy headed out the door. In the elevator, she asked, "So who was on the phone?"

"My brother and my sister."

"Sister?"

"Yeah. She lives in Boston, but she's home. Something's going on, so I need to head out. See you in the morning?"

"Sounds good, partner."

They parted ways and Jimmy called his brother when he hit the expressway, but Sean didn't answer. He thought about calling Moira but decided it would be better to wait until he knew what was going on at home. He didn't want to stand her up twice in one night.

He parked in front of his house and heard the yelling from the sidewalk. He raced up the stairs to see what the problem was. In the living room, Tommy screamed, "Who did it, Norah? I want to know now."

Looking past Tommy, he saw Norah standing in the dining room, tears streaming down her face. It didn't matter that she was twenty-two, in that moment, she was a toddler all over again, and he needed to make things right for her.

He slammed the door. "What the hell is going on?"

Sean came in from the kitchen with two beers in his hand. He came close, careful not to step between Tommy and Norah, even though they were on opposite sides of the room, and handed Jimmy a beer. "You're gonna need this," he said with a smile.

Jimmy accepted the beer and said, "Is someone going to tell me what's going on?"

Tommy turned to him and said, "Norah's pregnant."

The beer slipped from his grasp and bounced on the floor without shattering. He turned to face Norah, who finally stepped out from behind the table, and he saw the unmistakable bump. She was *pregnant*. She'd been keeping this a secret for months. More tears spilled down her cheeks, and she ran upstairs to Jimmy's room.

Sean and Tommy both started talking at the same time, and he couldn't understand either of them.

"Shut up."

He was met with immediate silence, which was a first. "Where's Dad?"

"Asleep," Sean answered. "I checked to make sure he took his meds without beer."

Jimmy couldn't believe he'd managed to sleep through

all the yelling. Then again, when they were kids, their dad often worked the overnight shift, so he'd gotten used to sleeping through their noise. "Did he see Norah?"

"Hell, no. That's probably the only reason why there was no blood or death when I called you. You got here just in time. I thought Tommy was about to lose it." Sean took a long pull on his beer.

Jimmy grabbed his bottle from the floor and set it on the table. This was exactly what he'd feared would happen to Norah when she was younger. Being raised in a house full of men without a mother was no way for her to grow up. By the time he'd left for the army, both Sean and Tommy were setting a horrible example for her by not going to school and getting into trouble. Jimmy had been afraid of what would happen to his baby sister, so he'd convinced their dad to send her to live with Aunt Bridget in Boston.

Their mother's sister would take care of her and make sure she finished school. She would look out for Norah because Jimmy wouldn't be able to.

Jimmy scrubbed a hand over his face. He needed air. He needed to think.

"What are we gonna do?" Tommy asked.

"Leave her alone." When Tommy jumped to say more, Jimmy raised his hand to cut him off. "For tonight, we give her space. We all need to cool off so we can deal with this."

"But—"

"Let it go, Tommy, or she'll leave and we'll lose her."

He walked past his brothers and trudged up the stairs. He knocked on his own door but didn't open it. Holding tight to his anger and worry, he forced his voice to be smooth. "Norah, honey, I just wanted to let you know that you can stay there." He paused, not sure what to do or say. "Do you want to talk?"

He waited, but she didn't respond. "Sean and Tommy will leave you alone. Get some rest and we'll talk tomorrow."

Jimmy grabbed some clothes from the laundry room and shoved them in a gym bag. "I'll sleep at Kevin's tonight and fill him in. Tomorrow after work, we'll deal with Norah. Find someplace for Dad to hang out tomorrow."

Sean nodded and gulped the rest of his beer. "I'll take him to work."

"Thanks, man. Don't forget his meds."

Sitting in his car, Jimmy felt overwhelmed by everything. He needed to let Kevin know about Norah, but he wasn't ready to go there. Kevin never wanted her to leave Chicago, so this would just be another fight. Instead of heading to Kevin's, he pointed his car toward Moira's apartment and hoped she wasn't as pissed as his family was.

MOIRA SAT CURLED on her couch with a huge bowl of buttered popcorn and *His Girl Friday* popped into the DVD player. It might not be the best date in history, but it didn't suck either. The opening credits rolled and Moira studied the frame.

It talked about how in the good old days, reporters did anything short of murder to get the story. There was something romantic about that idea. She wanted the fire of a great story to hunt down. She glanced at the mess she'd made earlier and still hadn't cleaned up. Her time would come for a great story.

Then, on the screen, Hildy entered and Moira was immediately caught up in the banter and fun.

A few minutes in, as Hildy ranted about Walter basically stalking her, a knock on the door almost caused Moira to drop her bowl of popcorn. She hit pause and went to the door.

She swung it open to see Jimmy leaning on the doorjamb. "Hi."

"You didn't check the peephole."

"Of course I did," she answered quickly, hoping he'd believe her lie. "Why else would I open the door?"

He pushed off the wall. "I had my hand over the hole. You had no idea it was me."

Knowing she was busted, she said, "Well, at least I had the door locked."

"You need to be more careful, Moira."

She crossed her arms. She did not need a lecture from a man who'd stood her up. "What are you doing here, Jimmy?"

"I came to apologize." He held up a brown paper bag. "I really was working. We got a break in the case and I couldn't leave."

She believed him. At least she wanted to. "What's in the bag?"

"Ice cream. Chocolate fudge brownie." He waved the bag. "It's Sunday, so Super Cup closes early. Otherwise I would've brought one of their brownies."

She snatched the bag from his hand and then took a long look at him. For a guy who should be celebrating a break in the case, he looked beaten down. "Want to come in?"

He nodded, so she stepped aside. Waiting for him to get in, she made sure he heard the lock click.

"What the hell happened in here?"

"That?" She pointed at the piles of crap. "I was searching for something." She didn't need another lecture about butting into his case.

"Any luck?"

"Not yet."

He stood in her living room, like he didn't know what to do or why he'd come.

"You can sit down. I just started *His Girl Friday*, but I can turn it off if you'd rather watch something else." She waited a beat, holding her breath. His answer would tell her a lot. She liked to use her choice in movies as a litmus test for guys.

Any man who would sit and watch an old black-and-white movie was definitely worth a second look. If a guy asked her to turn it off, he would not likely get another date. A guy who showed an appreciation for the movie would probably be a keeper.

Jimmy looked at the screen. "Cary Grant?"

"Yeah." Not too many men could recognize Cary Grant.

"I don't think I know that one." He settled on her couch, which was really more like a love seat given the size of her apartment. He took up more than half, especially when he spread his arms across the back.

Moira ducked into the kitchen to grab a couple of spoons. When she came back, she eyed the single chair that was more for appearance than comfort, but decided she could sit beside Jimmy without too much discomfort.

She sat and pried the lid off the ice cream, then handed him a spoon.

"I don't rate a bowl?"

"Why dirty a dish? This isn't going to take long." She dug her spoon in and scooped.

He did the same but waited until she sampled before he put it in his mouth.

She licked her lips. "Are you waiting to see if it's poison?"

"No, I wanted to see if it's worth extra miles of running to make up for the calories."

She scooped more. "Life's too short to worry about calories." She reached for the remote.

"Before you start again..." Jimmy reached and took the ice cream from her hand.

That wasn't a good sign.

"I'm sorry about blowing you off earlier."

"You didn't really stand me up. You called. That's more than I've gotten from some guys."

A muscle near his eye twitched. "I don't think this is a good idea."

"What? Sharing ice cream and an old movie?"

"Yeah. Us, dating."

"But if I get Liam's blessing, then we'd be okay?"

He shook his head and let out a small laugh. She grabbed her phone and dialed.

He looked over at her. "What are you doing?"

"Calling Liam."

"Christ." He reached over to grab the phone, but she scooted farther away. "Moira, hang up."

Liam's voice mail answered, so she disconnected.

His jaw clenched, which sent her into a fit of giggles. He rubbed a hand over his face, drawing out the look of exhaustion.

"I'm trying here, Jimmy. What do you want from me?"

"I don't know."

"Well, you need to figure it out." She pressed play on the remote and grabbed the ice cream off the table.

He glanced at the ice cream but picked up her forgotten bowl of popcorn. Walter and Hildy continued their banter, and Jimmy settled back against the couch. Like everything else he did, Jimmy watched the movie intently.

While he did, she stole moments to stare at him. Something troubled him, and she worried it was her. Maybe she shouldn't have pressured him into a date. But really, how long should a girl have to wait? If she were smart, she would've never given him a chance. They'd known each other for years, yet Jimmy hadn't made a move until he saw her dressed up playing a role that was far from her real life.

Maybe that caused his confusion. He was attracted to the Moira who schmoozed, but he knew the real her, the girl who talked too fast and too much.

Halfway through the pint of ice cream, she tapped his shoulder and held out the carton to him. He handed her the popcorn.

She ate a handful, but what she really had a taste for was him. She shifted closer to get his attention, and when he looked at her, she leaned in and planted her lips against his.

He bobbled the ice cream, and she leaned closer, swiping her tongue against his lips, urging them open. Salty sweetness, chocolate and popcorn. Delicious.

He touched her shoulder with his free hand and gently pushed her away. For a third time, they shared a kiss and he pushed her away. The message couldn't get any clearer.

"Sorry," she said, and retreated to her corner of the couch.

"No, Moira," he started, but then cradled his forehead.

"I get it, Jimmy. You're not sure if you want to go on a date with me. Kissing me makes you all kinds of uncomfortable. It—"

For such a big man, he moved fast. Suddenly, she pressed uncomfortably against the arm of the couch as he ravaged her mouth. The length of his body lay against hers, and muscles flexed and throbbed all around her.

He pulled away for a second, and she was sure she'd lost

him again. But he took a slow breath and came back to her lips and slowed his kiss. He rubbed his lips against hers gently and licked the seam. Then he traveled across her jaw and down her throat. His teeth scraped her pulse, causing it to ratchet up even more. He tugged her earlobe between his teeth and she arched against him. She wanted more. She wanted him to do this all over her body.

When they were both panting, he slowly backed away. His body still pressed hers, but he moved his face to meet her eyes. "You're right, Moira." His voice was ragged. "I am uncomfortable kissing you, but not for whatever reason you've cooked up in your head. I don't think I can do this right now."

Her heart sank. Jimmy was attracted to her. Never in a million years would she have guessed he would be. She felt it now in every move he made as he lay on top of her, but he was letting her down easy. What next? The it's-me-not-you speech? She stared into his eyes, willing him to tell her something, anything but the excuses he seemed ready to dole out.

He stroked her cheek. "I can almost see the thoughts in your head. Don't. This whole thing is far beyond what I know how to handle."

"It's not something to handle. It's life. We like each other. Let's see where it goes."

Now he did pull completely away from her. He sat back and sighed while looking at the ceiling.

She touched his thigh and he jumped. "What's going on?"

"Norah's back."

Moira hadn't expected that. "That's good, right?"

"She's pregnant and hasn't finished college yet."

Moira stared and tried not look as shocked as she felt. "Wow."

He shifted again. "Don't say anything to anyone. She showed up tonight. Tommy and Sean flipped out. She was crying and locked herself in my room."

Shit. His family was pretty screwed up. But then, she'd always known that. "You can stay here if you want."

He looked at her.

"I'll sleep on the couch and promise to keep my hormones to myself." She smiled brightly, maybe a little too brightly, but he looked miserable. She knew that look. Ryan had it every time he thought about Maggie.

What was it with older brothers thinking they could solve everyone's problems?

"Thanks for the offer." He tucked some hair behind her ear, skimming the sensitive spot he'd aroused with his tongue, and she shivered. "I'm going to Kevin's. I'll break the news to him and spend the night there."

"Want to at least finish the movie?"

He put forth the effort to give her a smile, but it was weak. "Absolutely."

Then he did something completely unJimmy-like: he pulled her against his chest and wrapped his arms around her. She sank against him and couldn't focus on the rest of the movie to save her life.

11

The final credits on the movie rolled, and Jimmy was afraid to move. Moira had fallen asleep on him, nestled against his chest. He didn't want to wake her, but he couldn't stay. Even if he had the willpower to control himself, he needed to talk to Kevin before Tommy did.

He slid out from under Moira and settled her on the couch with a pillow under her head. She stretched and moaned and snuggled the pillow. He wanted to be the damn pillow.

For all his misgivings about getting involved with Moira, tonight made him feel the possibility. Everyone, including him, had a hard time seeing Moira as more than a kid sister. She was a woman, and every kiss they shared emphasized that. If he could deal with Norah, maybe he and Moira could have something.

He covered her with a blanket and tried to imagine a life with Moira. Could they be a forever thing? He shook his head. His thoughts were running as crazy as hers usually did. He didn't even know if they wanted the same things.

And if they didn't?

She stirred again, and her eyes fluttered open. "Leaving?"

"Yeah. Good night."

She sat up, knocking the blanket off. She stood and stretched. Her shirt rode up, baring her stomach and tightening across her braless chest.

"Sorry I woke you." He kissed the top of her head and walked to the door. "Lock up."

She followed him and stood beside the open door.

He looked at her sleepy face and felt the pull to stay again. "I want a rain check for tonight."

"Rain check?"

"I didn't get my date, remember?"

The look of shock gave him pleasure. It wasn't too often he surprised her. He pulled the door closed and waited. She must've still been standing in shock. He thumped the door. "Lock up now, Moira."

The clunk of the lock was the only answer he got. He sent a text to Kevin to make sure he'd be awake. The ease of his evening with Moira dissipated with each mile he gained toward Kevin's apartment.

Kevin didn't respond to his text but met him at the door, wearing nothing but boxers.

"What's wrong?"

"I need to crash here. You don't have company, do you?"

Kevin walked away from the door. "Sean called."

Fuck. He'd asked them not to. "He told you?"

"He just said you'd be here, although that was hours ago, and that Norah was home." Kevin crossed his arms. "He didn't make it sound like she was visiting."

"She's pregnant. Very pregnant. Tommy flipped out because she wouldn't tell him who the father is."

"The fuck she won't." Kevin started moving around as if to get dressed.

"Sit your ass down." Jimmy flopped on the couch, exhausted. "She's home. She's safe. And she's scared."

"I told you we shouldn't have sent her to Boston. If she was here, we would've been able to watch her. This never would've happened." Kevin paced while he talked, making Jimmy even more tired.

"I was overseas, and Tommy and Sean were doing nothing but getting into trouble. You weren't much better. Who was going to stay on top of Norah? At least Aunt Bridget made sure she stayed in school. Norah could've come home for college. She wanted to stay in Boston. She made a life there." He leaned his head against the back of the couch and closed his eyes.

"More like Aunt Bridget is so old, she wouldn't know when Norah snuck out. At least if she was here, no guy would ever get near her. We all would've made sure of that."

An image of Moira yelling at her brothers over the bonfire reminding them she was an adult rang through his mind. Norah was technically an adult, too. Maybe they all needed to accept it.

He heard the shuffling of Kevin's feet as he paced.

"Are we flying or driving?"

"Where?" Jimmy asked without raising his head.

"To Boston. We need to find this asshole and drag him here."

With great effort, Jimmy sat straight. "We're not going anywhere."

When Kevin looked like he wanted to pounce, Jimmy held up a hand.

"She came home because she needs us. When she's ready to talk, she will. Like it or not, she's an adult and she has to make her own decisions." He sounded rational, which was not at all how he felt. Mostly he wanted to drive to Boston tonight, as if he had the energy for a ten-hour drive, and beat the shit out of whoever took advantage of his little sister. But he knew that was irrational. They didn't even know she had a boyfriend, or whatever. Jimmy talked to Norah weekly, sometimes more. It's not like he dumped her in Boston and forgot about her.

She had a life there that she enjoyed. He'd thought it was a good move.

Kevin continued to pace like he was stuck in a cage. All Jimmy wanted to do was reclaim some of the peace he'd had an hour ago. The thought struck him as odd—peace with Moira O'Leary? He almost laughed.

He really needed to get some sleep. "Where can I crash? I've got an early morning meeting with my boss."

"The spare room is open. If there's stuff on the futon, shove it off."

"What, no fresh sheets and a mint on my pillow?" Jimmy asked as he heaved himself off the couch.

"I might consider it if you were sucking my dick, but since I'm not getting lucky, you can set up your own damn bed."

Jimmy grabbed his bag and headed to the futon. Shove the shit off? Kevin had a pile of laundry Jimmy feared might not be clean. He swept it all into the corner of the room and flopped down. The hard mattress was far from comfortable, but his eyes closed and he drifted off before he could think about how much he missed his own bed. Moira's couch would've been a better choice.

THE FOLLOWING MORNING, Moira woke up, excitement still buzzing in her veins. Not only had Jimmy shown up to hang out with her, but he'd also watched *His Girl Friday* all the way through. She'd fallen asleep, and he could've stopped the disk and changed the channel, but he didn't. She'd known he was a keeper.

Plus, he wanted a rain check for their date. A date she worried she shouldn't have tried to force. She didn't know what change had taken place between her and Jimmy, but she was definitely on board for it.

She spent the morning straightening up the mess she'd made of her apartment yesterday. As she put away piles of papers and business cards, she made an attempt to organize them and maybe even file a few. The thing was, organization didn't come naturally to her. Controlled chaos was the order of her life. She attributed it to being the fifth child in a big family.

Flipping through another stack of cards, she realized she probably threw away the escort card. She remembered being insulted by the woman's assumption about her. And the card had no information other than a phone number. Maybe her best bet would be to seek the woman out. She checked her calendar for upcoming events. Moira knew the woman was particular about the events she attended. Moira never saw her at the smaller, more intimate parties. She needed to blend and hide, which was difficult to do with fewer people around.

The thing about summer in Chicago, though, was that the list of things to do was endless. It might be a total crapshoot, but if Moira packed her schedule and hit as many of the events as possible, she'd increase her odds of finding the woman. All she had to do was find her. Then she'd be able to get information and build a story.

She created a list that made her slightly dizzy, but would be doable. She'd be running across the city to at least two events a night over the course of the next few weekends. Then there were the midweek events to round things out. Who needed a social life when your job kept you social?

She sighed and tried to figure out where she was going to fit in a date with Jimmy. Normally, she'd drop an event to be able to go on a date, but this was her chance to get the scoop on not one, but two real stories. If she could break out with these, everyone would stop looking at her like she was playing at being a journalist. They'd respect her job.

And then what?

The same poking little question jabbed at her. She wished she had a plan, a road map for her life. She worked at a job she enjoyed, but she wanted more. The whole package: a family, great job, house, and husband to come home to. The problem was, she kept waiting for things to happen in her life. The closest thing to being proactive she'd been was asking Jimmy out.

Most of the time, she simply followed the current of her life. She didn't do much to try to change course. Did she want to now?

She returned to the articles she completed, did a final read through and submitted them. Then she settled in to write a proposal for the first half of her story, outlining the escort angle among the wealthy in Chicago. If she could get a foot in the door, she could write about being an escort.

Her gut tightened at the thought. She didn't know if she could go through with sleeping with some guy for money. No, she knew she couldn't. But how far would she go for a story? She left the barely written proposal open on her computer and decided lunch with Kathy was in order.

She texted her friend and then quickly dressed. Kathy

said she could meet in a half hour, so Moira headed out. She arrived at the flower shop a little early, so she checked out the arrangements Kathy had on the counter. "How's it going?"

"Busy," Kathy replied with a pair of scissors in one hand and ribbon in the other.

"If lunch won't work today, we can make it some other time."

"I'm going to make it work. I worked last night until after ten and came back again this morning at six. I need to get out of here. Just let me finish this." She cut the stem on a couple of flowers and shoved them into the vase.

Moira knew next to nothing about flowers, having hardly ever received flowers from a guy. That was something else she should add to her keeper list: a guy who sent flowers.

"Let's go. Anna will keep an eye on everything until we get back." Kathy yanked off her apron and tossed it on the counter. "What's up?"

"Nothing."

"Liar."

"Actually, a whole lot. Jimmy kissed me again yesterday morning. Then I asked him out on a date, which he backed out of at the last minute, and then he showed up at my apartment with ice cream." Moira slipped her arm through Kathy's and led her out the door of the shop. "And that's just my love life. I've got things going on career-wise, too."

They walked to a burger place on the next block, ordered food, and sat.

Kathy groaned. "God, it feels good to sit down." She sighed again and then said, "Finish telling me about Jimmy. I can't believe he kissed you again. What's his excuse for the on and off bullshit?"

"I confuse him."

Kathy laughed.

"He doesn't want to like me or get involved with me because of Liam. But it's there, Kath. The attraction, the zing, it's there big-time. And I'm comfortable around him, you know, since I've known him my whole life." She spun her drink in slow circles.

"But?"

"But nothing. I'm excited." She paused, still trying to ignore the doubts. "However, he made an excellent point. What if things don't work out? He was talking about his relationship with Liam, but I've spent so many years longing for him, that I'm afraid the reality won't live up to the fantasy."

"It never does. Why worry about it? I'm more concerned about where he thinks things will go between you. I know those O'Malley boys. You deserve to be more than a notch on a bedpost." She took a long drink of her pop.

Moira knew the remark came from Kathy's brief stint as Kevin's girlfriend or whatever she'd been. Moira had introduced them one year at the block party, and they had hit it off. Unfortunately, Kevin had neglected to explain his idea of a relationship, which mostly consisted of being friends with benefits. He was the sole reason Kathy no longer came to the block party.

Yet another reason to be annoyed by Kevin.

"Jimmy is nothing like Kevin."

Kathy raised her eyebrows, but then stood when the counter guy called their number. She returned with a bag holding burgers and awesome fries.

"In addition to bringing ice cream last night, he watched *His Girl Friday* with me. All the way through, even though I fell asleep."

"Ooo...that puts him in the keeper column." Kathy narrowed her eyes. "Why did you fall asleep? I don't think he gets keeper credit if it was a postcoital decision."

Moira laughed so hard she choked on her fries. "We kissed. A couple of times, and he pulled back like a gentleman. He has some family issues to deal with, but he wanted a rain check for our date."

Kathy bit into her burger, so Moira starting eating in earnest. She hadn't realized how hungry she was. Maybe ice cream and popcorn for dinner hadn't been the best choice.

After a few bites, Kathy said, "So spill. What else puts him in the keeper column? I know you've always had him there, but did you have a reason?"

Moira chewed and thought. She couldn't argue Kathy's point. Jimmy had always been in the keeper column because she just knew. Rather than try to explain her gut reaction, she went for the obvious. "He has a steady job. Jimmy has always worked. He did watch my favorite movie with me, which I think gets bonus points. He brought fudge brownie ice cream."

Kathy took another long drink, as if waiting for more. "Okay. Job, movie, chocolate. I'll just assume he has sexy arms since you've been drooling over him forever. What else?"

"Besides being able to kiss and knock my socks off?"

"Yeah. Is he nice to his mom?"

"She's dead. But he does take care of his dad. He's always taken care of his brothers." Moira thought about how he would take care of Norah, too. And her baby. A little spear of fear shot through her. What would that mean for them if he had to take care of Norah and her baby? He'd said he couldn't handle a relationship, and now she understood what he'd meant. He was talking about Norah.

"You're listing some pretty damn good stuff, but is he right for you?"

Moira shrugged. She didn't know. Although she'd always wanted him and known he was a keeper, she'd never thought anything would come of it. "That's what dating is for. He's a keeper. I never said he was my keeper."

But in her heart, she really hoped he would be.

JIMMY'S LIFE had become a flurry of activity. The property crimes cases he had been working on were shoved on the back burner again. Elks agreed to continue the investigation into the theft ring based on the information Len provided. What they hadn't expected was for two other men to come forward with information. Unsurprisingly, they were Len's friends, everyone except for Stan Decker. They expressed a sense of betrayal because Jimmy had lied about his identity, but the mayor admitted the undercover work had been his idea.

As excited as the new information should've made him, Jimmy felt overwhelmed. For every inroad they thought they found, they really hit four more obstacles. Every man had been with a different woman, different names, different descriptions, but they all had the same story. Each man's house was burglarized while he'd spent the night with the escort and his wife had been out of town.

He and Gabby waded through notes on three interviews and found few common threads. The women introduced themselves to the men at different functions. They all met at different hotels. They all had different burner phones that were no longer in service.

Even more perplexing was that the houses had no signs

of forced entry. They bypassed security systems. Jimmy and Gabby had no idea how they managed to get in. To top it off, because the houses were not treated as crime scenes, they had no evidence.

Frustration clawed at Jimmy. This investigation was turning out to be worse than some of the cold cases he'd encountered.

And now he had to go home and deal with Norah. She'd texted him earlier today and apologized for dumping on him without warning. Tommy had also texted letting Jimmy know he was still fuming. Like Kevin, Tommy wanted to go to Boston and beat the crap out of some guy. The problem was, they had no idea who the guy was.

Jimmy looked at the clock just as Gabby stood.

"We should call it a night. The commander will have guys pulled in tomorrow to run a task force. They'll probably want to run a full game for James Buchanan and set him up as a decoy. Don't you think?"

Jimmy nodded and then rolled his neck. Nothing would relieve the tension. A sudden flash of Moira's smiling face hit him. She involved a totally different kind of tension, but one he couldn't deal with. Not tonight. Maybe no time in the near future. "Yeah, let's go. We'll have to be here early to address this."

As they walked out, Gabby said, "Pretty cool way it's going, though. The case. It looks to be a big one. We break this, and we both might get a gold star next to our names."

"Mmm-hmm."

"Are you okay? You seem distracted, which isn't like you at all."

"Sorry. I am a little. I'll unfuck my brain tonight and be good tomorrow." He hoped he was telling the truth. He needed to be on his game to be on the task force.

He walked Gabby to her car and waited until she pulled away. His head ached from being pulled in too many directions. Sitting in his car, the heat pressed on him and he turned the air on high. He rolled the windows down and closed his eyes. Five minutes. He wanted just five minutes without something needing his attention.

The whir of the air blowing through the vents soothed him, and for the first time since he left Moira's apartment last night, his muscles unknotted a fraction and he was able to catch a breath. Thinking about sprawling on Moira's couch eased his muscles a little more. Before he developed a real thought, he pulled out his phone and dialed Moira's number.

At the sound of the first ring, the realization hit him that he didn't really know why he was calling. He couldn't spend time with her. Not now, not with the case taking off, and not with Norah being pregnant and hiding in his room. The third ring sang in his ear and he considered hanging up. But then he knew she would call him a coward.

Fourth ring and then her voice, light and bubbly came across the line. "Hey, can't come to the phone right now. I might be partying or writing or both. Maybe I'm just indulging in chocolate, but you won't know if you don't leave a message so I can call you back."

He rolled his eyes at her long message as he waited for the beep. "Hey, Moira. It's Jimmy. I was calling..." He listened to her long-ass message and hadn't come up with something to say. "Just hi."

After disconnecting, he tossed the phone into a cup holder and headed home. On the way, he tried to process that his baby sister was pregnant. She obviously planned to have the baby, but he had no idea if she wanted to keep it.

They needed to come up with a plan. She had some serious decisions to make in regard to her future.

When he pulled up to the house, he didn't see Sean's motorcycle at the curb, which was weird because he'd said he'd take Dad into work with him. Shit. Unless he didn't. Which would mean that Dad was home with Norah. Jimmy left his car and walked into the house, finding it eerily quiet. "Hello?"

No one answered. He went to the basement door first and yelled to Tommy and Sean, but still got no response. Dad's bedroom was empty as well, so he headed upstairs to look for Norah. His door was open and she sat in his study watching TV.

"Hey," he called softly.

She turned suddenly, her eyes wide. "Hi." She clicked the TV off.

"Where is everyone?"

"Sean came home from work with Dad. I don't know what he told him, but he dragged Dad and Tommy back out and took them to dinner." She rubbed her hands on her belly. She looked far older than she should. "I think they wanted us to talk alone."

Jimmy crossed the room and squatted in front of her. The anger bubbling just below his surface was held in check because she looked so vulnerable. "How did this happen?"

Norah kept her head down, refusing to meet his eyes. She coughed a laugh, and a tear streaked down and plopped on her hand. "You gave me the talk when I was eight, Jimmy. We both know how this happened."

"I also taught you about protection."

"Nothing is one hundred percent effective."

He reached up and tucked her hair behind her ear so he

could see her face better. "Why didn't you tell anyone? You could've called me. How far along are you?"

"Six months. I didn't tell anyone at first. I was scared, so I hid it. I was able to hide it pretty well. Then I started showing and couldn't hide it behind a big T-shirt. Aunt Bridget flipped out." She swiped at a tear and took a deep breath, still not looking at him.

"She didn't say anything."

"That's because I told her you already knew and you were okay with it."

He rose and pulled the ottoman close to the chair and sat in front of her. "But you didn't."

"Of course I didn't. I knew you'd freak out more than she had." Now she did look up as if to dare him to disagree.

He couldn't.

"What was your plan?"

"I left Aunt Bridget's house and crashed with some friends until the semester was over. Then I planned to come home, but I got scared all over."

"School was done over a month ago. Where have you been?"

"Mostly hanging with friends. I finally got tired of couch surfing. I quit my job and came home. I wanted to call, but I didn't know what to say."

She plucked at nonexistent threads on her shirt. He hated seeing her so unsure of herself. Norah had never been shy or afraid of anything. Now, she curled into herself and he wasn't sure how to reach her.

"What do you want to do?"

"I don't know."

He released a breath and tamped down the urge to yell at her. Tommy had done enough of that last night. "What about the father?"

"What about him?"

"Who is he?"

She shook her head before speaking. "I'm not going to tell you."

He stood, needing to move to work the frustration out. "He has just as much responsibility in this as you do."

"If I tell you, you guys are going to go crazy on him and that's not fair."

"You spent the last few months sleeping who knows where and you're worried about what's fair for him?" His voice started to rise.

"He doesn't know."

She spoke so quietly that Jimmy wasn't sure he'd heard right. "Did you say he doesn't know?"

She nodded.

Jimmy paced a few more steps. He breathed deeply. He didn't want to fly off the handle, but he felt it coming. "Why the fuck doesn't he know? You didn't call me, that's bad enough, but you sure as hell should've told him."

She stood and launched herself at him, holding him in a tight hug like she had after a nightmare when she was a kid.

Jimmy held her, feeling awkward with the baby bump hitting him. He brushed his hand over her hair. "Besides having a responsibility to you and the baby, he has a right to know, Norah."

"I know, but..." She sniffed and pulled away from him. She turned away before continuing. "He wasn't a one-night stand, Jimmy. He's a good guy. We met over Christmas break, and I fell hard for him. We had a great couple of weeks, but then he went back to school. We tried the long-distance thing. He visited a few weekends, but it didn't work. We ended on good terms, but then I found out I was pregnant. I was going to call him, but I didn't know what I wanted to do, so I waited."

She walked the room, absently touching shelves and books before stopping in front of the window that looked out over the street. "He came back to Boston for spring break. Just to see me. He gave up going to Mexico with his friends so he could spend the week with me. And I planned to tell him then. But it felt so good to have him back. I felt normal with him and I didn't want to lose that. I wasn't showing yet, so no one knew, which made it easy to pretend I wasn't. So I waited some more. Then I ended up waiting so long the decision was made for me. Kind of."

"I assume you know how to reach him?"

She nodded.

"You need to tell him. He should have some input."

"I'm afraid, Jimmy."

"Of what? You didn't do this alone."

"No. I'm more afraid he'll want to have this baby with me." She continued to stare out the window at their neighborhood.

"What's wrong with that? Nothing says you have to marry the guy." He shoved his hands in his pockets to hide his frustration.

"I'm afraid he'll give up his life, his dreams, his plans, for me and the baby. I don't want him to do that."

Jimmy sank onto the chair Norah had vacated. So his sister was trying to be noble? "You shouldn't have to give up your life and dreams either. This is something the two of you need to work out."

And if this guy bailed, he would have to answer to Jimmy.

Norah leaned her forehead against the glass but didn't argue.

Now Jimmy needed her to cross the next hurdle, so they could make plans. "Do you want to keep the baby?"

She offered a pitiful movement that tried to be a shrug. "I don't know if I want to be a mom. But when I think about not having this baby in my life, I can't imagine that either. I don't know what to do. That's really why I came home." She finally turned and looked at him. "What should I do, Jimmy?"

He pushed off the chair, feeling much older than he should. "I love you, Norah, and I'm willing to do anything for you, but that's one decision you have to make for yourself."

Jimmy left the room to wait for the rest of the family downstairs. The information would be better coming from him so Norah wouldn't feel bullied. Although they meant well, Tommy, Sean, and Kevin would run over Norah to the point she wouldn't be able to think for herself.

They all needed to step back and treat her like the adult she was—whether or not they were ready to admit it.

12

Moira's week flew by in a blur of events and people. Her schedule was more jam-packed than usual. The upside was that she had plenty to write about and wouldn't run out of words. The downside was that she hadn't seen the mystery woman once.

Except for his one lame message, Jimmy hadn't called or texted or shown up with a pint of ice cream. Not that he'd said he would, but she'd hoped. She wouldn't have been able to make up the date this week anyway because of her scheduled events either, so it was for the best that he hadn't called. At least that's what she kept telling herself.

All she had to do was get through this beach party for another animal shelter. Sunday would be a day off, except for family dinner at her mom's house. At least once a month, they all had dinner as a family. Their mom demanded it. It was her way of making sure they stayed close.

She'd been looking forward to this beach event. She'd missed it last year because of another function, which had been so boring she couldn't remember it. This fund-raiser garnered a lot of attention in the city. She could get behind any facility that worked to get animals into good homes. Plus, beach.

She loved North Avenue Beach. A crowd almost always filled the space, but the lake was gorgeous. She could watch people play volleyball. And the ocean-liner beach house was amazing. The blue and white building made her feel like she stood next to a cruise ship.

Today, many of the partygoers brought their pets, which made it more fun for Moira. As soon as her feet hit the sand, she took off her sandals, carried them by the straps, and walked barefoot. Maybe not the most professional, but again, beach.

A guy ran by with his dog on a leash, both kicking up sand that sprayed her ankles. She wove through the crowd and tried to decide whom she wanted to talk to. Radio personalities chatted with guests, and some TV news reporters interviewed shelter workers. She watched the scene before her and wondered if her job had become irrelevant. Being a reporter was all she ever wanted to be, but no one had any idea who she was.

Had she expected to be famous? She thought about it for a moment and knew she hadn't, but she'd always thought she'd at least be respected, and she didn't feel she'd accomplished that.

She felt someone standing behind her, a little too near, seconds before she heard his voice.

"Hey."

Jimmy's low, deep voice made her want to crawl onto him. How did he manage to do that with one syllable?

"Hi." She turned and smiled at him. "What are you doing here?"

He rolled his eyes. "My wife Gabby is a huge animal lover."

Hearing him call Gabby his wife made Moira twitch a little. Knowing it was a lie didn't ease the twitch. "I see."

She turned back to her path toward the party. Jimmy walked beside her.

"Sorry I haven't been in touch. I did call once. Left a message. Things have been crazy."

"I know."

"Are you pissed?"

"No. Why would I be?"

"I left things a little unsettled between us. I meant it when I said I wanted a rain check for our date. I just haven't had a free moment."

She squinted against the sun as she looked at him. "Believe it or not, I've been busy too. I have better things to do than sit by the phone and wait for your call."

As soon as the words slipped, she cringed. She hadn't meant to sound like that.

"See, you are pissed."

"No, I'm really not. I'm just tired. This is my eighth event this week. I'm talked out, I guess."

"I can't believe Mouthy Moira ever gets tired of talking."

The childhood nickname brought back childish feelings of being excluded, usually by him. She pasted on a smile. "Being mean again."

"That's not mean. It's a term of endearment."

"Better not let your wife hear."

He rolled his eyes again. "Why have you been so busy? I thought you only did a couple of these things a week."

She lowered her voice. "I've been looking for that escort woman I told you about. I know she's around—"

Moira stopped her feet and her mouth at the look he

gave her. The muscle in his jaw twitched, and she could almost hear his teeth grind. Really not good.

"I told you to stay away from my investigation." His whisper sounded more like a threat than a sweet anything.

She straightened her spine. He would not intimidate her. "I'm not doing anything with your investigation. I know nothing about it. How could I get in the way? I'm working on a totally different story, one that has nothing to do with you."

"Moira—"

She backed up and waved at him. "Sorry, have to go. People to interview. Talk to you later." Then she did her best not to stomp in the sand.

She wasn't treading on his investigation. At least not as far as she was aware. He hadn't given her enough information to know what was going on. His eyes burned a hole in the back of her head as she made her way through the crowd. She saw some people she knew and went to say hi.

After about an hour, Moira caught her second wind. She was having a blast playing with all of the dogs, throwing Frisbees and discovering all the good the shelter did. She enjoyed this part of her job most: talking to people who were passionate about something. It came across in every word they spoke, and their eyes lit with excitement.

She wanted to capture that passion on a page with words. Would she ever be good enough to accomplish that?

A gentle tap on her shoulder had her turning around. She knew it wasn't Jimmy before she turned. The air wasn't vibrating and she hadn't felt watched. The guy standing behind her was from the zoo last week. Mike. "Hi."

He wore khaki shorts, an olive-colored polo, and thick leather sandals. He smiled as he pushed his glasses farther up on his nose. "I'm glad you're here."

"Really?"

"Yeah. Our walk last week was interrupted, and I'd hoped we could continue."

Moira felt the burning stare rolling off Jimmy from the other side of the crowd. He neared, and Moira put her arm around Mike's elbow, leading him away. Jimmy had to be more careful or he'd blow his cover.

"I'd like to take you out on a date," Mike blurted.

"Well, I'm kind of seeing someone."

"Kind of?"

"We haven't actually had our first real date yet. You know, life gets in the way sometimes." The sand beneath her feet was starting to cool.

"He's not here tonight, is he?"

"No," she answered too quickly, afraid she'd blow Jimmy's cover. They'd moved away from the crowd and Jimmy. "I'm technically working today, so it's not the best time for a date."

"But we can walk, right? I'm not taking you away from an important interview, am I?"

She liked his thoughtfulness and consideration of her job. "No. I'm about done."

Jimmy was about to burst through the crowd to follow Moira. He knew it was a mistake, but his feet kept going. All he'd been able to hear of Moira's conversation was that she was seeing someone who wasn't here tonight. Then he felt Gabby's hand link with his and he stopped.

Maybe that's why Moira was pissed. Not because he hadn't called, but because he continued to show up at these parties with Gabby. As long as he was undercover, he couldn't be seen with Moira.

"Oh, honey, I saw the most adorable dog. They have a book showing the animals available. I think we should consider adopting." Gabby voice was a little high-pitched and whiny. Everything he knew Gabby wasn't. "Come on."

She tugged his hand and pulled him in the opposite direction from where Moira walked.

He grit his teeth but allowed her to lead him.

With a sunny, fake smile on her face, she said through her teeth, "No one is going to believe we're happily married if you keep chasing Moira."

"I know that. And I wasn't chasing her."

An eyebrow disappeared behind her bangs.

"She makes me crazy. I can't think straight when she's around."

"Falling for her already? I thought you hadn't even gone out yet."

"We haven't. I'm not falling for her. She keeps butting her nose into the investigation, and it's going to be a problem."

"What are you talking about? She's been nothing but helpful."

"Whatever."

Gabby led him through the crowd and then oohed and aahed over the pictures of dogs in the book provided. All he could think about was Moira trying to convince him to adopt a dog. A dog wouldn't be the worst idea. It would get his dad out of the house and walking every day. He let Gabby flip pages while he looked at the crowd for Moira. He didn't like her running off with some guy.

Knowing it was the same guy from the zoo made things worse. Moira had said she was going to kiss men until she found the right one. He didn't want her to even give this guy a chance. Not before Jimmy got another chance.

Chance for what?

The quiet little question reverberated in his brain, but used Moira's voice. He didn't know what he wanted from Moira or where it would go, but he wanted to see. She was certain Liam wouldn't care, and Liam had been his greatest concern. Could Moira be the woman he'd been looking for?

He had no idea. He didn't know what she wanted for her life, so it was time to find out. Scanning the crowd again, he found her on the outskirts, still holding on to the guy's arm, but now they faced each other. The guy fingered Moira's hair, brushing it from her face.

Jimmy's blood ran hot and he swallowed hard. He couldn't keep attending these parties and focus on his job as long as Moira was there, especially if she flirted with other men.

"James," a voice called, and Jimmy looked up to see Stan Decker walking toward him.

None of the usual people had arrived yet, so in a way, Jimmy was relieved to see Stan. The closer he could get to that clique, the better his chances for drawing out the thieves. "Stan, I was beginning to wonder if I'd run into anyone I know."

"The wife likes animals. Looks like it's the same with yours. Buy you a drink?"

"Definitely." He looked at Gabby who nodded. He kissed the top of her head. "Be back soon."

As they edged away from the shelter workers, Stan said, "Len told me what was going on. Is there any way I can help?"

Jimmy stiffened, not sure what Stan thought he knew.

All of the victims had been told not to reveal anything to anyone—especially Jimmy's role. "What do you mean?"

"I convinced Len to come forward. I know about all of them. I know who you are. I'm asking if I can help." Stan ordered a couple of beers. When the bartender handed over the bottles, Stan tilted his head to get them farther away from the crowd.

At least he wouldn't be able to see Moira.

"I appreciate the offer, Stan, but I can't comment on an ongoing investigation." He drank from his beer and watched the waves on the lake.

Stan studied the label on his bottle as he spoke. "I knew about Len, but I didn't know there had been other men. Otherwise, I would've pressed him to come forward sooner. I've done some discreet asking and I have this for you." He reached into his pocket and pulled out a piece of paper.

Jimmy took it. A list of phone numbers.

"I asked some people I know to refer me to places of business if I wanted some company. I thought the numbers might help."

Jimmy tucked the paper into his pocket and sighed. Everyone wanted to butt into his business, and it irritated him. "Thanks, but I need you to let me do my job. If I need some help or information, I'll ask, but the more people that start asking unusual questions or digging in the wrong place could spook the thieves. I don't want to drive them away. I want to bring them to me."

Stan nodded. "I just want to help."

Jimmy patted his shoulder. "I know."

They walked back to find their wives. Jimmy was itching to leave. He looked for Moira but couldn't find her anywhere. A sick feeling plunged into his stomach as he thought she might've left with that guy.

He and Gabby said good-bye to Stan and Karen.

"What did Stan want to talk to you about?"

"Len told him everything. He said he helped convince Bitger to come forward. Then he gave me a list of phone numbers to escort businesses that cater to this crowd."

"That's good. It might be promising, right?"

Jimmy shrugged. "If it were that easy, one of the victims would've given us a number. This outfit is too slick. They have a wide enough network of women that they're not overlapping."

They walked to the parking garage and to their separate cars.

"Do you want me to run the numbers?"

"Nah. It'll keep until Monday. Enjoy the rest of your weekend."

"You too. Doing anything interesting?" She wagged her eyebrows. "I noticed Moira wasn't at the party anymore. Is that where you're headed?"

"I don't know. Things are complicated."

"So what? Loosen up and have some fun."

"See you Monday."

In his car, his muscles tightened again. Moira had left the party while he had been busy with Stan. It didn't matter that they hadn't had a date yet—the intention was there and they'd agreed to go out. Why the fuck would she leave with another guy?

Jimmy sped to Moira's apartment, determined to find out. He didn't have it in him to play games. Her car was parked in front of the building, but she didn't answer her door. He knocked again, intent on interrupting whatever she had going on.

Afraid he'd lose his temper and draw attention from the neighbors, Jimmy went back to his car. Why would

Moira bring her car here and then not stay? He called her phone.

"Hello."

"Where the hell are you?"

"On my way home."

"From where?"

"Uh...North Avenue Beach. I saw you there, remember?"

"Try again. I'm sitting in front of your apartment looking at your car." He gripped the steering wheel, anger mounting again.

"I took the bus. I didn't want to deal with traffic and have to pay for parking."

He released a slow breath, glad she was alone, but then he realized she was taking the bus through the city. Alone. "Where are you? I'll come pick you up."

"I'm stepping off the bus now. I'm at the end of the block. Why are you at my house anyway?"

"I wanted to talk to you."

"About?"

"You continuing to flirt with other men. Especially in front of me."

A heavy breath came across the phone so hard he could almost feel it. "Just...ugh...give me five minutes."

He got out of his car and leaned on the hood. Looking down the block, he tried to see which shadow might be her as dusk fell and the sky darkened.

A moment later, the moonlight glinted on her head, but even without the help of her bright hair, he would've known it was Moira. She barreled down the sidewalk, and he could almost hear her sniping and mumbling.

As if she had a reason to be pissed. He hadn't been pawing Gabby. If he'd even tried, Gabby would've kicked his ass. He hadn't so much as looked at another woman since he'd kissed Moira.

He stepped away from the car and met her in the middle of the sidewalk in front of her apartment. Her eyes flashed, and before he could say anything, she started. "How dare you get huffy because I talked to—not flirted with—some guy? You don't own me, Jimmy. Hell, I'm not even your girl-friend. More often than not, you're dodging me and I don't even know why."

She paused, one hand fisted like she wanted to hit him. "I was not flirting. He asked me out, and I told him I'm kind of seeing someone. Not that I should have to explain a goddamn thing to you. You said you wanted a rain check for our date a week ago and then you dropped out. Except your two-second message saying hi."

"You said you weren't mad."

Her arms flailed. "I'm not."

"You sound pretty mad." He liked her best flustered and he smiled.

Her eyes narrowed. "I'm mad because you're accusing me of I don't know what. I've been busy and you not calling to make plans didn't make me mad, not until you start trying to assert some kind of control over my life."

She stared at him, chest heaving, and he had no idea what to say. Then she stormed up the stairs to her apart-ment without another word. She was in the building before he realized what happened.

His stunned disbelief kept his feet rooted where they were. She left him as if their conversation was finished. He turned and stormed after her, searching for the right words for his anger. He got to her door and turned the knob, but found it locked. Of course, today of all days, she remem-bered to lock up. Hell of a message to send.

His fist thumped against the wood, and she swung the door open without asking who it was. The cold look in her eyes made him swallow the reprimand. They had other issues to sort out. She stood with one hand on the door, braced to slam it on him, and the other on her hip.

"I'm not trying to control your life. I'm trying to do my job, and you're making it difficult."

"I've done nothing but help you."

He held up his hand to stop her. "Seeing you flirt with other men drives me over the edge. I can't concentrate on doing my job and being James Buchanan when all I can think about is being Jimmy and taking you up against the nearest wall."

Her hands fell away from their aggressive positions and he took it as an invitation to step forward into her apartment. The neighbors didn't need to hear any more than they already had. She stepped back, and for a change, Moira appeared to be speechless.

Her chest still rose and fell with heavy breaths, but her eyes softened. Another half step and then she pressed herself against him, pulling his shoulders down and his face closer to hers. Her lips twitched in a playful smile before they met his.

His arms circled her body and he grabbed her ass and pulled her into him. She was a foot shorter than him and their bodies were not lining up the way he wanted. He pulled her up and she wrapped her legs around him. God, she felt good. Better than good, but his brain couldn't find a word because her tongue erased his ability to think.

He spun and leaned her against the closed door. The flimsy dress she wore flew up to her waist and he groaned. His brain emptied of everything except for Moira's softness surrounding him.

13

Moira loved the feel of Jimmy holding her. His determination was definitely a plus in this situation. His hands explored under her dress, which bunched around her waist. His fingers were strong and insistent. As much as she wanted to touch him everywhere, all she could do was grip his shoulders, afraid he might drop her.

His lips trailed down her neck and he buried his face in her cleavage. One hand left her ass and moved to the front of her dress, tugging at the buttons. She tightened her legs at his hips, bringing him even closer to her center without being inside her. How she wanted that.

A series of little pops told her he'd ripped her dress. That was going to be hard to explain to Mom. His tongue rode over her breasts and she ran her fingers over his scalp. His short hair softly bristled against her palm. He sucked on her nipple through her bra and she wished she'd thought to wear something prettier.

He tugged her nipple in his teeth and she knew he hadn't even looked at what she wore. She thrust her hips, her nerves coiling and seeking release. He moved to her other nipple and she wiggled more. With a grunt, he pressed her fully against the door, not allowing her any more movement, and she almost whimpered.

She yanked at his shirt, pulling it from under her calves, using the door as leverage and balance to inch it up, but his arms were in the way as he continued to hold her in place. Heat spread everywhere and she wanted to get rid of any barrier between them, but he wasn't cooperating.

"Jimmy." Her voice was husky and barely more than a whisper. He didn't respond, so she reached for his face. When he looked up at her, she said, "Get naked."

He gently released her legs, setting her on the floor. She tugged at his shirt again, but he stepped back, staring at her.

The look on his face was one of utter fear. Her heart pounded. She swallowed and then smiled. She ran her hands under his shirt, around his back, pulling closer to her. "Kiss me."

Instead, he grabbed her shoulders and held her at arm's length.

"What?" she asked quietly, angry at the desperation she felt.

"Give me a minute." He turned away and adjusted himself, took a step, and then ran his hands over his head.

She could almost hear the conversation going on in his head. Walking up behind him, she ran her hands along his hips and slid them into his pockets. She meant for it to be playful, but he jumped. The movement forced her to yank her hands back.

"Talk to me, Jimmy."

He turned back to face her. His eyes roamed the length of her and she knew her pale skin blushed under his gaze. His lips tightened to a thin line and he pulled the gaping front of her dress closed. It was like he just realized what he'd done and his face twisted.

"Sorry about this. I'll buy you a new one."

She knocked his hands away. "I don't want a new damn dress. I want the guy who was manhandling me a few minutes ago to come back. I want him to screw my brains out."

"I'm sorry," he mumbled again. He pulled his keys from his pocket and walked out the door.

What do I do that keeps chasing him off? Emotion stuck in her throat, making it difficult to swallow. After locking the door, she leaned against it, trying to gather her thoughts, calm her emotions, and soothe her rampant hormones. Now that Jimmy was gone, her skin cooled.

She bent over and picked up the buttons from the floor. Maybe she'd just sew this herself. She had no reasonable explanation for how three buttons popped off. While squatting, she saw a piece of paper and picked it up. A list of five phone numbers, but no other information.

It must be Jimmy's. She looked out her front window and saw his car was still there, so she called his phone. "You dropped a piece of paper with phone numbers on it."

"Shit."

"Do you need it?" What she really wanted to know was whose numbers they were.

"Yeah." He paused.

She waited. "Are you coming back up to get it?"

"I can't."

"I see your car, Jimmy. You're still out front."

"No, I mean I can't walk up those stairs again. I'm very uncomfortable right now." He groaned.

She released a wicked laugh. "Guess you should've finished what you started then."

"Not like that, Moira." His voice was steady, but quiet.

She sighed. She had no idea what he was struggling with, but she didn't have the patience for it. "Do you want me to bring it down?"

"Not a good idea. I'll get it from you tomorrow."

"I have dinner at my mom's. I'll bring it and drop it off."

"Thanks."

She saw his headlights finally flick on and he pulled away.

"Did you lock the door?"

"Yes." She stared at his car until he reached the end of the block and turned.

"Good night, Moira."

"It would've been," she mumbled.

She turned away from the window, letting the curtain slide back in place. Too revved to sleep, she changed into her comfy sweats, turned on the radio, and went into the kitchen to make brownies. It was her turn to bring dessert to dinner. She'd planned on making the brownies in the morning.

Now, she intended to make a double batch: one to eat warm from the oven and one to share with her siblings.

Chocolate might not be able to take the place of a great orgasm, but in a pinch, it was an adequate substitute. She opened her cabinets and pulled out ingredients. Liam would be ashamed to see her kitchen and lack of supplies. She had the bare minimum she'd need for the brownies. A box of cereal she couldn't remember buying and a jar of peanut butter were the only other items in the cabinet. In her freezer, she had a pint of ice cream and a couple of frozen pizzas.

She should go shopping. Better yet, she should invite Liam over. He'd shop and cook her dinner.

After mixing the brownies on autopilot, she shoved them in the oven and settled in front of her computer. She thought back over her night and realized Jimmy wasn't the only person having a problem concentrating on his job. She wrote a couple of paragraphs about the fund-raiser, including talking about a couple of the pets up for adoption.

As an article, it wasn't much, but it would do for now. She'd add some filler later, when she was in a better mood, like not sexually frustrated. She shot a text to Kathy and Elizabeth and asked them if they wanted to come over for brownies.

Elizabeth answered first: Colin wants to know what's wrong.

Moira rolled her eyes.

The invitation was for you, not my brother. Brownies out of the oven in ten.

Colin says he'll cover me at the bar if he can have some.

Sure.

Colin didn't need to know he'd have to wait until tomorrow to get them. She had no intention of sharing this pan with any man.

Kathy hadn't responded, so Moira figured she might be on a date.

Chocolate scent filled the air. She checked the pan and caught sight of Jimmy's slip of paper. Curiosity always got the better of her. She picked up her phone and dialed the first number.

"Elite Escorts, how may I direct your call?"

Moira fumbled the phone and disconnected. *An escort service?*

Jimmy was following up on her idea. Had the mystery woman said the name of the company? Moira couldn't recall, but it seemed like she would have, even though it hadn't been on the business card.

She fingered the paper. Jimmy had told her to stay out of his investigation, but this was about her article on Chicago's wealthy men using escorts. She needed to find the right kind of service to get information. How did a woman decide to be an escort? If she kept her focus on the women, there might not be any overlap with Jimmy's case. And if there was, it wouldn't be until he was done anyway. She copied the numbers.

The timer for the brownies went off, and she pulled them from the oven, her mind racing on the topic of escorts. While the brownies cooled enough to eat, she went back to her computer.

She was a bit of a news junkie. How could she not be when journalism was her life? She'd seen a couple of news stories about prostitution on the Gold Coast, the Viagra Triangle as the neighborhood was called. Older men seeking younger women to provide services. Then, of course, there were the online personals with their coded messages for payment.

But she couldn't see any of the men she met regularly doing that. She began her research in earnest and came across the story of the Gold Coast Madam. The woman had just published her memoir.

What if someone else decided to take up the torch left behind from Rose Laws? There was a distinct possibility someone had. The business itself was too lucrative. The system would work; privacy was the name of the game in order to be successful. People would trust her. They would tell her things, like when they wouldn't be home, making burglary possible.

Stop. Thinking like that crosses over to Jimmy's investigation territory. If she stuck to the lifestyle and business itself, it would not only be a great piece, but if she could get it done quick enough, it would also be timely as the Gold Coast Madam paved the way with her publicity.

A knock sounded at her door, startling her from her thoughts. She'd forgotten about Elizabeth. She opened the door to find Elizabeth carrying a six-pack of beer, which Moira found funny since Elizabeth hated beer.

As she walked in, Elizabeth studied Moira. "What's going on? Both Colin and I figured it was man trouble, but looking at you now, you look more excited than bummed."

Moira took the beer and put it in the fridge. Beer and brownies didn't mix. "Man trouble was definitely the reason for the call and the brownies, but while I was waiting for you, I got distracted with work stuff and something just clicked right. The spark of a new story kind of thing."

"As much as I'd like to hear about the story, I'd rather hear about the guy."

Moira grabbed a knife and cut into the still warm and gooey brownies. She hefted an obscenely large piece onto a plate and handed it to Elizabeth. Then she repeated the action for herself. She pointed to the couch, and when they were settled, she thought about where to begin.

Elizabeth had met Jimmy at the block party, but she didn't know him. While she thought, she took a bite of brownie. Nothing surpassed the first bite of a warm double chocolate fudge brownie.

"God, this is good."

Moira nodded. "I'll give you the recipe."

"I don't cook."

"Not at all?"

"Nope."

Moira nudged her. "One more thing to like about you."

"So, guy. Spill."

"You remember Jimmy, Liam's friend. He lives across the street from Mom."

"Was he the one who soaked you?"

Moira shook her head. "No, that was Kevin, Jimmy's brother. Jimmy stopped me from killing his brother and then gave me his shirt. He's the one who wouldn't play truth or dare."

Elizabeth's eyes lit and she smiled approvingly.

"He kissed me when I ran into him at a work thing. Then he kissed me again last Sunday when I went to talk to him. I asked him out. Kind of, but he didn't show."

"He blew you off?"

"Yes, but it was work, and he did call. Then he brought me ice cream and we watched my favorite movie."

"Sounds good so far. Not that I'm upset about getting a brownie out of this."

"He's got some family stuff going on and he wants to go out with me, but he doesn't. And there's this intense attraction that he's constantly fighting. I'm not sure why and it's frustrating. He was here earlier, and I was sure we were going to get naked, but he stopped and ran away."

"Like in the middle of the act?"

Moira snorted. "No. We were getting warmed up and he pulled back. He's always pulling back. I'm trying to be patient, but come on. I was warm and way more than willing and he just left."

She shoved more brownie in her mouth thinking about the sexual frustration.

"Did he give a reason?"

"No. He apologized." She stopped with a sudden thought. "He does that a lot around me. Apologize. Even when it's unwarranted."

"Maybe his family stuff is getting in the way of him getting involved with you." Elizabeth shrugged and put her plate on the table. "Talk to him about it. Find out what he wants, what he's looking for, and see if it matches what you want."

Moira ate her brownie. What she really wanted right now was a to-die-for orgasm. She didn't think anything with batteries would deliver.

"And if that doesn't help, I know a bar with a fabulous ladies' night. Great place for dancing." Elizabeth smirked.

Moira knew she was referring to the bar where Moira had sent her when Elizabeth first came to town. "That is a great ladies' night. It's not my fault you were already hung up on my brother and couldn't appreciate the other men there."

With another bite of brownie she sighed. If Jimmy had never kissed her, she'd go to a bar to continue to try to find the right guy, but now Jimmy was all she could think about. It was like being twelve all over again.

Elizabeth kept her company and allowed her to vent about Jimmy and chat about the story she was developing. When a yawn escaped, Elizabeth stood.

"Get some sleep. Put Jimmy out of your mind. I'm going to help Colin close the bar."

Moira stood to walk Elizabeth out. "See you tomorrow at dinner?"

Elizabeth shuddered. "Yeah, I'll be there."

Holding the door open, Moira laughed. "We're not that bad. The more you're exposed to all of us at once, the easier it gets."

"I doubt it."

Moira locked up, unable to put Jimmy out of her mind.

SUNDAY AFTERNOON CAME MUCH SOONER than Moira was ready for. She'd spent the morning doing more research and thinking about interviewing Rose Laws. What was the likelihood the woman would agree? Before requesting though, she wanted to have questions prepared, to have a plan. Time escaped while she was planning, and then she was running late for dinner.

She pulled up to her mom's house and looked across the street at Jimmy's. Eyeing the clock, she decided she could run there and drop off his slip of paper and then go to dinner. It offered her a quick escape so she wouldn't have to deal with the awkward conversation after almost having sex.

She knocked on the door and waited. Mr. O'Malley answered the door. "Hi, Mr. O'Malley. I'm Moira from across the street. Is Jimmy home? I have something to return to him."

The old man nodded and yelled over his shoulder, "Jimmy, come to the door." Then he shuffled away.

Moira wasn't sure if she should go in, so she waited on the porch. The TV blared in the living room and she wondered if Jimmy heard his dad. Maybe she should shove the paper in the mailbox and text him.

Too bad she hadn't thought of that plan before she knocked.

"Hey," Jimmy said from the other side of the screen.

"Hi. I brought your paper." She held it up.

He opened the screen door and held it open with his leg. Taking the paper from her, he said, "Thanks. I need this for work. Want to come in?"

"No, thanks. We're having dinner at Mom's." She pointed over her shoulder as if he didn't know where her mom lived.

"Okay."

She edged away.

"I'm sorry about last night."

"Sorry about what? That you didn't finish what you started?"

"Yes. No. I'm sorry about the way I treated you."

What the hell was he talking about? "You're apologizing for getting me hot and bothered and then leaving?"

"No. I'm apologizing for pushing you up against a door and ripping the buttons off your dress. You're not the kind of girl—"

"Stop right there, Jimmy. Don't even think about finishing that sentence. The thought of you wanting me so much you almost took me up against a door was hot. I wouldn't trade that for anything. And before you start thinking anything about what kind of girl I am, know this. Every girl wants to have her buttons torn off on occasion." She turned away. Ten years since she attended a Catholic school and she was still being treated like a good girl. As if she wasn't supposed to have any desires. Like she should lead a passionless life. She might as well be a nun.

"Wait."

She stopped on the walkway at the bottom of the steps and turned.

"Can I take you out after dinner?"

"Tonight?"

He nodded.

"On one condition."

His eyebrows rose.

"You promise not to treat me like a nun."

He chuckled. "Trust me, that is never how I've thought of you."

She headed back to her mom's house and heard the

screen door slam behind her. Stopping at her car to grab the pan of brownies, she checked herself in the mirror to make sure she wasn't blushing. Answering her siblings' questions might ruin her plans for the night.

Moira stepped through the front door and heard Colin yelling. He and Liam were on the couch watching a baseball game. She never understood the appeal. They didn't even like baseball all that much. It was like they just wanted to have something to yell at.

"Guys," Quinn called. "I just put Patrick down. Please stop yelling."

Colin smiled. "He might as well get used to the noise while he's young. It's not likely to get any quieter."

Quinn rolled her eyes and went back to the kitchen. Moira followed, but slowed because she felt Liam come up behind her. "No, Liam, you are not getting any brownies until after dinner."

"Like I need your brownies. I can bake my own whenever I want."

She turned to face him and set the pan on the dining room table. "Then what do you want?"

"Why did you go to the O'Malleys' house?"

Nothing got by her family. At least not when she really wanted it to. "I had something of his I needed to return."

"Whose?"

Like she wanted to visit with any of the O'Malleys besides Jimmy? "Jimmy."

"How did you end up with something of his?"

"He dropped it at my apartment." As soon as the words left her lips, she clamped her mouth shut. One day, she'd learn not to talk so much.

Liam's usually serious face became more solemn. "What was Jimmy doing at your apartment?"

"I told you I'm helping him with some stuff for work. We ran into each other at an event last night. He had some questions and stopped by to talk." God, she hoped the partial truth was enough.

"Last night?" Colin called from the couch. "Elizabeth said you had man trouble last night."

"Aren't you supposed to be watching the baseball game?"

He laughed loudly. "I think the show in there is better than the one on TV."

Liam's jaw tightened. Through clenched teeth, he hissed, "Follow me."

If it had been any of her other brothers, she would've refused and headed defiantly in the other direction. But Liam wasn't like the others. He was levelheaded, so she followed him onto the front porch.

He inhaled through his nose a couple of times before speaking. "What's going on with you and Jimmy?"

"Truthfully? I'm not sure."

"Shit, Moira. I know you were stuck on him as a kid, but I thought you outgrew it. Please tell me you're not playing out some childhood crush."

"It's not one-sided, if that's what you're worried about. I'm not a stalker." She sat on the concrete step and waited for him to join her. "I've always been a little in love with Jimmy. You know that. But something changed between us. I'm not sure what, but he's attracted to me."

"You're sure?"

"I'm not stupid, Liam. The man kissed me. I know lust when it smacks me like a freight train."

"I don't want you to get hurt."

"What makes you think Jimmy would hurt me? He's a good guy."

"He is. I'm not sure you both have the same goals in life, that's all."

She bumped her shoulder against his. "That's what dating is for, isn't it? Figuring that stuff out. Please tell me you're not going to go bonkers about this because I already told Jimmy you'd be okay with it."

"You did, huh?"

"Of course. You're Liam the levelheaded. I've always been able to trust you with my secrets."

He threw his arm over her shoulder and gave her a noogie. She swatted his hands away.

"Moira, get in here and set the table," their mother called.

She sighed. "Like Colin is incapable of putting out dishes?"

"Come on. I'll help." He stood and held his hand to pull her up.

They walked back into the house together. Moira always felt comfortable with Liam at her back.

14

—————

Jimmy finished washing the dishes and checked the time. He had maybe an hour until Moira was done with dinner. He'd never attended an O'Leary dinner like Griffin had. Liam had invited him, but he never went because he didn't want the family's pity. Back then, he believed people were only being nice to him because his mother was dead.

He knew better now, and looking back, he wished he would've gone to some of those family meals. It might've taught him how to keep his family together. It would be nice to share time together over a meal instead of beers in the middle of the night. He longed to have what Liam always had.

He wiped his hands on a towel and headed upstairs. Norah had taken over his space, leaving him to sleep on the couch or at Kevin's, but having his stuff in his room gave him a reason to check on her. He knocked on the door and waited for her to welcome him.

"Hey, I just need to use the computer."

She sat on his chair in front of the TV, watching some

sappy movie. Without looking away from the screen, she said, "Who was the woman at the door?"

The question threw him as he booted up his computer. What woman? Then he realized she was talking about Moira. "Moira O'Leary. Do you remember her?"

"I remember the O'Learys." She shifted in the seat, dangling her legs over the arm. "So is she your girlfriend?"

"No."

"But you're taking her out."

"We're going on a date."

"Where?"

"That's what I'm trying to figure out now." He pointed at his computer screen.

"Don't take her to a movie."

He stared at the movie times he'd already pulled up. He needed to keep her nearby so there was no chance of his cover being blown. No one would look for James Buchanan in this neighborhood. "Why not?"

"This is one of your first dates, right? You have to go somewhere to interact. At a movie, you sit in silence for two hours. What's the point?"

How sad was it that he needed to take dating advice from his pregnant little sister? "Any suggestions?"

She shrugged. "I don't live here anymore, remember?"

The words were spoken with enough bite to let him know she was still bitter about him sending her away. He'd believed they'd gotten past that.

"There's a carnival," she said.

"Huh?"

"One of those neighborhood carnivals. There are rides and games and cotton candy. I saw it when I went for a drive earlier."

The way she said it told him she wanted to go. He looked

at her bulging stomach. "Want me to bring you cotton candy?"

She smiled, the first he'd seen since she arrived. "The blue kind."

"You got it." A carnival was the perfect place for Moira. He remembered her begging Liam to take her when they were kids. Her parents wouldn't let her go with her friends, so she begged Liam.

Jimmy hadn't wanted to babysit. That's what he told Liam anyway. They were sixteen, and he wanted to look for girls, not hang out with Liam's fourteen-year-old sister. In truth, Moira always distracted him in ways she wasn't supposed to.

But Liam had felt sorry for her and agreed. When they arrived at the carnival, Liam told Moira to go off with her friends, sure she'd be fine. Jimmy spent the night keeping an eye on her and ignoring every other girl there. Moira was young and beautiful and far too trusting. He needed to keep her safe.

He showered and changed and then went downstairs to make sure Dad had taken his medicine. He'd never thought that at the age of thirty he'd have to play nursemaid to not one, but two members of his family. Norah still hadn't said anything about what she'd planned to do about the baby, and he was doing his best not to pressure her, but it wasn't like they could pretend and it would all go away.

The pressure of having to do everything in the house pressed down on him, so he went to the porch to wait for Moira. He should probably go and pick her up, but then he'd be under the scrutiny of her entire family, and he wasn't ready for that. The heat and humidity outside pressed on him too, but it wasn't nearly as oppressive as the O'Malleys inside. He looked to the sky and saw some ugly gray clouds. He hoped the storm would hold off until after his date with Moira. It would be just his luck to get her excited over a carnival and then be rained out.

Voices across the street drew his attention. Colin and his girlfriend were leaving. Dinner must be over. He kept his eyes trained on the house, waiting for Moira. Ryan came out next, carrying a baby car seat, followed by his wife. Immediately behind them, Moira bounced out. She pulled back the shade on the car seat and made noises at the infant. Ryan gave her a little shove, but she walked them to their car anyway. Once they were settled, she looked across the street at Jimmy.

He couldn't stop the smile from forming. Moira always had that effect on him. She continued her springy step across the street without looking for cars. When she reached the lawn in front of his house, she said, "Anxious for our date?"

"No, just waiting patiently. I know how the O'Learys like their all-afternoon meals."

"Our family dinners don't take all day. We have lives, you know."

He stood and walked down the steps to meet her. The smile on her face caused something in his chest to swell. It strangled him in a different way than being in the house with his dad and Norah had, but his lungs still constricted.

"So what's the plan?" she asked as she grabbed his hand.

She was always so easy with affection. Most of the O'Learys were. They were the kind of family that hugged and kissed hello. The girls squealed in delight, even as adults. He had no idea if Norah was a squealer.

"Hello?"

His attention snapped back to Moira, who was staring up at him. "What?"

"I lost you to something there for a minute."

"Nothing. I hear there's a carnival we could check out."

Her eyes brightened, and she skipped a little next to him. "I love carnivals. I haven't been to one in a couple of years. Remember when they used to do one at Saint Matthew's? All the families would come out. The eighth-graders ran the games, and everyone won a prize."

"That's probably why they couldn't afford to continue doing it."

"It was fun."

He led the way to his car. "I'm surprised you liked it. They only had a handful of rides every year."

"But they always had the Tilt-A-Whirl. God, I love that ride."

The thought of spinning uncontrollably in circles held no appeal for him. Before he unlocked and opened the passenger door for her, he asked, "Is your car locked?"

She shrugged, but said, "Yeah."

"Go check and make sure."

"My car is a piece of crap. No one is going to steal it, and there's nothing of value inside."

He grabbed her chin to face him. "You're inside the car. If it's unlocked, someone could sit and wait for you."

She shuddered. "You have a lot of creepy thoughts."

But she pulled away and went to her car. When she tugged the handle, the door popped open. She slammed the door and pressed the button to lock it. When she returned, he held his car door open for her and tried not to look smug. Had her brothers taught her any personal security measures?

He settled behind the wheel and drove to the carnival. Moira chatted about dinner with her family and the new baby, Patrick. One thing he could count on Moira for was chatter. He never had to make small talk, and it didn't seem to bother her that he didn't need to fill every moment of silence.

The odd thought struck him as he half listened to her. For as long as he'd known Moira, she'd been a talker. Not forced and uncomfortable conversation, but something natural for her. She drew people out and into the conversation but never required participation.

She suddenly grew quiet. "Were you even listening? Or is this another 'shut up, Moira' moment?"

"I was listening. You're totally in love with your new nephew and you hope that Colin and Elizabeth get married soon and have babies. You're thinking about who you can set Liam up with because you don't want him to be lonely." He glanced at her fast enough to see her mouth hanging open. "If you want my input, leave Liam alone. When he wants to find someone, he will."

Personally, he didn't think settling down was even a blip on Liam's radar. He'd known Liam to have girlfriends, but nothing serious, and ever since setting his sights on getting a restaurant of his own, he'd focused all of his energy there.

"Are you kidding me? My brothers don't do anything without a bit of prompting."

"They seem to be doing fine."

He didn't have to look to know she was rolling her eyes at him. "Liam's different, you know? I always feel like he's a little lost."

Jimmy couldn't argue. The description fit Liam. Jimmy turned down Lawrence and hit a traffic jam. Looked like everyone wanted to get one last night at the carnival.

"Can't you turn on your police lights and zoom through?"

"No. First of all, this is my personal vehicle. Second, that would be abuse of power and wrong."

He cut down an alley and drove a couple of blocks. He managed to find a spot on the street that didn't require a permit to park. Unfortunately, they'd have to walk to get back to the carnival. Jimmy checked Moira's feet. Gym shoes.

"What are you looking at?"

"Making sure you can walk back to the carnival without breaking your ankle." He exited the car and walked around. Before he got to her door, she'd already stepped out.

"Who the hell would go to a carnival wearing heels? Or to family dinner at home for that matter?"

He shrugged and locked the car. They walked to the carnival in relative silence. As they neared, he felt his muscles tense. The crowd was thick and many were already drunk.

"Something wrong?" Moira asked as she took his hand and tugged on his arm.

"No."

"Liar."

"You look at this place and see lights and laughter, fun and excitement. All I can see are the drunks who are going to get belligerent and the gangbangers looking for an opportunity to start trouble or steal something. Parents who aren't paying attention to where their kids are wandering off to and the pedophiles who might strike at any time."

He expected her to shoot a cocky remark back at him, but instead she released his hand and circled her arms around his neck. He felt her sigh against his ribs. "I wish you could forget being a cop for a little while."

"I don't know how."

"I know, but it's got to be hard always waiting for the bad and not being able to see the good."

He hadn't thought about it quite like that, but she was right. His vigilance was always on high. Holding on to Moira reaffirmed the need for that vigilance, though. He despised the thought of anything bad happening to someone he cared about.

And just like that, she slid from his embrace and took a few steps. She turned and walked backward. "Come on, let's go play. I want to see if I can make you relax a little."

Then she winked and crooked her finger at him. He had many ideas of how she could help him relax, but a carnival didn't appear anywhere on the list.

Moira slid through the crowd without a care for all of the dangers he saw, even though he'd pointed them out to her. Part of him loved that about her, despite the fact it scared the shit out of him.

Of course, she walked straight to the Tilt-A-Whirl, but forgot they needed tickets to ride. He hooked right to the ticket booth while she stood in line. He bought enough tickets for her to go on whatever ride she wanted.

He joined her on the Tilt-A-Whirl and decided one trip was enough, but for the sound of her giggling as she spun, a queasy stomach might be worth it. As they stumbled down the metal ramp, clomping their feet toward the exit, he asked, "Where to now?"

She pointed toward the row of carnival games designed to take money and give little or nothing in return. "Let's play some games."

15

———

As Moira strode through the midway of games, Jimmy scanned the options. She hoped he wouldn't pick something like basketball; she sucked at basketball, and he was like a foot taller than her. It wouldn't be a fair competition. She walked a few steps in front of him, but he caught her quickly and put his arm around her shoulder. Other than kissing her, he hadn't initiated any displays of affection, but she tried not to read too much into it.

"This way," he said, and pulled her to the side.

When she saw where he was headed, she groaned. A shooting game. "This isn't fair. Obviously, you're going to be a better shot than me—you carry a gun for a living."

"I just thought you wanted a prize. I didn't know you wanted to play, too."

She stopped abruptly. "Have you met me? Of course I want to play."

He nudged her forward while pulling money from his pocket. "Pick a prize for me to win for you. Then we'll play something else."

She smiled and studied the stuffed animals hanging all around. Pandas, ugly clowns, and strange-colored gorillas stared back at her. Then she saw it: a lion that had to be three feet tall. The light brown mane fluffed around the golden fur. Its eyes were dark and watchful. It made her think of Jimmy and his protectiveness. She pointed to the lion.

"I should've known better than to think you'd take it easy on me."

In order for him to win the lion, he'd have to hit every target on three different turns. Jimmy set his money on the counter and then began to negotiate with the carny. Jimmy wanted free practice shots so he could get the feel for the gun. He argued that if he was going to spend twenty dollars to win a lion that only cost five at the store, he should get a couple of free shots.

The carny was a teen who looked more interested in ogling girls than whether Jimmy took a couple of free shots, so he let him. Both plastic darts flew wildly away from the target. Moira snickered. She should've felt bad about setting Jimmy up for failure, but she didn't. The man needed to have a few harmless flops.

He stared at the gun intently and then at the darts the teen stacked up next to him.

"Want a kiss for good luck?"

He looked at her from the corner of his eyes. "Luck has nothing to do with it, but I'll take a kiss anyway."

She moved closer and waited for him to lower his face to hers. She slid her arms around his neck and kissed him. Their lips interlocked, but he kept it pretty innocent.

When he stepped away, he said, "Stand behind me so I don't get distracted."

She ran her fingers up his bicep. "You find me distracting?"

"Always." He shoved her hips gently to get her moving.

She stood behind him, a little off to the side so she could see. If she stood directly behind him, it would've been like trying to see through a mountain. The set of his shoulders told her he was in deep concentration.

Slowly, methodically, he started picking off targets —*ping, ping, ping*—not missing one.

When all of the darts were gone, he pointed at the lion and the teen took it down. "Great shooting, man. That's the first big prize I've handed out all weekend."

Jimmy turned and handed her the lion. Figures. The man did everything perfectly. She hugged the stuffed animal, which was harder than it appeared, much like Jimmy. This was not a snuggly animal.

"Where to now?" Jimmy asked.

"Let's stay here. Teach me how you won." She set her lion on the counter.

Jimmy laid a ten-dollar bill beside it. While the teen gathered her darts, Jimmy picked up the gun and handed it to Moira. Then he stood directly behind her and wrapped his body around hers. Maybe he was a bit snuggly after all.

As if oblivious to how quickly her heart began beating and how nicely she fit into his frame, Jimmy lowered his mouth to her ear. He started talking about lining up sights and aiming. Squeeze. Don't pull. It took everything she had not to laugh.

When he was done instructing, he put a dart in the gun and guided her hands back toward the target. She pulled the trigger—correction—squeezed and jumped a little when the gun popped. The dart went wild, and Jimmy sighed in her ear, causing a tingle to dance down her spine.

"I said squeeze the trigger."

"I did. Maybe I could focus better if you weren't literally breathing down my neck." She shifted her shoulders like she needed to make space.

Instead of indulging her, Jimmy kissed her neck and worked his way over to her earlobe. Moira's eyes fluttered shut, and she didn't care that the horny teenager stood in front of them staring. Jimmy's quiet breath in her ear made her knees weak, so she leaned on him.

Then he grabbed her hips and thrust them forward, away from the warmth of his body. "You have a few more shots to take. I'll try not to crowd you."

She forced her eyes open and focused on the circling targets. The sudden realization hit her that she wouldn't be able to beat Jimmy at this game or any other. She squinted at the targets and attempted to aim, but all she wanted was to feel Jimmy's body around hers again, his tongue exploring, making her weak.

Releasing a pent-up breath, she tried to relax. The dart flew from the gun and pinged off the target. Since she missed the bull's-eye, the target didn't fly back.

"Not bad," Jimmy said.

She shot a look over her shoulder. "Better than you thought I'd do."

"Even Lois Lane had her good days."

Moira aimed the gun again. "And Superman had his off days." She shot the rest of her darts without hitting any of the targets hard enough to win.

Jimmy handed her the lion.

"How'd you manage to hit all of them?"

"I can't share my secrets." He led her away from the booth.

"Spill."

"The gun pulls down and to the left. I adjusted, knowing where it wanted to go, so I aimed high and to the right."

Moira slugged his arm. "Why didn't you tell me that?"

He put his arm around her shoulder again. "I tried, but you were too busy panting to listen. I didn't want you to hyperventilate."

Oh, God. He wasn't as oblivious as she'd thought. Now she felt foolish because he knew exactly how turned on she'd gotten just standing in his arms and having him whisper in her ear.

"You're pretty when you blush," he said and stroked his finger down the side of her neck. He pulled her closer and whispered, "If it makes you feel any better, you do the same to me. It just takes more to make me blush."

She smiled and wondered what it would take to make Jimmy blush. "Let's go to the Ferris wheel."

The line for the ride was shorter than most. Moira knew that comparatively, the Ferris wheel wasn't exciting, but she always thought it was romantic. To be up above the city with a guy you like, maybe stealing a few kisses where no one but the stars could watch. While they waited for the cars to empty so they could get on, Moira turned slightly in Jimmy's arms. She shifted the lion to her left arm, so she could wrap her right arm around his waist. Her hand encountered a hard lump, and she realized he had his gun with him.

She yanked her hand back.

He stiffened, but his hands rubbed her shoulders. "Don't freak."

In a whisper that came out more like a hiss, she said, "Why do you need to have a gun on our date? What do you think is going to happen?"

"I feel better knowing it's there, that I'm prepared for anything. I never know what's going to happen, so I'm ready." He kissed the top of her head. "It's no big deal. It's part of who I am."

They moved forward in line, next to get a car. "Do you always carry it with you?"

"Pretty much."

She inhaled deeply. Jimmy was a cop, before that a soldier. She shouldn't be surprised that he carried a gun.

With his hand at her lower back, the same place he carried a gun, he ushered her toward the Ferris wheel. He held her hand while she climbed in and then sat beside her. She squished the lion between her hip and the side, trying to give Jimmy as much room as possible. Sometimes she forgot how big he was.

Jimmy settled in with one arm along the back of the car behind her head. His knee bumped hers and the crisp hair on his leg tickled her. The attendant slammed the bar shut to lock them in, and the car jolted forward.

"You okay?" Jimmy asked.

"Yeah, just processing. I never thought about you carrying a gun all the time. I thought it was something you took off, like your badge." She twisted her body, further squishing the lion so she could look into Jimmy's eyes.

"I can. I choose not to."

"Doesn't it make it easier for you to stay in cop mode, though? Harder to be a regular guy?"

"I'm never a regular guy, I guess. I'm always a cop." He cocked his head. "You're always a reporter."

"No, I'm not."

"Sure you are. You might not print everything, but you're always interviewing people, getting their stories. It's as natural to you as scanning for danger is for me."

He had her there. She never quite thought about the fact

that she was always a reporter. It was so much more than just what she did; it was part of who she was.

"Speaking of which, Liam said you weren't happy with your current job. Do you have a plan?"

The Ferris wheel had picked up all of the new occupants and began to increase speed. The cool air smelling of an impending storm rushed up at her, flinging her hair around her face. She shoved it behind her ears, buying time to answer Jimmy's question. "It's not that I don't like my job. I like it a whole lot, actually. I'm just not sure it's enough. Everyone thinks it's not a real job, that all I do is party and then slap some words on the page."

She waited, sure he would agree with the statement, but he didn't. "I'm thinking about other possibilities, articles I could sell that will carry more weight and allow me to break into more serious markets. I have you to thank for that."

"Me?"

"Yeah, running into you because of this case has given me ideas."

The car reached the top of the wheel and paused.

"You need to stay out of my investigation."

"What I'm working on has nothing to do with your job."

Swoosh over the arc and down the back side.

"Then what is it?" He toyed with her hair that was still flying around.

Should she tell him? She never talked about stories with anyone, mostly because she always feared someone stealing her ideas. But this was Jimmy, not a fellow reporter. "It's a slightly different angle. I'm looking into sex for hire in the Viagra Triangle."

He laughed and the sound echoed across the carnival. The sound was rich and full and big, just like him. "Do I need to worry about the research you might be conducting for this story?"

She slapped his chest—his very hard chest—and let her hand linger. His hand caught hers and he leaned over for a kiss. His lips were warm and insistent. He didn't use his tongue at first, just his lips as if the kiss was a preview. She immediately wanted more.

Her hand dropped from his chest and landed on his thigh. When he deepened the kiss, she caressed his leg, moving higher, wanting to feel more of him. He stopped her progress without breaking the kiss. She felt his lips curve into a smile.

The ride stopped as they were halfway to the top. More people getting off. How she wanted to be one of those people. She wiggled her fingers beneath Jimmy's palm, and he pulled away from her mouth.

"I'm not going to let you stroke me on a ride in public." He laced his fingers through hers.

"Shows what you know. I was thinking of a hand job."

He groaned and moved in for another kiss.

Between the rush of her blood and the air swirling around them as the ride picked up speed once again, Moira felt dizzy. His kisses turned her on so much, she was ready to get naked in public.

Jimmy pulled away again and shifted, causing the car to rock. "This is getting out of hand."

"Out of hand can be fun."

His chest rose with a deep breath and his smile was strained. "Tell me more about your plans for work."

"I don't really know. I get restless easily, but I've always known I wanted to be a journalist."

"Where do you see yourself in five years?"

She sat back in the car, still holding his hand, but staring up into the cloudy sky. When did she last think about a five-year plan? College?

In five years, she'd be thirty-three. In the back of her mind, she'd expected to be married with kids, doing the mom thing. She'd never separated her job from that, though. Part of her assumed she'd always work.

"I think that's the longest you've ever been so quiet. I didn't mean for the question to freeze your brain." His fingers rubbed her gently.

"I got caught up in thinking about it. I realized I no longer have a plan. I have some hopes and dreams, but no real plan." Plenty for her to think about later. "How about you?"

"I'll still be a detective, making my way up the ranks. One day, I plan to be a commander, maybe even chief, although the politics of the position might be too much for me."

She liked hearing him talk. Jimmy had never been much of a talker, at least not while she was around, so having him open up warmed something deep in her chest. The conversation she'd overheard him having with Liam at the block party pushed her to probe. "What about personally?"

"What do you mean?"

"You have a plan for your career. What about your personal life?"

"I know what I want, but that's not something you can really plan for. I want to be married, soon, so we can have two kids."

The car shuddered, and Moira knew their ride was almost at an end. "What about your dad?"

"Tommy and Sean are both living in the house. Hopefully by the time I get married, they can handle taking care of my dad."

The car swooshed again and stopped in front of the attendant. The man yanked the bar and Jimmy stepped off. He held a hand out to help Moira. Always the gentleman. Except for when he'd had her pressed against her door. She decided she really liked both sides of Jimmy.

Jimmy's head swam in a haze of testosterone. The chemistry between him and Moira was more explosive every time they were alone. He tried his damnedest to keep it in check, but she didn't make it easy.

Discussing his plans with her was easier than expected. He'd had similar conversations with other women, and it usually ended in one of two ways: they either hit the road running or immediately looked for a diamond. Moira just listened.

"Where to now?"

She shrugged. A sudden flash of lightning blazed across the sky followed by a crack of thunder. It looked like their luck had run out.

"We should probably head to the car so we don't get stuck in a downpour. Let me get some cotton candy for Norah first." He pulled her toward the concession stand. "You want anything?"

Her eyes lit when she looked at the menu. "They have funnel cakes. Yes! Extra powdered sugar and chocolate drizzle."

Jimmy placed the order and added a lemonade for them to share. He handed Moira the paper plate with her funnel cake and grabbed the bagged candy and lemonade. Glancing at the sky, he said, "You want to take a chance and eat it here, or eat while we walk?"

"There isn't any rain yet. Plus, you still have tickets. They're not going to give you your money back."

"That's not a big deal. The neighborhood's going to be a zoo if a storm hits. Everyone will try to leave at once."

She ripped off a piece of fried dough and then looked up at the sky. "I say we chance it."

Her wicked grin returned as she tugged at the dough and held out a piece to him. "Want some?"

He let her feed him, her fingers grazing his lips as she put the dough in his mouth. He licked the chocolate glaze and sugar from her finger and the air around them electrified. The dough squished in his mouth, the sweetness reminding him of their kisses.

Moira stared at his mouth for a moment and then broke the spell by turning away. The beer garden was nearby with a few picnic tables spread out, so she took a seat.

He straddled the bench beside her and took a long drink from the lemonade. He reminded himself that this was technically their first date. Moira deserved more respect than for him to spend his time imagining the many ways he'd like to taste her body.

She held up another piece, but he said, "That's not a good idea."

She smirked and popped it into her own mouth. "You don't know what you're missing. The first taste isn't nearly enough."

Shit. He already knew that.

Leaning over the lemonade, she sucked through the straw. Her lips puckered and she arched her eyebrow as if she knew exactly where his mind was.

Another flash of lightning lit the sky and the boom of thunder shook the ground.

Moira grunted. "Fine. You win. Let's go." She stood

suddenly, threw the plate away, and folded the remaining piece of cake and bit it. Her lion was safely tucked under her arm.

He liked a practical woman. He tossed the lemonade and led the way out of the carnival area, pausing to give his leftover tickets to a few teens he figured would brave the storm. As a teen, he would've too. The carnival would restart rides as soon as the rain cleared and then the crowds would be gone. He was too old for that shit.

Moira made quick work of her dessert while walking. He tried to slow his pace to accommodate her short legs, but she did a good job of keeping up.

A block down, the clouds opened and dumped rain. There was no warning drizzle or slow raindrops. Just buckets splashing all around them. He grabbed Moira's hand and pulled her into a doorway of a closed business.

Her T-shirt plastered against her skin and her hair hung in waves around her face. Water dripped down her cheek, but she was smiling.

She tilted her head. "Guess you were right. We should've started walking sooner."

Looking at her now, he couldn't be sorry she'd taken the chance. The wetness of the shirt outlined her bra, and her nipples protruded through the cotton. When she shivered, he realized he was staring. "I'm sorry. Do you want to wait here while I get the car?"

She leaned out of the doorway a little and glanced down the block, then up at the sky. Looking down at how drenched she was, she said, "What's the point? I'm already soaked. Wanna run for it?"

Was she serious?

She didn't wait for an answer, but took off running down the block yelling and squealing in the rain. The woman was nuts. He took off, knowing it wouldn't take long to catch and even bypass her. He sprinted and then slowed to stay by her side. This was probably the stupidest thing he'd done in a long time. As soon as the car came into sight, he pressed the button to unlock it so they could get in as quickly as possible.

Reaching the car first, he opened the door for her and she jumped in. By the time he got behind the wheel, her whole body was shivering even though the temperature had been in the mid-eighties when they'd left for their date. He reached behind his seat and hoped he had a sweatshirt or jacket for her.

He found a sweatshirt, gave it a quick sniff, and passed it to her. "It's dry."

She pulled it over her head and then fastened her buckle. Her stuffed lion dripped in her lap, so she tossed it on the floor at her feet.

"Sorry our date was ruined again. I'm beginning to think we're cursed."

"Are you kidding? That was awesome. I haven't had that much fun on a first date in a long time."

He turned the key in the ignition. "Your dating life might be even sadder than mine."

She laughed. He drove back to his house trying to figure out how to keep the date from ending.

Her car was at her mom's house, so he didn't need to drive her home. Bringing her to his house didn't sound too appealing. Norah had taken over his living space, and he never knew what his dad would be up to. That was the best case. Worst case, Tommy and Sean would be sitting in the living room with Dad to rib him about his date.

But he couldn't take her anywhere else when they were both dripping wet. He turned the corner toward his house, giving up on the notion of extending the date. "You want to try this again some other day?"

"Maybe," she said teasingly. She looked down the block at his house. "Pull over."

"Why?"

"Just do it!"

He pulled over to the curb, but left the car in drive, scanning the road to figure out why he needed to pull over half a block from his house.

She pushed the car into park and reached across him and twisted the knob to turn off the headlights.

"What are you doing? It's pouring outside and we're still a half a block from where we need to be."

"Correction. We're a half a block away from witnesses." She leaned close to him. "Want to make out?"

His brain short-circuited. He felt her breasts pressing against his arm. He hadn't made out in a car since he'd been a teenager. Weren't they a little old for this?

But what were his other choices? Say good-bye to her now or invite her into his house?

Her breath fluttered across his cheek, and she whispered in his ear, "Don't think too long and hard about it, Jimmy. You'll give me the idea that you don't want to."

He turned and captured her mouth. Her lips were cold and her hair dripped on his cheek. She tasted sweet like the sugar he'd sucked off her finger at the carnival. He plunged his tongue into her mouth, meeting hers, swirling, loving the touch and texture of her.

She pulled away from him and said, "This isn't going to do. Come on." She turned off the ignition and then stepped over the console and settled on the backseat. She patted the spot next to her. "I'm waiting."

No way he was climbing over; he'd never fit. He stepped

out and opened the back door to reenter. She slid over to allow him to get comfortable and then she pounced on him.

Her body lay on his as she pushed him against the door. Her cold fingers touched his face and then ran into his hair. Her lips were no longer freezing, but her hair continued to drip so much that it soaked his sweatshirt.

"Do you want me to put the heat on?"

"Uh-uh. I'm pretty sure you're capable of warming me up."

He refused to release the moan that would tell her exactly how much he wanted her. Instead, he took her mouth again, this time threading his fingers into her wet hair and angling her head to give him the access he desired.

She spread her thighs and straddled his leg, rubbing against him from hip to chest. "Touch me," she whispered.

"I am." But he knew what she wanted. He wasn't going to fuck her in the back of his car.

"Not like that."

She bit his lip to get his attention, as if she didn't already control his every thought. She grabbed his hand and moved it under her shirt. Her skin was slick from the rain, but warm under the extra layer of his sweatshirt. He didn't need any more coaxing.

Pulling her closer, he swung her other leg over his so she fully straddled him. He straightened and forced her to lean back against the driver's seat. He peeled the wet shirt away from her skin and followed it up with warm, wet kisses.

The rain beat a rhythm against the roof of the car matching the one in his head. Moira tasted so good. He reached her bra and pushed it up, revealing the whitest skin he'd ever seen. The globes of her breasts were full and her nipples stood out demanding his attention. He rolled the right nipple between his thumb and finger while he sucked on the left.

Moira's hips began to wiggle against him, making him harder. She put her hands on his shoulders for balance as she pushed her pelvis against his and thrust her breasts up. "God, Jimmy, that's so good."

He switch to suck on the other breast now and she grabbed the back of his head, keeping him close. He kissed and nibbled his way across her ribs. The fucking car was not big enough to accommodate everything he wanted to do.

He paused, leaning his forehead against her shoulder. His breath came quickly. Moira, on the other hand, had no intention of taking a break. She began yanking at the back of his shirt.

"What are you doing?"

"I want to feel your skin. I want you up against me."

"We can't, Moira. We're not going to fit."

"Sure we will. I'll show you." She flopped over the side and shimmied against the seat until her shoulders were against the opposite door. "Keep your knees bent and we can make this work."

He wanted to believe her, but if he fucked her in the back of his car, that's all it would be. Plus, with his luck, Mrs. Corrigan, whose house they were parked in front of, would call and report them. He'd hate to get caught literally with his pants down.

Once again, he'd taken too long to think, and Moira was already unbuttoning her shorts and sliding them over her hips. He twisted and grabbed her wrists to stop her.

"Do *not* do this again, Jimmy."

Something in her voice said more than the words did. If he quit, he'd lose her. Didn't she know how hard it was for him to walk away?

She jerked her hand from his grasp. "Forget it," she snapped, and her fingers began rebuttoning her shorts.

Christ. He covered her hand again to stop her progress. "I want you. You know I want you."

"Funny way of showing it."

He looked over her head at the now fogged-up window. He couldn't put into words what she did to him, why this would never be enough. Glancing back at her face, he saw the moonlight glint off her eyes. Anger had replaced lust, but she was still as sexy as ever.

He tightened his grip on her hand, forcing it away from her pants and back up against the window. He crushed his mouth to hers and ground his hips against her to show how much he wanted her. The sweatshirt had dropped back over her chest when she laid down. He remedied that so he could run his mouth over her exposed skin.

She didn't attempt to free her wrist. Her breath quickened as he rained kisses down her neck and then back to her breasts. She rubbed herself against him, so he pinned her down. He wouldn't let her rush him.

16

———

od. She'd never been so hot and wet. Between the rain and the cramped car and the heat from Jimmy's body pressed to her, she couldn't find enough oxygen. At least that's what she told herself. But she knew it was the effect his mouth had on her. And she wanted more. So much more, but he wouldn't give her any control.

The hand pinned above her head was losing circulation, but she didn't care. With her free hand, she reached for the snap on his pants. Her fingers brushed the juncture where their bodies joined, and even with all the fabric between them, she felt her heat and his hardness. A deep groan rumbled from him.

He pulled away from her and shifted her body, angling it so one of her feet planted on the floor and the other wrapped around his waist. He released her hand, and she thought for sure they were finally going to get naked enough to have sex, but Jimmy disappointed her again. He teased her mouth with his tongue to lull her and then captured both of her hands.

Holding her hands above her head, he slid his free hand to her waist where her shorts were still open. He leaned back to stare into her eyes as he slid his hand into her pants.

Fingertips grazed her hair, sending tingles throughout her body. He stroked her outer lips, teasing her. His eyes were devilish. She licked her lips and forced her body to lie still. He wanted control; she could give him that.

Finally one long finger slid over her slit, skimming over her clit, the barest touch. Then back with a little more pressure. Her breath caught in her throat, so she opened her mouth to capture more air. She focused on Jimmy and saw a smirk cross his lips.

His finger circled her clit and then rubbed it in a delicious swirling motion. She sighed a moan. One finger entered her, drawing out and then back in. As much as she tried to give Jimmy control of her body, her hips had their own idea and she thrust up to meet his hand. Tension coiled deep inside her, and sparks of pleasure shot through her system as his palm collided with her body.

Jimmy let go of her hands, but she kept them in the same place. He circled an arm around her waist and every bit of his attention focused on her pleasure, her needs, as a second finger joined the first, his slick movements drowning her. Quickened pace followed by torturous strokes. Her body had no idea what to expect. Hard then gentle. Fast then slow.

She closed her eyes to absorb every movement, to focus on his hand, to try to predict, anticipate, participate. She couldn't focus. Her brain was hazy and her nerves were strung so tight, she was afraid to move.

Suddenly his finger curled inside her, while his thumb pressed on her clit, and she was lost. He covered her mouth with his, probably to swallow her scream. Her muscles clamped down on his hand, and moisture flooded her panties and his palm. Her entire body shuddered, but Jimmy continued holding her, touching her, stroking her.

Moira had no idea how long she lay there in Jimmy's arms, panting and kissing him mindlessly. His hand was still in her shorts, as drenched as she was after the downpour. He'd reduced her to a relaxed puddle of nothing. She couldn't move.

Jimmy chuckled as if he could read her mind. He pulled his hand out and buttoned her shorts. With what little energy she had left, she pushed herself up. "What are you doing?"

"Taking you to your car."

"But—"

He popped the door open and exited before she should formulate a complete thought. He restarted the car and flipped the rearview mirror down to look at her splayed in his backseat. "That's a good look on you."

"What look is that? Pissed off?" She tried for snarky, but failed miserably.

He chuckled again. "Well sated."

"You could be too if you gave me a chance."

Pulling back into the street, he said, "I'm fine."

But the words sounded strangled. He wasn't fine. He couldn't be even if he'd been only half as horny as she'd been when they started. When he parked again, this time right in front of her car, she leaned over the seat and slid her hands down his chest. "We can continue this."

He picked up her hand and kissed the palm. "Not tonight. I don't have a bed."

"We were doing pretty good right here."

He responded with little more than a grunt. Like it had

been her fault he didn't get off. He wouldn't let her do anything. That's what she'd thought he wanted. Damn man needed to learn to use his words.

The door beside her swung open and Jimmy held his hand out to help her up. Good thing he was such a gentleman; she wasn't sure her legs would work. She stood and flexed her thigh muscles. Working. The rain had finally stopped, leaving cool air and sweet smells behind. He held her hand and walked her to her car.

She ran a hand down his chest. "Why do you keep stopping? We both want this. So much."

"I know."

"Talk to me."

She watched his throat work as he swallowed. Then he lowered his head and kissed her, melting her knees again. She leaned against the car, glad for its support. His kiss was gentle and smooth and left her wanting more when he pulled away.

"Good night, Moira. Call me when you get home."

She nodded but wanted to prod him for answers. She found it hard to argue when he kept answering her with kisses instead of words. Once she was inside her car, he backed off and watched from the curb as she pulled away.

Moira drove on autopilot, but when she was down the block and around the corner, the nagging sensation of questions unanswered hit her. Jimmy hadn't answered her. All she wanted to know was why he wouldn't fuck her. A pretty simple question.

He wanted to, that much was clear. She knew he wasn't a virgin, so he certainly wasn't saving himself for marriage.

That left her.

Why did he refuse to have sex with *her*?

That single question wormed its way into her brain and chomped away at all the remaining effects of a great orgasm. By the time she parked in front of her apartment, she was feeling sorry for herself, convinced Jimmy saw something innately wrong with her that made her unfuckable.

She got ready for bed, knowing Jimmy expected her call, but she knew she couldn't talk to him without sounding pitiful or accusatory, so she crawled into bed alone with her thoughts.

JIMMY STRODE into his house and was greeted with blissful silence. Of course, the one time he assumed he wouldn't find it, quiet surrounded him. He turned back to look at the street as if he could catch Moira, even though he'd watched her drive off.

His dick throbbed in his jeans, rubbing uncomfortably against the denim. He went to the bathroom to take a shower. Setting his phone on the toilet tank in case Moira called, he stepped under the spray, seeking relief. The hot water poked at his sensitive skin. Images of Moira writhing against him, pale skin flush with pleasure, while moaning his name made his dick twitch. He stroked his cock, hearing Moira's panting breath in his ears. He closed his eyes and smelled her musky scent.

His breath quickened as his hand moved faster. He imagined sliding into Moira, hearing her sigh, feeling her wet warmth pull him closer. Bracing his forearm against the cold tile, he groaned his relief as his cock spurt.

After catching his breath, he lathered up and washed. Moira's quiet voice echoed in his head. *Why do you keep stopping?*

He felt like an asshole now, after the fact, but in the moment, he knew it wasn't right. Hell, yes, he wanted to fuck her. He wanted to fuck her blind.

And that was the problem. Moira wasn't some chick to fuck. They were already more and he didn't want to screw it up. Maybe she was the woman he'd been looking for, the mother of his children, in which case, she deserved better than to be treated like a weekend fling, fucked in the back-seat of a car.

But maybe she wasn't his future wife. In which case, she was still Liam's little sister and fucking her would cause a rift he might not be able to repair.

The worst part was that he wasn't sure which way he hoped it would go. He didn't know what he wanted.

He twisted the knobs to shut off the water. As usual, they squeaked and the old pipes rattled. The sound reminded him that he wanted more than this.

He wanted a home that would hold his family comfortably, where the appliances worked without a kick, where he could relax. Ever since moving back in with his dad, he hadn't been able to relax at all. Between steadily progressing on the job and carefully watching Dad's diabetes and policing his brothers when necessary, he never had time to step back and breathe.

Moira made him want to breathe.

With a towel wrapped around his waist, he grabbed his phone. She should've been home by now, and she hadn't called. He dialed and waited for her to answer and hoped he could tell her about the realization he'd had in the shower. The phone rang and went to voice mail.

He couldn't leave a message, so he disconnected. He weighed his options and decided to send a text to make sure she got home safely. Taking the phone with him to the living room and the couch, which had become his temporary bed, he sat in the dark and waited. Twenty more minutes passed before he got a response.

I'm home. Already in bed. Good night.

The text was short and gave him the information he needed, but not what he wanted. He expected Moira to say more; she always did. He should start a conversation, but didn't know how, so he sat staring at the screen. Then it lit with another text.

I had a great time tonight. Thank you.

Maybe that was the only opening he'd get.

He ran his fingers over the screen of his phone and thought about a response. He could say good night and leave it at that. Or he could answer her question as a text and not have to see her reaction or hear her laugh at him.

I had a great time too.

He waited, wanting to continue the conversation.

Could've fooled me.

It was one of the best first dates I've ever had.

While waiting for Moira to answer, he dropped his towel, pulled on a pair of underwear, and settled on the couch for the night.

You didn't answer my question. That said plenty.

Shit. She thought he didn't want her or some other ridiculous imaginary reason. He lay against the pillow propped on the arm of the couch.

I didn't answer because I didn't know. I didn't want to say the wrong thing. Sounds like not saying anything was just as bad.

Didn't know...but now you do?

Figured she'd pick up on that. One small word and she found it.

Maybe. I want to take it slow. Figure out how we feel. I don't want to screw things up between us.

His finger hovered over the send button. Sharing his thoughts rarely worked well for him. He didn't come from a family that talked about their feelings, but Moira did. Knowing that gave him a little advantage. Plus, she was an obvious talker. He hit send and then set the phone on his chest, as if the slight added weight would calm his heart.

He waited for the vibration of an incoming text, but felt nothing. His eyelids drifted shut and he wondered what Moira was thinking. One good thing about her: he didn't usually have to guess about what she thought because she said every freaking thing aloud.

A sudden buzz jolted him awake. He must've dozed. He rubbed his eyes and stared at his phone.

I know how I feel—horny.

The tightness in his chest lifted. Flirtatious banter with Moira he could handle.

You're exaggerating. You were well taken care of tonight.

That sure of yourself?

I took a shower hearing you moan my name and smelling you on my hand. I'm damn sure of myself.

The words reminded him of her sounds and smells, and he got hard again.

What did you do about it?

Was she really wanting to have text sex? This was weirder than phone sex.

You have an excellent imagination. Figure it out.

Spoilsport. Want to know what I'm doing?

She was killing him. Rather than just thinking it, he told her.

No. It might kill me and I need to work tomorrow.

As soon as he sent it, he could almost hear her laughter.

Maybe I'll just show you next time we see each other.

Her answer was enough to set his mind at ease that she wanted to see him again.

I don't know when I'll be free. I have to check both my schedule and James Buchanan's.

Let me know when and I'll make myself available. Good night for real this time.

The reality of his life settled in again. Going to work in the morning didn't bother him. It was having the dual identity after he signed out for the night. He felt like he was treading water as James Buchanan. He just wanted to catch a break to solve the case.

With any luck, he and Gabby would make some headway with the escort services Stan Decker had given him. He let his eyes close, but thoughts of high-class hookers and thieves followed.

He wondered what would drive a supposedly happily married man to hire an escort. Whether for company or sex, he didn't understand. If you're not happy with your marriage, change it or divorce. What lies did these men tell themselves to make their behavior acceptable?

MOIRA SPENT her morning calling the escort service numbers she'd copied from Jimmy. He'd probably have a cow if he knew, but she hadn't lied to him when she said her story wouldn't interfere with his case. Part of her hoped she'd hear and recognize the mystery woman's voice at one of the services, but life wasn't that easy.

She'd planned to speak to whoever answered the phone at each place and ask about possible employment. If she could at least get an interview, it would get her foot in the door. She could find women to interview anonymously. Unfortunately, with the exception of the first, each of the numbers led to a generic voice mail stating nothing more than the phone number.

But before she could get ahead of herself, she had to develop a plan. She had to become someone other than Moira O'Leary, reporter. She had to be a nobody.

Creating a phony life was more fun than Moira anticipated. Her imagination rolled with it, and within the hour, she had a cover story. She studied her calendar, which had filled up once again. Since her last week of hitting every possible event hadn't given her anything, she didn't plan on trying again. But even with what she was expected to cover, adding in job interviews would fill the gaps.

Maybe she wouldn't be seeing Jimmy this week after all.

After her fabulous orgasm and then his texts, she felt relaxed. For a change, she thought Jimmy was opening up, at least a little bit. She didn't know what to make of his excuse that he was afraid of screwing things up with her, but it was better than where her mind had gone on its own.

Thinking of Jimmy made her horny all over again, so she blocked him from her thoughts. She had work to think about. A cocktail reception at a college library tonight. She owed one editor a couple of stories from her incredibly busy week last week, so she sat down to churn out the words.

A paragraph in, her phone rang. Ryan. He pretty much only called these days when he needed a sitter. She didn't mind since he'd always done everything for everyone in the family, but she almost missed the calls he used to make just to check on her.

She answered while still typing. "Hey, Ry. What night do you need a babysitter for?"

"Who said I needed a sitter?"

Her fingers froze on the keyboard. "What's wrong?"

"Nothing's wrong. I wanted to check on you."

Shit. Colin and his big mouth. "I'm fine."

"I talked with Liam last night."

Liam? Liam never ratted her out. He'd always been the one brother she could count on to treat her like a regular person.

"He mentioned that you're going out with Jimmy O'Malley."

Bullshit. She knew Liam never casually *mentioned* anything. "I am. So?"

"I like Jimmy, he's decent guy, but that whole family is a little messed up. Are you sure you want to get involved with him?"

"I've always liked Jimmy. He's a good guy. What's your problem?"

Ryan sighed. "Liam's worried and asked me to talk to you. He seems bothered by the idea of you and Jimmy dating."

"Uh-uh. I talked to Liam yesterday, and he was totally okay with it. I mean, there was the usual big brother crap you all spew out like robots, but that's it. What are you talking about?"

Nervous flutters churned in her stomach. Nothing ever bothered Liam. He was a live-and-let-live guy. He didn't butt in to other people's business. She sure as hell didn't understand why he'd go to Ryan instead of talking to her.

"Jimmy's his friend. If things go south, he probably doesn't want to have to choose between his sister and his friend."

"I wouldn't make him do that. If it doesn't work out, Jimmy and I would just avoid each other. Liam wouldn't be stuck in the middle." She toyed with the pens on her desk, lining them up like prison bars.

"Then maybe he knows something about Jimmy that you don't and he figures you won't listen to him."

This entire conversation made no sense. Why was she talking to Ryan if Liam had the problem? "Thanks for checking on me. I'm fine. I'm having a great time with Jimmy, and I'll deal with Liam myself."

"I'm pretty sure he wanted to avoid that."

"Too bad." She disconnected, but the irritation still flared in her chest. She was used to Ryan coddling her. But not Liam. She couldn't believe he'd gone behind her back to Ryan like he was tattling on her.

At least the event tonight would put her near downtown, so she could go to the restaurant and confront Liam at work. He'd be extra pissed because he hated to be interrupted while cooking, but that was too damn bad. He was lucky she planned to wait until after the dinner rush. And if the stars aligned for him, she might not make a scene.

Refocusing on the article on her computer, she pounded out paragraphs, fingers flying over the keyboard. She was tired of O'Leary men trying to run her life. She was capable of taking care of herself.

After a productive afternoon of writing, Moira stood and stretched. She poured herself another cup of coffee and glanced over at the TV while considering popping in a yoga DVD. Her body could use a good stretch, especially after sitting for so many hours. She looked longingly at her mug of caffeine.

Which did she want more—the coffee or the relaxed muscles?

Never good at making decisions, she decided she could

have both. She turned on the TV and slid the disk in. While it started, she chugged her coffee.

She liked it when she got everything she wanted. Something to remind Liam of.

LATER THAT EVENING, Moira felt accomplished. She'd not only done an hour of yoga, but she'd managed to go to the reception and interview people about the new collection at the library. Between the leftover calm from yoga and the quiet peacefulness of the library, she thought her conversation with Liam had a real chance of being civilized.

She drove to Porter's and pulled into the lot. Before leaving her car, she carefully considered her approach. With Ryan or Colin, she always had to run headfirst into a confrontation with all of her weapons drawn. She wasn't quite sure what to do with Liam because she couldn't recall a time when she'd had to fight him.

Too bad Liam wasn't married. If he was, she could call her sister-in-law and get the scoop. Moira realized how lame it sounded that she was wishing for a fake in-law because she didn't know what to do with her own brother.

Planning her argument wasn't going to work in this case. She needed to confront Liam and take her cues from him. Inside the restaurant, she asked the maître d' to seat her near the kitchen. When her waiter approached the table, she asked him to get Liam, and then braced herself for Liam to be pissed off. One thing he demanded from the family was that they never bother him at work.

But Liam worked crazy hours and she wasn't about to let this sit until they had dinner again as a family.

Her waiter brought her a glass of water and told her Liam would be out in a minute. While she waited, she looked around the restaurant. She'd been here before, not long after Liam had gotten the job. It was a high-end steakhouse with a nice atmosphere, but that was it. Nice was adequate.

Maybe she'd spent too much time eating and drinking with Chicago's high society. She didn't want nice; she wanted relaxed and fun. After walking in heels and a formal gown for hours, she'd much rather have gone to Colin's bar and bowling alley to relax. That is, if Colin didn't own it.

She never had too much fun with her brothers around. Which brought her full circle to her mission for the night. Liam.

"What's up?" he asked as he took the seat across from her. "You never come here."

So he wasn't pissed off. "I needed to talk to you, but I wasn't sure when you were off."

"You could've called. Then you'd know I'm off on Wednesday."

"This couldn't wait." She toyed with her fork and spoon. "Ryan called me today. He asked about me and Jimmy."

Liam said nothing. Figures.

"Why did you tell Ryan you were worried about me dating Jimmy?" She spoke quietly, hoping it would help Liam respond.

"Because I am." He leaned back in his chair and crossed his arms.

"We talked yesterday and you were okay with it."

He raised an eyebrow.

"You were!" Her voice jumped and she swallowed to calm herself. "Maybe you weren't excited about the prospect, but you certainly weren't demanding that I not see him."

"I know better than to demand anything when it comes

to you. You'd continue just to spite me." His voice and his posture were filled with steel.

"What's wrong? Jimmy's your friend, and everyone agrees that he's a good guy. Why wouldn't I want to go out with him?"

Liam leaned forward, placing his crossed arms on the table. "I've known Jimmy most of my life. He's a great friend, but you're not what he's looking for and he'll end up hurting you."

"What do you mean, I'm not what he's looking for? I'm a woman. I have a pulse. And I like him. What else could he want?"

Liam's face turned scarlet. His voice became a harsh whisper. "Obviously, he'd like to bang you. Long term, you can't be what he wants. And if you were, you'd never be happy."

"What the hell are you talking about? You're talking in codes and mysteries. Spit it out, Liam. What's Jimmy looking for that I can't be?" Her chest tightened as she waited for the anvil to crush her. For Liam to be this upset, Jimmy must be hiding one hell of a secret.

"He wants to marry a doormat, Moira. And I'll be damned if I'll let him turn you into one."

Moira opened her mouth to argue, but Liam's hand shot up. "I have to get back to work. I don't have time for a stupid argument. You need to trust me on this. He wants someone he can control, and that will never be you." He stood and carefully pushed in his chair. "I don't want to know what it would take for him to make you be that way." Liam kissed the top of her head. "Give me a call later this week and we'll have lunch."

Her mouth dried and the ability to form words fled. She

dropped a five-dollar bill on the table for the waiter and left. No way could Liam be right about this.

But how could he be wrong? Liam and Jimmy had been friends since elementary school.

She drove home without thinking about anything. Her mind was like snow, a fuzzy, white blur.

17

―――――

Moira woke the following day not feeling any better than she had when she'd crawled into bed. Instead of restful sleep, she'd been plagued by thoughts of Jimmy having ulterior motives. Liam said Jimmy was looking for a doormat, but he'd never treated Moira with anything other than respect. If anything, he was too...polite. Damn, she didn't even have an adequate word for him. It was more than courtesy.

If he viewed her as a doormat, wouldn't he have exhibited those tendencies? Granted, they'd only been on one real date, but she'd known him most of her life.

While she'd been at the reception and fighting with Liam, she'd forgotten to turn the volume up on her phone and she'd missed a call from one of the escort services. At least she assumed that's who they were. A very polite woman left a cryptic message about available appointment times and an address. No need to confirm.

She stood before her bathroom mirror and tried to make herself look presentable for an escort service. She wanted sexy business. Like the secretary every CEO wanted to fuck.

A black pencil skirt and a tailored white blouse showing a hint of cleavage. And of course, a pair of fuck-me pumps. She had no idea what an interview would entail, so she texted Kathy the address where she'd be just in case.

It was a system they'd developed when they went on dates in college. Always let someone know who and where. She got an immediate response.

An afternoon date? Go you!

She debated whether she should burst Kathy's bubble. Neither of them had been having much luck dating as of late, but she didn't like lying to her friend.

No date. Just a work interview that's a little shady.

Too bad. I've got your back, though. Can't wait to hear about the shadiness.

Moira finished primping and headed out. She rehearsed her story as she drove and prayed she didn't end up sounding like an actress spewing lines. She parked and hoped they'd validate because this story might eat her rent money. Suite 509. Nothing on the directory named the business located in 509.

The elevator zoomed up to the fifth floor and her stomach plummeted. Maybe her nerves would work in her favor. On five, the doors pinged open and she faced a small reception desk. A young woman greeted her with a wide smile.

"Hi, I'm Moira Donnelly. I have an appointment."

"Hi, Moira. I'm Lisa. I left you the message. Follow me, and I'll give you a quick tour." Lisa stepped from behind the desk. "We have a small office, but some girls come in to hang out and chat over coffee."

Moira wanted to see the coffee room. A good place to meet her interviewees, but she couldn't ask yet.

Lisa led the way down a short hall. She pointed to one

door. "That's the conference room. We hold meetings there occasionally." At the next door, she stopped and knocked.

"Come in."

Lisa pushed the door open and said, "Your one o'clock is here."

Moira followed and swallowed her surprise to see an older woman, maybe around sixty years old sitting behind the desk. For some reason, Moira never considered anything other than the images of young, beautiful women working here.

The older woman stood. "Hi, I'm Billie."

Moira felt like she was being put in an x-ray machine. She gulped and pushed out, "I'm Moira. Nice to meet you." She led with her hand extended.

Billie shook briefly and sat, so Moira followed.

"How did you get our number, Moira?"

"A friend."

"Does this friend have a name?"

Moira's lips tightened. She hadn't thought they would ask about how she found out about them. "Yes, but I'd rather not say."

The answer seemed to satisfy Billie because she settled back into the chair. "What do you know about what we do?"

"Not much. All I know is that you're an escort service for selective clientele."

Billie gave a short nod. "Why would you want to work here?"

"I just moved to Chicago. I followed my boyfriend here against my family's advice. After a month, he dumped me. I've tried working different jobs, but it's hard. A friend suggested I consider being an escort because I have the right attributes."

Billie leaned forward on the desk. Her sickly red lipstick

smudged unevenly on her lips. The wrinkles around her mouth didn't suggest happy laugh lines, just the leftovers of a hard life. Billie's gaze raked over Moira's body again, as if the first look hadn't been enough. "When was the last time you read a newspaper?"

"I read the online versions everyday."

"So you can carry on an intelligent conversation with a man? Something beyond tabloid headlines?"

Moira nodded. On this, she was sure of herself. "Give me a topic."

Billie flicked her finger over her mouse and glanced at the computer screen. "Syria."

"That's a pretty big topic." Moira inched closer, balancing on the edge of her seat and launched into a monologue about the most recent Syrian uprising.

Two minutes in, Billie held up a hand. "Okay."

Then she just stared at Moira.

Moira felt like she was sitting in front of her mother after breaking curfew when she was sixteen.

"Do you have any questions?"

"Yes." Moira's mind raced with ideas, but she knew she couldn't push it. "Is everything here legal?" She paused for a half second and then rushed on with, "I don't mean to imply anything, but we all hear stories and I don't want to do anything that will land me in jail."

"We provide a legal service."

That wasn't much of an answer. If everything they did was legal, why the secrecy? "How do you find your clientele? Do you vet them? How do you know that the next Craigslist killer hasn't just hired you?"

Billie let out a raspy chuckle. "There are no guarantees in life. People discover us the same way you did: word of mouth."

Moira played with her hands in her lap and hoped the next question wouldn't ruin it. "What am I expected to do on a date?"

"You're expected to dress appropriately for the date, usually on the formal side. These men are not looking to go to the movies. It's the theater, opera, et cetera. You need to be able to hold up your end of the conversation. You're more than arm candy; you're an actual date. In addition, there will be times when we'll have you attend a party or reception with a few other girls to work the room. Beyond that, anything else is up to you."

"How do I get paid?"

"The price is based on the length of the date and what the client expects. After the date, you'll receive payment from me."

"How often will I work?"

"You let us know when you're available, and as dates are needed, we'll contact you with the pertinent information. Some clients will specifically request you, and we'll do our best to accommodate that, if you're available."

Moira nodded, unsure if there were other questions she should ask. The thought of attending parties made her remember the mystery woman and all of the people who knew her as a reporter. "One more thing. You mentioned parties, so I was wondering if it would be okay for me to change my appearance."

"Why?" Billie's expression shifted, but she hadn't gone cold, more like she was intrigued.

"I've attended some parties with my stupid ex. I wouldn't want people to recognize me. I'm starting a new life and don't want to be associated with him."

"That's fine. Some of the girls have different personas

they take on depending on where they're going or who their dates are."

Air seeped from Moira's mouth in relief. She was afraid she'd gotten this far and had blown it.

"Well, Moira, I think you'll fit right in here. Are you interested in a job?"

"Yes, I think I am."

Billie stood and shook her hand again. "Go back out there, and Lisa will take your picture for our portfolio and get all of your information. Welcome aboard."

Moira tried not to wobble on her heels on the way out of the office. She shut the door behind her and leaned against the wall to take a deep breath.

From her station by the elevator, Lisa smiled. "How'd it go?"

Moira walked the length of the hall and said, "I'm supposed to see you about taking my picture and getting my information."

"Excellent." She stood again. "Come this way." This time, she walked around her desk and down the opposite hall, which wasn't much of a hall, more like a cubby with three doors.

One door stood open. Break room. Unfortunately, no one was there.

"It's early. Girls usually trickle in later in the day. Most prefer to have their dates pick them up here. That way, they don't have to drive themselves or give out their home addresses." Lisa turned the handle on the adjacent door. "This is a smaller office we use to take photos. Can I get you a cup of coffee or water or something?"

"Coffee would be great. Cream and extra sugar, please."

Moira sat at the small round table. Behind her were

photographer screens. Lisa returned with a Styrofoam cup of coffee and a high-end digital camera.

"We'll snap a couple now, but next time you're here for a date, we'll get some more of you all dressed up."

Moira nodded and stood. Lisa snapped on a few more lights and then positioned Moira. It was all a little surreal. After she took four photos, Lisa told Moira she could sit. She left the room again and Moira took a slug of coffee.

Lisa returned with a one-page information sheet. Moira began to fill it out. She used the address of O'Leary's Pub to be safe.

"If you want to come back later, I'll introduce you to some of the girls. They can give you the real scoop, like standing around the watercooler at the office."

Moira lit up. "I'd love that. What time?"

Lisa looked up to the ceiling as if calculating. "We have four girls booked tonight. Three of them have early dinner before a show, so if you come by around four thirty, they should be here."

"Awesome. Thank you so much." Moira finished filling out the paper and shook Lisa's hand. Getting her story didn't seem like it was going to be so difficult after all.

JIMMY STOOD on the outer edge of the conference room and stared at the group of men in front of him. Gabby stood by his side, surveying the same. She was the only woman in the room. The commander had developed a full-blown task force in the days since the victims had come forward.

Jimmy figured many of the men had probably come from vice since they had the whole escort angle. No one believed for a second the escorts wanted to sleep with these men for free. The men had probably been advised by their attorneys not to admit to sex for money.

The whole situation bugged him. Rich men hiring prostitutes and everyone was going to look the other way because someone had stolen from these men. He couldn't argue that the theft was the bigger crime. More than a hundred thousand dollars in jewelry had been stolen from the three households. All jewelry belonging to the wives.

Jimmy couldn't help but think that in addition to wanting the cash the jewelry would bring, the thieves also wanted to send a message to the men. And from what he'd observed, the men received the message loud and clear: stay with your wives and away from escorts.

The commander yelled for everyone to quiet down so he could brief them on the case. Jimmy only half listened since he'd been in on it from the beginning. Elks introduced the new players and named someone the head of the task force. He should've paid closer attention to that part, but he knew the man in charge would make himself known repeatedly.

Then Elks called Jimmy to the front of the room. He slid along the wall and felt everyone's eyes on him. When he got to Elks's side, he made eye contact with anyone looking his way. He wouldn't be looked down on because he was newer at this job than most.

"Detective O'Malley has been undercover for the past three weeks as James Buchanan. He's been introduced as a friend of the mayor and as a result has become acquainted with the victims. They are all now aware of his position, and in fact, it is partially due to his involvement that the men came forward." Elks paused and stepped to the side.

It took a second for Jimmy to realize that Elks wanted him to say something about the case. A little heads-up would've been nice.

"As Commander Elks said, I've been undercover, attending different society events. My partner, Gabby Ruiz has been posing as my wife so I can appear as much like the victims as possible. They are all wealthy and married with a roving eye. We were given a list of possible escort services to look into."

Another detective stood with a raised hand. "We have that. We've checked the numbers and cross-referenced with addresses and business licenses. We have locations and have sent officers to check things out. We don't want to rush in and spook them."

Elks stood forward again, so Jimmy stepped back. "The likelihood of the business being behind the thefts is small. We think it's a smaller group of escorts possibly working with more experienced thieves. We're going to get O'Malley set up with a property that looks like an easy target so we can catch them."

Someone in the back of the room yelled, "That means O'Malley has to convince a hooker to come on to him."

The room filled with laughter.

Elks raised his hands to quiet them. "Yeah, well, we're working on that too. Do we have any idea how the escorts are targeting these guys?"

The same detective, who had to be from vice, stood again. "We don't have evidence, but these shops target the Viagra Triangle. The Gold Coast has seen a large uptick in business this year. It's hard to crack down on it because so many of the hotels turn a blind eye, especially when palms are greased."

Viagra Triangle. Where had he heard that before?

Elks continued to outline the plan, and Jimmy's brain scanned memories. As Elks wrapped up, it hit him. Moira.

She'd made jokes about doing a story on the Viagra Triangle.

Damn it. Everything kept coming back to her. She'd said she wasn't doing anything to interfere with his investigation, but this sure as shit would get in the way. The room began to clear, and Jimmy stayed back, debating whether he should tell Elks about Moira.

What would he say? A reporter is working on a story about prostitutes on the Gold Coast? He had no idea what Moira was doing. He shook his head and decided to talk to Moira first. Then he'd decide what to do about it.

"Did you need something, O'Malley?"

The brusque question had him jerking his head up to look at Elks. "No, sir. Except I was wondering where we were going to get a mansion that would belong to James Buchanan."

"I have no idea. There's no money in the budget."

Jimmy thought of Griffin Walker. It was a long shot, but they didn't have much else. "I have an idea. A guy I kind of grew up with might have a place we could use."

Elks's eyebrows shot up. "Who's that?"

"Griffin Walker. We know each other through mutual friends. I know he recently moved to a house in Oak Park, but he might still have something in the city we could borrow."

Jimmy had never used personal connections for anything. Even when he first joined the force, he'd never used his father's reputation to try to get ahead. But this was different. In his gut, he felt like this case could propel his career forward, give it a jump start, rather than waiting patiently for years for things to click.

"Talk to him and let me know what he says." Elks picked up his files and left.

Jimmy turned and saw that Gabby had waited for him by the door. "I guess you get to be Mrs. Buchanan a while longer."

She cocked her head to the side. "Not really. In order for the thieves to strike, I need to be conveniently out of town, so I'll probably only have to appear with you a couple more times to make sure everyone in the world knows you're married. Then I'm off the hook and back to just being me."

Jimmy walked back to his desk and found the task force lead sitting on the edge of the desk. "Can I help you?"

The man extended his hand. "O'Malley, I wanted to personally introduce myself. Kittner. I wanted to make sure there are no hard feelings about me heading the task force."

Jimmy shook his head. "I didn't expect to be given lead. I don't have enough years on the job."

"Elks told me about this reporter who knows your cover. You grew up with her?"

This was not going in a positive direction. "Yeah. Moira O'Leary."

"She's been able to help?"

"She made a point of talking to me and Gabby in front of the guests to make it seem like we belong. She also gave us insight into the guests, some of whom turned out to be victims."

"Are you feeding her information?"

"What? No. When we approached her because she'd seen me on my first night as Buchanan, we agreed to give her the exclusive on the case if it developed into something."

"Have you seen her outside of the society events you attend as Buchanan?"

"Yes."

"In what capacity?"

"We're friends."

Kittner narrowed his eyes. The man might be in charge of him while on duty, but he had no business trying to tell Jimmy who he could spend his off hours with. "Do I need to explain the sensitive nature of this case? In my experience, reporters cause trouble."

"I don't discuss the case with anyone." Not really, not with actual details.

"Make sure you don't. I'm working on a list of events you'll be attending. Make sure you check with me before you go home tonight."

"Will do."

One more thing for him to worry about. After Kittner left, Jimmy tried to recall every conversation he'd had with Moira over the last few weeks. Had he given her any fuel? She'd said he'd inspired whatever she was working on. This wasn't looking good.

oira had checked her phone for the umpteenth time. Jimmy hadn't said when he'd call, just that he would when he was free. Her brain was so stuffed with ideas she felt like she'd burst and talking with Jimmy was top of the list. She'd had an entire day to think about what Liam had said.

While she never saw any indication of Jimmy's determinedness to find a doormat, Liam's reaction warranted a discussion. She needed to know what Jimmy thought they were doing. She knew he'd been hesitant about a relationship with her because of Liam, but she couldn't fathom that this was behind his thinking. She had a mountain of laundry to do, and she needed to go back to the escort service.

She loaded her dirty laundry in her car and called her mom to let her know she'd be stopping by later to use her machines. If Moira timed it right, she'd get dinner and a visit in with Mom and then be able to catch Jimmy when he got home from work. Sounded like a hell of a plan.

Still wearing her dressy clothes from earlier, she headed

to the escort office. When she strode in, Lisa greeted her with a smile.

"I'm so glad you came back. The break room is filled with girls. Also, we have a function Billie would like you to attend on Friday. Will you be free?"

"Uh…I think so, but let me check." She pulled out her phone and accessed the calendar. She was supposed to attend something, but she could skip it. One minor article for a blog wouldn't break her career, but getting the scoop on high-class hookers might take her to the next level. "I'm free."

"Excellent. Let me introduce you to Jenny. She'll be your partner for the night, and she has all the details." Lisa led the way to the break room.

Moira's palms sweat. It was just a room full of women. Why was she nervous? The minute she stepped into the room, she knew exactly why. It was like sixth-grade gym class all over. Every pair of eyes in the room swept up and down her body to measure her as competition. She forced the corners of her mouth up and widened her eyes and hoped it made her look more friendly than crazy.

Lisa made quick introductions and then left to man her desk and the phones. Jenny flipped her long blond hair over her shoulder and pointed to a chair, so Moira sat. The other women in the room returned to their own conversations.

"So," Jenny started, "we'll be partners on Friday."

Moira quickly wiped her hands on her skirt. "I'm sorry. This is probably a stupid question, but what does it mean for us to be partners?"

Jenny let out a quick little laugh and her dark blue eyes crinkled. "You really are a newbie."

Moira nodded.

"When we work a party, Billie sends us in with partners

in case of trouble. Sometimes a guy will get handsy, and having another woman there is backup. She can call Billie and let her know of a problem without causing a scene. Your partner is also there to get information about where you'll be in case a guest takes a liking to you." She crossed her long legs, and her skirt rode a little higher on her thigh.

"When Billie hired me, she said I would be paid to go on dates and that was it. Anything else was up to me. Working a party makes it sound like I'm expected to sleep with whatever man wants to."

"Oh, God, no." Jenny leaned forward, one elbow balanced elegantly on her knee. "Billie's clients all know the score. They can look all they want, but if they want more, it's the woman's choice. Billie sends security to each party, so there's backup for our backups. If you choose to extend your date, Billie needs to know who the guest is, so she can bill appropriately."

Waves of overwhelming nerves cascaded over Moira. She didn't know if she could pull this off.

Another light laugh from Jenny. "You look like a semi ran over you. Don't be nervous. It's just a party. Talk to the men, maybe dance if there's music. That's all Billie requires."

She could do that. She did it every week as a reporter. Well, maybe not the dancing part, but talking to people was her specialty. "I have a quick question. I talked to Billie about changing my appearance for the parties. If I'm on a one-on-one date, I'd go like this, but I've attended some social functions with my ex, and I wouldn't want him or his friends to recognize me. Any suggestions?"

"Get yourself a wig. Your hair is going to be a selling point for many men, but it also makes you stand out. Maybe spray-on tan and new makeup. Trust me, most men won't get beyond the hair color."

"Okay."

"I'll meet you here at seven. Eat a decent dinner before, but nothing that will bloat you. Cocktail dress. During the party, limit yourself to one drink. Drink it slowly and then switch to water. Billie will square up with you at the end of the night, unless you make other arrangements to extend a date. In that case, you can stop by here on Monday and she'll pay you." Jenny glanced at her watch. "I have to get going. My date will be here in a minute."

Moira stood. "Thanks for all your help. I appreciate it. I kind of expected everyone to be catty and mean."

"There's no need. As long as you don't try to poach someone's regular, there are plenty of dates to go around."

"Thanks anyway." Moira watched her leave. Although Jenny had been very helpful, there was no way she'd be a source for Moira's article. Jenny was too together and appeared to enjoy the job. She needed to find a weak link, someone who would talk freely and not get suspicious.

Three other women, each dressed to the nines sat around the small table chatting. Another woman stood by herself by the sink, cradling a cup of coffee. She wasn't dressed as nicely, so Moira made the assumption she wasn't on her way to a date.

"Hi, I'm Moira."

The woman nodded, although now that Moira got a closer look, she appeared much more like a girl.

"Piper. Nice to meet you."

"Have you worked here long?"

The corners of Piper's mouth turned down for a second and she said, "A few months."

"Do you like it?"

"Way better than other places I've worked. Billie's fair, and anytime you want to stop by for a cup of coffee, her door is open." Piper held her cup up.

"You came here just for coffee?"

Piper smiled. "I came to pick up my pay. Billie was busy, so I grabbed a cup." She dumped the rest of the contents and washed out the cup with a dab of soap and couple of quick swishes of a rag.

When she turned back, Moira said, "I'll walk out with you."

In the hall, they waved at Lisa and stepped on the elevator. Once the doors closed, Piper said, "A little heads-up, one new girl to another. Watch your back with Jenny. She's nice, she knows what she's doing, but she'll steal any guy you have on the line."

"She just finished telling me that there were plenty of dates to go around."

"There are, but she wants first pick."

Moira laughed. "I like you. Can I buy you a cup of coffee?"

"I just had a cup."

"I meant some other time. Billie said I should talk to some of the other girls to get the scoop, and you strike me as a straight shooter."

The elevator stopped on the first floor and they stepped out. Piper pulled a card from her pocket. "Sure. Give me a call. Right now, I'm free on Thursday and Friday, but that could change."

Moira turned the card over in her hand. Was she supposed to have business cards? "Thursday would be great. I'll give you call."

Piper waved down a cab and Moira walked to the lot. Next time she'd park at a meter. It had to be cheaper.

Moira drove to her mom's house and ran different scenarios in her head. While she did her laundry, she tried to figure out how she could change her look for the party on Saturday. Maggie had her coloring, except for the hair, so maybe Moira would get a brunette wig. And new makeup. Then she realized Jenny hadn't given her information about where they were going, only that they'd meet at the office.

Her mother made small talk about work she wanted to get done around the house, and Moira helped her make a list. Ryan and Colin would be thrilled. Every time Mom mentioned paying someone to do something, they jumped in, sure she would get ripped off. They ate dinner and Moira thought she was going to escape personal questions, but she never had that kind of luck. Eileen always had questions.

"You're dating Jimmy O'Malley?"

Moira rolled her eyes. "Who told you?"

"It should've been you. When did this start?"

"A week or two ago. We've only been out twice, kind of."

"Kind of." Mom sniffed. "What man takes you on a *kind of* date?"

"We had a real date at a carnival Sunday. Before that though, he had to work late, so our plans fell through. He came over to my apartment and we watched a movie."

Her mother's stare bothered her almost as much as Liam's anger. *What's with this family?*

"I expect a man you know through Liam to offer more than showing up to take advantage of you. He should still be putting in the effort."

Moira pushed the food around on her plate, no longer hungry. "He's not taking advantage, Mom. He came over to apologize and he'd had a bad day, so I invited him in."

"Is it serious?"

Moira dropped her fork, unable to pretend anymore. "I

don't know. I haven't had the chance to find out because everyone in this family is trying to push me away from him. He's a good man, damn it. What the hell is everyone's problem?"

Her mother's eyes blazed at her language, but she couldn't care. She shoved away from the table and brought her plate to the kitchen. After giving herself a moment to calm down, she returned to the dining room. "I'm sorry I swore and yelled at you."

Eileen nodded. "I know you've always looked at that boy with stars in your eyes. I want to make sure he's not taking advantage."

Her language was crisp with a bit of an edge, and if she listened closely, Moira could hear the hint of the brogue, which meant Mom was angry.

"I'm not a starry-eyed kid. I'm a grown woman and I still like Jimmy. I don't know where our relationship will go, if anywhere, but it should be up to us to figure that out."

"You're right. A mother can't help but worry."

"Can you tell my dumb brothers to back off?"

Eileen smiled and stood to clear her plate, but Moira took it from her.

"I'll get you a cup of tea. My laundry should be about dry, so I'll be heading home." In the kitchen this time, she found a little peace. If Mom understood her need to do this on her own, there might be some hope for her brothers. She put the kettle on the stove and went to the basement to pull her clothes from the dryer. By the time she had them folded, the kettle was whistling.

She poured her mom's tea and delivered it to the living room. As she carried her laundry basket to the front door, Eileen's eyes focused on the clothes on top.

Jimmy's clothes.

Moira followed her mother's gaze. "We got caught in the storm Sunday night, and he gave me a sweatshirt to wear home." No need to mention the fabulous orgasm he'd also given her. "I'm going to drop it off now."

Her mother simply nodded and turned on the TV.

Moira lugged the basket to her car and slid it into the backseat. Pulling Jimmy's sweatshirt and the T-shirt he'd given her at the block party, she scanned the street for his car. He was home.

She closed her car, remembering to lock it just in case Jimmy quizzed her, and headed across the street.

A HEADACHE POUNDED behind Jimmy's eyes on the way home from the station. He didn't like Kittner's implications. When he walked in the door, Kevin was sitting on the couch with their dad, watching a ball game. They each had a beer.

"Did you test your blood?"

"Yeah, yeah. It's fine."

Jimmy knew that brush-off answer. He gathered the test stuff and shoved it at his father. "It's not fucking fine. We've been over this."

Seamus grumbled but pricked his finger. Surprisingly, the test came back normal.

"Ha," Seamus shouted. "Now get outta the way. The Sox are gonna win this one."

Kevin pushed up from the couch and followed him into the kitchen. "What bug crawled up your ass?"

"Nothing."

"Right. My guess would be a sexy, little redhead."

Jimmy grabbed a beer from the fridge and looked at Kevin. "What are you talking about?"

"Dad told me you're going out with Moira."

Jimmy didn't answer. He hadn't wanted to deal with his family about Moira. Not now. He went to walk around Kevin to go upstairs, but Kevin grabbed his elbow.

"Of all the fucking women you could go after, why her? You know I've liked her for years."

Jimmy snorted. "She can't stand you. It was never going to happen. Besides, my relationship with Moira is complicated."

This time, he did push past, but Kevin yelled, "Bullshit. You're either going out with Moira or you're not."

"I am, but..."

"But what? You're just looking to fuck her? It's nothing serious like every other girl you've ever had? Shit, I could get behind that. In fact, when you're done, maybe I'll get my turn."

Jimmy turned back to face Kevin, rage boiling. "Shut the fuck up."

"Are you really into her?"

He wanted to punch Kevin for talking about Moira like she was nothing more than a piece of ass, but he had no idea what they were to each other. The last person he wanted to talk to about Moira was Kevin. "I'm undercover and she's part of the assignment. I don't want my cover blown."

"I'm sure you want something blown."

His fist cocked back, but a sharp intake of breath caught his attention and he dropped his arm. He spun and saw Moira standing in the living room in front of his father, who wore a smirk. Her mouth hung open for a second and he saw the hurt in her eyes. It lasted exactly one heartbeat and then her eyes narrowed and color rose in her cheeks.

"Thanks for clearing that up." Her voice was tight, too

controlled for her. She tossed some clothes on the couch. "Those are the shirts I borrowed."

She turned on her heel and slammed the door. Kevin chuckled behind him. He set his beer on the table and shot a dirty look at his father who had obviously let Moira in and thought the situation was funny.

Jimmy ran out the door and called, "Moira."

She was at her car across the street, yanking on the door handle. Then she pressed the button to unlock it.

"Moira. Stop."

She looked up at him, stark anger in her bright eyes. Then she got behind the wheel and peeled out.

"Fuck." He fumbled for the keys in his pocket. By the time he got behind the wheel of his car, Moira was nowhere in sight. His hands gripped the steering wheel, muscles in his hands tight to the point of almost cramping. He forced his fingers to loosen.

While at a red light, he pulled out his phone and called her. No answer. He hoped she was going straight home. He had no clue where else to look for her, and he needed to fix this. As he drove through the streets, he wondered how much of his conversation with Kevin she had heard. She'd definitely heard him say she was nothing more than work for him. If she heard everything Kevin had said, he didn't know if he'd be able to smooth that over.

Kevin had a way of pissing her off just by breathing. For as long he could remember, he'd had to force Kevin to apologize to Moira for one thing or another.

When he pulled up in front of her apartment, her car was there, and he released a relieved breath. He went to her apartment and knocked, but she didn't answer. He waited, hoping that she wasn't ignoring him, and then knocked again. Then he tried the knob. Locked.

At least she listened about something.

He knocked again, a little louder this time. "Moira, open up. I know you're in there. Stop acting like a kid and let me in so we can talk."

"I have nothing to say to you."

She was right on the other side of the door.

"I have things to say."

"No one's stopping you. Talk to your heart's content. Knowing you, it'll be short."

Her ride home hadn't taken the edge off her anger. Jimmy rubbed a hand over his head. He didn't know where to start, but he was sure that he didn't want to be in the hallway. Bracing a hand on the door, he hoped she was still there when he said, "I wasn't ready to talk to my family about us. Especially Kevin. I didn't know what to say to him."

The lock clunked, and he removed his hand a half second before she tore the door open. "How about 'I'm dating Moira. I like her'? Would that have been so painful?"

"When it comes to Kevin, yeah. Can I come in?"

"Why? People might get the impression you actually *want* to be around me."

He shoved the door wider, forcing her back with his size, and closed it behind him.

She sputtered for a moment and then said, "I didn't say you could come in."

"You didn't say no either. You were too busy with smart-ass comments. I do want to be around you and you know it."

"Then why lie to Kevin? That's bullshit. I've been killing myself to defend our relationship to my family, and you can't even admit we have a relationship. I deserve better than that."

Her words struck him, and he stepped back until he was against the door. "What? Defend what to who?"

"Us. My family has questioned whether I know what I'm doing and if I really want to get involved with you. Liam was actually pissed. He doesn't get mad about anything."

"Shit." His shoulders sagged. He'd wanted to believe her when she'd said Liam wouldn't care. Jimmy should've talked to Liam himself before he even thought about a date with Moira.

"That's your only response?"

Right now, Moira was the priority. He straightened from the wall just as she pulled back to hit him.

He snatched her arm at the wrist and pulled her into him. She was breathing hard and her chest collided with his torso. She pulled back her other arm to swing, so he caught it and held both arms behind her back. Her eyes blazed and her nostrils flared.

She was so fucking hot when she was mad.

He lowered his head and kissed her hard. She fought against him for a minute, but then her lips softened. In her stubbornness, she refused to participate in the kiss, though. He moved his mouth to her ear. Her hair fluttered with his breath and she shivered.

"I lied to Kevin because I didn't want him to know about us. I wanted to keep this for myself. I want you so fucking much I can't think straight."

Moira stopped struggling in his grasp, but he didn't turn her loose. Using her bound arms to push her forward, her soft flesh pressed into him. "You've been tormenting me for longer than I can remember. Sunday night my cock was so hard it hurt. I jacked off in the shower thinking about you. Smelling you on my hand."

Her shoulder twitched with another shiver and her

breath quickened again. She swallowed hard and he pressed a kiss to the pulse on her neck. "I want you every time I see you."

"So show me," she rasped out.

She tugged her hands, and this time, he released her. She stepped back and started unbuttoning her blouse. Her eyes were hot with lust instead of anger now. She licked her lips, and when he groaned, her fingers fumbled on a button. He'd seen the bared skin before when she'd been in a fancy dress and again when he ripped her dress open, but it was no less erotic this time.

He stepped closer and she retreated. She wanted him to watch, but she wasn't moving fast enough for him. No man had enough control for that. He reached out, using his size to his advantage again and tugged her closer. His fingers curled in the waistband of her skirt to hold her in place and his other hand yanked the blouse free.

She finished opening the last two buttons and shrugged out of the shirt. It slid soundlessly to the floor.

Jimmy kissed the white freckled skin above her bra and trailed down to her waist. He knelt in front of her. His hands went to her thighs and shoved the skirt up. He could smell her arousal as he pulled her panties down. With them removed, the patch of red curls was revealed and he brushed his fingers over her mound.

Her hands came down on his shoulders abruptly and her fingers dug in with every slight stroke. He spread her lips and flicked his tongue against her, tasting her, savoring her. Shouldering her thighs wider, he ran his tongue down her seam and she moaned. Her thighs trembled, so he shifted her entire body to make her lean against the wall. Her shoulders thumped against the wall as he lifted her knee over his shoulder, giving him better access.

Her pink center was warm and wet. After a couple of swipes of his tongue, he sucked on her clit, drawing it into his mouth. Her body jerked and then settled against him again when he pressed his tongue inside her. Her gasps and moans urged him on. His teeth scraped gently across her sensitive flesh causing another little jump.

He licked and sucked until she went up on tiptoe as if to escape while pushing at his head to keep him on target. He sank two fingers into her and stroked while his tongue focused solely on her clit. A string of *ohs* and *fuck yeahs* and *oh my gods* rang in his ears. Her hips bucked and her thighs trembled. Her walls tightened on his fingers as she came. He pulled them out and replaced them with his tongue tasting her juices as she rode the waves of her orgasm.

When her body began to calm, he pulled his face away and wiped at his chin. He kissed her inner thigh and it twitched. He held her in place with his hands on her hips mostly to hold her up, but also to ground himself as he looked at her. He'd thought she was beautiful after she came in the backseat of his car, but that was nothing compared to this.

19

Jimmy pressed his body against her, and it felt like it was the only thing keeping her upright. The orgasm had shaken her so hard that she felt boneless. Her entire body tingled and trembled at every touch. Jimmy's hands moved to her breasts and rubbed at her nipples through her bra. Everything was so sensitive it almost hurt.

"I don't think I can take any more," she whispered weakly.

He tilted her chin toward him and waited until she made eye contact. "You wanted this. You wanted me to show you and I'm not nearly done."

The power of his words shot through her and she shivered. He crushed his mouth to hers, and she tasted herself on his lips, mixed with the taste of Jimmy. That alone was enough to turn her on again. His tongue, that magical, talented tongue plunged into her mouth, and his hands dove into her hair, gripping tightly.

Everything Jimmy did, he accomplished with gentle forcefulness that made her want to surrender. He made love to her mouth. She couldn't remember the last time she'd been kissed so thoroughly.

"I'm taking you to bed now." His voice was gruff and hoarse with need.

Smiling, she said, "Give me a minute so I can regain the ability to walk."

"I don't have another minute. I need to be inside you now."

Then he scooped her up. He actually picked her up and carried her to her bed. Of course she knew he was a big guy; he towered over her. But never in any of her dreams had she thought about him using that brute strength to carry her to bed. It gave her a little rush.

He placed her on the bed and while he stripped down, she reached into the drawer of her nightstand and pulled out a condom. She set it on the bed beside her and wiggled out of her skirt, taking her pumps with it. Then she unclasped her bra to set her breasts free. Jimmy had gotten his shirt and pants off, but when he saw her breasts, he groaned and dove at her. He still wore his boxer briefs and his erection pressed into her leg.

"These are amazing," he said as he palmed one breast and sucked the other nipple into his mouth.

His mouth, now that was amazing. She arched into him. The slow ache began to build in her again. With barely moving his body off her, he managed to get his underwear off. He kissed her hard and insistent as he lay between her legs.

Jimmy stroked her cheek and asked, "Is anything off limits?"

The question startled her. Was there?

The look on her face must've revealed something

because he muttered, "Shit. You're not a virgin." He said it with just a hint of question.

She laughed. "No."

"Is there anything I can't do to your body?"

She stared into his eyes and felt it through to the center of her being. "I don't think so."

He leaned his forehead to hers. "You're killing me here." Inhaling deeply, he levered himself up a bit and said, "If I do anything you don't want, you have to say so. Okay?"

Her eyes were wide and her imagination sped through possibilities. She'd read about enough kink that a flood of thoughts blipped by. She swallowed hard and a thought hit her. "Wait." It came out sharply and he froze, muscles taut. "Don't pee on me."

He burst out laughing and collapsed on top of her. He weighed a ton, but feeling his hard muscles and long limbs surrounding her was delicious. His laughter filled the room, breaking some of the tension, and she felt her own giggle rise. "I didn't think it was that funny."

Pushing up on his elbows, he looked into her eyes, his smile filling his face. "I don't think I could do that right now even if I wanted to, which I don't."

She laughed at the ridiculousness of what she'd said. He quieted her with another searing kiss and her mind emptied of all thought. Her legs curled around his hips.

He kissed her neck and pushed her legs away. A whimper bubbled up in her throat. If he backed away again, she was going to cause some serious bodily harm. He chuckled and said, "I've waited too long for this. Don't rush me."

With some men that would be an empty promise. With Jimmy, she had no doubt he would deliver. He explored her entire body, touching, squeezing, kissing, and licking. Every time she moved to touch him, he gently removed her hand and held it for a minute.

Using his hands, he brought her to the brink of orgasm again and managed to hold her there. Her mind swirled out of control and her body moved instinctively to find release. Jimmy, however, continued to toy with her.

Finally, she croaked out, "Jimmy, I can't."

"You can and will."

She closed her eyes and grasped at what little sanity she had left. That's when she heard the condom wrapper. Finally.

She waited for the glorious pressure of his body pushing her into the mattress, sinking into her. But it didn't happen. He'd pulled away again and massaged her thighs, his thumbs working their way up. He touched her, caressed her, but didn't enter or touch her clit. She thrust her hips up, but he used his forearms to hold her down.

Then his sweat-slicked body was on top and gliding into her. One long, strong stroke and he buried himself. The shock startled her and her intake of breath was sharp.

His gentle, slow motions disappeared and he hammered into her at a frantic pace, but the collision of their bodies was needy and fulfilling. She bucked up to meet his thrusts, planting her feet flat on the bed beside his hips. Her fingers dug into his shoulders.

He thrust his hands under her shoulders and pulled her entire body to him. The bed shook and slid into the wall. Their faces were barely an inch apart, their breath mingling, sweat dripping, flesh slapping.

The ache in her was gone, replaced by a tight coil of nerves, and when Jimmy shifted, the orgasm ripped through her. She climbed onto him, wrapping her arms and legs around his body, every muscle strained, riding the wave of the orgasm. Jimmy released a guttural groan and went rigid.

Moira didn't know what happened, but she couldn't breath, couldn't see, couldn't swallow. Somewhere in the recesses of her brain, she registered that Jimmy had slowed his pumping to a final few jerks of his hips, but she couldn't feel her limbs. She told herself to move, respond, but her body wouldn't listen.

"Holy fuck," Jimmy said. He lifted off her body.

Her arms and legs slid away from him, totally useless. Her brain finally came back online as he rolled to the side. With him gone, she became cold, but her body was too exhausted to even shiver. From the corner of her eye, she saw Jimmy's chest still heaving. He didn't say anything, but reached out and held her hand.

She fell in love with him all over again. It was stupid, starry-eyed kid stuff, so she closed her eyes. She didn't want him to see. His weight shifted on the bed and she knew he was getting up. He kissed the back of her hand before letting go.

"You okay?"

She forced a swallow and licked her lips. "Uh-huh."

Without opening her eyes, she knew he left the room. She felt the absence of his buzzing energy. Jimmy had imprinted himself all over her. She rubbed her hands over her face and into her hair. She struggled against heavy muscles to sit up and open her eyes. Glancing down at her body, she saw no signs of a difference, a change caused by Jimmy, but she felt it.

He came back into the room and studied her. "What are you thinking?"

Knowing she couldn't explain what she'd been searching for, she returned to her flirtatious roots. "I was thinking you asked about things that might be off limits, leaving my imagination to wander to all sorts of depraved things, but as amazing as that sex was, it wasn't kinky."

He smiled and sat beside her. "I wanted to be up front about expectations. Tonight was about getting to know your body."

"What else did you want?"

His face became serious and he kissed her. On her lips he whispered, "Everything."

The word settled heavily in her brain and in her chest, but she refused to acknowledge its weight. "Will you spend the night?"

He lowered his eyelids. "I can't tonight. I have something I need to take care of."

She tried not to feel disappointed.

"I would, but this can't wait."

"Who says *I* can?"

"You'll have to." He bent over and pulled on his underwear.

"Can I ask where you're going and what you have to do?"

"You could, but I won't answer."

She shifted away from him, but he caught her wrist. "You need to accept that there are things I won't talk about. My job tops that list. I'll never be accused of oversharing."

"Fine, but don't get mad at me when I withhold information, too."

Laughter burst from him again. "You'd explode if you couldn't share. You don't know how to keep your mouth shut."

She swung her arm to thump his shoulder, but he caught it and held it over her head as he pushed her back into the mattress. His laugh faded into a sigh as he kissed her. His lips were still curved in a smile and Moira's heart floated. As much as she liked the strong, silent, brooding Jimmy, happy Jimmy was a crap ton of fun.

His free hand trailed down her neck, across her collarbone, and down to her breasts. "I have plans for these."

"If you expect me to wait, I suggest you get off me now, or I might be tempted to use your handcuffs to keep you here."

He stood, sliding away from her body. "Tease."

She watched as he stepped into his pants. His muscles bunching and twisting. He pulled on his shirt and started to button it. "Stop staring at me like I'm dessert."

"I bet you're a tasty treat."

He closed his eyes and shook his head. "Come lock me out before you make me forget I need to go."

"Fine." She stood and pouted, having lost the battle of getting him to stay.

Jimmy stepped into the hall and stopped. "Put on a robe."

"What? I'm going to lock you out and then I'm going to take a shower. I don't need a robe. You've seen it all."

He pointed across the living room. "I prefer for your neighbors not to see it all."

She rolled her eyes. "I'm on the third floor, Jimmy. Unless there's a giant out there, no one is seeing anything."

He still didn't move, so she gave in and grabbed her robe from behind the door. As soon as the satiny material kissed her overly sensitive skin, she thought about the last time Jimmy had seen her in the robe. It was the first time he'd gotten close to her and she'd been sure he was going to kiss her.

Satisfied she was covered, Jimmy walked toward the door.

"That first night you came here..." She followed his foot-steps slowly.

Jimmy paused at the door.

"When you wanted me to lock up. Were you going to kiss me?"

His shoulders tensed and she was sure he wouldn't answer. He turned and grabbed the belt of her robe, pulling her into him. "Not only did I want to, but I almost did. It's a sexy robe. Not to mention having a jar of wax thrown at me was extra hot."

He gave her a brief kiss and walked out the door. "Lock up." He knocked once and she locked it behind him.

In the silence of her apartment, smelling of sex and feeling satisfied, her brain went back to Jimmy's statements earlier. What did he mean when he said he wanted every-thing? More importantly, could she give it?

Jimmy walked to his car and checked the time. If he drove fast, he'd make it before Liam left work. As much as he didn't want to, he had to have the conversation that should've taken place before laying a hand on Moira. He drove into downtown and parked down the street from the restaurant. Before getting out, he checked his reflection in the rearview mirror. He hoped he looked the same instead of like a guy who just got laid.

He walked to the restaurant's lot and found Liam's car. He waited, growing impatient, when restaurant employees began filing out the back door. Some gave him a look but they said nothing. Jimmy heard Liam's voice before he saw him. Liam said good-byes and headed his way. When he saw

Jimmy, there was a hitch in his step. "What are you doing here?"

"I need to talk to you. Want to grab a beer?"

Liam shoved his hands into his pockets and shook his head. He stepped closer.

Jimmy blew out a breath. Liam knew the reason for his visit and now he wanted to make him squirm. He rubbed at his head and searched for the words. He'd always been honest with Liam. No reason to change that now. "I slept with Moira."

Liam jumped, and his fist connected with Jimmy's jaw before he saw it coming. The punch knocked him back a step, but Jimmy regained his balance and put up his arms in defense. He didn't want to fight Liam, but he refused to get his ass kicked. Liam already dropped his fist, so Jimmy rubbed his sore jaw.

"What the fuck, Jimmy? You could have any woman. Why Moira?"

"I don't know. She does something to me, man. I can't explain it. I've stayed away from her for a long time, but this case has put her in my path time and again."

Liam's eyes narrowed. "What do you mean you've stayed away?"

"Shit, she caught my attention when she was a teenager. I felt guilty as hell thinking about her like that. She was a kid. *Your* kid sister. So I steered clear of her."

"So you're going to fuck her and then what? You're going to hurt her and I'll fuck you up. Friend or no."

"She's more than a fuck, and she's not a kid anymore, Liam. This was as much her decision as mine. I have no intention of hurting her." He leaned against Liam's car, absorbing the conversation.

"Rarely do people intend to hurt someone. What do you

think is going to happen? She's going to walk away from her career to sit around the house waiting for you?"

"I don't know what's going to happen. We're figuring things out. I care about her."

Liam paced in a tight circle. "Don't do this."

"It's already done. I'm not asking your permission. I was just informing you." This conversation headed downhill fast. Who knew it could get worse than his friend leading with a punch?

"Then there's nothing left to say. Get off my fucking car." Liam approached with his keys in hand.

Jimmy said nothing, but he stepped aside. Liam would be fine once he cooled down. With any luck, that would happen before Liam rushed off to the other O'Leary boys to send a mob to his house. He walked back to his car.

With the euphoria of amazing sex subsiding, Jimmy could think, but he didn't like where the thoughts headed. Liam had a point. How did Moira fit into his life plan?

She was definitely the married, settled down with kids type, but she had a career she not only liked, but was good at. She was in the middle of striving to take her career higher. He remembered her excitement in talking about her new story.

Which reminded him that he was supposed to learn more about the story to make sure he didn't get into hot water at work. He didn't have a shot of thinking about work when Moira was warm, wet, and willing in his arms. He pushed thoughts of a naked Moira from his mind and focused on how he could learn about her article. A casual conversation over dinner should do it.

And if by chance, she was too close to the investigation, he'd tell her to back off before his superiors found out. No problem.

Moira slept soundly and woke in a storm of mixed emotions. She and Jimmy were a couple. Excitement and anticipation trickled through her as thoughts of Jimmy bombarded her every move. No matter what she did or where she moved, she thought of him. As she walked out of the bathroom after brushing her teeth, she stared at the wall where he licked her until she came. In the living room, she saw the couch and remembered snuggling against him while watching a movie together. Her front door reminded her of being wrapped around him as he tore her clothes from her body.

It didn't matter that they'd only actually had sex once; she began to imagine going all the way in each of those scenarios. And Jimmy was phenomenal in every scene.

She dressed and loaded her laptop into her bag. Work was so not going to happen in her apartment today. She'd work at the coffee shop, and hoped that once she had more of Jimmy, she'd be able to function like a regular human being.

The late morning air was cool, a nice change of pace from the sticky humidity they'd had for days, so she walked to Starbucks. After ordering her coffee and finding a comfy chair to work in, she shot a text to Liam. He'd said that he was off on Wednesday, and given this new development with Jimmy, she needed to get things straight with Liam.

She didn't expect to hear from him for a couple of hours because he liked to sleep in on his days off, so she booted up her computer and sipped on her sweet brew. Before starting any new articles or proofing things she needed to submit, Moira spent time gathering her thoughts on the escort services she'd called.

In a new file, she took notes about Billie and Lisa and Jenny and Piper. They all seemed like totally normal people, like regular people she might meet and interact with on an ordinary day. Part of her article should address the perceptions people have about escorts. That got her wondering about the clients. Would they be considered johns? Probably not unless they had sex for money, but most of the girls seemed to act like that was a given.

How desperate would she have to be in order to have sex for money? If she didn't have her family to fall back on in hard times, would she have considered it? Letting her mind wander to the what-ifs was not going to get her work done, so she closed the file and opened the articles she needed to proof one last time.

Proofreading was by far the most boring part of her job, and her mind continued to wander, but it didn't go to hookers.

Jimmy starred in every image and thought.

Moira always liked the new lust and fascination stage of a relationship. The way the feelings consumed her and energized her was intoxicating. Everything with Jimmy was exponentially potent, and even as she reminded herself that she was in public, heat crept into her cheeks and hormones surged.

Then her phone rang, drawing her attention. Liam. "Hello."

"Where do you want to meet for lunch?"

"You still sound pissed off, so maybe you should pick."

"Choosing where we eat isn't going to make me feel better. Why don't you head over here and I'll cook?"

"You cook all the time. Today's your day off. Let someone else do the work."

"I love what I do, so it's not a chore. Besides, cooking relaxes me, which might work in your favor."

She sighed. Why she thought she'd be able to lay down the law to any of her brothers eluded her. No matter what, she'd always be their little sister. "Fine. Want me to bring anything?"

"Nope. See you in an hour or so." Then he hung up.

She wasn't used to Liam acting like this. He'd always supported her against their brothers, and a sinking feeling settled on her. What if he couldn't accept her relationship with Jimmy? What then? She couldn't go there. Not now. Cutting the legs off a relationship that had barely started was not her style.

Refocusing on the article in front of her, she forced her attention to stay on the words on the page. At least until her phone rang again. She considered ignoring it, but then she saw it was Jimmy. "Hey."

"Hi. What are you up to?"

"I'm at Starbucks working."

"Why there?"

"I was too distracted in my apartment. But then I discovered the distraction followed me and it's really hard to focus." She toyed with her cup and felt foolish for being so happy that he'd called.

"If it makes you feel better, I'm off my game today, too. I was calling to see if you're free for lunch."

She winced. For once, she planned something and now she'd miss out on a better offer. This was why she liked to keep her options open. "Sorry. I'm having lunch with Liam."

"Shit."

"What?"

"I saw Liam."

"When?"

"Last night. After I left you."

She stopped playing with her coffee and straightened in her chair. "You left my bed to go hang out with my brother? We might need to talk about your priorities."

His breath was heavy and strained in her ear. "Liam had a right to know that we've taken our relationship to the next level."

She closed her eyes tightly and asked the question she didn't really want the answer to. "How did he react?"

"He punched me."

"He what?" Her voice rang out across the room, and five people looked up from their work bubbles to observe the commotion.

"I had it coming. You're his little sister. He's mad, but you know Liam. He'll cool down and be more rational."

"That would've been good information to have before I made plans to see him for lunch. He's still pissed." She dropped her head onto her hand.

"Are you regretting last night?"

"Not for a second," she mumbled. It was the truth. No amount of grief from her family would make her regret sleeping with Jimmy.

"Is there anything I can do?"

"No. It's time for my brothers to accept they can't decide who I have in my life or who I choose to sleep with."

"Good luck. Are you free for dinner?"

"If I'm still alive, sure."

"I'll pick you up at six."

"What should I wear?"

"Whatever you want." He paused and then added, "Nothing too sexy. I want to make it to dinner."

"Grubby sweats it is then."

"Sweatpants are easy access—no buttons or zippers. Just slide them down."

Christ. How did this man make sweatpants sound sexy? Her breath quickened because she imagined him doing just what he said.

"Makes quite the picture, doesn't it?"

"Get out of my head, O'Malley. I'll see you at six."

He chuckled softly as she hung up.

She finally finished proofing the article in front of her and submitted it. Then she packed up her computer and prepared for lunch with Liam.

20

———

Liam's apartment was tidy. An odd word to describe a man's apartment, but it was the first one to come to mind whenever she visited him. Moira attributed it to the fact that he worked crazy hours at the restaurant, but today, she suddenly realized the space was devoid of Liam. He had the barest essentials for living room furniture. Nothing comfortable and inviting, just utilitarian.

His kitchen, on the other hand, was amazing. Here was the color and luxury and decadence. He didn't say anything as he chopped vegetables and dripped oil into a pan.

And Moira knew better than to start a conversation. Other than a perfunctory greeting when he let her in, Liam was in his zone. A radio mounted under the cabinet provided his sound track. As he worked, mouthwatering smells filled the air and the tension in his shoulders visibly eased.

She figured the act of cooking produced the same results in him as eating brownie à la mode did in her. She snagged a carrot and crunched while watching.

Liam in the kitchen was fascinating. She had no idea

where he'd gotten his love for food, but she was glad he did. Many times over the years, he took over everyone's cooking chores. All he asked in return was for someone else to do the dishes.

After she'd been there about fifteen minutes, about the same time the silence started to get to her, Liam began humming along with the radio. It was a bubbly pop song, and she knew he managed to release a good portion of his anger through the knife in his hand, the same way she'd pound on her keyboard in a flurry of words.

This was why she was closest to Liam. They were a lot alike. Beyond the physical attributes of red hair that their siblings had all dodged, Moira and Liam created. They used different tools, different media, and produced different results.

But they understood each other.

She sat at the counter and waited, knowing the food was almost done. Liam plated the food, chicken with some sauce and veggies, and even though it was just the two of them, he made it look pretty. If she were in charge, the food would get slopped on and passed around. He carried both plates to the kitchen table so she followed.

Many discussions in their family occurred at the table over food. It somehow made things less threatening. At least that's what she wanted to believe. Her previous boyfriends who had been brave enough to come to an O'Leary family dinner might disagree.

Moira tucked into her food quickly, afraid she'd lose her appetite once Liam starting talking.

"Jimmy came to see me last night."

"So I heard."

"Did you send him?"

She laughed and almost choked on her chicken. "Hell

no. Why would I? He didn't even tell me. He just said he had something to do."

Liam went to the refrigerator and pulled out a couple bottles of water, handing her one. The cool liquid soothed her throat and she continued to eat.

"I told you Jimmy was a bad idea."

She shrugged. She didn't come here to fight with Liam.

"He's going to hurt you."

"How can you be so sure? I've spent time with him, and he's never shown any sign of treating me badly."

"What the hell do you see in him that you can't find in some other guy?"

She shot him a devious look. "Besides his smokin' hot body?"

Liam's face crinkled in disgust. "Don't go there. I've known Jimmy long enough. I've heard his stories. I don't need to imagine you starring in any of those accounts."

If Liam hadn't been her brother, she totally would've pumped him for more information. She'd love to know more about the mystery of Jimmy O'Malley. "Look, Liam. I know you worry about me, and maybe it's a little weird for me to be with your friend, but I like him. We connect and it's...wow. I haven't felt wow in a long time."

"You're looking for the whole package. Jimmy's not it. You're wasting your time and his."

"There are worse ways to waste some time."

"I'm not going to change your mind about this, am I?"

"Not unless you can offer some compelling reason I shouldn't go out with Jimmy. You've given me nothing concrete. A strange foreboding isn't enough."

Liam seemed to go back to his irritated self, but stopped talking long enough for them to finish their lunch. Moira took her dish to the sink and rinsed it before filling the dishwasher.

Liam joined her and began wiping down the counter and stove. "Jimmy is looking to settle down with a wife who will wait on him and raise their children without having a life of her own. He's determined to find a wife who won't work outside the home."

The comments gave her pause for thought. She remembered overhearing Jimmy's conversation with Liam at the block party, so she kind of knew that.

Liam touched her shoulder. "Are you ready to give up your career to have Jimmy? And even if you were, what if it doesn't work out? Then what?"

"Then I guess I move myself and my brood of kids in here to keep you company so you can support us all." Her joke wasn't met with a smile.

"I'm serious, Moira. You've worked hard to build your career. What happens when you walk away from it?"

"Jimmy and I have barely started dating. We haven't discussed the future." But Liam's points crawled into her brain and took root. Would she be willing to give up her career for the marriage and family she wanted?

"Maybe you should've had that conversation before sleeping with him."

"He told you we had sex?"

"That's why I punched him."

"Did it make you feel better?"

"A little." He threw the sponge in the sink at the same time she closed the dishwasher. "I asked him to back off, and he refused. Said it was too late."

Her heart fluttered a little. So maybe she wasn't the only one defending their relationship. She hugged Liam hard. "Thanks for worrying about me, but I'll be fine."

"Famous last words."

She left Liam's apartment feeling slightly less anxious. Her family would probably never stop worrying about her and there was nothing she could do about it. Instead, she'd focus on her career and her budding relationship. Life was good.

THE ENTIRE SITUATION was fucked up. Jimmy sat at his desk and hoped to avoid Kittner for the remainder of the day. The man had felt the need to point out to Jimmy again that allowing Moira access to information on the investigation would be problematic for everyone. Jimmy took that to mean Kittner would hang him out to dry if something went wrong with the case.

Jimmy put in a call to Griffin Walker to ask about any property he might have in the city he might allow them to borrow. It was a long shot to even ask, but Jimmy wanted to put in the effort to make this case.

He'd built a rapport with the mayor. High profile cases could go either way and make or destroy a career. His father had stayed away from anything that would draw attention. Seamus was a nose-to-the-grindstone, head-down, and do-the-job kind of guy. Nothing wrong with that, but it limited the advancement opportunities. No one would offer a hand up if they had no idea who you were.

In that respect, Jimmy wanted to be known. He wanted to be the guy who could get things done. If Liam wasn't pissed at him, he would've asked him to call Griffin. Griffin was tight with the O'Learys and would probably do the favor if Liam asked.

The task force was split up, tackling different aspects of

the case. Some built victim profiles they would use to incorporate into James Buchanan's life. Some worked diligently on discovering what they could about the escort services Stan Decker had alerted him to.

Jimmy was the only one without a specific job. He didn't want to sit around pretending to be James Buchanan. He left the station after a quick good-bye to Gabby. He needed to go home and talk to Norah. The girl hadn't told anyone what she planned. She was obviously having the baby at this point, but she sat in his room every day, leaving only to eat.

Waiting in his personal life didn't sit any better than in his professional life. He walked into the house and froze. The living room was clean, smelling of pine cleaner. The hockey equipment that usually piled in front of the door was stacked neatly. He crept into the living room, unsure what to expect.

There was Norah, checking Dad's blood. Without seeing the number, Jimmy knew it wasn't good based on the look Norah gave him. Then she swiped the bottle of beer from their father. "If you can't take your meds and monitor your shit, you can't have beer."

"Give me my beer, girl. You can't tell me what to do."

Norah straightened, planted one hand on her hip, and pointed at him. "I might not have been around much, but I know what I'm talking about. If you don't start doing what you're supposed to, I will dump every beer in this house. I grew up without a mother. I'm not about to lose you too because of stupidity."

Their dad grumbled but stopped arguing.

Jimmy stood dumbfounded. He'd gotten so used to Norah slouching around, in near tears, not really speaking, that he'd forgotten how bossy she could be. With the exception of her bulging belly, she looked like she did as a toddler when she would stomp her foot and demand the world revolve around her.

"Hey."

Norah spun and threw her hands up. "You need to deal with him. He doesn't listen to anything."

"Tell me something I don't already know." He looked around the living room. "The house looks good."

"Well, someone had to clean it. Men are pigs."

As much as he wanted to argue, he couldn't because he hadn't had time to clean and Sean and Tommy never lifted a finger. "Thanks."

She shook her head and walked into the kitchen.

He followed, digging into his pocket for the information he'd gotten from Gabby. "Here," he said, thrusting the paper at her.

"What?"

"I found a doctor for you. You have an appointment tomorrow morning. Luckily, they had a cancellation."

"I don't need you to make doctor appointments for me. I'm not a child." She scrubbed the table as she talked.

"You're pregnant. You've been here for a couple of weeks and have barely left the house. Have you ever seen a doctor?"

She nodded. "Back in Boston."

"You're here now, and you didn't seem like you were moving forward. Go to the appointment."

She nodded. He was surprised she gave in so easily.

"Do you know what you're going to do once you have the baby?" He leaned against the refrigerator to stay out of her way while she cleaned.

"I don't know. It's just so overwhelming. I don't know if I'm ready to be a mom."

"What about the father? Have you called him yet?"

"No. But I will. Soon. As soon as I figure out what I want."

The strength he'd heard in her voice when she yelled at Dad had disappeared. Jimmy wondered what it was about her ex-boyfriend that made Norah shrink back.

She dried her hands on a towel and leaned against the table. "I appreciate you giving up your room. I was thinking that if I sort through the crap in the spare room, I could buy a bed and move in there."

"No hurry. The couch isn't so bad." Plus, he planned on spending some nights at Moira's. He liked the thought of waking with her in his arms.

"Where did your mind go just now?" Norah prodded.

"Nowhere."

"I call bullshit. You were all stern and serious and then it kind of melted away. I don't believe for a second that it was because you want to give up your bed for me. Who were you thinking about? The hot redhead?"

"None of your business, Squirt. I'm going to shower and change. Then I'm going out. Thanks for keeping an eye on Dad."

She smiled and the whole room brightened. Jimmy smiled back. He didn't know how not to. His baby sister was finally on the mend.

MOIRA STRAIGHTENED up her apartment and hoped Jimmy planned to spend the night. He'd texted earlier to make sure everything had gone okay with Liam and to make plans for dinner. She'd changed the sheets on her bed and put on a cute summer dress. Then she tucked all of her research notes into drawers so the chaos wasn't quite as noticeable.

Jenny had called her with the details for the party they were attending on Friday. It was the same one she was supposed to report on, and she thought she might be able to do double duty. She definitely had to change her appearance because if people recognized her as a reporter, it would ruin her chances for getting the scoop. Plus, she didn't really want people she knew to think of her as an escort, even if it was just for a story.

Pushing work from her mind, she lit a couple of candles and waited for Jimmy. She knew she didn't need a whole seduction scene, but she hoped to convince him to eat in and hang out at her place. She wanted to have him all to herself.

When the knock sounded at the door, she reminded herself to check the peephole instead of ripping the door open, even though she knew it was him. She opened the door and he handed her a bouquet of mixed flowers. Hmmm...a guy who brought flowers. Jimmy was checking off items on her keeper list without even trying.

"Thanks. This is a nice surprise. In my world, a guy only brings flowers when he's fucked up and needs to apologize."

Jimmy halfway smiled. "This is an apology. How did things go with Liam?"

"As well as could be expected."

She went to the kitchen to put the flowers in a vase. As she reached over her head into the cabinet, Jimmy let out a low whistle telling her just how short her dress was. Her inner diva gave a self-satisfied smirk. "Liam thinks you're going to hurt me because you're looking for a wife who will stay at home and be at your beck and call."

Jimmy winced. "For the record, I don't expect beck and call service, but I do want a wife who will stay at home with our kids."

He got points for honesty instead of brushing it aside.

"I explained to Liam that we haven't gotten to that point in our relationship." She paused. "I can't believe you told him we had sex."

"I told you I talked to him."

She slapped her hand on the counter beside the flower arrangement. "You said we were taking our relationship to the next level."

"After dating, sex is the next level."

"But he's my brother. You could've shown a little more tact." She leaned forward and buried her nose in the bouquet.

"He's also my friend. I never thought about censoring myself."

She moved away from the flowers and stepped on tiptoe to kiss his cheek. "You also never dated his sister before. New game, new rules."

His arm circled her waist, pulling her closer. "Where do you want to go for dinner?"

"We can order in."

He grunted in her ear and kissed her lips. His hands found the hem of her dress and inched it up. She curled her calf around his.

"I like the way you think. Pizza will give us a good forty-five minutes."

She laughed and stepped back to grab her phone. "What do you want on it?"

"Something with meat." He wrapped his arms around her again.

She turned in the circle of his embrace and tried to focus on talking to the pizza guy. Jimmy made it increasingly diffi-cult by nibbling on her neck. She breathlessly rattled off her address for delivery and tossed the phone on the counter. "Forty minutes," she said as she faced Jimmy.

He captured her mouth again and she sighed. She ran her hands over his head, allowing his soft hair to bristle against her palms. Lost in the heat of his body exchanging breath with him, Moira melted as he deepened the kiss.

21

Moira studied herself in the mirror and wondered if the dress she wore was nice enough. Piper had texted that she should dress for a date, even though they planned to meet for coffee. The cocktail dress would work for most dates, she assumed. Her idea of a good date was shorts and gym shoes for riding the Tilt-A-Whirl. Remembering her first date with Jimmy brought a blush to her cheeks, which wasn't entirely unflattering.

Screw it. Her dress would have to do. She wasn't good at auditioning repeatedly. Billie had hired her, so she must've done something right.

She checked the time, and a stab of panic hit her. She had to hurry and pray for no traffic on her drive into downtown. Shoving her keys into her clutch purse, she rushed out the door.

Forty minutes later, she stood in line to order coffee and kept looking for Piper. She ordered a grande with a double shot. As much as she enjoyed having Jimmy spend the night, she needed an extra boost of caffeine to keep going, and it was only four in the afternoon. It was probably good that she'd told Jimmy she had work to do tonight.

Piper strode through the door wearing expensive jeans and a glittery top. Not quite what Moira would consider a date outfit. The barista handed her a cup and she went to join Piper.

"I thought you said dress for a date."

"I did."

Moira pointed at Piper's jeans.

"You need to be ready for a date because I'm giving you my client for the night."

Moira's heart leaped into her throat and she couldn't swallow. For a moment, she forgot to breathe. She wasn't ready for this, a date where a man might want her to have sex. She took a gulp of hot coffee hoping it would dissolve the lump so she could talk. The scalding her tongue received earned her a few seconds to think as Piper laughed at her.

After Piper ordered, Moira regained her ability to form words. "What do you mean, date?"

Piper shrugged. "I talked to Billie and told her I thought Mr. Lee would be a good initiation into the business."

Moira walked slowly to a table and sat, waiting for Piper to get her coffee and offer an explanation. In the meantime, Moira focused on how to respond. Piper was being generous to give up a paying job, but Moira hadn't quite thought this through. She'd believed she had time to develop a plan. She already knew the type of clients the service catered to; Moira just knew them in a different setting. For her, the escorts were more interesting. She wanted to know what made them take this job.

Piper sauntered over. Long legs leading out from swaying hips. She was the kind of woman who had men stopping to look at her. She flipped her hair over her shoulder and pulled out the chair across from Moira.

"So this date..." Moira started.

"Mr. Lee has been a client of mine since I started. He's a good guy. He's old and wants a beautiful woman on his arm for a fancy dinner."

"Just dinner? That's it?"

"Yeah. I like the old guy. If you can make it through a date with him, you'll ace Friday night. The men at the party will be younger and smoother. Mr. Lee will let us know if you come across as plastic."

"When is this date supposed to happen?"

Piper glanced at her watch. "About an hour. We'll walk over to the office, and Mr. Lee will pick you up there."

"Won't he be mad if he's expecting you?"

Piper crinkled her nose. "He's my regular, but he some-times gets another girl if I'm busy. He'll be okay with it, unless you screw it up."

"Okay." Moira sipped her coffee. She could do this. Dinner was no big deal. "Do you like working for Billie?"

"Yeah. She's fair and she runs a clean operation. I mean, stuff happens, but Billie never forces you to take a date with a guy you don't like, and she vets the guys pretty well."

Moira didn't want the sales pitch; she wanted the nitty-gritty. "What's the weirdest date you've ever been on?"

"Shoot. That's a pretty long list." Piper narrowed her eyes and looked up. "Lots of kinky weird stuff, but the weirdest had to be a woman who wanted me to take a guy out and spend the night at a hotel with him. She paid me five grand to keep him happy for the night."

"What do you mean, some woman? I thought all dates came through Billie." An idea caught in the back of Moira's brain, like an itch she couldn't quite scratch. She was on to something.

"This was after a party Billie had sent us to. A guy was hitting on me pretty hard. When he went to refresh our drinks, this woman talked to me. She had twenty-five hundred on her, with the promise that if I could convince this guy to take me to a hotel, she'd meet me the following morning with the rest."

"Wouldn't Billie get mad about that?"

Piper shrugged. "Some girls work for more than one service, so I didn't see the problem."

"How did you know the woman would show?"

"I didn't, but I was late with rent, and the twenty-five hundred would make me straight. I wanted the rest, but if I didn't get it, no big deal. But I did get it. First thing the following morning, the front desk called and let me know I had an envelope waiting for me. Some people are into weird stuff. I figured she was setting her husband up to either get off because things weren't good in the bedroom or get caught because he was a cheater. I half expected someone to be taking pictures while we were fucking."

Moira almost choked on her coffee. Piper talked about being a prostitute in a regular conversation as if it wasn't illegal and no one would think anything about it. Moira glanced around to see if anyone was eavesdropping.

"Chill out. You don't have to screw a client if you don't want. But if you do, a bit of advice. Don't expect earth-shattering orgasms. Think like a porn star. You're there as a tool to get them off. Anything you get is bonus." She finished her coffee and tossed the cup.

Moira had had some lousy, selfish lovers, but she always held out hope that things would improve. She supposed if she viewed it as a business transaction, the disappointment would be kept at bay. Her mind wandered briefly to Jimmy. After the way he'd handled her last night, she could never view him as a simple transaction. And she'd come to expect an excellent roll in the hay.

Jimmy's intensity made her shudder. How would he react if he found out about this date? Would he accept it as part of her work, much like being James Buchanan was part of his?

"What are you thinking?"

"About a guy I'm seeing. How he would react if he knew I was doing this."

"There is nothing to be ashamed of. We're providing a service. Would you be ashamed to be a cook or waitress who serves food to a man who can't cook? Of course not. These men don't have time to play the field and the games that go along with dating. They just want a woman on their arms when they go out." Piper tilted her head to signal it was time to go. "Besides, the boyfriend will feel like a god after he makes you come because a client didn't."

Moira widened her eyes at Piper's comment. The woman talked much too loud in a public place, which was saying something coming from Moira.

"Shoot, it's a good thing Mr. Lee will be your first. You blush much too easily." Piper led the way out of the coffee shop.

They walked briskly down the street, dodging pedestrians who were leaving work. Revolving doors on each office building spun spilling businessmen into the street. Everyone talked on phones or into Bluetooths. The flow of bodies reminded her exactly why she preferred to work from the comfort of her apartment. She might never have the income these people had, but she'd never have the stress either.

At the next corner, Piper stopped and pulled out her phone. "You don't need to go up to the office unless you want to. You can shoot Billie a text from the door when Mr. Lee shows up. He'll have a driver who will open the door for you."

"How will I know it's him?"

"It'll be a limo." She glanced down the block. "In fact, that might be him now." She typed quickly on her phone. When it buzzed back, she said, "Yep, that's him. Go forth and have fun. When you get back, it'll be early enough that Billie will still be here and she'll pay you."

Moira turned to go but asked, "Why are you giving up your work? Don't you need the money?"

Piper lifted one shoulder. "I'm okay. I think everyone needs a break, a hand up. Pay it forward kind of thing. See you tomorrow night."

"Thanks." Moira hustled down the block as quickly as her heels would allow. When she stopped in front of the building, the driver standing at the limo nodded to her and then stepped back to open the door.

Moira walked carefully over, not quite sure what to expect. What she saw was a bit of a shock. When Piper had said Mr. Lee was an old guy, Moira figured she was talking about a man in his fifties. Mr. Lee had to be pushing seventy. His fluffy gray and white hair ruffled in the breeze the open door let in.

"Mr. Lee?" she said in the sweetest voice she knew how to project.

"Get in, girl. We have a reservation."

She started a little at his sharp tone, but she slid into the limo. The leather cooled her bare skin, which was warm from both the weather and the quick walk. "Hi, Mr. Lee, I'm Moira. It's nice to meet you."

He eyed her up and down and nodded. "You got a brain in that head?"

"Yes, sir."

"Don't call me sir. I ain't your daddy."

She smiled at his frankness.

"Pretty smile. Did you go to college?"

"Yes, s—to study journalism." She didn't feel the need to lie. She figured the closest she came to the truth the easier it would be.

The limo pulled out into traffic, and she relaxed against the seat a little. Mr. Lee appeared to be a harmless old man, if a bit on the cranky side.

"We're going to a steakhouse for dinner. Do you have any *special* requirements?"

He sneered the question, so she knew her answer had better be no, so she shook her head.

"I don't abide by people who refuse to eat food, all vegetables or no bread or tofu crap. I never understood why people can't just eat."

"Well, studies have shown that a balanced diet is healthy. Too much of anything isn't good. Moderation is what most people haven't figured out, which is why obesity is an epidemic in American society."

Mr. Lee snorted. "People are just plain lazy."

"I can't argue."

THREE HOURS LATER, the limo pulled up to the curb in front of Billie's office again. Moira's stomach was full and her cheeks were sore from smiling. She actually enjoyed her dinner with Mr. Lee. Of course he wasn't the type of man she would ever think to date for real, but she would've spent that time with him for free, and yet she was getting paid for it.

She went up to see Billie and collect her money. As she peered down the hall, she noticed a couple of girls chatting over coffee, and as much as she wanted to pump them for information, her body was too tired and her brain too busy. She'd thought her story was going to be about these filthy married men who cheated on their wives with hookers, but it was so much more.

Lisa called out as Moira headed toward Billie's office. "Moira, I have your pay here."

Moira pulled up short and doubled back. Man, her feet were killing her in these shoes. "Thanks, Lisa."

She didn't want to be tacky and open the envelope in front of her, so Moira stepped back onto the elevator. The thought of walking back to her car made her cringe, but the prospect of walking down the street barefoot wasn't any more appealing. The route back to her car took twice as long because of her slow pace, but it allowed her to think about something Piper had said.

We're providing a service.

Tonight, with Mr. Lee, she believed that. If she hadn't gone on a date with him, he probably would've spent the evening alone. Didn't everyone deserve to have company and an enjoyable evening out? So many people were lonely, and Mr. Lee simply had the means to pay for some company.

Was this how prostitutes convinced themselves that what they were doing was okay? She arrived at her car and sighed as she sat behind the wheel. Driving through the city to get home, Moira let the ideas turn over in her head. The more she thought, the more she realized this story had the makings of something really great, if she could just find the right angle, the right focus. If she did the proper legwork, she could create a series of articles. One would focus on the girls working as escorts, another on the men who hired them, and then the third, Jimmy's case. A featured series would definitely get her name recognized. With that on her résumé, she'd be able to sell articles almost anywhere.

She pulled up next to her apartment still in a daze trying to figure out the next move for her story. Her feet screamed as she walked into the building. What she wouldn't do to have an elevator right now. Instead, she took off her shoes and trudged up the stairs. As she rounded the landing, the sight before her made her heart skip a beat. Jimmy sat leaning against her door, looking as beat as she felt.

"Hey," she said.

"Hey."

"What are you doing here? I told you I had a work thing." The incomplete truth tugged at her.

"I wanted to see you." Jimmy's gaze ran the length of her. "You look amazing. No shoes?"

She dangled the shoes from her fingers. "My feet are killing me. Too many hours in these damn things."

He levered himself against the door and stood. "How about a massage?"

She thought of where a foot massage would lead and couldn't withhold the hum in her throat. He took the keys from her and opened the door.

22

Jimmy pushed the door open into the living room, and when Moira walked past him, he grabbed her and pulled her into a kiss. He meant for it to be a quick hello kiss, but his tongue had other ideas. Once he tasted a little of her, he immediately wanted more.

But tonight he had a mission. He needed to talk to her about the story she was working on. So with his hands on her hips, he pushed her away from him. "Why don't you go take a quick shower? I'll grab us a couple of beers and find something on TV."

"Want to join me?"

He sighed. If he got in the shower with her, he'd never get to the damn conversation. "Not tonight." He kissed her nose and turned her body toward the bathroom.

In the tiny kitchen, he grabbed the beer and a bag of chips and took them to the living room. Her apartment was blessedly quiet. One of his favorite things about spending time at her place—besides being with Moira—was the quiet. He'd lived with his dad for so long, he'd forgotten how quiet a home could be.

With the sound of the water running in the other room, he flicked on the TV and flipped through channels looking for something Moira would like. He settled on some old black-and-white movie on AMC.

He settled into the corner of the couch and drank his beer. Moments later, the water turned off, and he sincerely hoped Moira would return wearing something more than the short little robe she favored. When the bathroom door opened, steam billowed out and she rounded the corner wearing shorts and a tank top.

Thank God.

Her face scrubbed clean of all makeup made her look even younger. She smiled and sat near the center of the couch, stretching her legs to set her feet on his lap. As if he would forget offering a foot massage, she wiggled her toes to get his attention. He took another swig of beer and then touched the cold bottle to the arch of her foot to mess with her.

She jerked her foot away with a yelp. "That wasn't nice."

"Couldn't help it." He put his bottle down and began to rub her feet.

She leaned back, closed her eyes, and sighed. "That feels so damn good. I think every woman who has to wear heels should have a personal masseur waiting when they get home."

"I can be your personal masseur." The words slipped out, and then he thought about the implications. Was he willing to be here every day?

Moira reached over and grabbed her bottle of beer. "You never told me why you're here."

"I need to talk to you about the story you're working on."

"I thought we agreed talk of work was off limits."

She started to tug her feet away, but he held fast to her

ankle. He rubbed his thumb down the arch of her foot, and a look of pleasure stole across her face.

"My boss thinks I've fed you some information that will interfere with our investigation."

"You haven't. In fact, you've been pretty damn tight-lipped since early on, when you weren't even sure if it was going to be a case." She drank from her bottle.

"I need to know what this other story is that you're working on. When we went to the carnival, you said you had me to thank for it. You're doing a piece on the Viagra Triangle. What exactly are you doing?"

"I can't tell you."

Tension tightened his shoulders. Why couldn't she make this easier? Moira normally talked nonstop. The one time he needed her to talk, she decided to clam up. "Why?"

"I have a whole host of reasons. The first being that you'll be pissed off and I don't want to ruin a perfectly good foot massage." She said it with a smile as if she could lighten the conversation.

"How about I keep massaging even if I get pissed off? I need to know."

This time she did pull her feet away and stood. "You don't need to know. You want to know. Why?"

"I just told you."

"And I told you my story isn't part of your investigation. Why can't you trust me?"

Why couldn't he trust her? He had no easy answer. "You're a reporter."

"So? Do you treat every reporter this way? Do you go to the newspaper and grill the journalists to see what they're working on? No, of course not. But because you know me, you want information. Why?"

"I have to know with certainty that your story will not clash with what I'm working on."

"How about you tell me all about your case and I'll verify that we won't clash?"

The frustration grew and he stood. "What's the big fucking deal about telling me about the story, Moira? Since when do you keep anything a secret?"

"I shouldn't have to justify my work or my decision not to share that work." She paused, staring at him. "I think it's time for you to leave." She crossed her arms, bracing for a fight.

He didn't know how to respond, so he walked out. He stopped briefly in the hall to wait for the click of the lock. Satisfied when he heard the snick, he stomped down the stairs and out to his car.

By the time he started the engine, he was grinding his teeth. He had no idea what to tell Kittner. He wanted to believe Moira wasn't doing anything that would interfere, but he couldn't be sure. However, he did know he hadn't given her any details.

He thought about how he'd approached the situation to see if there had been a better way. A way that wouldn't have gotten him thrown out. Maybe if he'd lulled her with the massage a little longer or waited until she drank more of her beer. He'd come on pretty strong.

If she'd come at him like he'd done, he'd be pissed. But he was a cop trying to solve a crime. She was a reporter.

In that moment, he knew he was as guilty as everyone else in her life of not respecting her job.

Shit. He'd screwed the pooch on this one.

By the time he pulled up at home, he was feeling guilty.

He hadn't given Moira's career much thought. He didn't actually know what she did. In truth, he saw her much as everyone else did: a partygoer who slapped some words on a page. Which was completely unfair to her.

Inside the house, he slipped into his room and grabbed his laptop. In the dark quiet of his living room, he stared at the glowing screen as he searched and read articles Moira had written.

They went on for pages. Her name appeared on blogs, in magazines, and in newspapers.

By two in the morning, he had a new appreciation for what she did. Her words did more than tell the story of rich people at parties. She managed to make him laugh, tug at his heart, and in some cases, make him want to pull out his wallet.

She definitely did more than type letters on a screen.

Now he needed to figure out how to show her he understood that. He stared at his phone. Moira usually stayed up late working, but he had no idea if she'd still be up. He sent a text. You awake?

She answered with a quick yes, so he called and hoped she wasn't still so pissed off that she wouldn't answer.

"Why are you up so late?" she asked instead of saying hi.

"I could ask you the same."

"I'm almost always up late. It's a good time to work. Plus, I was too cranky to sleep."

"Sorry." He took a breath. "I'm awake because of how I handled things. I got caught up reading all of your articles. They're really good. You've been writing real stories for a long time."

"Yeah, my party attendance makes for excellent reading."

"Don't." It came out harsher than he had planned, but he despised when she put herself down. "You're a good writer. I'll admit that until tonight, I didn't pay attention to what you do. But it's more than just parties, so don't belittle it. Be proud of what you do."

She was so quiet he thought he'd lost his connection.

Her voice was small when she asked, "You really read them?"

"I've got the bleary eyes to prove it."

"Why?"

"Because I realized after we argued that I was doing the same thing as everyone else. Treating you like your job doesn't matter."

"Compared to a job like yours—"

"Stop. If you want people to respect what you do, you have to take it seriously first. You flit through life acting like nothing matters, but when I read your articles, I heard your voice and I knew that it all matters too much. Instead of talking about the parties as your job, which I know you don't even like all that much, tell people about the causes and charities. They'll listen." Again, she became so quiet, he was sure he'd angered her. She never liked being told what to do. "You there?"

"Yeah. I'm just stunned." There was a slight creak in her voice. "You're pretty amazing when you do more than bark orders or speak in one-word answers." She sighed instead of laughing. "All jokes aside, thank you."

"Don't tell anyone or you'll destroy my image."

"Don't think that's possible, O'Malley." She paused again. "Good night, Jimmy."

Jimmy went to sleep hoping Moira understood his position, that he wasn't trying to hold her back from her career. He needed her to be safe and away from his investigation.

But as he dozed off, Liam's voice bounced around his brain. He couldn't imagine Moira walking away from her career. Moira was such a twist in his life plan that he no longer knew what to expect. Could he learn to live with her having the career she loved if it meant he could be with her every night?

AFTER HER ARGUMENT WITH JIMMY, Moira worked on her notes for the article because she couldn't sleep. She wasn't even sure why she fought with him. She'd never been secretive about her work, but this felt different. And part of her deep down knew he'd be mad, not because her story interfered with his case, but because of what she was doing to get the story. He'd given her an opening when he called and apologized, and she probably should've taken that chance to tell him.

But he didn't ask about her story again, and it was the last thing on her mind after he talked about how good she was at her job.

Of course, all the arguing and talking and not sleeping meant she overslept, which led to her running around like a maniac all day trying to prepare for her evening.

She shopped for a new dress, makeup, and a wig, and by the time she got home, she began to doubt every purchase. Unfortunately, Kathy was busy working on a big wedding order, so Moira called Elizabeth for help.

Elizabeth arrived with a confused look on her face. "Why do you need help getting dressed for a party? Don't you do this every week?"

Time to bite the bullet. "It's complicated, and I'm going to explain it to you, but you have to promise not to tell Colin."

Tossing her purse on the couch, Elizabeth cocked one eyebrow. "How bad is it?"

"Not that bad, but if you tell him, he'll tell everyone else and my brothers will all freak out. It's a work thing and they won't like it."

"I agree conditionally. If I think you're being unsafe, my promise goes out the window."

"Fair enough. I'm working on a story about high-class escorts and the men who hire them. In order to get the inside scoop, I applied to work at an escort service."

"You did what?"

The alarm on Elizabeth's face was priceless, and Moira immediately knew her brothers could never find out. She decided the best course of action would be to spill the whole story. "I'm not going to actually be a prostitute if that's what you're thinking. Some escorts really only go on dates. I went on one last night. Tonight, I'm going to an event with a few girls to work a party. The problem is, it's an event where people might know me, so I can't look like myself."

Elizabeth leaned against the arm of the couch, like she needed to absorb the information. "Why am I here?"

"Because I need help to not look like me."

Elizabeth waved a hand. "Wait a minute. You said you went on a date? What does Jimmy think about all this?"

"He doesn't know. We agreed not to discuss work because he doesn't want me digging into his case. In turn, I refused to give him details about what I'm working on."

"And you think Colin will be the problem? From everything I've heard about Jimmy, you'd better think again."

Moira rolled her eyes. As if Elizabeth was telling her something she didn't already know. "Are you going to help me, or what?"

"Of course I'll help, but you need to give me all of the details about where you're going, and you have to promise to touch base with me so I know you're safe. Otherwise, I call in the cavalry."

"No problem." She'd been planning on texting basic details to Kathy as always for backup. "Now make me look like someone new."

Moira led the way to her bedroom where she had her new purchases.

"Brunette, huh?"

"There's no way I can stay a redhead; it's too distinctive, and I thought going dark would be fun. Do you think it was a bad choice?"

"I don't know. Let's try it on and see."

Moira pinned up her hair and fit the wig on her head. She looked in the mirror and thought she looked like a kid playing dress up. "This is never going to work."

Elizabeth circled her. "Don't give up yet. You're looking a little ghostly right now. The dark hair is too harsh for your skin, but makeup can fix that. Sit."

Moira plopped on the bed and relaxed in Elizabeth's capable hands. They'd only been friends for a couple of months, but Moira trusted her. Plus, Elizabeth was one of those women who always looked put together even when she wasn't trying.

After what felt like hours, Moira looked at herself in the mirror again. It was her, but different. Her family would recognize her—probably—but the guests at the party would have no idea who she was. She looked like she had a gorgeous tan, which was impossible with her fair skin. She burned every summer, and when the burn faded, she went back to being white.

"What do you think?" Elizabeth asked.

"I think you're amazing. I can't believe you did this with

makeup. Where were you when I was sixteen and dying to hide my freckles?"

Elizabeth laughed but sobered quickly. "Are you sure this is something you want to do?"

"Yeah. It's going to be a good story. Some news outlets have skimmed the surface of the escort trade among the rich, but no one's had the inside scoop."

"It doesn't sound like the kind of stuff you usually do, though, so it worries me."

For someone who wasn't a big sister, Elizabeth definitely had the routine down.

"The whole idea of me getting this story is that it *is* different. It's not some fluff piece everyone tosses aside." Moira picked up the dress from the bed and held it against her chest to make sure it would look right with her new appearance.

"And then what?"

Moira shrugged. "I'm not sure. I want this story, though."

Elizabeth heaved out a sigh. "Do you need anything else from me?"

"Don't tell Colin." She gave Elizabeth a quick hug. "Thanks for everything. I'll text you the details and call you when I get home tonight. No worries."

Elizabeth shook her head. "I think this is why my parents stopped at two kids. There's always something to worry about."

Elizabeth left, and Moira slipped into the dress and scarfed down a bagel before heading out the door. When she arrived at the office, Lisa let out a wolf whistle.

Moira hoped her makeup would cover the blush creeping up her cheeks.

Lisa came around her desk for a better look. "We need to

take a photo of you like this. The guys who like exotic will definitely go for you."

Exotic? Never in her life had anyone accused her of looking exotic. Different was good. Maybe. She followed Lisa and let her take a couple of photos.

"Do you have a different name you want these posted under?"

Shit. She hadn't thought about that. "How about Grace?"

"That's fine. Just remember to always be Grace tonight." She replaced the lens on her camera and then said, "The limo will be here in about ten minutes. The other girls are in the coffee room."

"Limo?"

"Yeah. Didn't Jenny tell you? When Billie books us into a party, everyone shares a limo there."

"And back?"

"Yep. Unless of course you make other arrangements at the party."

So they had to socialize during the party, but they could go home with whomever they wanted. A shiver of unease ran up Moira's back. It was the first bit of doubt she'd experienced since Piper pushed her into her first date.

Before heading to the break room, Moira checked her phone, hoping for a text from Jimmy, but there was nothing. He couldn't possibly still be mad because of her refusal to tell him about her story. Although it hadn't come up, she thought they were good. Maybe he had a break in the case, so he couldn't call.

Taking initiative, she sent him a text. Working late. Want to catch up tonight?

Then she stood like an idiot, waiting for a response as if it was supposed to be instantaneous.

I'm working too. I'll call when I'm done.

Hmm...he didn't sound angry—not that a text could hold a tone. Maybe the argument they'd had was nothing more than butting heads like they always did. He must be over being pissed off because he wanted to see her. Feeling better, she turned her phone off and went to wait for the limo with everyone else.

23

———

Jimmy switched his phone to vibrate and hoped his message to Moira was enough that he no longer sounded like the dick he'd been last night. He tugged at the damn bow tie again. He hated the formal events more than anything. The pet events were bad enough, especially with Moira pushing him to adopt a dog, but being dressed like a penguin took him too far out of his element.

One member of the task force sat in a car with Gabby to check out the guests as they arrived. The team decided Jimmy needed to go solo to be a target. The main problem was that no one had any idea which escort service, much less which particular escort, might target him. So he was expected to swim through the crowd of beautiful people, smiling his phony smile, and making small talk about how his wife was out of town. They hoped word would spread to make him an appealing and immediate target.

Although they were aware of three thefts, the police had no idea how big the ring was, how many people they had in play, or how many more victims they might come across. An hour into the party, Jimmy swirled the whiskey in his glass just to hear the clink of the ice.

Boredom dragged him down. Anything would be more productive than this. As he leaned against the bar, he surveyed the crowd. Most of the guests were paired off, having arrived as couples. The unpaired women and men wandered. Jimmy studied the women to try to figure out if any were escorts.

It's not like they looked like the average streetwalker. These women fit right in. They carried themselves as if they completely belonged in this crowd, secure in their positions. Jimmy straightened his shoulders. If they could fake it, so could he.

In his peripheral vision, something caught his attention. He turned and scanned. Three women stood in a group chatting it up with three men. Definitely a pickup scene. A brunette had her back to him, and as she shifted her weight from one foot to the other, that same something tugged at him.

A familiarity nagged him. His gaze wandered the length of the woman and landed on her ass. Her torso twisted as she looked beyond the man in front of her and her profile sucker punched him.

He knew that profile in his gut. Her makeup and clothes didn't matter. He knew Moira.

Jimmy stepped away from the bar forcing his temper down. She'd assured him her work wouldn't interfere with his. Yet here she was.

But he hadn't told her he'd be at this event.

Regardless, he needed to keep his cool in order to keep his cover intact. He slid into place beside Moira, intent on joining the conversation just like any other man who wanted to hook up with a single woman.

Her awareness of him was immediate. Her eyes flicked wider for a second before she forced her mouth to curl into a welcoming smile. "Hi, I'm Grace."

He had no clue what game she was playing. He took her extended hand and stroked the inside of her wrist. "James."

Moira's smile remained steady, but her eyes held fear. Yeah, she knew he was pissed. He took his hand away and pushed it into his pocket. The grip on his drink tightened as he felt the glare coming off the man next to him.

Moira licked her lips nervously and her nose wrinkled. She probably forgot she had lipstick on.

The guy beside him edged forward, in a weak attempt to take the lead. Jimmy stood straighter, towering over the man, and angled his body so that the disparity between the two of them would be obvious.

"James," she began, "Tim and I were just talking about movies. What were you saying, Tim?"

He glanced down at Tim whose mouth opened and closed ineffectively.

Jimmy sipped his whiskey and then said, "Personally, I don't think they make movies quite the way they used to before any of us were born. Don't you agree, Grace? The true storytelling and amazing dialogue of the old black-and-white movies remains unparalleled."

Her jaw dropped. Even he didn't know he'd be able to lay down the bullshit as thick as everyone else. This was becoming second nature, and although he didn't like it, he definitely enjoyed the look on Moira's face. "Let me buy you a drink."

Before she could protest, he grabbed her elbow and guided her toward the bar.

"I'm fine, James. I just finished a drink. I wouldn't want to get tipsy."

"Then have a glass of water and let me get to know you better."

At the bar, she yanked her arm back with only enough force to let him know she was irritated. The bartender filled orders at the other end of the bar. Jimmy and Moira quickly faced each other and said simultaneously, "What are you doing here?"

Her nostrils flared, and he knew the skin across her chest would be pink. He closed his eyes and shook the thought. He needed to focus. "I'm working. Didn't you get my text?"

"Yes. You didn't say where you were going."

"Neither did you."

"I played by your rules. No talk of work." The fake smile she presented grated his nerves. Only he would recognize the nastiness simmering beneath.

He flicked the black wig she wore. "What's this about? You never play dress up when you come to these things."

Her eyes darted away and he had his answer. She was working on her secret story. *Fuck.*

"I told you to stay the hell away from my case."

"I am." Her angry whisper hissed at him. "I'm doing my own thing here. You're the one who just inserted himself into my conversation."

The bartender came over, and she asked for a glass of water. Then she turned back to Jimmy. "We both have jobs to do. It's probably best if we pretend not to know each other."

"We know what my job is, but I still have no clue what you're doing. What the hell kind of story are you chasing?"

She inhaled deeply. "I'm working on a story about high-class escorts and the men who hire them."

In one fell swoop, the pieces came together and his

muscles locked. He forced his jaw to move, praying that he was jumping to conclusions and she'd call him an idiot. "Are you here as a fucking hooker?"

She raised an eyebrow. "No, I'm here as an escort. Now, if you'll excuse me, I have to go mingle."

Moira stepped around him and walked away. He set his glass on the bar so he wouldn't crush it in his hand. Counting to twenty, he took slow breaths and willed his body to relax. She was going to make him explode, and his cover would be shot to shit. It would be career suicide to fuck it up now.

He grabbed his glass again and swallowed the contents in one gulp. All he had to do was pretend he didn't know Moira. What was a little more acting when he was in this deep?

For the next twenty minutes, he walked the perimeter of the room making eye contact with few people. The banquet hall felt like a cage, and the other men in the room were his enemies. He watched as Moira interacted with a variety of men. One by one, guys sidled up to her, handing her a drink, which thankfully she was smart enough not to consume.

She'd tilt her head and let out a light little laugh that reached his ears over the noise of conversation around him. His entire body was in tune with her.

Then Tim returned and that was when Jimmy's last ounce of patience slipped away. Tim slid his arm around Moira's waist and tried to lead her away from the crowd. She danced sideways and patted his chest, but Tim wouldn't let up.

Jimmy began his trek toward them, trying to figure out how to approach without blowing his cover when another woman entered the picture and distracted Tim. As soon as Tim turned his back, Moira ducked away.

She wasn't quite quick enough to escape Jimmy, though. He caught her elbow and propelled her toward the elevator. "We're done partying for tonight."

"Wait." She relaxed the arm he held and cuddled up next to him. "I think she's here."

He started, confused. He'd expected her to yell at him. "Who?"

"The mystery woman I told you about. I think I caught a glimpse of her, but then that asshole Tim got in the way." She ran a finger down the front of his jacket and looked up at him from under heavy lids.

Who the hell was she putting on a show for?

"Get the hell out of here and I'll go back and look."

Her forehead crinkled. "No way."

"What does she look like?" He stepped away from her and craned his head to look at the crowd in the room. It was too coincidental for it not to matter. "Are you sure she's here?"

"No."

"Shit. Come here." He pulled Moira flush with his body and pulled out his phone to text Gabby. If James Buchanan was supposed to be interested in escorts, texting instead of groping one wouldn't help his case. He kept the phone low to their hips and sent the text.

Gabby responded immediately that she had surveillance and photos of each guest so they could figure out the woman's identity.

Jimmy lowered his head and whispered in Moira's ear. "We're leaving now."

"You can leave. I'm not. I'm working."

"You're wrong on multiple counts. You are leaving, and you are most definitely done with this kind of work." He'd already pressed the elevator button, and when the doors swooshed open, he pushed Moira inside, blocking her escape with his own body.

"This is kidnapping."

He pressed his body against hers, pushing her against the wall. Her body was familiar, even though the face wasn't. Except the eyes. She still had Moira's eyes. "You can have me arrested later. There is no fucking way you're staying at a party where the men all think you're a hooker."

She rolled her eyes and he growled. He wrapped his hand around her jaw and forced her to look at him. "This isn't a game. You think Tim back there was bad? That was nothing."

The elevator dinged when they approached the lobby, but neither of them moved. Fear had returned to Moira's eyes, and he didn't know if it was the realization of the truth he spoke or him that put it there.

He released her and stuck out his arm to hold the door. When she joined him, he put an arm around her shoulder and said quietly, "I'd never forgive myself if something happened to you."

MOIRA SWALLOWED HARD. Anger and tension rolled off Jimmy so hard she thought they might knock her over. Of course she'd known that pretending to be an escort had some risk involved, but she hadn't truly considered it. She attended the party with a group, she had backup, and it was a public place. She had no intention of going home with anyone.

Oh shit. She left the party without letting Jenny know. "Wait," she said to Jimmy. She dug out her phone and sent Jenny a text letting her know that she was leaving. She thought briefly about making a joke about Jimmy having to pay her for leaving with him, but she knew he wouldn't find it funny.

Something in his eyes, the intensity with which he spoke in the elevator unraveled her. This wasn't just about his case, no matter what he said.

"Do you have your car here?"

"Nope. I arrived in a limo." Crap. She should've just said she got a ride. Her freaking big mouth.

His step faltered for a minute. "Why?"

"Because the girls I came with all shared one."

"The girls you came with." He handed his valet ticket to the attendant. "What girls?"

She put an arm around his waist and went on tiptoe to kiss his cheek. "I missed you last night."

"Don't change the subject. What girls?"

"I'd rather not say."

"Don't fuck with me, Moira."

"I'm not trying to, but you're already kind of mad, and I'm fairly certain this will only make it worse."

He spun her so they were face-to-face again. "Kind of mad doesn't begin to describe me. I'm fucking furious, pissed off, and borderline homicidal."

She gulped again, not doubting a word he said. Luckily, the valet pulled up in his car and held the door open for her. She offered him a friendly smile and sat down.

After tipping the valet, Jimmy joined her.

"Promise you won't yell."

"I can't promise that." He pulled out into the weekend traffic of downtown Chicago.

She closed her eyes and spoke as quickly as her tongue would allow. "After I got the idea for the story on high-class escorts, I contacted a few companies to interview for a job.

One called me back and hired me. I was at the party tonight as one of their escorts." She sucked in a breath and then remembered to add quickly, "There's no requirement to be a prostitute, and I had no intention of sleeping with anyone."

Moira kept her eyes tightly closed, prepared for the bellowing. Her hands fisted in her lap, and she tried to remember she shouldn't have to defend her actions or her career to Jimmy. They'd barely been on a couple of dates.

When silence continued to press on her, she squinted her left eye. Jimmy's hands gripped the wheel so tightly the veins on his hands bulged. His severe intensity was focused on the road in front of them, and she prayed no one would do anything like cut him off.

Moira watched cars drive past them, people dressed for a night out on the town. She and Jimmy matched the attire but this wasn't them. They would never be the couple who dressed in fancy clothes to hang out at some downtown bar.

A faint buzzing sounded, and Jimmy's hand left the wheel briefly to fish out his phone. He still said nothing. The silence clawed at her. She was never good at being quiet.

"Yeah," he snapped out. "What? Who?"

Moira turned in her seat to gauge what was going on. Jimmy glanced at her.

"Fuck. Okay." He jammed the off button on his phone. "Change in plans. We're going to another hotel."

"Why?"

"Because we have a tail. Someone is following us and we don't know who or why. Our best guess is someone is following because they bought your act as hooker. Good job."

She shrank back into her seat. This was the side of Jimmy she'd heard about but never witnessed.

Muttered curses continued to stream from his mouth. He pulled into another fancy hotel and handed the valet his keys. He strode into the hotel with his arm around Moira, but she'd never felt him so distant.

At least not since they'd kissed the first time. She watched him closely as he paid for a room. Most people would see James Buchanan, stiff businessman, but she saw Jimmy O'Malley, uptight cop. With the key card in one hand, he put his other arm around her shoulder again. Until they got into the elevator.

He dropped his arm, pulling his warmth away with him. She knew better than to say anything because they both needed to put on a show, but in the privacy of the hotel room, she'd tell him exactly what was on her mind.

Which was what?

She stared openly at him, turned on in a way she knew she shouldn't, but bossy Jimmy doing his cop thing was pretty sexy.

Shaking her head when the elevator stopped, she formed more appropriate thoughts. Jimmy had no right to pull her from the party. She had every bit as much at stake as he did. They were both trying to build their careers. His was not more important.

He slid the key card into the door, and she followed him into the room silently. She pushed the door closed with a loud thud, and he reached behind her to utilize the extra locks.

Moira didn't even get a chance to make her argument. Jimmy's body pressed hers against the door and he kissed her. Hard and desperate. His tongue invaded her mouth and woke up every nerve in her body.

Her anger dissipated and melted away as she took everything Jimmy gave her. His hands were frenzied on her body as if they hadn't seen each other for months. As if he needed to memorize everything about her. He was rough, but not mean as he grabbed her and rubbed against her bare skin as he reached under her dress.

When his hand reached for her panties, her eyes fluttered closed. He never moved more than mere inches away from her, his entire being assaulted her senses, overwhelming her. Somewhere in the distance, she heard buzzing and thought she was losing consciousness. Was it possible to get so turned on she could pass out?

Jimmy dragged away from her with yet another mumbled curse. His hand cradled her jaw until she opened and focused her eyes on him. His other hand held his phone. "Don't move."

She swallowed hard. Moving wasn't an option. Some of her faculties weren't in working order. She no longer had the ability to think or function when his dick was in touching distance—she'd been dickmotized.

The phrase popped into her head and Moira giggled. Jimmy shot her a confused look over his shoulder. She would never let him know he held that power. She'd known girls in college who had been dickmotized. Moira and Kathy made jokes about it. How could a cock make a girl stupid?

But now she knew.

Jimmy began pacing farther and farther from the door, and although he'd told her not to move, she was pretty sure the spell had been broken. He rubbed a hand roughly over his head and then tugged his tie off.

She eased away from the door and went to the bathroom to get herself together. The dynamic between her and Jimmy was off the charts. She'd been right when she told him at the block party that things between them would be explosive. Somehow in her head, though, she thought the sexual charge would replace the rest of the head butting and snipping they participated in.

After filling a glass with water from the sink, she sat on the edge of the bed. Jimmy had finished his call and stood in front of the windows.

"Our tail is sitting outside waiting, so we have to be in here a believable amount of time. Then…" He scrubbed a hand over his eyes. "Fuck. I can't go home if they're still here. James Buchanan wouldn't live in that neighborhood." He continued talking as if to himself. "They must not have followed me before if they're still interested. If we're lucky, the thieves plan to follow me home in order to break in after they assess my house. See if I'm a good target."

Moira didn't respond. If he couldn't go home, could she? Would it mess up his case?

"I hate to do this, but do you think you can call Griffin and ask him if I can use his condo? I called earlier in the week, and he hasn't responded. I need someplace for James Buchanan to live." Jimmy still hadn't turned around to face her. His entire body remained tense like he was in a constant battle.

"Sure. I think Ryan said he's been out of town, but I can call." She dug her phone out again and dialed Griffin.

"Hi, Moira. What do you need?"

Why did people always answer the phone like that when she called? Then she looked at the clock and cringed, wondering what time it was for him. "Hey, I hope I'm not calling too late, but I have a huge favor to ask. It's gonna sound weird."

"I'm used to your weird. Shoot."

"Can Jimmy O'Malley use your condo?"

"Shit. I got a call from him earlier in the week and I sent

the request onto my lawyer. I totally forgot about it. Why are you calling for him?"

"It's a long story, but he needs to pretend to be rich, and I'm kind of involved in a story that looks like it's overlapping with his case. I wouldn't pressure you right now, but we're in a hotel room and he can't go home because he's being followed, so he needs to keep up the act."

A grumble sounded on the phone, and Moira felt like she was talking to one of her brothers. "What the hell have you gotten yourself into?"

"No more than usual. This would be a huge help. Free babysitting whenever you need it."

"You do that anyway." He sighed. "I'll call the building and get him a key. Give me an hour or so. Just make sure that nothing is destroyed."

"Thanks. I owe you. Again." She ended the call and looked at Jimmy who had finally turned away from the window. "You're in. A key will be waiting for you in about an hour. Don't ruin the place."

Jimmy opened his mouth and then shut it. Relief shone in his eyes, but she wanted the words he held back. He was always holding back. He turned back to the window and dialed his phone. "Walker agreed. Yeah. No. You follow her. Get someone else then. It's not negotiable." His voice dropped to a near growl. "I don't give a fuck what Kittner says. We don't know who's in that car. Thank you."

He disconnected. Moira wanted to go to him, to soothe him, to ease the edginess, but she had a feeling she was the ultimate cause of the tension.

"Thank you for asking Walker." His voice was quiet and still held the sharpness from his phone conversation.

"No big deal. The O'Learys always say if you have a big

family, use it." He came from a big family, but she didn't get the impression it was the same for the O'Malleys.

"It's still more than you had to do. More than most would do."

She still studied his reflection in the window. The only light in the room came from the bathroom where she'd left it on.

"Want to talk about it?"

He shucked his jacket and laid it on the chair in front of him. "You know I can't."

Her jaw tightened in frustration. "For right now, can't you just pretend I'm your girlfriend, not some reporter you don't want to give information to?"

His head jerked a little when she called herself his girlfriend.

"But you are a reporter. I can't afford to forget that."

"I can forget if you can. Jimmy, you look like you're about to shatter you're so wound up. I won't write a damn thing about this unless you say I can. I would never intentionally do something to screw up your job."

He sank into the chair where he'd laid his jacket. Resting his elbows on his knees, he hung his head. Moira crossed the room and knelt in front of him. She took his hands and said, "You can trust me."

When he looked up, she was lost in the depth of his eyes. Desperation and something else stared at her, but she couldn't figure out what. She couldn't play this guessing game with him. She leaned up and kissed him, pouring the love she'd always felt into it.

His hands framed her face again, and she stroked up his legs until she found the button on his pants. She stroked his dick through the material and then reached in. He groaned into her mouth. She pushed him back into the chair and tugged the pants down enough to release him.

He watched under heavy-lidded eyes as she stroked the length of him. Then she licked her lips and swirled her tongue over his tip, tasting his saltiness. She sucked the tip of his head into her mouth and then ran her tongue up and down the length. She caressed his balls and then took his entire cock into her mouth, tapping the back of her throat.

A deep growl rumbled in Jimmy's chest, and she opened her eyes enough to see his face contort. Even with his dick in her mouth, he held back. She began to bob, using her hands and her tongue.

He grabbed her head and said, "Fuck. Get this thing off."

Until that moment, she'd totally forgotten about the wig. She was always so much herself around him that she'd forgotten her disguise. She straightened and his dick slapped up against his belly. Pulling out bobby pins as quickly as possible, she tossed them on the table and yanked the wig off.

Jimmy still looked pissed, so she unwound her hair from the bun and let it wave crazily around her face and down to her shoulders. When she put his dick back in her mouth, he responded with a yes as he threaded his fingers in her hair all the way to her scalp.

As usual, Jimmy took control and set the pace he wanted for release. Firm but gentle. It didn't take long and his already tight muscles became rocks. His hands fisted but stilled on her head.

Still fucking holding back.

She shot him a look of challenge. She wouldn't let him hold back now. Forcing her head down on his cock, she knew he'd either have to loosen his grip or pull out her hair. She rammed him into the back of her throat, ignoring the automatic gag reflex. She scraped her nails gently on his balls, and he jolted, then settled into the sensation.

"Moira, babe, just—" The sounds of his panting filled the room as his balls tightened in her hand.

The first spurt shot into the back of her throat and she swallowed. He growled and held her head, pumping into her furiously.

When he finished, her lips and jaw were a little sore, but the complete look of relaxation that took over Jimmy's body was worth it. She tucked him back into his pants, but didn't attempt the button or zipper.

"Holy fuck," he said as he still panted with his eyes closed.

His head lolled back on the chair and Moira crawled up his body. "Feel better?"

"Hell, yeah."

"Good."

"Come here." He pulled her up until she was on his lap.

His eyes were barely open, but she looked into them. "Don't hold back. Not with me, okay? I can't live like that."

24

Jimmy's chest tightened, his heart constricting so much he thought it might be a heart attack. Then Moira settled her head on his chest, tucking in under his chin, and every nerve in his body eased. He loved the feel of her body against his, not just sexually, but all the time.

Fuck, he was a mess.

He swallowed and cleared his throat. "Just so you know, Gabby's going to follow you home to make sure no one else follows."

Moira played with buttons of his shirt. "Why would someone follow me?"

"We don't know who's doing the following. We have no idea who the players are and I'm not taking any chances with you." He kissed the top of her head. She was safe now and he'd make sure she stayed that way. "You need to back off this story, Moira. Not only is it not safe, but it's stupid and it's getting mixed up in my case."

He felt her body stiffen, but he held her in place and

rubbed her back, down her arm, keeping physical contact because he wasn't ready to let her go.

"My story is not stupid, and it's not my fault *you* got mixed up in my story. If you hadn't gotten all grabby at the party, we wouldn't be here now."

He sighed. She was right, but he didn't feel any better about it. "I know your story's not stupid. The way you're trying to get it is what I take issue with."

This time she did sit up to pull away, but he locked his arms on her hips.

"If I was a journalist embedded with soldiers in Afghanistan, I wouldn't be called stupid."

"Maybe not by some, but it is stupid. A civilian doesn't belong on the battlefield anymore than you belong acting like a hooker."

"I'll do whatever I have to do to get a real story."

"I wasn't talking shit when I said you've been writing real stories for a long time."

She snorted. "Yeah, my real stories are taking me far. No one knows my name and no one takes me seriously. I'm not some airhead taking notes on my palm. I'm a journalist."

Her voice rose as she continued and her eyes flashed. Jimmy cupped her jaw. "I know your name and I take you seriously."

"No, Jimmy, you don't, or you wouldn't assume I should walk away from a story—a valid, good story—just because you say so." She stood now and slid back into her sexy high heels. "I assume it's safe for me to go? I mean, if I were really a hooker, we'd be finished, right?"

He laughed. "I think we both know that if we were actually having sex, I wouldn't be anywhere near finished."

She looked pointedly at his crotch. "If you say so."

He stood, adjusting himself back in his pants. He didn't

want her to go. James Buchanan had the money that he could afford to have her spend the entire night. The simple thought of anyone treating Moira like a prostitute burned in his gut. "You don't need to leave yet."

The look she shot him was cold and so unlike Moira. "Yes, I do."

Jimmy knew he'd be working with Gabby, so he couldn't have her stay. "Let me call downstairs and have them get you a cab."

She nodded.

"I would drive you, but James Buchanan wouldn't be taking you home."

She hummed a minor response while she pinned her gorgeous red hair up and tucked it under the wig. He hated everything about this night.

Well, except for the blow job. That had almost made up for the clusterfuck he was in the middle of.

He called down to the front desk and had them arrange for a cab. Then he called Gabby to let her know Moira was on her way down.

"All set?"

Jimmy stared at Moira, knowing he should say something else, but he had no idea what. Remembering what he'd discovered about her and her writing, he searched for words, but they were buried beneath his roiling emotions looking at Moira pretending to be a hooker. The entire image was so wrong. "Moira."

She looked up at him, and if he could ignore the makeup and the hair and stare into those baby blues, he could focus and see her. Only her. And what he saw twisted him. She was wounded. He kissed her gently, hoping to ease the uncertainty from her, to let her know he'd meant what he said. "I take you seriously. You're amazing. But this is complicated. Even if I wasn't working an overlapping case, do you think I'd ever want to see you dressed like this? Pretending to be a prostitute? Putting yourself in danger?"

It was the last one that pushed him over the edge. Experience taught him that no prostitute led a safe life.

"I'm an escort, Jimmy, not a hooker. I'm arm candy and conversation for guys with money who don't want the dating scene."

When he opened his mouth to protest, she held up a hand. "Don't treat me like I'm stupid. I know most of the girls sleep with clients for money. I have no intention of doing that or putting myself in a situation where I'm vulnerable. I don't even plan to do this for long. I'm gathering information."

"I can't handle the thought of you doing this, Moira. It's not like you're interviewing people to get the story. You're doing the job, and it's not safe. Whatever protocols you think are in place to protect you, they're not enough."

The sadness never left her eyes and now he saw a hint of worry. Worry was good. It might be enough to protect her. She pressed a kiss to his cheek and left without saying anything else.

He paced the length of the room, feeling useless. He stared out the window as if he could see Moira leave, watch for someone following her, but that too was useless. The room didn't even face the front of the hotel. Impatience tugged at him. Why hadn't Gabby called with an update?

He gripped his phone in his hand and forced himself not to dial. Gabby would call as soon as she knew something. The phone buzzed and he answered.

"The tail is following Moira's cab. Kittner wants you to stay put in case there's a second car."

Right now, he didn't give a fuck what Kittner wanted. He needed to make sure Moira was safe.

"I know you care about her, Jimmy, but she got herself caught up in this. It's not necessarily a bad thing. She'll be more forthcoming with information than some random girl. We can use this to our advantage." Gabby was right. He was thinking like a boyfriend not an undercover cop.

Fuck. If Moira had been any other girl, he would be using her, but this *was* Moira and they had a personal relationship. This was exactly what Kittner warned him about. "I don't like it. We still don't know who we're dealing with and what they're capable of. If something happens to her, the entire O'Leary clan will descend on me and the whole department. It'll be ugly."

Gabby laughed. "We'll make sure she stays safe."

"What the hell am I supposed to do? I don't have any clothes or anything. I'm stranded in this room until Walker arranges a key for his place."

"I'll go to your house and send some clothes and stuff to Walker's by morning. In the meantime, enjoy your night off."

She disconnected and he flopped back on the bed. He called home and let Norah know he wouldn't be home tonight, but that Gabby would be dropping by. She assured him she'd keep an eye on Dad. He should feel more relief knowing that, but since he was still so worried about Norah and her pregnancy, the turnaround he'd witnessed just confused him.

For once, it would be great if things in his life would go the way he planned. This was supposed to be the year things would smooth out and he'd move forward. Instead, he was hit with one twist or turn after another.

MOIRA HAD the cab drive her back near the escort office so she could pick up her car. When she'd left the hotel, a flurry of emotions stormed through her. For every step she made with Jimmy, it felt like he'd given her a shove back.

She'd believed something shifted between them when they'd spoken on the phone last night. He'd taken the time to actually read her work. Jimmy understood her more than she'd given him credit for. She thought he understood how important her career was to her.

She'd allowed people to make jokes about her job for so long that she'd forgotten how much she did love it. When was the last time she talked seriously about writing with anyone? Jimmy had been the first person she could remember wanting to share that part of herself with.

Yeah, she had it bad. And it no longer felt like the teenage crush she'd always harbored.

And then tonight he ruined all the progress. She must've only been a good writer when she covered safe topics like abandoned animals.

He'd actually called her stupid.

The cab pulled up in front of the building and Moira stepped out. She glanced up to the office and debated going in to see Billie. At some point, she'd have to let Billie know who she left the party with. It was too much for her right now.

"Excuse me," a soft elegant female voice called from the curb.

Moira turned and tried not to swallow her tongue. It was the mystery woman she'd been looking for, leaning against a sleek sedan. Moira cleared her throat. "Yes?"

"My name is Gail. You're Grace, right?" The woman spoke with confidence, the question just a formality.

Moira nodded, feeling quite uncomfortable with this woman knowing her name, fake or not. She had to have followed Moira in the cab, which meant she'd followed her and Jimmy when they left the party. How did they not notice?

Gail pushed back her auburn hair, darker red than Moira's, and tilted her head. Light brown eyes focused on her. "I don't mean to alarm you. I spoke with some of your colleagues at the party and they passed on your name."

Moira waited. She pictured Jimmy playing James Buchanan and masked her expression as best she could, but her heart slammed in her chest.

"I can't help but feel we've met before."

Moira swallowed hard, grateful for the long shadows on the street. Even with the disguise, Gail might be able to put two and two together. "I don't think so." She pulled her keys from her purse. "Was there something else?"

"You left the event with James Buchanan."

Moira straightened her back. "I don't think it's any of your business who I left the party with."

Gail waved her hand as if Moira needn't answer, and then stepped closer. "I wasn't asking. What I'd really like to know is whether you have a personal or business relationship with Mr. Buchanan."

Moira summoned every ounce of courage she had. She cocked an eyebrow and pointed up at the building behind her, where Billie's office was located. "Like I have time for personal relationships?"

Gail smiled then and a scheming look came into her eyes. "If you think Mr. Buchanan will be contacting you again for your services, I might have a proposition for you."

Intrigued, Moira stepped closer to Gail and lowered her voice. "I know he'll be calling me. He made sure to get my number and asked when I'd be available."

"Do you already have plans?"

Moira shook her head. Her heart continued to pound and her palms were sweaty. She had no idea where this conversation was going or what the right answers were. "He's supposed to call me tomorrow." Moira paused, remembering what she knew of the other victims in Jimmy's case. "His wife is out of town, and he's trying to squeeze in all the fun he can."

"Perfect." She held out a business card. "Call me when you set up the date with Mr. Buchanan. You will be compensated well for your help."

Moira took the card. "I'm not doing anything illegal like drugging him or blackmailing him. This is just a job to me like anything else. No one is worth going to jail for."

"It's nothing like that."

"Then why are you so interested in...James?" Shit. She'd almost said Jimmy.

"We'll talk more when you call me." Then she spun on her incredibly high heel and returned to her car.

It was like something out of a movie. Secret meetings, hidden agendas. This might be the information Jimmy needed for his case. A nervous flurry skittered through her body. Moira raced to her car. She needed to see Jimmy.

No, she couldn't see Jimmy, especially if Gail continued to follow her. Plus, she didn't know where Jimmy would be. Probably still at the hotel. She flipped the business card between her fingers. No name, no identification, only a phone number.

As she sat behind the wheel, a wave of nausea rolled through her. Taking a deep breath, she started the engine and blasted the air-conditioning. The unexpected meeting had her so rattled her hands shook.

Being undercover definitely wasn't her strong suit.

How did Jimmy do this without having a nervous break-down? She closed her eyes again and focused on Jimmy. Always cool, controlled. Those were words that didn't apply to her.

Thoughts of Jimmy in cop mode kind of turned her on again. As much as she didn't like being bossed around—she'd had more than enough of that growing up—his demands stirred something beside the usual resentment in her. A chill shivered down her back, so she turned the air down. That had to be the cause. She pulled out into traffic and headed home. She'd calm her body and her imagination and then she'd call Jimmy.

JIMMY STRODE through Griffin Walker's condo and stared at the expensive furnishings. The place was immaculate and made him feel completely out of place. Not that he preferred the mess his brothers left all over their house. Middle ground would be good. This place looked like a model home where no one actually lived.

At least the TV was kick ass. He had nothing to do but sit on his ass and wait. Of course, no one knew exactly what they were waiting for. He itched to get back to work, but Kittner didn't want to take a chance on Jimmy's cover being blown.

When his phone rang, he was glad for the distraction and he didn't care who it was, but seeing Moira's name on the screen made him smile. She must've cooled off. He wondered why Gabby hadn't called again. Unease still clawed at him because he knew Moira was being followed. "Hey."

"Are you sitting down? You need to sit down because I have amazing news."

He loved her voice when she was pumped about something. It was like she could get high by talking, as if oxygen were a drug. "I've been sitting on my ass for hours."

She blew out a long breath. He braced himself for the onslaught of her rapid speech.

"I had the cab drop me off by the escort office so I could pick up my car. I was walking down the street and you'll never guess who came up to me." She paused to take a breath.

He paused to absorb the information. She went back to the damn escort office even though he'd expressed how it wasn't safe for her to be playing these games. Plus, where the fuck was Gabby?

"Mystery woman. Her name is Gail, by the way. No last name. I'm sure she has one; she just didn't tell me. Anyway, she was very interested in you, Mr. Buchanan, and the fact that I left the party with you. She gave me her card, which only has a phone number on it, just like the one she gave me last year that I couldn't find. She kind of remembered me but couldn't quite figure it out. Isn't that great, though? I mean the new contact not the not remembering me part. Although that's probably good, too. This is what you've been looking for."

His head spun and he got off the couch to pace, which only added to the dizziness. Moira proved she hadn't lost her ability to be Mouthy Moira. His muscles tightened and he saw red. After their argument, he was sure she understood how worried he was about her and that she'd have enough common sense to back off.

"Jimmy? Did you hear me?"

"I heard all right. I heard that you ignored everything I said and continued to stick your pretty little neck out without a care."

"I didn't do *anything*. I went to pick up my car. Like I said earlier, you're the one who brought attention to me. She approached me because you led me away from the party. This is all on you. Asshole."

He didn't give a shit if he was being an asshole. He knew that a good portion of her involvement in this mess was because of him and his inability to stay away from her. "Give me her phone number. Don't leave your house and don't tell anyone about this."

"No 'thank you, Moira, for getting me the information I desperately need for my case'?"

"I asked you to stay away from this."

"Actually you told me to, demanded that I stay away from your investigation. What you don't seem to grasp is that I wasn't trying to get tangled in your mess. It just happened. And I certainly didn't have to come to you with any information. I've done nothing but help you from the beginning and I've done it for nothing."

"Don't take a righteous attitude, Moira. You helped because you were promised a story. You've had an ulterior motive from the get-go."

"If you believe that, you don't know me at all." She hung up.

He stared at the phone, not believing that she had hung up on him. What were they, twelve? As he was about to call her back, a text came through from her with the phone number she'd gotten. He took a deep breath and called her back, determined to stay calm and make sure she understood the importance of staying out of sight.

The call went to voice mail. Damn it. "Moira, do not tell anyone about this phone number and absolutely do not use it. And stay home in case you're being watched."

Fuck. He stared at the number. He had no idea how long he stood there debating his next move when his phone rang again. He answered without looking, assuming it was Moira, but it was Gabby.

"Quite the exciting night, huh?"

"Fuck no." He had the phone number for the best lead they'd gotten since the beginning of this damn case and he was sitting on it.

Gabby sighed in his ear. "Don't worry. Things are looking up. Moira is safely in her apartment, and the tail left her when she got to her car. The interesting part is that they made contact with her when she got out of the cab. I wasn't close enough to hear, but I figured I'd talk to Moira. To my surprise, she called me."

His stomach churned. He'd told Moira not to talk to anyone.

"Aren't you going to ask?"

"Just tell me. I'm not in the mood to play games."

"Moira gave me the phone number to a woman named Gail who asked her about you." Gabby waited for his response. "You knew, didn't you?"

"She called me with this information a little while ago."

"If this woman approached Moira, you know we have to use it, especially since she asked about you. They're setting up another burglary. This is probably our best chance. Everything's falling into place."

"This is Moira, though." He didn't know what else to say to give weight to the pressure he felt to keep her safe.

"I know, Jimmy. Let's have her make contact and see how they run it. If it looks dangerous, we won't follow through."

"She's not a cop. She's not trained."

"That's probably working in our favor. She's not suspicious."

For being in such a huge condo, Jimmy felt like he was trapped in a closet. Breakable things surrounded him and he had to remind himself they were not his to smash. He probably wouldn't be able to afford to replace anything either. So he continued to pace. He knew Gabby was right. Moira was the best thing they had.

"I want you to run this. Personally. Make sure she's safe."

"I can't see her. I'm Mrs. Buchanan. If they have eyes on her, I can't be there. I'll figure it out. You sit tight."

Sit tight. As if that was even a possibility. Every nerve was taut, every muscle a rock, and thinking of Moira intentionally and repeatedly putting herself in the middle of this investigation turned him inside out.

He couldn't continue this back and forth, push and pull. She didn't want him to hold back. Moira was in for one hell of a battle this time.

MOIRA FELT A LITTLE GUILTY. After having Jimmy tell her to keep Gail's information to herself, she knew he'd try to cover it up to keep her out of it. She couldn't let him do that. She understood why, but this case was important to him and he would throw away something that was potentially useful. She didn't want him to get into trouble, so she'd called Gabby. Gabby would get through to him.

He listened to her.

A pang of jealousy shot into her. She knew there was no romantic or sexual relationship between Jimmy and Gabby, and Moira really liked Gabby, but she couldn't help but be jealous of the fact that Jimmy listened to what Gabby said. He valued her opinion and didn't brush her off.

Then the logical voice in the back of her head—man, she hated that voice—reminded her that Jimmy did listen to her and that was part of what had gotten her into trouble. She'd told him about her Viagra Triangle story and he'd listened. He also spent time reading her work to understand her better.

And now he probably hated her. But he'd get over it, right? He'd have to realize at some point she did it to help him. Her phone rang and she half-expected it to be Jimmy calling to yell at her, but it was Gabby.

"Did you talk to Jimmy?"

"Yep."

"Was he mad?"

"Upset, but he knows we need to utilize this information. Besides, just think of the kick ass story you'll have a front row seat for."

That little nugget should have her dancing through her apartment, but all she could think about was how angry Jimmy really was. But they both had a job to do. "What's the next step?"

"Right now, nothing. Go about your regular life and I'll call you when we have more information."

Her regular life? Her regular life now included dating and sleeping with Jimmy. The most interesting part of her life lately was now off limits. "How long until you have a plan? I'm assuming I'm going to need to tell Gail something."

"We'll have you call her after we have things set up for Jimmy. I have to get back to work now."

"Wait." Moira took a slow breath so she wouldn't sound

too eager. "Can I talk to Jimmy? I know I can't see him, but it's not like our phones are bugged."

"For now, no contact. If you need to get a message to him, call me."

Yeah, sure. Hey, Gabby, tell Jimmy how much I want to get naked with him next time we're together. "Okay. What about his family? Is someone checking on his dad?"

"He said his sister has it handled."

"Oh. Okay. I'll talk to you later I guess." Moira hung up and itched to call Jimmy. Instead, she crawled into bed alone.

THE FOLLOWING MORNING, Moira sat down to work, but she couldn't do an article on last night's party since she'd been there as an escort not a reporter and she didn't stay. She checked her e-mail and played around on social media, but she was antsy and bored. She grabbed her keys and her laptop and headed out for a change of scenery.

A block from her apartment, her phone jingled with a text. From Jimmy.

Where the hell are you going? I told you to stay at home.

For a man who wasn't supposed to have contact with her, he was still being pretty controlling.

Gabby said we can't talk. She also told me to live my regular life. I'm going to get a coffee.

How the hell did he even know she'd left? She stopped in her tracks and spun around. People on the sidewalk brushed past her. She looked up and down the street, not even knowing what she was looking for. He was having her followed. Gabby said nothing about being followed.

She turned back and walked the next block to the coffee shop. She ordered a large iced coffee and settled at a table.

Although she didn't have any articles due, she had a few ideas to play with. Then she went back on social media to spread the word about Colin's bar and bowling alley.

Her phone jingled again, and she was determined not to engage Jimmy. But it wasn't from Jimmy. It was Lisa. They had another date for her tonight, and they wanted to know if she could take it. She stared at the message.

She didn't know if she could stomach playing the role of an escort again. The first couple of times turned out okay, but she didn't want to press her luck. But Gabby told her to continue on with her regular life. Being an escort was part of her regular imaginary life.

Everything was much too complicated.

She called Gabby. "Sorry to bother you again, but I have a slight problem."

"What?"

"First, is someone following me?"

"Jimmy wanted us to keep an eye on you to make sure everything's okay. Did our guy screw up so bad that you saw him?"

Moira mulled that for a minute. If she said yes, some poor guy she didn't know would get into trouble. If she told the truth, Jimmy would get into trouble.

"You talked to Jimmy."

"He texted to ask where I was going. I figured someone had to be following me for him to know. The real problem is that the escort service has a date for me tonight. I wasn't planning on going on more dates, but..."

"Shit." Gabby blew a breath across the line. "If you don't go, they might suspect something is up. We're still piecing together all the players. I can't make you do anything, Moira. It's your call."

"But you think I should go."

"I didn't say that."

Moira turned her cup in slow circles. "If you were me, you'd go."

"I'm a cop. I'd get paid to go."

"Will your friend be watching me tonight if I went?"

"Absolutely. But I don't want you to do anything you're not comfortable with."

"What can one date hurt? Tell your guy my date will pick me up in front of the escort office at eight." There, decision made.

"Be careful."

"Of course." She texted Lisa to let her know she'd take the date. If her luck held, maybe it would be a nice old man like Mr. Lee.

Moira finished her coffee and walked back home, acutely aware that someone was following her and watching her every move. Maybe two people if Gail was watching, too.

This life was way too complicated. She longed for the days of attending parties, chatting with people, and being herself. Her job did matter even if she didn't win prizes or garner awards. She made a difference in the lives of those affected by the charities and organizations she helped publicize.

She trudged up the steps to her apartment and prayed there would be no more surprises.

25

───────

Jimmy had a late lunch with the mayor, with Kittner in attendance. Everyone agreed Jimmy should continue to play his part and sit on his ass. Everyone except Jimmy of course. Gabby had already filled them in on Moira's involvement, and Jimmy felt Kittner's irritation throughout the meal.

When the mayor excused himself to go to the washroom, Kittner leaned over and spoke quietly. "I told you being involved with a reporter would be a problem."

"Her work happened to cross into our investigation. She didn't stick her nose into it intentionally." Jimmy's hands fisted under the table.

"And you know this how? Because she said so? Reporters will do whatever's necessary to get a story. She'll sell you out in a heartbeat."

While Jimmy might question whether Moira intentionally stuck her nosy body where it didn't belong, his belief in her loyalty held fast. "Moira has said nothing to anyone about this case and my involvement. She wouldn't risk it."

"You're fucking her."

Jimmy put his napkin on the table and leaned close enough to Kittner to be taken seriously. "Who I fuck is none of your damn business. I've done nothing to compromise this case, and you won't insinuate that my personal relationship has interfered."

The entire situation ate away at Jimmy. His personal relationship *had* interfered, but Kittner didn't know that. Moira and Gabby made sure of that. He hated the way Kittner viewed Moira, and he was disgusted with himself for letting things go this far.

When the mayor returned, he thanked Jimmy and Kittner for all the hard work they'd done on the task force. "When do you think things will wrap up?"

Kittner jumped in before Jimmy could say anything. "We plan to get Mr. Buchanan out of the condo within a couple of days. We think the hired escort is the key, but we're not sure how. Once we have things in place, we'll have her make the call and see how the thieves approach it."

"Any chance you're barking up the wrong tree?"

"Given the intel we have right now, no."

Jimmy widened his eyes, waiting for an explanation. No one informed him of any intel, other than Gail being the contact person, and that had come from Moira. When Kittner didn't expand, Jimmy pushed. "What intel?"

"The information we have on Gail Thuringer. We have an idea of who her partners are and how they'll proceed based on previous crimes." Kittner pushed his plate away and slid his chair back.

Jimmy held out a hand to halt him. "Why haven't I been told any of this?"

Kittner didn't answer. He just shot him a look. Jimmy was being left out of the loop because of Moira.

They both rose and said good-bye to Mayor Park. When

they were outside the restaurant, Jimmy continued, "How am I supposed to do my job if I don't have all the information?"

"I make sure you have what you need to know when you need to know it. The information you need is that you're to call Moira and make a date for tomorrow night, your last night of freedom before your wife comes home. We'll take it from there." Kittner walked down the block to his car as the car service pulled up for Jimmy.

He'd rather have driven his own car, but Buchanan would use a service. Jimmy settled into the backseat and then realized Detective Joe Barkley was his driver. "What the hell are you doing here? You're supposed to be watching Moira."

Barkley eyed him in the rearview mirror. "Gabby and I switched places. She wanted to get you information." Barkley handed him a file.

Most of the pages were copies of official reports, but Gabby included her personal notes. As far as they could surmise, Gail Thuringer worked with a ring of thieves. They'd hit a handful of people and then went underground for a while before resurfacing.

As Barkley pulled up in front of the condo, he said, "Gabby also wanted you to know that I'll be following Moira all night tonight, so you don't have to worry. She'll be safe."

Yanked from his concentration, Jimmy looked up. "Why wouldn't she be safe in her apartment? I told her to stay put."

He needed to call her and tell her to ditch her family dinner tomorrow.

Barkley was unusually quiet.

"What?"

Barkley cringed as Jimmy watched in the mirror.

"I thought Gabby told you. Moira has a date."

"What?"

"The escort service called—"

"No." Jimmy leaned forward and pressed on Barkley's shoulder. "Call it off. She shouldn't be going on some fucking date."

A date? What the hell were they thinking?

Barkley twisted to look at Jimmy. "It was her choice, but it makes the most sense. If she's being watched, it would be suspicious for her to turn down work. I'll be there. She'll be fine."

Jimmy clutched the file in his hand and got out of the car. He slammed the door behind him, but it offered no relief. He wanted to beat the shit out of something, but he was stuck in some overpriced condo filled with things he couldn't afford.

Once he got upstairs, he changed into sweats and went to the building's fitness center to work off some of the tension and frustration. If he called Gabby or Moira right now, neither of them would listen. He needed to be rational.

MOIRA SLIPPED into her favorite cocktail dress and put on some makeup. The only information Lisa had given her was that she'd be going out to dinner. She assumed that since the client had money, it would be a fancy dinner as opposed to Olive Garden, so she hoped her choice in clothing was appropriate. When she left her apartment, the sun was setting and it created a pink-orange glow in the sky.

Before climbing into her car, she looked around and tried to figure out if Gabby's guy was watching. What if he didn't pay attention? She should've gotten a phone number or at least a description so she'd know what to expect. Then she shook her head. She'd never needed a babysitter before, and this was just a date.

She drove to the office and went to the break room to have a quick cup of coffee, as if that would quell her nerves. Two other girls she hadn't met before sat at the table in front of textbooks. Moira looked, but didn't say anything. In the reception area, she asked Lisa, "What's with study hall?"

Lisa looked to where Moira pointed. "Oh, a bunch of the girls are working their way through college. They'll get a degree with no loan debt. Sometimes they bring their books here and squeeze in some studying." She went back to working on the computer.

Moira wandered up and down the hall, sipping on her coffee. She wanted to be as cool and nonchalant as Piper and Jenny were about this job, but it ate her up.

Tomorrow at dinner, she'd thank her family for putting her in a position where she would never have to do this kind of job to get ahead in life. Lisa's phone beeped.

"Moira, your date's downstairs."

Moira dumped the rest of her coffee and headed down. Quick dinner, pleasant conversation, and then back home to crawl into jammies and watch a movie.

A car sat at the curb, and when she exited the building, the driver swung the back door open. She slid onto the seat and assessed the man beside her. He was younger than she'd expected and relatively good looking. He had short, dark hair and dark brown eyes, and his smile was just this side of leery. Of course, it didn't help that he stared at her chest.

"Hi, I'm Moira." She extended her hand.

He took it and stroked and petted her hand instead of shaking. "I'm Terry."

"Nice to meet you. I wasn't sure where you had dinner planned. Am I dressed appropriately?"

"You look fine."

He continued to ogle her but said nothing. The silence irked her more than the gawking. At least other men feigned an interest in her as a person. They started conversations and asked questions. Even old Mr. Lee did more than stare.

Terry shifted his body and angled closer to her, feeding her discomfort. His index finger traced a pattern on her shoulder at the border of her dress, skimming across from fabric to bare skin. She suppressed the need to recoil.

"Where are we headed for dinner?"

"Mmm...I was thinking we'd go straight for dessert." His hand landed heavily on her thigh.

She slid a couple of inches until she hit the door. "I'm sorry, Terry, but I think you have the wrong idea about what's happening here."

"I know what's happening. I pay a hefty fee and I get an evening with you." His hand slid to the hem of her dress.

She slapped her hand on top of his to prevent movement. "You hired me to be your date for the evening. A nice dinner out with a woman on your arm. That's all."

His head jerked back and incredulity filled his face. Then he let out a hearty laugh. "I like a girl with a sense of humor, but I'm not in the mood to play games."

Her heart pounded and her stomach twisted. "I'm not playing games. I'm an escort, not a hooker."

He stared at her like he was waiting for a punch line. All she heard was Jimmy's words of warning.

Terry reached out and roughly palmed her breast. "You're a hooker with a fancy title. That means if I pay, you fuck me."

Air trapped in her lungs and panic gripped her. She

shoved at him, but he wouldn't budge. "I am not fucking you. Get off me."

His body pressed closer, and tears pricked the backs of her eyes. No way was this happening. She sucked in a gulp of air and slammed both hands against his chest, dislodging his position. "Stop the car!"

The driver looked in the mirror, but didn't answer. Terry leaned closer, just as Moira jumped forward to make the driver understand that he needed to pull over.

Moira's elbow connected with Terry's face, and he yelled, grabbing his nose. "Bitch."

"That was an accident. Stop the car."

He shot a look at the driver and snapped, "Pull over."

The car came to an abrupt stop, and Moira didn't wait for the invitation to leave. She stood on the curb as the car drove off. Her breath hitched as she tried to inhale. Her entire body felt wobbly. Another car pulled to the curb and she took an automatic step back. The window rolled down.

"Hey, I work with Gabby and Jimmy. Are you okay?"

She nodded, not trusting her voice.

"You don't look good. Can I give you a ride?"

She shook her head.

He waited a moment and then threw the car into park and got out. He stood in front of her, assessing her. What was one more guy staring at her? A lump the size of Texas lodged in her throat. She couldn't even tell this guy to leave her.

He opened the passenger door. "If I leave you on the street looking like this, Jimmy'll have my ass. Get in."

She jerked at the command, but didn't move her feet.

"I'm going to take you home."

She took a step back. After she swallowed hard, she

thought maybe she could speak, so she forced out, "I'll take a cab."

He had his phone in his hand and spoke to someone. She couldn't hear what he said, but then he thrust the phone at her. "Gabby wants to talk to you."

She held the phone to her ear.

"Moira, what happened?"

"I can't talk."

"What. Happened."

"My *date* decided all he paid for was to fuck and that's what he planned to do." Tears clogged her throat.

"Shit. Are you okay?"

Moira nodded and then realized Gabby couldn't see her. "Yeah."

"Listen. The guy standing awkwardly next to you is my friend. His name is Joe and he's going to give you a ride home."

Moira didn't say anything else. She handed Joe his phone and sat in the car. Neither of them spoke on the way to her apartment.

When she got home and locked the door, the full force of what had happened screamed through her. Her hands still shook and tears streamed down her face. She sank onto her couch and waited for the worst of it to pass.

Her phone buzzed in her purse as it had multiple times since leaving her date. She was afraid to see who was calling.

Billie would probably be pissed because the date had been ruined, but Billie had told her she never had to do anything she wasn't comfortable with.

Gabby would want to check on her again, but Moira was barely functional. She didn't want to fall apart even worse under Gabby's questioning.

If it was Jimmy...she couldn't talk to him. She wouldn't be able to handle his I-told-you-so attitude. So he was right. Big freaking surprise.

And if it was anyone from her family, she couldn't let them know.

So she ignored the phone and went to take a shower. She wanted to wash away every remnant and memory of this whole stupid thing. This would go down as by far one of the worst nights of her life.

JIMMY CALLED and left a message for Moira to make a date. He didn't know why she wasn't answering. Gabby and Barkley were being closedmouthed about Moira's date. All they would say was that she was back at home safely. But something was up. He studied the file Barkley had given him while waiting for Moira to call back.

After an hour, he called again. Then he sent a text telling her not to go to her mom's house for Sunday dinner. He wasn't sure how often they did it, but she was in his neighborhood often enough for him to notice.

When another hour passed and Moira hadn't called, he called Gabby.

"I know you're bored, Jimmy, but there's nothing for you to do."

"What's going on with Moira? She's not answering her phone or calling me back."

"She's not supposed to have contact with you."

"As my date for tomorrow night, she is. Besides that, Moira answers. Always." He flipped on the TV and watched news headlines scroll past.

"I'll call her and check. Maybe she's following the rules."

That made him laugh. "Moira never follows the rules. What happened with the date?"

Gabby got quiet. His gut twisted. He knew it. Something had happened. "Tell me."

"I didn't get the whole story, but the guy got handsy in the car and she got out. She never made it to dinner."

Visions of some asshole pawing at Moira filled his head and rage coursed through him. "Who is he?"

"We don't know. She only got a first name. The car was a hired service."

"Fuck that. The escort service knows."

"Jimmy, I know how to do my job. This idiot isn't part of the plan. Moira's okay. Joe Barkley was following the whole time."

But Barkley hadn't been in the car. What if it had been more than some groping? His head swam with the possibilities. He hung up on Gabby and texted Moira. Call me if you want to talk. It doesn't matter if Gabby said not to.

He waited, but his phone didn't ring. Long minutes dragged by and finally, Moira texted Okay.

The single word sent another wave of panic through him. He needed to see her, to know she was all right, but Kittner would never let him get near her right now. Not when it looked like they were going to be able to close this case tomorrow.

He paced the room again and then called Liam.

"What do you want, Jimmy?"

How could Liam still be pissed? "Moira's in trouble."

"What?"

"I can't give you any details, and I can't check on her because I'm stuck at work. Go to her apartment and check on her."

"How do you know something's wrong?"

"She hasn't returned my calls or my texts all day, until a few minutes ago, when she answered with one word."

"And?

"Do you even know your sister? Moira never uses one word when she can use fifty. I can scroll through pages of texts from her and never does she use only one word." His heart thumped against his ribs. How could Liam not trust him? "Please, Liam. I don't want her alone right now."

"What aren't you telling me?"

"I can't say."

"You're an asshole."

"Tell me something I don't know. Are you going?"

"Of course I am. She's my sister."

Moira stared at the TV, not absorbing anything she watched. A knock sounded at her front door and she jolted. Her first thought was Jimmy. Then she heard, "Moira, open up."

Liam? What was he doing here? She hesitated, not sure if she wanted to see him.

"I know you're home. Jimmy told me to come here."

She went to the door and checked the peephole, which made her feel stupid since she knew it was Liam. Another wave of disappointment swept through her at seeing her brother. Until that moment, she hadn't known how desperately she wanted to see Jimmy. She opened the door, but said nothing. He walked in and she locked the door behind him.

"What happened?" Liam's eyes narrowed as he looked her up and down.

His voice was soft, so different from the last time they spoke. She wanted to be brave and shrug off her night.

"It's a long story." Her voice wavered, and she knew she wouldn't be able to tell it without crying again.

"Then I guess I'll put on the tea." As he rumbled around her tiny kitchen, he asked, "Is this something I'm going to have to kick Jimmy's ass over?"

"No. He didn't do anything." She leaned against the wall adjacent the kitchen and tried to figure out what she could tell Liam. She wasn't supposed to talk about Jimmy's case, but what to include?

"Start at the beginning."

So she did. Liam, as usual, didn't interrupt, other than to give her a cup of tea when it was ready and lead her to the couch. He listened and she was grateful. By the end of the story, tears trickled down her face at the memory of Terry groping her and pushing for more. She swiped at the tears. Her hands shook and tea slopped over the brim.

Liam took the cup from her. "What the hell are you doing?"

"About what?"

"Why would you put yourself in a position like that?"

"It wasn't intentional. Things snowballed so quickly. I had the idea for the story, and working as an escort would give me a push others don't have. It's fascinating, but I didn't realize, at least not fully, how dangerous and soul cutting it is."

"So you're done then."

She shook her head. "No. Tonight taught me that I need to write this story. You wouldn't get it. These girls, who you and every other man see as a pricey piece of meat, are people. Some are working their way through college. Just because they're paid for a date doesn't make them property for a man to treat like trash."

Liam edged forward on the couch. "Not that I don't agree with you, but you're not keeping this job as an escort."

She bristled for a moment because she hated being told what to do, especially by one of her brothers, but then she realized she'd already decided she wouldn't be going on any more dates. "I want to tell their stories and the stories of the men who hire them. They're not all bad. My first date was with an elderly gentleman who wanted company over dinner. But there's no way to know what you're getting into. And the thing that's really digging into me right now is that Jimmy is pursuing these thieves, but no one bats an eye at the men who hired escorts to sleep with them."

After finishing, she felt better, more like herself, and her restlessness manifested itself in the need to write.

Liam's face scrunched up. "You're not seriously saying that a man who hires a hooker is the same as a thief."

"No, but do you think Jimmy would hesitate to throw one of the escorts in jail if he caught her? Of course not, but everyone looks the other way when it comes to the man. Like somehow he's better than she is."

"I can see you're feeling better and I'm not about to get into this conversation." He stood and gathered the teacups.

She followed him to the kitchen. "Thanks for coming by."

"That's what brothers are for."

"Hmm...and I thought your sole job was to boss me around."

"Nah. That's just a perk." He tucked his hands into his pockets. "About Jimmy."

"I don't know what we're doing or where things are going. They're not in a good place right now because my story got all enmeshed in his case." She wouldn't tell him how much she wished it had been Jimmy at her door or how much she missed talking to him over the last couple of days.

Liam looked defeated. "See you at dinner tomorrow?"

"I can't. Jimmy told me not to go."

"So you listen to Jimmy but not your brother."

"It's not like that. I don't want anyone to know my real last name or where my family lives. My part in Jimmy's case should be over tomorrow night. Maybe we can do lunch next week. Okay?"

He pulled her into a sudden hug. "Be careful."

Although she'd been careful, it was Jimmy watching out for her that made her feel safe. "I will."

Liam left and she got to work writing the article that could change her career.

26

———

Moira spent the night in a caffeine-induced writing session. The words took all her focus, making it easier to push Jimmy from her mind. She'd barely managed a brief nap before waking from a nightmare with Terry as the star. She made another pot of coffee and then got ready for her date with James Buchanan.

Since James had taken her Friday night while she wore the wig, Moira figured she'd better pretend all over. She didn't bother with the bronzer since the only man she had to be with was Jimmy and he knew what she really looked like. The wig gave her enough of a disguise.

When she parked her car and rounded the corner in front of Billie's office, Gail was already waiting.

Gail handed her an envelope, and as much as Moira itched to open it, she held it for a moment. "What's this for?"

"That's the first half of your payment. All you have to do is convince Mr. Buchanan to spend the night with you in a hotel. All night, no matter what it takes."

"I don't think that'll be a problem."

A huge man walked up behind Gail. Unease skittered through Moira. The man said nothing and didn't move.

Gail smiled and said, "Don't disappoint us."

Then they walked to a car waiting at the curb. The man held the door open for Gail and then he got behind the wheel.

When they pulled away, Moira put the envelope into her purse and stood in front of the building nervously, like all the world was staring at her. Even her insides were fraught with tension, everything stiff and not working quite right.

Then another car pulled up, and Jimmy opened the back door and held it open for her. The sight of him alone released something in her and she wanted nothing more than to jump into his arms, but she knew she couldn't. And even if she didn't know it, his body language would've sent the message. She joined him at the car, and his lips barely swept past her cheek with a kiss.

She slid into the car.

After closing the door, Jimmy pointed to the driver and said, "Moira, this is Joe Barkley."

Moira nodded. "We've met." To Joe, she said, "Nice to see you again. And thanks for the ride yesterday. I wasn't quite myself, but I do appreciate it."

The air in the car shifted. Anger rolled off Jimmy and she wondered how much he knew. She assumed he knew everything since he told her to call him to talk, which was a weird offer to begin with given how often he told her to shut up, but if he'd known, why was he angry now?

She sat close enough to feel the heat of his body on her thigh, and she longed to curl up against his chest. She wasn't sure why she couldn't, or shouldn't, but she knew it would be unwelcome. Jimmy wasn't just his usual quiet self; he'd become a statue.

They rode in the car for a while and she had no idea what the plan was. Then she remembered the envelope in her purse. She pulled it out and dropped it on Jimmy's lap. "Here. Gail paid me half up front. I'm supposed to get you to spend the night with me at a hotel. The entire night and I'm to do whatever is necessary to make that happen."

Jimmy picked up the envelope and tapped Joe's shoulder. Joe took it and left it on the seat beside him.

"I don't suppose I get to keep that, do I?"

Jimmy slid her a look that effectively told her to shut up.

When they pulled up to an expensive downtown hotel, Jimmy said, "We have reservations at the restaurant and then we'll go upstairs. You ready?"

"Sure." This was so much easier than her previous escort jobs.

An hour later she was kicking herself. Jimmy was making this date impossible. She talked her way through dinner like she would any other time, but no matter what she said or did, he wouldn't engage. There were brief flickers of something in his eyes, a heated gaze that sent warmth through her, but then he'd mask it.

If Gail was watching, she would assume Moira would fail at her mission. Jimmy didn't look like a man who wanted to get laid. The waiter stopped at the table to remove their empty plates and asked if they wanted coffee.

"I'd love some."

"No, thank you. We're good."

When the waiter left, she kicked his shin under the table. "I wanted a coffee."

"By the way you're talking, I know you've already had a few pots too many. Judging by the look on your face, you also didn't sleep. And it wasn't because you were having fun."

So he noticed she hadn't slept. Jimmy noticed every-thing. "Well, if you're so smart, why don't you realize that you aren't acting like a man on a date?"

"What are you talking about? I picked you up. We've shared a nice meal and a bottle of wine. Sounds like a date."

She rolled her eyes and then slid her foot up his calf. "You might want to make it look like you're interested in taking me upstairs. Anyone watching us right now would think you're my brother for all the physical attention you've directed at me."

She was pushing it, and the little tic in his jaw was the only evidence. Another flash of heat in his eyes. Without breaking eye contact, he waved the waiter over for the bill and signed it to their room. He stood and held out his hand.

His fingers closed tightly over hers, and when she stood, he moved their joined hands behind her back and brought her body to his. He lowered his mouth and claimed her with a kiss.

And God, did she melt. This was what she'd needed last night. This touch, this belonging, to make her feel right and normal. He was better than brownie à la mode. Besides giving her comfort and safety, he turned her on with a simple swipe of his tongue.

She was breathless when he pulled away, and it took a moment for her to focus.

"Show's over" was all Jimmy said before leading her to the elevator. They got off at the fourth floor, Moira still out of sorts, confused by the juxtaposition of the steamy kiss and Jimmy's distance.

Inside the room, he locked the door, and when he turned to her, she wrapped her arms around him and pressed her face to his chest. She needed this more than she knew. He gently removed her arms from him and said, "I need to call Gabby."

Jimmy stepped around her and tugged off his tie while he made the call.

It was like she wasn't even there with him.

"We're in the room. I have no idea if she has eyes on us, but it's possible." He mumbled a few more things, and Moira stood rooted in place.

When he disconnected, she asked, "So what do we do now?"

"Wait and hope they break into Walker's condo, so we can arrest them." He shed his suit coat and unbuttoned the first two buttons on his shirt. He sat in the chair and turned on the TV.

Of all the things they could be doing after not seeing each other for a couple of days, he wanted to watch TV? Although he sat still in that uncomfortable chair, she felt the storm brewing around him. That same whirlwind she never understood before.

"What's wrong?"

He slid her a look and returned his attention to the TV.

As if that would work. She grew up with four brothers. She stood in front of him, blocking his view of the screen. "Talk to me. What's the matter?"

"What's the matter?" His voice barely rose, but he was seething. He stood from his spot and tossed the remote onto the table with a clang. "How about I'm sitting in a fucking hotel room while everyone else is about to make an arrest that should be mine? I'm sitting here doing nothing. With you."

It was like a punch to her heart. He didn't want to be with her. That's why he sent Liam to her apartment last night. It certainly explained the chunk of granite he'd turned into. But she had no idea why. "Why?"

"Why what?"

"Why are you treating me like this? I thought we had something good going."

"We did."

Her heart stuttered and sank. *Did.* Past tense.

Jimmy kept his distance, but for a change, continued to talk. "Then you had to push. You had to go after a story that put you in the middle of my investigation. And last night, in the middle of a dangerous situation."

He was pissed about his stupid job? "I went on that date last night for you, not me. I didn't need to continue the charade for my article, but I didn't want to mess up your investigation. I was totally freaked out and scared last night." Her voice cracked and she swallowed hard. "Do you think I would put myself in danger for a story?"

"I obviously have no idea what you'd be willing to do for a story. But I know you rush into things without thought. It's who you are."

A wave of iciness swept over her. He was doing what Liam had warned her of. He needed to control everything and he couldn't control her. "I'm sorry I'm so difficult. I'll leave you to your business."

She turned and picked up her purse from the dresser. She couldn't face him anymore and didn't want him to see the tears that threatened.

"You can't go. Someone will be watching to make sure we spend the night in the room."

For a second, she thought he wanted her to stay, but it was just the job. She didn't turn around. Instead, she went to the bathroom and locked the door. With the water for the bath running, she sat on the toilet and cried tears of heartbreak, which were somehow much worse than the tears of fear and disgust she shed last night.

Fuck. The woman drove him insane. When Jimmy saw her standing on the street waiting for him to pick her up, irritation dug into him because she wore that fucking wig again, which just accentuated the fact that she was playing a hooker. But then, when he looked into her eyes as she walked to the car, he saw pure happiness.

He'd wanted nothing more than to bundle her up and take her home to be safe, but it wasn't an option. He had a job to do and Moira would never go for it. He'd been harsher than he'd wanted to be when she confronted him, but he was grasping at his last threads of control. She stood in front of him looking vulnerable and feisty at the same time, luring him in with the touch of her body, but he couldn't let go of the fact that she was standing there in a wig pretending to be a prostitute.

Something, that while it ultimately helped his case, she started on her own for an article. She wouldn't be happy to stay where she was with her job. They weren't so different; they both wanted to excel, be more, get further. But he couldn't live with her like that.

He spent two days tied in knots worrying about what she was doing, not being able to talk to her, knowing she wouldn't listen if they could talk. He looked at the bathroom door. The water was running, but no other sounds seeped under the door.

He'd never get used to a quiet Moira. She talked to herself while she worked, typing away at the computer. She sang while she made coffee in the morning. She moaned and called his name while they had sex.

Turning up the volume on the TV, he hoped to drown out all sounds from the bathroom and the images in his head. He settled back on the bed and fell asleep knowing that for at least the next few hours, Moira was safe.

JIMMY WOKE to the sound of his phone buzzing across the table where he'd left it. He rubbed his eyes and sat up to grab the phone. The TV was off and Moira was curled into the armchair across the room. He answered the phone as he checked the time. Three a.m. "What's up?"

Gabby answered, "We got 'em. Meet you at the station?"

He looked at Moira sound asleep, using his jacket as a blanket. "Yeah, I'll be there."

He pulled the blanket back on the bed and then picked Moira up. Her face showed evidence of crying and a stab of guilt poked him. He didn't want to hurt her, but Liam had been right, they didn't belong together. As he shifted her weight to get her into the bed, she wrapped an arm on his shoulder and snuggled into his neck.

If only he could keep her right there.

He set her down, removed his jacket from her, and replaced it with the blanket. He scribbled a note and left it on the nightstand. Kittner would need her to come into the station as a witness, but it would wait until morning.

Plus, he couldn't stomach seeing her look at him with hatred for breaking her heart.

THE NEXT TWO days were filled with interviews and forms

and statements before Gabby came to Moira and gave her the promised details so Moira could write the article she'd been working toward for a month.

Then she allowed herself a week of pity. A solid week of homemade brownies and fudge brownie ice cream, late night black-and-white movies, and sleeping until the rest of the world was well into their workday and she could pretend they all ceased to exist. Kathy came by after work and let her complain and whine about Jimmy and how stupid he was. Elizabeth dragged her out for a manicure and pedicure before going to ladies' night at a club.

When she wasn't pining away over Jimmy O'Malley, she worked her ass off well into the night to write the article on the theft ring that targeted wealthy men with a penchant for high-class hookers. She queried the *Chicago Tribune* since they'd printed her article on Griffin last year as well as the first one she'd done on the Bostwick Charity. The editor wanted it for the Sunday edition and also wanted first shot at her follow-up on the escorts. Working for the *Trib* even as a freelancer would open doors.

It was everything she'd been hoping for, but she couldn't quite get excited.

Surprisingly, none of her brothers came to visit. She didn't know if Elizabeth warned them off, or if by some chance, they didn't know Jimmy had broken her heart. Her mother wanted her to come over for dinner because she'd missed the last family dinner, and since it was the middle of the week, Moira wouldn't have to face her brothers yet. Especially Liam. Although he wasn't a told-you-so kind of guy, she didn't want him to hate Jimmy.

She also wasn't sure she wanted to see Jimmy's house and run the risk of bumping into any of the O'Malleys. Pulling into her old neighborhood, Moira decided to park around the corner from her mom's house and use the back door to go unnoticed.

Unfortunately, that meant she didn't see Liam's car parked in front and was unaware she'd find him standing in the kitchen. She wanted to back out the door, but he'd already seen her. "Hi. What are you doing here?"

"Mom told me you were coming for dinner and I wanted to check on you."

"I have a phone. You know where I live."

"But you wouldn't have answered. How are you?"

She joined him at the small counter and cut up vegetables for dinner. "I'm good. The *Trib* is going to run the story I got from working with Jimmy." She smiled, both because she was proud of herself for the accomplishment and because she managed to say Jimmy's name without getting choked up.

"That's great, but how are you holding up? Elizabeth told me Jimmy broke it off. What happened?"

"I really don't know. It's not like something happened— it was more that you were right. Jimmy and I are different, and those differences were too much for him. As usual, I had no idea what was going on in his head because he can't open up and just talk." She scooped carrots and cucumbers into the bowl of lettuce.

Liam took the knife from her hand and turned her to face him. "I don't want to make excuses for the guy, but you scare him."

Moira snorted. "I am like the least scary thing in his life. He's a cop."

Liam shook his head. "He's a cop because it gives him the chance to get the bad guy and protect people. You scare him because he doesn't think he can protect you. He can't control you."

"Did he tell you this?"

"He didn't have to. I've known him my whole life. Ever since his mom was killed, he's been looking for a way to control everything." He rubbed his hand over his short hair. "The thing is, I hadn't considered that you would push back. That you might show him how to loosen some of that control."

"What are you saying? After all your *stay away from my little sister* shit, you think Jimmy and I belong together?"

Liam took a big step back. "Do you love him?"

Another step while he waited for her to answer, making her suspicious.

"Yeah, I love him. I've loved him since I was ten. Lot of good that has done me."

Another step.

"Then maybe you should continue your pushy ways and go after him."

Her hand balled into a fist and she realized why Liam had been backing away. He knew she was ready to hit him. "For weeks both Jimmy and I have been listening to you tell us how we shouldn't be together and it's this colossal mistake and now, after he's dumped me, you're saying I should fight for this relationship with a man who's afraid of me because he can't control me?"

She inhaled deeply and stepped forward. Liam stepped away.

"I worry about you, but Mom was right and I should've stayed out of it."

"Great time to choose to listen to Mom. You couldn't have had this epiphany, I don't know, a *week* ago, so I could've struck while the iron was hot? While Jimmy and I were still caught up in the emotions of what we had? It's been a week and he's probably over at his house thanking God I haven't stalked him."

Liam burst out laughing.

She rushed him and smacked his arm. "This is not funny."

"Listen to yourself. It is pretty funny." He grabbed Moira's shoulders and sobered his expression. "This isn't one of those things where within a week, it blows over. Part of what made me wig out when Jimmy told me he'd slept with you was the look in his eyes. You were never some fling for him to scratch an itch. Prove it to him because he's obviously too stupid to see it."

Her shoulders sagged. She looked down at her wrinkled T-shirt, shorts, and ratty flip-flops. Not exactly a go-get-a-man outfit. "What if you're wrong? What if he doesn't want me? I don't know if I can put myself out there for him to stomp on my heart."

"Then put the ball in his court and force him to make a choice. If he knows he still has a shot, that might be all the incentive he needs."

She rolled her lower lip and bit into it, thinking. Force him to make a choice. Then it hit her. Jimmy still owed her one favor. All she had to do was push to collect. It would give him a chance. "Hold dinner for me. I'll be back in a few minutes."

She walked out the front door and across the street before she lost her nerve. The front door to the O'Malley house was open, and she heard the TV blaring with a base-ball game. She pounded on the screen door.

The look of shock on Jimmy's face when he came to the door was priceless. "Moira."

As if she didn't know her own name. Push him, Liam

said. She knew how to push. "Friday night, pick me up at six thirty. Wear a suit."

"What?" Panic replaced the shock.

"You owe me. You promised to be my date to my reunion. It's this Friday."

"But...I thought..."

"No, Jimmy, you didn't think. You didn't talk. You didn't open up, which was all I asked of you." She was eternally grateful for the screen separating them because the look of pain in his eyes made her want to wrap herself around him. "If just once, you had said, 'Moira, don't go after this story because I'm worried about you' or 'I can't think straight if I don't know you're safe' I would've given you whatever you wanted. But you barked orders and made demands. If you had given me that piece of you, Jimmy, let me see your vulnerability, I would've given you anything because I love you."

His jaw dropped and she turned and walked away. She felt his gaze on her back as she crossed the street and forced herself not to turn around.

Ball firmly in his court.

FRIDAY AFTERNOON, Jimmy sat thinking. Norah came into the room and Jimmy noticed she was starting to do the pregnant woman's waddle. She was in a better place over the last couple of weeks, smiling more, talking about finishing school here in Chicago. She still wouldn't name the baby's father, but overall, she was happier.

"You are such a wuss."

Still his snotty little sister, though. "What?"

"You're screwed up in love with Moira and you're sitting

here staring at your suit like it's the Wizard of Oz. Get dressed and go get her."

He'd been toying with that exact idea. What was supposed to happen after this one date?

"I don't know what's holding you back, Jimmy, but whatever it is, talk to her. Work it out."

Moira said she loved him and would've given him anything if only he'd asked. He jumped off his bed with the idea. "You're right."

A broad smile spread across Norah's face. "Words every sister lives to hear."

"Whatever. Now get out." He dressed, and on his way to Moira's apartment, he stopped for flowers and chocolate. Maybe not the best negotiating tools, but they'd get him heard.

At five forty-five, he knocked on Moira's door, but tested the knob. Locked. It brought a smile to his face. The door swung open and Moira stood in front of him wearing the skimpy robe again.

"You're here."

The surprise in her voice stung. If nothing else, he always held up his end of a bargain. "Of course I'm here."

"But you're early. I said six thirty. I'm not ready."

He took a step, forcing her into the apartment. "I figured we would need the extra time for negotiations."

Her face scrunched. "There's no negotiating. You either take me to the reunion, or you get out of here."

He sighed. His words failed again. "Sorry." He put the candy and flowers on the table.

When he turned to face her again, her arms were crossed on her chest. She'd obviously

forgotten the move caused a tantalizing gap in her robe.

Before attempting to speak again, he did the one thing

he'd been longing to do for days. He threaded his fingers into her hair and lowered his lips to hers. How could he expect to live without this?

Her mouth yielded against him and he kissed her with the fervency of every emotion he'd kept bottled up for far too long. When she moaned into his mouth, he knew he had to pull away, or he'd never get around to talking.

He held her at arm's length and the unfocused look in her eye turned him on. He released a slow breath and concentrated. "Negotiations," he said, as much to remind himself what his goal was as to clue her in.

She blinked slowly but stepped forward as if to kiss him again. He held fast. "You wanted to talk. I'm talking."

He dropped her arms and stepped back. His heart kicked up and nerves tingled at the base of his skull. "I love you, Moira."

Her face melted into all kinds of desire and he gave in and kissed her again. One sweet, swift kiss. He leaned his forehead against hers. "I was an asshole and I should've talked to you. Here's the deal. If this is going to work, no more crazy, dress-up, dangerous stories to chase after. I get that your career is important to you, but I can't function when I'm worried about you."

She snorted. "Did you just plagiarize the speech I gave you the other day?"

He smiled, so happy to have her smart-ass comments. "Cut me some slack. I'm new to this whole verbalize every emotion thing. I can't lose you."

She started to tear up. "Done."

"That was too easy." He pulled back to check to see if she was teasing. She wasn't.

"After pretending to be an escort, I decided I didn't like that work. I can't promise I'll keep the job I'm doing forever, but I can promise to stay away from dangerous things." She stepped closer to him and he started to lose his train of thought. "You can't tell me what stories I can do, but I want to share that part of my life with you."

He sighed. "You have to move out of this apartment. I hate this building."

She laughed. "Where the hell am I supposed to live?"

"I was thinking we could look for a place near our parents."

"You want to move in together?"

He nodded. "Maybe buy a house."

She moved away with a stunned look on her face and he liked being the one to deliver a shock for a change. "What about your dad?"

"Tommy and Sean are both adults. They need to start acting like it and chip in. Plus, Norah's home and she's doing better. She's actually really good with my dad. He listens to her more than anyone."

"What are you saying?"

"I'm saying I love you and I don't want to lose you." No words had ever been as scary as those.

"I'm not giving up my job to be a happy homemaker. I don't know if I'll ever want that."

His heart beat double time. He knew this and had tried to come to terms with it. "I get it. I'm sorry I tried to tell you what to do with your career. I just...I need to know that you're willing to build a life with me." He swallowed hard. "You said you'd give me anything if I asked. I'm asking for you."

"Damn. I just wanted you to give us a chance. You really know how to throw a girl."

"I'm confused. Is that a yes?"

She smacked his arm. "Of course it's a yes. But don't

think that asking for me now gets you out of a ring and getting down on one knee at some point."

"Wouldn't dream of it." He grabbed her and started kissing her again, losing himself in everything she had to offer. She hopped up and wrapped her legs around his waist. As she pressed into him, he groaned. "How much time do we have?"

"As long as we want."

"I love the way you think."

NOTE TO READERS

Thank you so much for taking time to read my book. I hope you enjoyed hanging out with the O'Learys in Chicago. Keep reading for an excerpt of the next book in the series, *Just a Taste*, where Liam O'Leary falls for his mentor's daughter when they both inherit a taco truck.

If you could spare a moment, I would appreciate you leaving a review of this book.

If you'd like to stay up-to-date on my releases and have the chance to win some prizes, click here to join my newsletter.

27

JUST A TASTE EXCERPT

Liam O'Leary walked through his apartment and peeled off his sweaty T-shirt, one that smelled of grease and onion soup that a clumsy line cook had spilled on him. The kid had no idea what he was doing, couldn't keep up with the pace of the kitchen, and Liam knew the owner would have to fire him. Exhaustion tugged at every muscle. Thoughts of the line cook—Liam didn't bother learning names until one proved himself—made Liam shake his head.

He'd asked Jonathan if he could sit in on the interviews for the last round of new hires, but Jonathan refused, saying he wanted Liam to focus on running the kitchen. The man might be a brilliant businessman, but he had no idea what it took to run a kitchen. Liam had been working at Porter's for more than two years and he still didn't understand how Jonathan managed to own a restaurant.

Jonathan had graduated from culinary school, but had never taken a job in a kitchen. He bought Porter's and hired a kitchen staff. Liam had been his fourth executive chef. It didn't take long to figure out why: Jonathan didn't want to work the kitchen, but wanted the credit for what happened there. He created the menu but rarely listened to new ideas.

Every now and then, though, Liam made small changes without Jonathan's knowledge. Tonight had been one of those nights. Unfortunately, Jonathan chose tonight to grace them with his presence, and the small addition of some herbs to the soup had turned into an explosive argument.

Liam stepped under the hot spray of the shower and tried to figure out what he wanted to do. He'd been thinking about opening his own restaurant for over a year now, but had yet to make a move. Unlike his older brother Colin, who would jump into anything that looked good, Liam needed to weigh his options.

One thing he knew for sure was that his time at Porter's was coming to an end.

With a towel wrapped around his waist, he went to the kitchen and popped the top on a beer. He fished his phone from his jacket pocket and checked messages. He'd heard the phone earlier in the evening, but since it wasn't a number he recognized, he bumped it to voice mail.

He carried his beer back to his room to pull on a pair of boxers while he listened.

"Hi, Liam, this is Carmen Delgado. I don't know if you remember me, Gus's daughter. I'm calling to let you know that my dad passed away."

The barest hitch caught in the girl's voice. She continued talking, but Liam no longer heard. Of course he remembered Carmen. She'd been a sweet kid who'd always played at giving him a hard time when he worked for Gus.

Gus.

Liam sank to the edge of his bed. Gus was dead?

Gus had been his first mentor. He'd given Liam his first real job, understood his love of cooking and food, taught him how to create. Liam's chest felt heavy. He took a swig of his beer and pushed it past the sudden lump in his throat.

"Here's to you, Gus." He lifted his bottle and drank again. He'd been a bad friend in recent years. He couldn't remember the last time he went to see Gus. How long had it been? Maybe once or twice since Gus's wife had died. Liam had gotten busy with his own life and few friendships survived his hectic schedule.

When they had spoken by phone, Liam knew Gus understood that. He'd lived a similar life. His last conversation with Gus flooded back into his head. A food critic did a write-up about Porter's and said wonderful things about Liam.

Gus had called to congratulate him. Liam had heard the pride in the old man's voice. That had been over a year ago. Guilt crept into Liam for letting so much time pass. Picking up his phone from where he'd dropped it on the mattress, he pressed the buttons to listen to the message again, needing to find the information to pay his respects to a great man.

***

After two days of making phone calls, Carmen's throat was scratchy and her voice almost nonexistent. Making all of the other arrangements for her father had been simple enough. But the phone calls nearly did her in. She'd found herself praying for answering machines and voice mails so she could leave the practiced message instead of having a real conversation.

Everyone had loved Gus. He'd had friends everywhere. Her family arrived on her doorstep and tried to take over for her. Her aunts and uncles meant well. She knew that, but taking care of her father was her job and she couldn't let anyone else do it. Her whole house was crammed with people, just like it had been when her mother had died.

Gus had felt like they'd needed that support and it was simply the way of her family, but she wanted peace. She needed to be alone and she couldn't find space anywhere. It was part of the reason she made the wake only a few short hours on Sunday. People would attend the wake and come back to the house to share a meal. The faster they got her dad to his final resting place, the faster they would all move on.

So she could move on.

She didn't know what that even meant. The idea made her feel light-headed. She'd been taking care of her parents for so long, she hadn't been able to think about herself. For now, she pushed the heavy thought away. She had details to attend to, people to speak with, arrangements to make.

Her cousin Rosa popped into the kitchen. "Hey, girl, how are you doing?"

"I'm okay. I think all the calls are done."

Rosa crossed the room and wrapped her arms around Carmen. "Let's get out of here. Go have a drink, do some dancing."

Carmen pulled away from Rosa. "What are you thinking? I can't go dancing. What would people think? My dad just died and I'm going out to party?"

Rosa rolled her eyes. "What do you care what people— forget that. It shouldn't matter what people think. Everyone needs a break. Especially you."

"I can't. I still have things to do to get ready for the wake."

"Well, I'm going out. You have my number." Rosa swished out of the room in her super-skinny jeans and kitten heels.

As much as Carmen loved her cousin, they had never had much in common. No matter how different they were, though, Rosa was the closest thing Carmen had to a best friend. She was an excellent confidant, but Carmen could never keep up with Rosa's social life. Heck, Carmen didn't even have a social life. She was the only twenty-seven-year-old spinster she knew.

Pouring herself another cup of coffee, she reclaimed a seat at the kitchen table. Her uncle and cousins were still sitting in her living room, watching something on TV. They had all pitched in doing various things, but she craved space and peace. She was used to being alone most days. Her dad went out on the truck and she handled the house and the office end of the business. The extra people were suffocating.

With the sounds of the TV from the other room, she focused on making a list of things she still needed to do. She had to update the web site and let customers know that the truck would be out of commission for a while. Maybe forever? She hadn't thought about what to do with Dad's business. He'd loved the food truck, but Carmen couldn't imagine running it.

Maybe Pete would want to take it over. Her younger cousin often went out with her dad to work. He knew most of the operation. Pete, however, was immature and she didn't know if she could trust him to work consistently. Her uncles had already mentioned selling the truck and the house and having her move in with one of them.

As if she wasn't a grown woman capable of taking care of herself.

She forced her head back to the task at hand. No decisions had to be made right now. She added Update Web Site to her list, followed by Clean Out Dad's Bedroom. That would be a huge task. When her mother had died, Gus would only let Carmen get rid of a few things. He clung to every item of Inez's that he could. He hadn't been ready to let her go. Over the months, Carmen snuck and removed things her dad might not notice, but overall, she knew she would now have to clear out the belongings of both of her parents.

Those two items alone weighed her down. She knew there would be more. Her father had a will, so she would have to talk to his lawyer about that. Then the outstanding bills for both the house and the business. At least her dad had been smart enough to add her name to everything after Inez's death.

She blinked back the tears and focused on the details. She'd be able to hold her shit together as long as she had a job to do.

***

Liam walked into his childhood home, so glad to feel the calm and comfort of family when he knew he would face sorrow later in the day. The O'Leary family dinner was mandatory at least once a month. Eileen O'Leary expected her children to share a meal as a means to keep close. It was something his parents worked together to achieve as soon as he and his five siblings neared adulthood and branched out to have their own lives.

He walked straight to the back of the house. The living room was empty, so he must've beaten his brothers to the house today. In the kitchen, he knew he'd find his mother standing over the stove. He wished she would let him help with the meal preparation, but she never would. They took turns bringing dessert because as much as Eileen loved her sweets, she didn't make them. Dinner was her job and she refused to share it.

"Hi, Mom," he called as he opened the refrigerator to slide in the cheesecake he'd made for after dinner.

She peered around his shoulder to see what he'd brought. "Don't tell your brothers and sister, but I like it most when it's your turn for dessert."

"That's no secret, Mom. I always make your favorites. That's why I'm your favorite."

She slapped a towel at his arm. "Don't say that. I love all of my children equally."

"No one else is here. You can tell the truth." He looked down at her, suddenly struck by how small she appeared.

Her face grew serious. "What's the matter?"

"What do you mean?"

"Something's wrong. What is it?"

He hadn't been trying to cover his grief, but he hadn't planned on talking about it either. "Remember Gus Delgado? He owned the Mexican restaurant I first worked at?" Eileen nodded. "He died. His daughter called and left a message. After dinner, I have to go pay my respects."

Eileen didn't say anything, but she patted his arm. As far as physical affection went, that was about it for his mom. His dad had been the hugger in the family.

She turned back to the stove. Judging by the smells, they'd have roast for dinner. "Is there anything I can help with?"

She shook her head. He heard the front door open and he went to see which siblings had arrived. Moira pushed through the door and Liam hoped she brought Jimmy with her. Although he hadn't been thrilled with his friend entering a relationship with Moira, he'd appreciate seeing Jimmy today.

Unfortunately, Moira entered alone. "No Jimmy?" he asked.

She sighed. "Don't look so disappointed. He'll be here in a few minutes. He went to check on his dad."

"I'm not disappointed in seeing you." He squeezed her hard until she gasped.

"Why are you all dressed up? What's going on?"

"Nothing." He released her.

She crossed her arms and raised an eyebrow. Like their mother, she didn't need words to call him a liar.

"I found out an old friend died. The wake is today. I'm just feeling out of it."

Her whole face changed, filling with sadness for a friend she hadn't even known. She wrapped her arms around him in a gentle hug, unlike the playful one he'd forced on her. Jimmy opened the door without knocking, assessed the situation, and asked, "What's going on?"

"Nothing," Moira answered. As she stepped away, she ran a hand down his arm in reassurance. She would understand his desire to not discuss it.

Jimmy's gaze went back and forth between him and Moira, and then landed on him, questioning. Liam smiled. "Any luck on the house hunt?"

"I thought so." Jimmy took off his coat and hung it in the closet. "Your sister's too picky."

"I am not," Moira retorted.

Before the discussion could go further, Eileen called from the kitchen, "Moira, come help with the vegetables."

She shot Liam a dirty look.

He shrugged. "Don't look at me. I offered to help when I got here. She doesn't want my help."

Moira moped out of the room. Liam knew it wasn't fair that their mother assigned traditional gender roles.

"What was the hug about?" Jimmy asked when Moira had left.

"I don't want to talk about it. Tell me about the house." Anything to keep his mind off his plans for later that afternoon. He and Jimmy didn't have long to talk alone. Before he knew it, Ryan and Quinn arrived with baby Patrick and Michael and Brianna came in. Colin arrived solo.

Moira came out of the kitchen as Colin sat on the couch beside Liam. "Where's Elizabeth?"

"At the bar."

"Why do I get the feeling she's avoiding family dinner? Doesn't she know it's a requirement? Shoot, if I have to be here, she should too."

"You're blood. No escaping it. She likes to point out that she's not an O'Leary and is therefore not required to be here."

Moira headed back to the kitchen, but shot over her shoulder, "Then maybe it's about time you made her an O'Leary."

Liam watched Colin and smiled. He recognized the look on his big brother's face.

"What are you looking at?" Colin asked.

"Did you already buy the ring?"

"What are you talking about?"

"You go ahead and play it cool around Moira because we know she'll flap her jaws to everyone, but I saw your face change when she suggested marriage."

Colin leaned closer. "Is it that obvious?"

Liam shook his head. "Probably not to everyone. But you don't get nervous and that's what I saw."

"The damn thing has been burning a hole in my pocket for a couple of weeks now. I can't figure out when to ask. Or where to ask. It seems like it would be a big deal for a woman, you know? I don't want to screw it up."

"I've got nothing for you there, but let me know if there's anything I can do to help."

Colin picked up the remote and turned the TV on to a football game. The Bears were losing to the Packers as usual. Within minutes, all four O'Leary men along with Jimmy O'Malley were sitting in the living room, screaming at the television at football players who couldn't hear them.

HOURS LATER, Liam drove through the Humboldt Park neighborhood, dreading his destination. He'd missed the viewing at the funeral home intentionally. He didn't want to see Gus like that. The thought alone brought too many memories of his own father's funeral. The street in front of the Delgado house was filled with bumper-to-bumper cars. He drove around the corner and searched for a spot.

The flowers he bought wobbled in the passenger seat and part of him wanted to leave. But he couldn't. It wouldn't be right. Not for Gus and not for Carmen. At the end of the next block, he squeezed into a spot. As he stepped from his car, a blast of cold air hit him. He pulled his jacket tighter around him with one hand while he cradled the flowers in the other.

He walked into the harsh wind down the block toward Gus's house. He hadn't been a guest at Gus's house often, but he'd eaten dinner there a few times. Of course, he'd been there when Gus's wife had died. He hadn't stayed long. His own grief had been still too fresh and he couldn't stand it.

It had been years and he thought by now it would be easier, but with each heavy step, his doubt increased. He climbed the steps to the porch and knocked. No one answered. The noise from the other side of the door was loud. He knocked harder and then turned the knob.

He entered the house and looked around. People packed the entire living room. He stood still for a moment, allowing the air of the room to warm him. He studied the faces and realized he didn't know anyone. No one approached him, but many looked in his direction with open interest.

Then he spotted Carmen. She bustled around, taking plates and delivering coffee to older men and women around the room. He crossed to her and followed until she went into the kitchen. He waited in the doorway.

The kitchen was empty of guests. She put the dishes in the sink and then braced her arms on the counter and released a breath that shuddered through her. Guilt poked at him. He was interrupting a private moment and he should leave, but his feet wouldn't listen.

He cleared his throat. "Carmen?"

She straightened slowly before turning to face him. A slow smile formed on her face. "Liam."

He hadn't been sure she would remember him. "How are you holding up?"

She lifted her shoulders in answer. The question was dumb. That was one of the worst parts of dealing with people after his father had died. The dumb questions from people.

"Here." He held the flowers out to her. "I know it doesn't help or ease the pain in any way, but I couldn't come here empty-handed."

"Thank you. They're beautiful." She took the vase from him and looked for a free space on the counter. The entire kitchen table and the length of the counter held trays and bowls of food. The smells made his mouth water even though he wasn't hungry.

"Can I get you something to eat?" she offered after she stashed the flowers in the corner near the refrigerator.

"No. Can I help with some of this? Do something for you? You look like you have your hands full with all of your guests." He removed his jacket and hung it on the back of one of the kitchen chairs. He rolled up the sleeves of his shirt, prepared to help.

She blinked a couple of times. "Uh... In all honesty, I'll probably end up throwing most of this out. There's just too much." She turned in a circle. "Coffee. I need to make more."

Liam moved forward. The girl looked dead on her feet. How could her family not see this? He pulled a chair out from the table. "Sit. I'll make it."

"No, it's okay."

"Carmen, sit down. Take a break and relax for a minute." While not harsh, his tone was firm and she sat.

He remembered when Gus's wife, Inez, died and the house had been filled like this. Gus loved having the family here, but Carmen had hidden in the kitchen, overwhelmed. Liam had joined her then too. He moved around the kitchen making coffee and then washed the dishes that were in the sink.

"You don't have to do that, Liam."

"I know. I like to feel useful. And I don't think anyone in your family wants to chat me up." He rinsed a dish and put it in the drain. "I came here to see you, Carmen. I don't know anyone else. Your dad was my friend."

He heard her hiccupping breath. When he turned, he expected to see her crying, but she just stared off at nothing. Drying his hands quickly, he squatted in front of her. "What do you need, Carmen? I watched you run around here, taking care of everyone. What can I do for you?"

Her focus shifted until her eyes met his. So much sadness. He wanted to wrap her in a tight hug, but they had never had that kind of relationship. They'd had a teasing, laughing one with minimal contact. And that had been years ago.

"Could you take the coffee into the living room? I just need a few minutes."

He patted her knee before rising. "Take all the time you need."

***

Of all the people to see her, really see her, no way had Carmen expected it to be Liam O'Leary. She had called him out of respect for her father, but she hadn't thought he'd come. Maybe to the funeral home, but certainly not to the house. She'd escaped to the kitchen because she needed to get away from the looks and comments, the rubs against her hand meant to reassure her that things would be okay.

So many people filled her small house. The air became oppressive and she couldn't breathe. When Liam caught her in the kitchen, she felt her nerves unraveling and he'd seen it.

"Who's the white boy pouring coffee? Tia Rosalie wants to know," Rosa said.

So much for a minute of peace. Carmen turned to face her cousin. "It's Liam O'Leary. He stopped by to pay his respects and offered to get the coffee for me."

Carmen pushed away from the table. If Rosa was in the kitchen, others would surely follow. Especially if Liam drew attention. And how could he not? He didn't exactly blend with her family. Once on her feet, she swayed.

Rosa caught her arm. "Hey now. Are you all right?"

She nodded weakly. "I'm fine. A little worn out. It's a lot to take in at once, you know?"

Liam returned with the coffeepot, still half full, which was a good sign. Maybe people were planning to leave soon. She took the pot from him. "Thank you."

"What else can I do? Want me to wrap up the food?"

She glanced at Rosa. If she mentioned throwing it all away, Rosa would get nosy. "Why don't you make yourself a plate to take with you? I'll never be able to eat all of this."

"Rosa," someone called from the living room.

Rosa waited, looking at Carmen's face. "Are you sure you're okay? Mom and Dad are probably ready to go."

"I'm good. Thanks." She forced a smile that she hoped would pass the test for her cousin.

"Call if you need anything." She grabbed Carmen in a hug and added in her ear, "I mean it."

"I will," Carmen whispered back. The brief respite she'd taken had to be enough. She followed Rosa back into the living room to say good-bye to her family and walk them out. Luckily, when Rosa's family decided to leave, the rest of the family followed suit. It had taken another hour, but Carmen closed the door on her last cousin and sank against the door.

Blissful quiet.

Except not. Water was running in the kitchen. Who? Then she remembered Liam. She'd completely forgotten about him. She shoved away from the door and walked to the kitchen. In the doorway, she froze. The entire room was clean. Dishes stacked neatly on the drain and counter. Liam hadn't noticed her presence and she watched him for a moment.

He was bigger now than he'd ever been. Broader. But his red hair and freckles hadn't changed. And those blue eyes still had the ability to mesmerize her.

A flash of memory struck her: Liam, elbows-deep in the

stainless sink at her father's restaurant. Physically he'd always stood out in that kitchen, the one white guy among a bunch of Mexicans, but he fit in somehow. His love for her father's food brought him into the fold.

"Everyone gone?" he asked without turning around.

"Yes." She walked to him and leaned against the counter. "Thank you for cleaning up. You didn't have to do that."

"It didn't look like anyone else was going to help." He winked at her. "Besides, it was like old times."

"I had the same thought when I saw you standing at the sink. You're far from being a dishwasher now, though, right? My dad was always bragging about what a great chef you are." She crossed her arms over her middle. For all the details she'd handled over the days, she'd spoken very little of her father.

"I wouldn't be where I am today if your dad hadn't fostered my love of cooking." He dried his hands on the towel at the edge of the sink, then picked up a glass dish filled with food. "My to-go container. I'll return it when I'm finished."

"No problem. Thank you for your help. Really."

"I know you said you were going to throw the food away, but I broke it up into meal-sized portions and put it in the fridge. If you freeze some, you probably won't have to cook for weeks."

She shook her head with a smile. This man, who was a virtual stranger, had helped in ways that her family couldn't. They meant well and she couldn't hold that against them. But Liam let her be. She briefly recalled her dad talking about Liam's father dying. It had been while Mom was sick and Carmen had been overwhelmed. She hadn't even really paid attention.

"I'll see you tomorrow." He gently touched her shoulder with his free hand and gave a little squeeze.

Tomorrow. At the funeral. She offered a weak nod, not trusting her voice. He grabbed his coat and left without a sound. Carmen locked up and stood in her living room, a room she'd grown up in, and the silence assaulted her.

She'd wanted the silence, the peace, but now she felt like it would swallow her whole. She turned the TV back on, found the telenovelas her mother loved to watch, and then she curled up on the couch.

RECIPE

Moira's Super-Fudgy Brownies

1½ sticks of butter
    1¼ cup sugar
    1 cup unsweetened cocoa powder
    ½ teaspoon salt
    1 teaspoon vanilla
    3 eggs
    ¾ cup all-purpose flour
    ¼ cup hot water
    1 cup semisweet chocolate chips

Preheat oven to 350 degrees. Grease bottom of 9-by-13-inch pan.

Melt butter in microwave and let cool slightly. In a bowl, mix sugar, cocoa powder, and salt. Stir in melted butter and mix well. Stir in vanilla. Add eggs one at a time, mixing after each. Batter will be shiny. Stir in flour and mix well. Mix in hot water. Stir in chocolate chips.

Spread evenly into pan. Bake 35 to 40 minutes. Cool on a rack. Cut and enjoy with ice cream or a glass of milk.

ALSO BY SHANNYN SCHROEDER

More Than This

A Good Time

Something to Prove

Catch Your Breath

Just a Taste

Hold Me Close

For Your Love

Under Your Skin

In Your Arms

Through Your Eyes

From Your Heart

Stand Alones

Between Love and Loyalty

Meeting His Match

Daring Divorcees Series

One Night with a Millionaire

My Best Friend's Ex